Next Exit, No Outlet

CW Browning

Copyright © 2019 by Clare Wroblewski

All rights reserved.

Cover design by Dissect Designs / www.dissectdesigns.com
Book design by Clare Wroblewski

No part of this publication may be reproduced, stored in or introduced into a retrieval system, or transmitted, in any form or by any means (electronic, mechanical, photocopying, recording or otherwise), without the prior written permission of the copyright owner, except by a reviewer who may quote brief passages in a review.

This is a work of fiction. All of the characters, organizations, and events portrayed in this novel are either products of the author's imagination or are used fictitiously. Any resemblance to actual persons, living or dead, or events is entirely coincidental.

CW Browning
Visit my website at www.cwbrowning.com

First Printing: 2019

ISBN-13: 9781650581729

Author's Note:

To all my readers who have anxiously followed Viper and Hawk through their journey, laughed with Angela and Stephanie, cried over John and grown to love Michael and Blake – this one is for you.

Next Exit, No Outlet

"But if there is harm, then you shall pay life for life, eye for eye…"
~ Exodus 21: 23-24

Prologue

Alina Maschik inched forward in the bumper-to-bumper traffic clogging Route 70 East. Red and blue lights flashed continuously ahead and she glanced at the navigation system, noting the time. There had been an accident during rush hour on a Friday. Fantastic.

Returning her gaze to the traffic before her, she inched forward again. Two lanes were merging into one to circumvent the collision ahead. She could see two ambulances in the middle of the intersection but, beyond that, her view was blocked by the pickup truck in front of her.

She sighed and shifted in her bucket seat. She had known she'd hit rush hour on her way back from Pennsylvania, but she hadn't expected to spend over half an hour on a four block stretch of highway. Alina pressed a button on the steering wheel, skipping the rock song blaring from the speakers. A new song began and she leaned her head back against the headrest, her eyes on the back of the truck.

Damon was at the house in Medford, waiting for her. She should have been there long before now. The plan was to go straight to the house after the operation in Independence Park. He'd followed the plan. She hadn't.

Alina's eyes wandered to her left, watching as what little traffic that had been able to get past the accident flew along the westbound side of the highway.

Leaving the city after their successful mission, she had seen a man walking away from the area around the FBI building. Recognizing him as an assassin she'd seen last fall in Rittenhouse Square, she'd aborted the plan and followed him. He got into a vehicle three blocks away and headed out of the city. She'd lost him outside Conshohocken, about thirty minutes northwest of Philadelphia.

The traffic on the other side of the highway began to slow and move to the side. Alina shifted her gaze. One of the ambulances was pulling away from the intersection, lights flashing. As the left lane cleared to give it space, it picked up speed and the siren began to wail. She watched it fly down the left lane, noting the name of the service and the ambulance number absently. Good. Maybe now they would start moving.

She turned her attention back to the road and eased forward a few feet, following the truck. She was almost at the intersection now. Once she passed the accident, the traffic would speed up again. She glanced at her watch. Finally, she would be moving again.

A uniformed police officer was standing in the intersection, directing traffic as Alina drew closer to the light and looked at the wreckage. A black Escalade was half on the grass median separating the east and westbound lanes, the front end completely smashed in. Her gaze shifted curiously to the other vehicle. She froze and her blood ran cold as a wave of shock rolled over her.

Alina's hands clenched involuntarily on the steering wheel as she stared at the maroon Mustang GT in the center of the intersection. It had been spun around, presumably by the accident, and was facing her. The license plate was untouched by the collision, and the number was clear. It was a number she knew well. The car had spent many hours in her driveway.

The front end didn't have a scratch. It was the rest of the car that told the story. The passenger side was completely smashed in, and the window was shattered. On the driver side, the back quarter panel had been hit, and the back bumper was off the car altogether. Stephanie Walker's Mustang looked as if it had been hit by a train on both sides.

Alina's eyes moved to the black Escalade and she dropped her gaze to the license plate, memorizing the number quickly. Fury replaced the shock and, as she crawled forward, she watched as the second ambulance slowly maneuvered around Stephanie's car and eased into the westbound lane to follow the other one.

Alina glanced in her rear view mirror and then behind her to the right, checking the narrow shoulder beside her. Seeing that it was clear, she wrenched the wheel sideways and hit the gas. Pulling out of the line of traffic, she shot into the shoulder and to the corner. Turning down a side street, she reached out and hit speed dial on her phone. A moment later, Damon Miles' voice filled her car.

"Yes?"

"Change of plans," she said shortly, flying down the narrow road. "I need you."

There was brief silence on the line and Alina could almost see

Next Exit, No Outlet

his grin.

"Last night wasn't enough for you?" he finally drawled.

"At the hospital," she said, ignoring him. "Leave now."

"That's doesn't sound good." The amusement left his voice. "What hospital?"

"That's what I need you to find out. It's got to be either Cooper or Our Lady of Lourdes. I'm driving and can't access anything, so you'll have to tap into the scanners for me."

"Tell me."

"Accident in Cherry Hill on Route 70. Two inbound ambulances, one of them transporting Special Agent Stephanie Walker." Alina recited the ambulance numbers to him and made another turn, cutting through a residential neighborhood as she doubled back towards the river. "Find out which hospital, then meet me there. Take the bike. It's faster."

"Anything else?"

"Yeah. Come armed for a fight."

Chapter One

Special Agent Blake Hanover followed the nurse down the wide emergency room corridor, a forbidding scowl on his face.

"Here we are," she said over her shoulder as they came to the cubicle at the end. "She's right in here."

Blake nodded to her in thanks and strode into the small room. Stephanie Walker was in a bed with an IV hooked up to her arm, and a monitor keeping track of her heart rate. She had her head back on the pillow with her eyes closed, but when he walked in, she opened them and lifted her head.

"Hey."

"Hey yourself," he retorted, walking over to stand next to the bed.

He looked down at her and his scowl eased a bit. Her face was pale, and a nasty bruise was beginning to discolor half of her forehead. A few superficial cuts on the side of her face had been cleaned and left uncovered, with the exception of one which had a small gauze bandage over it.

"You just can't keep out of trouble, can you?"

His words were softened by a half smile, and her lips curved in response.

"You know me. I like to keep busy."

Blake shook his head and looked around. Spying a chair off to the side, he pulled it over to the side of the bed.

"Have you seen a doctor yet?"

"Yes. He was in about twenty minutes ago. I have another concussion and he wants to send me down for an MRI. I also have whiplash and a twisted wrist." She held up her left arm, bandaged up to her elbow. "They already did a CT scan. No broken bones or signs of internal bleeding. It could have been much worse."

Next Exit, No Outlet

"Rob wanted to come, but I talked him out of it," he said, getting up and going to the opening of the cubicle. He reached up and closed the heavy privacy curtain before returning to his chair. "I told him the less people involved, the better." Blake lowered his voice. "Tell me what the hell happened."

Stephanie shrugged, wincing in pain at the movement.

"You're not going to believe it," she said tiredly. "I'm not even sure I believe it. If it wasn't for the witness and the statement he made to the police, I'd be inclined to think I dreamt the whole thing."

"What witness?" Blake asked sharply.

"One of the guys that hit me. He couldn't avoid it. I spun into his lane. The cop said he saw everything and was willing to give a statement. I can pick up the report on Monday, if I'm still alive."

He made a face. "Don't talk like that."

"Well, let's face it, Blake. Things aren't looking all that great. This afternoon someone tried to shoot me, and a few hours later someone else tried to kill me with some kind of toxin!"

Her voice rose as she spoke and he heard the tremor of panic in her tone.

"Ok, slow down. Let's go back to what you remember from the accident," he said soothingly, glancing at the monitor as her heart rate increased significantly.

She took a deep breath.

"I was on my way to Alina's, as we agreed. I was going through a green light when I saw something black out of the corner of my eye and then, BAM! I never even saw them come into the intersection. He hit the passenger side and threw me into a spin. I ended up on the other side of the highway. A pickup truck would have slammed into my door, but he managed to swerve enough to hit the back quarter panel instead. The impact spun me back into the middle of the intersection and out of the line of traffic."

"That was the witness?"

She nodded. "He stayed with me until the cops got there."

"Then what?"

Stephanie shook her head and leaned back on the pillows.

"That's where it gets crazy. Some guy, the driver of the black SUV that hit me in the first place, comes up to the car. I thought he was checking to see if I was okay."

Blake raised an eyebrow questioningly when she stopped and she shrugged again.

"He wasn't. He tried to stick me with a needle. We struggled and I hit him with the butt of my gun. He dropped the syringe and I grabbed it."

"Why do you think it had a toxin in it?"

"Because I stabbed him with it and he died."

"What?!"

"I told you it was insane."

Blake got up impatiently, running a hand through his hair. He did a quick turn around the small cubicle, then stopped and faced at her.

"How do you know he died?"

"I asked the cop when he was questioning me. He didn't want to tell me, but I told him I out-ranked him. Besides, I saw the dude fall, and he didn't move again the whole time they were getting me out of the car and into the ambulance."

A grin pulled at Blake's lips. "You told the cop you out-ranked him?"

Stephanie smiled ruefully. "Well, I do."

Blake sank down into his chair again.

"How the hell did they know where you were going?" he demanded, shaking his head. "Even if they followed you, they couldn't have planned an interception. How did they know you'd be on that road? It's not even the route you take home!"

"I'm more concerned with who they are, and why they want me dead," she replied. "You realize if I'd been knocked unconscious, I'd be dead right now, right?"

He scowled. "Yes."

They fell silent for a long moment, Blake looking like thunder and Stephanie chewing her bottom lip thoughtfully.

"Who knew I was going to Alina's?" she asked, finally breaking the silence. "You didn't tell anyone at the office, did you?"

"Of course not. Even Rob didn't know where you were going, only that it was a safe house. Hell, he doesn't even know it's in New Jersey."

"I told Angie in the car, but I'd just hung up when I got hit," she said slowly. "Even if someone was listening, they couldn't have known what road I was on or where I was heading, let alone have time to get there."

Blake shook his head, sighing in frustration.

"None of it makes sense. Have you called the Black Widow?"

Stephanie looked a little guilty. "Not yet."

He stared at her. "What are you waiting for?"

"I don't know." She rubbed her forehead, her brows wrinkled. "I keep thinking she's got enough to worry about, and now this is

Next Exit, No Outlet

taking it to the next level. I mean, someone tried to blow her head off last week, *and* the week before that! Now, I'm going to foist myself on her when people are shooting at me too? That hardly seems fair."

Blake shook his head.

"I don't think a few extra bad guys will make much difference at this point, do you?" he asked.

She sighed.

"Probably not, but I don't want it on my conscience. Maybe I should just go into one of our safe houses like Rob wants. They're uncomfortable and depressing, but at least I wouldn't be putting anyone else at risk."

He studied her for a long moment.

"Is that what you want to do?" he finally asked.

Stephanie raised troubled eyes to his. "I think so."

He was silent for a moment, then he glanced at the monitors and the IV in her arm.

"Before we tackle that, let's talk about all this," he said, making a movement with his hand that encompassed the cubicle. "The longer you stay here, the more you're at risk. It won't take them long to figure out which hospital you came to, if they haven't already. They've tried twice now. They're not going to stop just because they're a man down."

Stephanie's eyes widened. "You don't think they'll come here, do you?"

"I don't know, but it's not a chance I'm willing to take. Are you?"

She stared at him for a beat, then lowered her gaze to her IV. "No."

Blake nodded and stood up. He looked over at the clear plastic bag on a table inside the opening that contained her clothes.

"Where's your gun?"

She reached under the thin blanket covering her and pulled out her Glock. He grinned, his eyes creasing at the edges, and a warm glint lit his brown eyes.

"That's my girl," he murmured. "I'll go find the nurse and tell her you want to be discharged. If anyone comes in here without me, shoot them."

Michael O'Reilly rubbed his eyes and sat back in the chair.

After staring at the laptop screen for another minute, he picked up his empty coffee mug and got up, turning to carry it into the kitchen. When Alina asked him to discreetly dig around in a man's past, he didn't really think he'd find anything. The man was a household name, a permanent fixture in Washington, DC, and an old war-hero to boot. He'd got the impression that even *she* was skeptical in the beginning, asking him to do it more out of an effort to cover all her bases than from any thought that he might actually find something.

Michael shook his head and put the mug in the dishwasher. A year ago, he would have helped her out of loyalty to her dead brother and his best friend, Dave. But over the past ten months that he'd gotten to know Alina, a lot had changed. When she asked him to do it over a week ago, he'd agreed out of loyalty to her.

Turning to open the fridge, Michael pulled out a beer and used the bottle opener he kept on the door to pop the top off. Taking a long sip, he turned to go back into the dining room, where he had his laptop on the table.

Now, he was doing it for himself.

Until tonight, he hadn't been able to turn up anything on Mr. X, as Alina called him. She said he was the X factor. Michael grunted as he settled himself back in front of his laptop. X factor or not, up until now, Michael had been unable to find anything on the man. He was as clean and upright as they came these days. Alina was of the opinion that no one was that clean, and so he kept looking. If nothing else, his time with the Secret Service had taught him patience, and tonight that patience had paid off.

Michael was just reaching for the mouse when his cell phone rang. He frowned and picked it up.

"Hello?"

"Hey Mike," Blake greeted him. "When did you say you were getting your ass up here?"

Michael's eyebrows shot into his forehead and he reached for his beer.

"Tomorrow. What now?"

"I'm at the hospital." Blake lowered his voice. "The bastards tried again."

Michael scowled. "Stephanie?"

"She's banged up, but alive for now."

"I thought she was going to Alina's house?" Michael said, standing up and pacing the length of his dining room with his beer in his hand. "What happened?"

"They got to her on her way there. Drove right into her and

forced her off the road. She says the driver then came over to the car and tried to stick her with a needle. She managed to get it away from him and stabbed him first. He died in the road."

Michael swore softly. "Now what?"

"She wants to go to one of our FBI safe houses. I still want her to go to Viper's, but she says it's bringing more threat after Alina. She won't budge."

"Oh, she'll budge when Lina gets involved," he assured him. "What about you?"

"If we go into a safe house, I'll go with her. If she goes to Alina's, I don't have a choice. Viper won't let me anywhere near her secret lair."

"True enough. I can try to talk to her, but no promises on what good it will do. She's got some strange idea that she's responsible for anyone who comes into her world."

Blake snorted. "I can handle myself."

"Agreed, but try and convince her of that." Michael ran a hand over his short hair and took a long drink of beer. "What about tonight? What are you two going to do?"

"Right now we're waiting for her to get discharged. The nurse put up a fight, then the doctor came in and did the same. They want to admit her."

"I thought you said she was just banged up!"

"She is, but it's her head that's banged up. She's double concussed, and they want to run tests and scans and all the doctor crap that costs thousands."

"She can refuse."

"And she did. So now we're waiting, but of course they're not rushing to process the paperwork."

"And when you finally get out of there?"

"I'll check us into a hotel and try to figure out what to do. We can't move to a safe house until tomorrow. If I contact Rob now, he'll insist she stay here and go through the tests, and I don't think it's safe. If they're willing to shoot up the inside the FBI parking lot, they won't think twice about coming into a hospital. Look what happened to John. At this point, Steph wants to take her chances with the head and get to safety, and I don't blame her."

"Has she called Lina yet?"

"No. She's waiting until we get out of here." Blake cleared his throat and lowered his voice again. "Any idea what's going on there? Why are they acting so cagey with each other?"

"I wish I knew," Michael replied, going back to his chair and sinking into it. "Every time I ask, I get shot down. Alina claims there's nothing wrong."

"That's a crock. Stephanie says the same thing, and she can't lie to save her life. Not that it's any of my business, but it's sure making this a lot more complicated than it needs to be."

"Well, let me know when you get into the hotel. I'll leave early tomorrow, although I don't see what help I can be if you're disappearing into a Fed safe house."

"I'm still hoping she'll go to Lina's, wherever that is."

"Keep me posted."

"Will do." Blake paused. "Hey Mike?"

"Yeah?"

"Be careful. My gut tells me this is just getting started up here."

Michael set his beer down on the table next to his laptop.

"Yeah, mine too," he murmured, looking at the screen on his laptop.

He hung up and set the phone down, staring at the financial statements on the screen.

"Mine too."

Chapter Two

Stephanie stepped out of the elevator with Blake, and the smell of oil and stale urine greeted her. She wrinkled her nose in reaction and glanced at the tall man beside her. Her head was buzzing, her whole body felt like it had been battered by a heavy-weight champion, and her leg was back to being unbearable. She leaned on her cane, taking some of the weight off the leg that had suffered a gunshot wound the week before, and paused to look around the parking garage.

"How far is the car?" she asked.

"On the other side of the garage." Blake looked down at her. "I'd go get it, but I'm not leaving your side. How are you holding up?"

"I feel like I was in a car accident," Stephanie replied dryly. "I'll be fine."

He grinned. "Maybe you shouldn't have turned down the wheelchair."

"I wasn't about to be pushed out of there like an invalid. I'm perfectly capable of walking," she said with a scowl.

Her cane chose that precise moment to slip on the smooth tarmac, and she gasped as she lurched forward, her bad leg giving out on her. Blake grabbed her and hauled her up against his side, unable to keep a chuckle from escaping.

"I can see that."

Stephanie laughed despite herself and straightened up, pushing his supporting arm away.

"Well, under normal circumstances, anyway," she said. "The only reason they wanted to stick me in a wheelchair was to reinforce the fact that they were pissed I was checking myself out."

"We probably should have waited until they did the MRI," he said after a moment. "This is your second concussion in a week and a half, and they don't even know about the hit you took the other night in your apartment. Your brain could be jelly for all we know."

She looked at him in disbelief. "Thanks for the vote of confidence!"

He shrugged, a teasing smile on his face.

"Hey, I'm sure you're fine. Probably."

Stephanie choked back a laugh. "You're an ass."

"Yeah, but you're glad I'm here," he said. "Who else would make you laugh after someone tried to kill you? Twice?"

"I *am* glad you're here," Stephanie admitted, sobering. "I don't know–"

She broke off as the relative silence in the parking garage was shattered by a muffled pop. It was a sound they both knew well: the sound of a suppressed gunshot, followed a second later by a thud. Because of the acoustics in the enclosed parking garage, it was impossible to tell where the noise actually originated.

Blake whipped out his Beretta and spun around, scanning the garage while moving into a protective position behind Stephanie. She shifted her weight to her good leg and reached for her Glock, her heart pounding as her eyes searched for the threat. They were about halfway across the parking level and she could see Blake's black Challenger at the end of the row. There was no one near it.

"Do you see anything?" Blake demanded.

"Nothing."

He let out a low curse.

"Me either. Move toward the car."

Stephanie began to move toward the Challenger, her eyes darting around the garage. The places an attacker could conceal themselves were numerous, and she felt the overwhelming pressure of panic start to tighten her chest. She took a deep breath, trying to calm herself.

An eerie silence fell as they moved across the pavement. They had gone about three feet when an unnatural cry echoed across the garage, terrifying in its suddenness. Stephanie looked up and her mouth dropped open as a man dressed in dark jeans and a black jacket free-fell from the level above, a gun still in his hand and his head twisted at an impossible angle. Before she had time to even gasp, the body hit the pavement behind a white service van with a sickening splat.

"What the hell?!" Blake spun around and stared over her shoulder. "What was that?!"

"A…man," she stuttered, "…with a gun."

"Where?"

"Behind that van. He just fell…from up there!"

She pointed to the cement barrier along the level above them.

Next Exit, No Outlet

"Like hell he just fell," Blake muttered, putting a hand on her back and propelling her forward. "Move!"

Stephanie grunted as pain shot up her leg and she traded her Glock for her cane, switching the gun into her non-dominant hand. She forced her legs to move as fast as her pain-ridden body would allow, fear constricting her throat and making it hard to breathe.

God, I don't want to die!

She felt Blake stiffen behind her and then his hand left her back as he spun around. Stephanie started with a gasp at the deafening sound of his Beretta as he fired, his back to hers. Dropping her cane, she moved her Glock to her right hand and swung around to face the threat with him, raising her gun.

A man had fallen to his knees, a semi-automatic dropping out of his hand as blood spread across his chest. Behind him, two more figures moved out from behind a sedan, their weapons pointed straight at them. As soon as they broke cover, *pop-pop* echoed dully through the parking garage and they swayed for a moment with stunned looks on their faces. Almost as one, they fell, blood pouring from holes in their foreheads.

"What the—?!" Blake glanced at her Glock.

"It wasn't me!"

Tires squealed behind them and they both swung around, their guns ready, to find a black van careening straight for them. Blake reached out and wrapped his arm around Stephanie's waist, turning to half-push, half-throw her out of the way. Glancing behind him at the oncoming van, he threw himself against her, propelling them both behind the cover of a Honda civic.

Stephanie had a momentary sensation of flying through the air before she slammed into the side of the car with a grunt. Blake crashed into her before they both fell to the cement. Pain ripped through her as she hit the ground, the air knocked out of her, and she lay on the tarmac, momentarily stunned. Beside her, Blake groaned and lifted his head to look at her.

"You okay?"

All she could manage was a nod. He rolled onto his back, his arm still around her, and she went with him. They stared at the van, watching as it slammed on the brakes and skidded to a stop a few feet away. The windowless back door slid open, revealing three large men dressed in black body armor and holding assault rifles. Blake swung up his Beretta and aimed. Before he could get a shot off, the one on the far right fell backwards into the van, a bullet hole in his forehead. The middle one jumped out and Blake squeezed the trigger, aiming for one of the few vulnerable spots on the assailant. His shot was true, and the man stumbled and fell, blood pouring from the base of his throat.

Stephanie watched in bemusement as the last man fell back into the van at the same time the middle one took Blake's bullet. Tilting her head back, she scanned the cement barrier on the level above their heads and was just in time to see a rifle barrel disappear from the edge. Another *pop-pop* brought her attention back to the van and she gasped. Two bullet holes were in the windshield.

Blake jumped to his feet as the driver side door opened and the driver rolled out, returning fire down the aisle. He moved in front of Stephanie, protecting her with his body, but she struggled to stand, using the Honda for support. Glancing at her swiftly, he pushed her behind him again, then scowled. She was staring to their right, her face draining of what color it still had.

Turning his head, he watched as a blonde woman with short hair advanced down the middle of the aisle toward the van. Her face was unrecognizable, her lips pressed together and her eyes intent on her quarry. Blake had seen a lot in his time, first with the Marines and then the FBI, but despite it all, he felt a chill go through him at the look of deadly promise on her face. She ejected a clip from her gun and slammed a fresh one in, never breaking stride.

Pop-pop-pop.

Without missing a beat, as soon as her clip was engaged, she fired through the open door, keeping the driver pinned beside the van, unable to return fire until she was upon him.

Reaching the bullet-ridden door, she slammed it shut with one hand and delivered a kick with the full force of her leg to the figure on the other side of the van. Then she disappeared from view, concealed by the van itself. They couldn't see her, but they could hear, and that was enough. A male scream of pain was suddenly cut short, followed by an unholy silence. When she reappeared a second later, she looked directly at Blake.

"Get her back behind the car and against the wall!" she commanded, her voice flat and hard. "Now!"

Blake reacted to the steel in her tone and turned to propel Stephanie toward the cement wall a few feet behind them. As he did so, a black SUV skidded around the bend from the ramp leading from the lower parking level, roaring down the aisle towards them. At the same time, a motorcycle shot down the ramp from the upper level, flying around his Challenger at the end of the row. Pressing Stephanie against the wall, Blake spun around and watched as the woman grabbed one of the assault rifles from the back of the van. She turned, took a few steps

Next Exit, No Outlet

towards Blake, and tossed the rifle to him without a word.

"Is that...?" Blake began, catching the weapon with one strong hand.

"Viper," Stephanie replied, her voice shaking.

The motorcycle stopped behind the van and the rider got off, striding forward. He swung a rifle off his back in one smooth motion and joined Viper next to the van.

"This should be the last of them," he said, his voice carrying to Blake and Stephanie.

"I want one of them alive."

The man nodded as the SUV stopped and a long barrel emerged from the passenger window.

"Who's the guy?" Blake demanded, blocking Stephanie's view by moving in front of her, effectively using himself as a shield.

"He's with her." She sounded resigned. "His name is Damon."

Damon fired through the windshield on the passenger side of the SUV while Viper strode toward the vehicle. She held her gun in both hands, and when the driver's door opened, she raised it and fired. Her shot went through the window and into the shoulder of the emerging man. The back window slid down and Viper dove under the driver's door as a hail of bullets flew out.

Stephanie gasped and grabbed the back of Blake's jacket, peering over his shoulder. He glanced at her, his face grim. She didn't notice, intent on watching the live-action nightmare unfolding before them. Her heart was back in her throat, but this time she was terrified for the friend she had known since she was six years old.

Damon disappeared around the passenger side of the SUV, and they heard glass breaking then more gunfire. Viper somersaulted below the back door, out of the effective range of the automatic weapon being waved from the window, and stood against the back quarter panel of the SUV. She reached over and wrenched at the door. As soon as it cracked open, she fired three rapid shots inside before jumping out of the way again as a body fell out, the rifle falling to the ground with him. She leaned against the back side of the SUV again as silence fell.

"Clear!" Damon called from the other side.

Viper glanced into the back of the SUV and stepped over the body on the ground, moving back to the driver's door. The injured driver was pressing one hand against his shoulder, trying to stem the tide of blood, while his other hand was in his lap. As she moved to the open door, the hand in his lap came up holding a gun.

He fired, but it was a split second too late. The butt of Viper's gun had come down hard on his wrist and the shot went wide, missing her. The pistol fell to the ground with a clatter, and Viper grasped the back of his head, slamming it into the steering wheel.

Blake grimaced at the howl of pain that echoed out of the SUV, then watched as Viper did it again, stunning the man. Gripping his shirt, she pulled him out from behind the wheel and threw him onto the ground, kicking the pistol out of reach. He shook his head as if to clear it and tried to grab her ankle to pull her off balance. Instead of falling, she pivoted on her other foot, spinning and bringing her knee down onto his chest. He grunted in pain, growing still as the air was forced out of his lungs. Pulling a long, serrated blade from the vicinity of her ankle, Viper leaned down until her face was inches from his, pressing the tip of the blade into the side of his neck.

Stephanie couldn't hear what was being said, but she could see her friend's face and that was enough. The terrifying assassin was there, and Alina was nowhere to be found. Damon rounded the back corner of the SUV and looked toward Blake and Stephanie, his face impassive. Stephanie shivered at the arctic chips that had replaced his blue eyes. These were the two assassin that were complete strangers to her.

While they watched, he said something in a low voice to Viper. She nodded briefly and tossed him a set of keys. He turned to stride toward them, effectively blocking their view of what was happening behind him.

"Blake Hanover?"

Blake nodded.

"We've got about three minutes to get her out of here and somewhere safe," Damon said, nodding towards Stephanie. "Come with me."

Blake didn't move.

"Who the hell are you?" he demanded.

Stephanie took one look at Damon's face and moved out from behind him, putting a hand on his arm.

"It's ok, Blake," she said, her voice calmer than she felt. "Let's go."

"We'll go in my car," Blake said stubbornly.

"Then you'll be dead within the hour," Damon said bluntly. "They have it tagged with a tracking device."

Blake stared at him speechlessly.

"You Marines really need to learn to move and think at the same time," Damon continued, bending down to pick up Stephanie's discarded cane. He handed it to her. "Go!"

Stephanie fought an insane urge to laugh and pulled on Blake's arm to get him moving.

"We're not all fitting on that bike," she said, following Damon along the cement wall, away from Viper and the last man left alive.

"We're taking Viper's car," he said shortly.

Blake reached out and pulled her to a stop. Stephanie looked at him in surprise, then her eyes widened as he swung her up into his arms.

"We'll move faster without you walking," he said briskly.

Damon looked at them and she thought she saw the faintest glimmer of a laugh in the icy blue eyes of the assassin. But it was gone as quickly as it came. He turned his head and led them swiftly along the barrier wall, around the corner, and up the down ramp. From her perch in Blake's arms, Stephanie could see Viper clearly over his shoulder. She was still bent over the driver on the ground and Stephanie turned her eyes away quickly. She didn't want to know what was happening there. She'd seen that side of Alina before, and decided that she never wanted to see it again. Now here it was, in all its terrifying glory.

She shivered and Blake glanced down at her, squeezing briefly. He thought she was upset over the attack, and she was willing to let him believe that. It was better than the truth: that she was terrified of the killer her best friend had become.

Chapter Three

Alina rode through the security gate and into the parking lot off North 8th Street in Philadelphia. A high-rise towered above the lot and, straight head at the end of the aisle, her Shelby GT 500 was backed into the assigned spot against a brick wall. Damon leaned against the hood, his arms crossed over his chest and one ankle crossed over the other, looking dark and forbidding. The passenger side door was open and Blake stood next to it with one arm braced against the roof. As she pulled into the lot, he looked up.

Damon watched as she pulled up in front of the Mustang and turned off the motorcycle, pulling the helmet off. The look on his face was unreadable, but she knew from the set of his shoulders and the clench of his jaw that he wasn't happy. He uncrossed his arms and tossed her keys over as she got off his bike.

"Any problems?" he asked.

"No. You?" She caught her keys with one hand and tossed him his with her other.

"No."

Alina nodded and looked at Stephanie through the windshield. "How is she?"

"Shaken up, but not hurt." Damon straightened. "Do you have all your safe houses programmed into your onboard Nav system?"

Alina flashed a grin. "It got you here, didn't it?"

Damon grunted.

"And now those two know one of your safe spots," he muttered. "Not good."

"I didn't have much of a choice," she retorted, turning toward Blake. "How is she?" she asked, raising her voice and walking around the front of her car.

"She's completely freaked out, but fine," Stephanie called from inside the car, bringing a smile to Blake's otherwise grim face. Blood had dried around a gash on his cheekbone and he looked ready to go to war.

Next Exit, No Outlet

Alina reached the open door and looked in at Stephanie. She was seated sideways with her cane leaning against the dash and her purse on the floor.

"Good. Let's get you inside and away from the cameras."

"Where are we?" Blake asked, reaching a hand to help Stephanie out of the low sports car. "Are you sure it's safe?"

Alina looked at him, a very faint look of amusement on her face.

"It better be. It's one of my safe houses."

Blake glanced at her, surprised.

"You have a safe house in Philly? Why? You live across the bridge!"

"Why not?"

"How many safe houses do you keep?" Stephanie demanded, gaining her feet and leaning on her cane.

"Enough."

Alina glanced around the dark parking lot and moved towards the entrance to the building, beeping the Shelby's car alarm on as she did so. Damon waited for Blake and Stephanie to follow her, then turned toward the motorcycle.

"Where's he going?" Stephanie asked as they reached the double glass doors to the lobby.

Alina opened the door and motioned them inside, not even glancing back at Damon.

"To secure the perimeter."

Stephanie made a face at the brief answer and went into the brightly lit lobby, looking around. It was small with a row of elevators directly in front of them. On the right was a wall of mailboxes with call buttons, and on the left was a row of plush, comfortable chairs for waiting visitors. Alina went to an elevator and pressed the button, glancing at her watch.

"What time did you actually discharge from the hospital?" she asked.

Stephanie thought for a minute.

"I guess it was about seven-thirty," she said slowly, looking at Blake. "Right?"

"It was closer to eight, I think," he answered. "It'll be on the paperwork. Why?"

The elevator opened and they got in. Alina swiped a fob on her keychain in front of the pad and the doors slid closed silently. A second later, the car began a swift and silent ascent.

"The death squad got there right after you discharged," she

said, turning to face them. "That means someone told them you were being released."

"What if I had stayed?" Stephanie asked. "They wanted to keep me and do some scans. They didn't want me to leave."

"They were going to admit you?"

"Yes."

Alina's lips tightened and her face took on the impassive mask that Stephanie hated. She turned back to the doors as the elevator came to a gentle stop and they slid open. Stephanie and Blake followed her into a wide corridor with hardwood floors and fresh, white walls. Without a word, Alina led the way to the door on the right and unlocked it. Flipping the switch inside the door, she moved aside so they could enter while she typed in the code on the alarm keypad.

"How do you know they weren't there before we discharged?" Blake asked, following Stephanie into the condo and closing the door behind them.

Alina turned away from the keypad and dropped her keys onto a sideboard table against the wall in the entryway.

"Because I was already there."

She strode down the short hallway into a large living room with a wall of windows overlooking the city and Blake and Stephanie glanced at each other.

"How…? Why…?" Stephanie stammered, following her. "What do you mean you were already there?"

Alina turned on the lamp next to the couch and picked up a remote. Pointing it at the windows, she pressed a button and thick, red shades slid down to cover the windows, blocking out the night.

"I was on my way home when I passed your accident," she said, turning to face them. "One of the ambulances was just pulling away. Damon picked up the EMT call from your ambulance to the hospital, so we knew where you were."

"And you just hung out in the parking garage?" Stephanie dropped onto the couch. "Why didn't you come in?"

"Because I had a feeling they'd try again." Alina looked at Blake. "Your car was tagged. They were following you as well."

"So your friend said," he replied, sitting next to Stephanie. "Why would they follow me?"

"As a fail-safe to get to her." Alina walked to the galley kitchen on the left and went in. "They know you're working together. In fact, they probably know everything about you, right down to what kind of dog food Buddy eats."

Stephanie gasped.

Next Exit, No Outlet

"Oh my God, Buddy!" she exclaimed. "He's all alone at the apartment!"

"I know," Blake said. "I'll have to go get him but, without my car, I don't know how."

Alina looked over the open bar that separated the kitchen from the living room.

"You're not going anywhere," she said flatly. "You're both staying here until I find out who's behind this. I'll get Buddy."

Blake stared at her. "What?"

"You heard me." She opened the refrigerator where a case of water was stocked on the top shelf. "I'll take care of him."

"Oh, that would be awesome," Stephanie answered before Blake could object. "Will you bring him here?"

Alina pulled out two bottles and turned to leave the kitchen.

"That's not possible. No animals allowed." She walked over to hand them each a water. "I'll take him to my house. He'll be fine there. Raven won't take on a dog of his size."

"Raven?" Blake asked with a nod of thanks for the water.

Alina smiled for the first time. "My hawk."

He choked. "Your hawk?!"

Stephanie laughed outright.

"I guess it does sound weird," she said, opening her water and taking a long drink. "It's really just a pet bird, only bigger," she added when she was finished.

"What the hell are you doing with a pet hawk?" Blake demanded, staring at Alina as if she had three heads.

She shrugged.

"He seems to like me." She went over to an armchair and sat down, fixing Stephanie with an unreadable look. "Tell me what the hell is going on. Start from the beginning."

Stephanie sighed and sat back on the couch, shifting her leg uncomfortably.

"I wasn't going to tell you any of this," she began. "You have enough going on without worrying about me."

Alina raised an eyebrow. "I do?"

"Yes, you do!" Stephanie exclaimed, disgruntled. "Good God woman, are you even human?!"

"That's a little harsh," Blake murmured, "even if her hair *does* look like something out of a Cold War thriller."

Alina's lips twitched, the only acknowledgment she gave the weak jab.

"I like it," Stephanie told him. "I think it looks good. It suits her."

"Hm," Blake grunted, sipping his water.

"What do I have going on that you think is more important than someone sending a hit team after you?"

"You have people trying to kill you!"

"I can assure you, there's nothing new in that."

Stephanie glowered at her.

"Damon got shot when someone was aiming for you. Then they shot up John's funeral, and God knows what they'll do next. Don't tell me this is just another day at the office for you."

"Actually, it is." A deep voice spoke behind them, and Stephanie and Blake visibly jumped. "Viper seems to attract fans wherever she goes. I can't imagine why."

Damon walked into the living room and glanced at Blake and Stephanie on the couch. Seeing their water bottles, he looked at Alina.

"You have water?"

"In the fridge."

He turned to go into the kitchen.

"Well, I wasn't about to add to the number of people throwing bullets her way," Stephanie tossed over her shoulder in his direction. "What kind of friend would I be if I put her in danger like that?"

Alina stared at her impassively, not trusting herself to look into the kitchen where Damon was at the fridge. She knew she'd see her feeling of disbelief mirrored in his eyes.

"Trust me, you're not putting me in any more danger than I'm already in," she said after a moment of silence, the faintest hint of steel in her voice.

"Well, you know everything now, anyway," Stephanie said with a shrug. "The other night, someone broke into my apartment and was still there when I got home. They hit me over the head, and when I came to, Blake and Buddy were there."

"Buddy?" Damon asked from the kitchen.

"His pit bull. You'll meet him later," Alina said. She turned her gaze to Blake. "What happened when you got there?"

"Buddy went berserk and tore through the apartment to the back door. It was just closing, and I never saw them. By the time I'd checked Stephanie, they were gone."

"And nothing was missing?" Damon asked, coming back into the living room with two bottles of water in his hand. "Are you sure?"

Stephanie nodded.

"Yes. The next morning, I discovered that they'd copied the hard-drive from my laptop. That was it."

Next Exit, No Outlet

Damon walked over to Alina and handed her one of the bottles. Sitting on the arm of the chair, he looked at Stephanie.

"What was on your laptop?"

"That's just it! Nothing! I have no idea what they were after."

"The safe wasn't touched? You're sure?" Alina asked.

"Yes. Nothing was missing."

"Nothing else happened the next day?"

"No. I went to physical therapy and was home the rest of the day. Then today I went to work. When I tried to leave this afternoon, someone shot at me. Ballistics dug a high-powered rifle round out of the car, so I would never have seen them. Thank God I dropped my keys and they hit the car."

Alina and Damon glanced at each other.

"What?" Blake asked, seeing the glance pass between them. "What are you thinking?"

"If she was home all day yesterday, that would have been the perfect time to go after her," Damon said reluctantly. "Why didn't they? Why wait until she was at work and have the added risk of trying to do it in a Federal building?"

Blake frowned. "I have no good answer for that."

"Something changed," Alina said slowly, opening her water and taking a sip.

"What?" Stephanie asked, her brows coming together in a frown. "What do you mean?"

"Maybe they didn't take the easy target you presented because they weren't going to come after you again."

"What could possibly have changed that made them want to kill me?!"

"They didn't find what they were looking for on your laptop, for one," Damon said.

"That would be all the more reason *not* to kill her," Blake pointed out. "If they think she knows something or has something, she's no good to them dead."

"He's right," Alina murmured. She looked at Stephanie consideringly. "This doesn't have anything to do with what they're looking for, at least not entirely. Something else changed to make her a target."

"What about the car accident?" Damon asked. "Tell us what happened there."

"A black SUV plowed into the passenger side and spun me through the intersection into oncoming traffic. I got hit again. When the car finally stopped, the driver approached me." Stephanie paused and took a long drink of water. "He tried to stick me with a needle."

"What?" Alina asked sharply, her eyes narrowing sharply. "A syringe?"

Stephanie nodded tiredly.

"He tried to grab my arm but I managed to fight him off long enough to get my gun out and knock the syringe out of his hand. There was a struggle for it and I stabbed him in the arm. He backed up a couple of steps and went down. He stayed down, and when police got there, he was dead."

Damon looked at Alina, his face grim.

"Neurotoxin?" she suggested, her eyes on his.

"It could have been a couple different things," he replied slowly, "but if it happened that quickly, my money's on SUX."

"SUX?" Blake repeated.

"Succinylcholine," Alina explained. "It's a paralytic drug. It works on the neuromuscular system."

"Basically, it paralyzes all the muscles in your body. They stop functioning altogether, and that includes the lungs and respiratory system. The victim asphyxiates in seconds," Damon explained. "Certainly less than a minute. It's usually undetected because the enzymes in our body start breaking it down immediately. Most doctors think the victim died of a heart attack."

Stephanie stared at them speechlessly, stunned.

"Who *are* you people?" she finally exclaimed. "How do you know this stuff? Hell, I didn't even know potassium chloride was still a thing until Lina said someone shot John full of it!"

Despite the grimness of the situation, Alina felt her lips pulling upwards.

"It's our job to know this stuff," she said.

Damon shifted on the arm of the chair and stretched his arm along the back, behind her head.

"We wouldn't be very effective if we didn't," he agreed, his eyes dancing.

"Well, you're definitely effective," Stephanie muttered.

Alina saw her shiver and felt a twinge of remorse. Stephanie had caught a glimpse of Viper once before, and their friendship had changed because of it. Tonight, she saw her again, but this time it was much worse. This time Stephanie had seen Viper attacking multiple enemies as effortlessly as she had been trained to do, without emotion or compunction.

Blake shook his head.

"I can't wrap my head around this," he muttered. "You're

Next Exit, No Outlet

saying John was killed with potassium chloride, and then someone tried to shoot Stephanie up with a paralytic drug. Who has the resources for all this? They showed up tonight in full gear, with assault rifles. Who do they think Stephanie is?"

"A priority one target," Alina said, her voice hard.

Damon looked at her sharply. "Again? That term's popping up a lot lately."

She nodded. "I know."

Blake cleared his throat.

"Care to loop us in over here?" he asked. "We don't speak assassin."

A look of amusement crossed Damon's face and Alina smiled faintly.

"It means someone wants her dead yesterday, at any cost," she told them, her brief smile vanishing. "Whatever it is that changed, it bumped Stephanie to the top of their most wanted list. They won't stop until she's dead."

Chapter Four

Alina's words hung heavily in the air, all the more sinister because everyone in the room knew they were true. What color that remained in Stephanie's face drained away and Blake's jaw tightened as he scowled. Before he could open his mouth to say anything, Alina felt her phone vibrate against her hip and she frowned, reaching into her pocket. She glanced at the screen and let out a soft sigh, raising the phone to her ear impatiently.

"Yes?"

"Where the hell have you been?!" Angela Bolan demanded without ceremony. "Where is everyone?"

Alina was silent for a beat, irritation washing through her at her old friend's tone.

"Excuse me?" she finally asked, her voice dangerously soft.

Damon looked down at her sharply, his brow creasing, while Stephanie and Blake glanced at each other then back to Alina.

"I went to Stephanie's at seven to meet Blake and waited for half an hour, but he never showed up," Angela told her furiously. "So I drove all the way out to the boondocks where you live, expecting to find him there with Stephanie, but no one was there either! Not Stephanie, not Blake, not you, not even Damon! I tried calling Steph, but it goes straight to voicemail. I tried calling you earlier, but it went straight to voicemail. No one's picking up, I've been all over South Jersey tonight, and I want some answers!"

Alina slowly raised her eyes to Stephanie's face.

"Why were you meeting Blake at Stephanie's?"

Stephanie gasped and her hand flew to her mouth as her eyes widened in dismay.

"Oh my God!" she exclaimed. "Angie! We forgot about Angie!"

Blake looked at her.

"We?" he repeated. "I didn't know anything about this! Why was I meeting Angela at your house?"

Stephanie waved her hand, motioning him to be quiet, and

Next Exit, No Outlet

pointed to Alina's phone.

"Put her on speaker," she said. "I can't believe I totally forgot about her!"

"I can. You almost died," Blake said dryly as Alina lowered her phone and tapped the screen.

"You're on speaker," she told Angela, resigned.

"Why am I on speaker? Is she there? Stephanie?"

Alina leaned forward and set the phone on the coffee table. When she sat back again, she glanced at Damon to find his eyes on her. She gave a barely imperceptible shake of her head and his lips quivered.

"My God, Angie, I'm so sorry," Stephanie exclaimed. "I forgot all about you."

"Where the hell are you? Why aren't you at Lina's?"

"I never made it there. I'm sorry. I should have called you sooner."

"What do you mean you never made it there? Where are you?"

"I'm –" Stephanie stopped and looked at Alina questioningly.

Alina shook her head and Stephanie frowned.

"I can't tell you," she said. "I'm somewhere safe."

"What do you mean you can't tell me?!" Angela's voice rose an octave and Stephanie grimaced. "I just spent two hours driving around looking for you!"

"Let's start at the beginning," Alina interjected, her calm voice a direct contrast to Angela's. "Why were you meeting Blake at seven?"

"Because Stephanie asked me to!"

Alina pinched the bridge of her nose and felt one of her eyelids begin to twitch.

"I called her on my way to your house," Stephanie explained, realizing that Alina was very close to losing what little patience she had. "I wanted her to go pack some clothes and grab some things for me. I was going to ask Blake to meet her there so he could let her in."

"Except he stood me up!" Angela piped up.

"He didn't even know about it!" Blake exclaimed. "How is this my fault?"

"Is that Blake? He's there too? What the hell, Steph?! Are you all having a party without me? Next you'll be saying Mr. Hunk O' Mysterious is with you!"

Alina felt strong fingers brush the back of her neck, sending an inconvenient shiver of awareness down her spine. Damon leaned down, his lips brushing her ear.

"Mr. Hunk O' Mysterious?" he murmured.

Alina felt a laugh welling inside her and she shot him a look of sheepish amusement. Damon's eyes met hers, and the look in them promised lots of questions later when they were alone. She turned her head away and he straightened up again, leaving his hand on the back of her neck. His fingers rubbed the muscles there, sending shockwaves through her, and she bit the inside of her lip. Yep. She wasn't getting out of explaining that nickname.

"He's here too," she said, a slight tremor in her voice.

"Of course he is!" Angela was working herself up into a full-blown temper now. "You're all together and no one thought to call and give me a heads up that plans had changed?"

"Ang, I'm sorry," Stephanie said earnestly, leaning forward. "It's been a long night. I was in an accident. Someone ran me off the road and tried to kill me."

Silence followed that announcement, and Alina waited for the explosion she knew was coming. She didn't have to wait long.

"WHAT?!" Angela screeched, making them all wince. "And NO ONE CALLED ME?!"

Alina dropped her forehead into her hand and closed her eyes. Damon increased the pressure on her neck and she could feel him laughing silently beside her.

"I was taken to the hospital in an ambulance. Honestly, calling you wasn't a priority at that point in time," Stephanie said, a hint of impatience creeping into her voice.

"Well, are you okay?"

"I'm banged up, but I'll be fine. I have a double concussion, whiplash and a twisted wrist. Other than that, I'm just dandy."

"What hospital are you at? Did they do an MRI or cat scan? How long are you going to be stuck there?"

Stephanie looked at Alina like a deer in headlights and she shrugged as much as to say, 'you're on your own.' Stephanie made a face.

"I signed myself out of the hospital," she said reluctantly.

"You what?!" Angela's voice rose again. "Steph, your brain could be turning into jelly!"

Stephanie shot an accusing look at Blake and he raised his eyebrows innocently.

"Good grief, Angie, my brain's not turning into jelly! Why is everyone saying that? I'm fine."

"Well, where are you? I'll come see for myself."

Stephanie looked at Alina expectantly.

"You can't," Alina said flatly. "Don't worry. She's fine."

"What do you mean I can't?" Angela demanded. "Why not?"

Next Exit, No Outlet

"She's somewhere safe, but it won't stay that way if people know where she is," Alina replied. "The people trying to kill her aren't stupid. They'll be watching you in case you lead them to her."

"Don't tell me I can't...wait, what? Are you saying I'm being *watched?*"

"She's not saying you're being watched," Stephanie said, shooting Alina a look of reproach. "She's just pointing out that it's a remote possibility. There's no point in risking anything."

"Why aren't you at her house?" Angela asked after a moment of thought. "That was the original plan. What changed?"

"This was more expedient," Alina said.

"Expedient? What the hell kind of answer is that?!"

"What she's trying to say is that when I left the hospital, I had to get somewhere safe fast," Stephanie said, shooting Alina another exasperated look. "Her house was too far away."

"Well, if you think I'm going to stay away from Stephanie indefinitely because you didn't want to take the time to drive her to your house, Alina, you're out of your mind," Angela said roundly. "Expedient or not, she's my best friend and I want to make sure she's ok. Where are you?"

"You're not coming," Alina's voice took on a steel edge. "It's too dangerous, for both of you."

Stephanie shook her head and sat back on the couch, a look of resignation on her face. Blake raised an eyebrow and looked at her questioningly.

"This is about to get ugly," she whispered in explanation.

"Well, if you'd taken her to your house like originally planned, we wouldn't be having this issue. I mean, seriously! I'm always coming and going from there, so no one would think anything of it. Stephanie would be comfortable and I can come see her."

Alina took a deep breath and counted to ten, willing her eye to stop twitching.

"I think you're forgetting that Stephanie was attacked on her way to Alina's house," Damon said dryly. "You really want to test fate and try again?"

"You mean to tell me that you two can't get Stephanie there safely?" Angela demanded in a deceptively sweet voice.

Blake choked back a laugh and then quickly sobered when Alina shot him a deadly look.

"This isn't up for discussion," Alina said, her voice tight. "Stephanie's staying here and you're not coming near her until we find out who's doing this and why. End of story."

"Like hell it is! I don't care what you do or who you are, Lina, you're not bossing me around this time. My best friend almost died twice today. I have every right to be with her and see for myself that she's okay. The most logical solution is to move her to your house where I won't lead anyone to her, whatever that's supposed to mean. I think you're being paranoid, personally, but I'm willing to compromise and play along. If you're not going to compromise as well, we have a big problem."

"She has a point," Blake said. "Your house *is* the safest place. I've been saying that all along. After what happened tonight, I see why you don't want to move her again, but Angela does have a valid argument."

"Don't encourage her," Alina said, standing up impatiently and pacing around the living room.

Damon watched her, his face impassive, and remained silent.

"Will you all please stop talking about me as if I'm not even here?" Stephanie spoke up. "Don't I get a say in this? It's me that's under fire, after all. I think I should be able to decide where and how I keep myself safe."

They all looked at her and Alina raised an eyebrow.

"Well?" she asked when Stephanie didn't continue.

"Honestly? I'm torn. They're right. Your house is the logical choice. The place is virtually a compound, and your security system rivals the Pentagon's. A person can't flick a booger on your property without you seeing it."

"But?"

Stephanie shrugged.

"I don't want to bring more trouble to you. We've already been over it. I'm not trying to get you killed along with me."

The smile that crossed Alina's face was downright terrifying.

"Oh, when I go, it won't be because you got me killed."

"Then it's settled," said Angela. "When should I bring her things?"

"It's not settled. I need to think about this."

"What's there to think about? We all agreed it's what's best, and it's what Stephanie wants!"

"I never said it's what I want!" Stephanie exclaimed, throwing her hands up in the air. "In fact, I thought I just made it clear that it *isn't* what I want to do!"

"But you said —"

"Enough!" Damon finally spoke, his voice slicing through the arguing. "It's late and Stephanie's been through enough today. Lina and

Next Exit, No Outlet

I will figure this out. In the meantime, Stephanie's staying here until further notice. Clear?"

"Agreed," Blake seconded, surprising both Alina and Damon. "It's not safe to move her tonight and I, for one, am not willing to make a decision this important when I'm tired, pissed off, and just want to kill someone."

"I really think you guys are making this much more complicated than it needs to be," Angela said, disgruntled.

Alina closed her eyes and counted to ten.

"*We're* not complicating anything," she bit out when she had finished. "Steph will call you tomorrow with an update."

"Don't you dare hang up on—"

Alina leaned down and pressed end, cutting off Angela's furious words. Stephanie stared at the phone for a second, then raised her eyes to Alina's face.

"Well, if she wasn't mad enough already, she is now," she said dryly.

"I'm surprised she waited that long," Blake muttered, standing up and stretching. "Good Lord, is she always like that?"

Stephanie nodded. "Pretty much, but she has a good heart. She only means the best."

"No doubt, but she needs to stay out of this," Damon muttered, standing. He looked at Blake. "Give me your keys and I'll take care of your car."

Blake tossed him the keys reluctantly and glanced at Alina. "You've got Buddy?"

"Yes. He'll be fine." She motioned to a set of double doors on the far side of the living room. "Bedroom's through there. There are towels in the closet, and chargers on the nightstand. Keep your phones off until I can take care of their GPS chips. We have to assume whoever's after you can track them. Let's not make it easy on them."

"You're not going to take them?" Stephanie asked, surprised.

Alina shook her head.

"No. If I disable them, whoever's behind this will know I'm the one who got you out of the hospital alive, and they'll know I'm still in the area. I want to postpone that as long as I can. If you power the phones off, they can still track you, but it will take longer and they'll assume you're working alone."

Blake nodded and pulled out his phone, powering it off. He looked at Stephanie and she reluctantly pulled hers out of her purse, doing the same.

"How will we contact you?" she asked, looking at Alina.

"There's a laptop in the bedroom. It's secure enough to send me a message if you have to. I'll send you an email tomorrow. You can check it on that. It will be encrypted, and the encryption software is already on the laptop." Alina turned and headed toward the short hallway leading to the door, Damon beside her. When they reached the door, she paused and turned back to look at Blake. "I hope you live up to your reputation, gunny. Michael speaks very highly of you."

Blake caught the warning in her tone and his jaw tightened. Before he could answer, she and Damon were gone, the door closing softly behind them.

Alina watched as Buddy circled in front of the sliding door a couple of times before finally flopping down and laying his head on his front paws.

"Are you sure about him being here with Raven?" Damon asked, setting a plate with leftover pizza on the bar in front of her. "I don't see this ending well."

"Raven will ignore him," Alina replied, picking up a slice of pizza. "He's too big to be anything other than an annoyance to him."

Damon circled the bar and sat on the stool next to her with his own pizza.

"I hope you're right." He bit into his slice and they ate in silence for a minute. "How long do you think you can keep Stephanie safe in that condo?"

Alina shook her head. "Not long enough. She'll have to be moved tomorrow."

Damon glanced at her.

"That was a full wet team at the hospital. You think it's the same people after you?"

"Yes." She got up and went into the kitchen to pull some paper towel off the roll by the sink. "It's too much of a coincidence."

She wiped pizza grease off her hands and went back to her seat, handing him a piece.

"Why Stephanie?" Damon asked, sipping his beer. "What do they want from her?"

"My guess is the leak found out about John's hard-drive. I think that's what they were looking for in her apartment. If she saw what was on it, she's now a liability."

Next Exit, No Outlet

"And they don't know she didn't," he finished. "Fantastic. What did you get out of the one you questioned tonight?"

Alina scowled.

"Not much. She's a priority target, and they were told not to fail again. He couldn't tell me anything more than that."

Damon looked at her in disbelief.

"Nothing about who ordered it?"

She shook her head.

"They were mercenaries. He only answered to the head of the team. He had no idea who hired them or why."

Damon cursed softly.

"I liked it better when he was using his own men," he muttered. "Why the switch? Why send one of his own to the FBI building, then move to hired mercenaries a few hours later?"

"To be fair, he's got to be running low on men," Alina said after a moment, a brief, cold smile crossing her face. "We must have made a dent in his reserves in Atlantic City. That was sixteen right there."

Damon flashed an answering grin.

"That's true." The smile faded. "It won't be long before they check CCTV and traffic cams and pick up the Shelby. He'll know it was you who saved her at the hospital, and the Shelby was parked outside the safe house for over an hour. At most, you only bought yourself a couple hours."

She nodded. "I know."

Damon finished his pizza and looked at her.

"I hate to say it, but the only logical place is here," he said, his voice low. "I don't trust her, and I don't see it ending well, but at least we can contain a war here, and she'll have a fighting chance."

Alina pushed her empty plate away.

"I've been trying to think of an alternative, but I keep coming up empty. Every alternative involves travel, and that involves cameras. Even getting her here will be tricky, but at least it's manageable."

They were silent for a long moment.

"I can get her here in the Audi. That's clean and won't raise any flags," he said finally. "I can take her out a side door and disable the cameras in the immediate area ahead of time. What about Blake?"

She shook her head.

"No," she said flatly. "I don't need another soul on my conscience."

Damon frowned.

"He's a Marine, not a civilian. You're not responsible for him.

Stephanie, maybe. Angela, definitely. But the gunnies? No."

Alina looked at him.

"And have yet another person know about this house?" she demanded. "You're the one who keeps saying too many people know about me as it is!"

"What's one more at this point?" he countered. "Besides, let's be honest. When this is all over, this house is blown. You already can't stay here."

Alina got up and picked up their plates, carrying them over to the dishwasher.

"I know."

Damon watched her with his bright blue eyes. "And how do you feel about that?"

She shrugged and opened the dishwasher to put the plates inside.

"I've been feeling out of place and restless here for a while now," she said slowly. "You know that. It was only a matter of time before I'd have had to move on. At least this way, it's on my own terms."

"Then you might as well let Blake come with Stephanie. It's better to have them all where we can keep an eye on them."

Alina closed the dishwasher and looked across the kitchen, her eyes meeting his.

"And if things go sideways?"

"If that happens, it won't make any difference if they're here or not." Damon got up and crossed the kitchen to stand in front of her. "But if we can find the bastard before it all goes to hell, then they'll be safer here than out there."

She was silent for a moment, her face impassive, then she sighed softly.

"Do you have any idea how much of a circus it will be?"

He grinned. "No one ever said life was easy, but at least we can be entertained along the way."

Alina snorted. "You say that now. Just wait. You have no idea."

Next Exit, No Outlet

Chapter Five

September 28 - Iraq
Hi John,
I don't have much time. I'm moving out in an hour with a team for a search and rescue mission. A corporal went missing last night and intel says he's being kept in a town a couple of hours from here. It's a known insurgent stronghold, and I'm not sure how long it will take to locate him. I want to send these before I leave. Two attachments. Keep them safe.
My buddy Michael is getting suspicious. I think he knows something is going on, but I can't tell him anything. I can't tell anyone, but especially not Mikey. He's Irish, and has the temper to match. He'll go off and get himself killed if he gets wind of what's going on. I need you to make sure of one thing: if anything happens to me, don't let Michael O'Reilly know any of this. He's too hot-headed to approach it calmly, and I don't want him getting hurt. He's already promised to look out for Lina if anything happens to me, so you might meet him. A word of caution: he'll be even more protective than me, so make sure you treat her right!
I managed to get a few minutes alone with that war hero I told you about last letter. He's in intelligence now, and he was very interested in what I had to say. He said I did the right thing in bringing it to him, and he's going to look into it. He

thinks he can take care of it without my involvement getting out, so there might be hope yet.

I'm running out of time. Someone's watching me. I can feel it. I'm glad I'm getting out of here on this mission today. A couple days away will give me some breathing room. Maybe when I get back, it'll all be over. But just in case, keep these files safe. Remember, don't tell anyone - not even Lina.

I'll write again when I have news. At least now I'm not the only one trying to figure this out.

Give Lina my love,
Dave

Dawn was just breaking when Alina came awake, her eyes opening slowly as something pulled her from sleep. Damon was beside her, propped up on his elbow, one finger tracing the puckered incision on her abdomen. His lips were pressed together in a line as he stared broodingly at the healing wound.

"Hawk?"

He raised his eyes to hers and Alina found herself looking into deep, emotionless pools, his thoughts effectively concealed from her.

"It's healing well," he said in a low voice.

After digging out a bullet that went through him and into her, an infection had set in, necessitating a trip to a surgeon to have the wound cleaned out. The doctor had stitched it up last week, but the skin was still puckered and angry as the antibiotic he prescribed worked its magic. The muscles gave her pain every time she moved but, all things considered, Alina would take that over the alternative.

"It's getting there."

His gaze shifted to her left arm and the two holes that were now almost completely closed. Those had been courtesy of a bullet that went through her outer bicep. Alina frowned at the look on Damon's face.

Next Exit, No Outlet

"Three new scars, all in the past month."

She raised an eyebrow. "Since when do you keep track?"

"Since they started happening stateside. Injuries in the field are one thing. I get my share, too. These are different. These happened because you were here."

Alina studied his face for a long moment, trying to figure out what he was getting at.

"These are nothing compared to this," she finally said, pointing to the incision on his left side. "This should have killed you. Mine are simply flesh wounds."

"Flesh wounds that should never have happened." Damon sighed and rolled onto his back, staring up at the ceiling. Long shadows fell across his face. "It's safer working ops on foreign soil than being home. I went to Georgia, got in, got my target, and got out - all without getting shot. Hell, you went into a Taliban camp in Afghanistan alone, killed everyone there and walked out without a scratch."

Alina rolled onto her side to face him.

"Not exactly without a scratch," she disagreed, pointing to a faded scar on her jaw. "And either one of those could have gone very differently. You know that. We can't choose when things will go according to plan. We can only control how we react when they don't."

He smiled faintly. "Are you quoting Harry to me?"

She thought for a moment.

"Was it Harry who said that? All the instructors from the training facility blend together in my mind now."

"It sounds like something he would have said, right after he just dealt us a blow that probably had us in the infirmary for hours."

Alina studied him for a moment. "Why the sudden introspection?" she asked softly.

Damon was silent for a long moment, then he exhaled.

"This has to end," he said, his voice just as soft. "We have to find the bastard and finish this. There are only so many times we can get shot before our luck runs out."

"We will. I'm getting close."

Damon looked at her sharply. "What?"

"I haven't had much time to keep you up to date. I'm making progress."

"How much progress?"

"More since I got into John's hard drive. The emails make sense now, and I've been able to put together a timeline and a map."

"The troop movements," Damon said, sitting up and propping a pillow behind his back. "I saw them on your computer downstairs. Is that what this is all about?"

She sat up beside him and nodded.

"Among other things, Dave sent John copies of manifests with missing artillery and equipment. He also sent him maps and satellite images. I thought they were all highlighting troop movements, but they weren't. Most were of areas where the troops were, but a couple were areas where the military never went."

Damon frowned. "What?"

"Dave thought someone was taking military equipment and selling it to insurgents. The manifests he sent back that up. They were all shipments that were reported lost or destroyed, but Dave believed they were actually stolen and sold."

"Did he have proof?"

Alina nodded.

"In at least one instance. Two crates that were supposedly destroyed showed up on the back of a truck in a village. Dave saw them himself."

Damon whistled. "Where did they go?"

"Into the mountains. Here's the kicker. He sent photos that he managed to get of two men with the truck. You'll never guess who was in the photo."

Damon eyed her warily. "Who?"

"Al-Jibad."

He stared at her, his face suddenly impassive.

"Are you kidding me?"

"No."

"That bastard got his weapons from *us*?!"

"Not just us. We were working jointly with British forces. And it gets better. The manifests that Dave sent, just the ones he was able to get copies of, totaled over twelve million dollars worth of weapons," she said grimly. "There were more that he wasn't able to copy and send."

Damon leaned his head back against the headboard and gazed across the dark room.

"That's certainly reason enough to put a bullet in his head. No offense."

Alina glanced at him. "You need to stop saying that. Why would I take offense? It's how he died."

Damon shrugged. "Yes, but there's more tactful ways for me say it."

"Dave's been dead for twelve years. You can sugar coat it all you want, but he'll still be dead."

Next Exit, No Outlet

Damon looked at her and his lips twitched. "What about the troop movements?"

"I'm still trying to figure that out, but it looks like it wasn't so much the troop movements that were important, but what was happening at the same time."

He raised an eyebrow questioningly. "Well?"

"Each time they moved, it coincided with activity in the mountains and the insurgent camps."

"So whoever was selling the equipment knew when they were advancing. That's not surprising."

"No, but it also coincided with diplomatic activity," she told him.

"Well, we know the leak is from Washington," he said slowly. "So, again, no surprise there."

"In the second to last letter, Dave said someone was visiting and he was going to try to get a meeting with him."

Damon's lips tightened. "And?"

"In the last letter, written the day before he died, he said he got the meeting and told him everything."

"Why the hell would he do that when he didn't trust anyone?" Damon demanded. "Hell, he practically committed treason by sending the information to John because he didn't trust anyone."

Viper's mask slid into place and her eyes hardened.

"As far as Dave was concerned, there was no reason *not* to trust him. The man was a war hero."

Damon sucked in his breath and looked at her sharply.

"You think…"

"Not only that, but he worked in intelligence. If anyone could help him, Dave believed it was him."

"It will be a beautiful spring day today with a high of eighty degrees and plenty of sunshine. What a way to start the weekend! Grab the kids and head outside. There are plenty of events going on around the city, and the weather will be perfect all weekend."

The morning news droned on in the background as the smell of frying bacon filled the kitchen. The man at the stove set down a pair of tongs and picked up a splatter screen, setting it over the frying pan. Turning, he glanced at the small television in the corner and watched as the meteorologist went through the weather for the upcoming week. Spring was on its way out, and the days were getting longer and warmer. Soon summer would be here, and he would be looking for ways to escape the city and the oppressive heat.

That is, he would be if he was still here.

His phone vibrated on the counter and the man glanced at the screen. Sighing, he reached for his Bluetooth, hooking it into his ear.

"Yes?"

He turned back to the stove and lifted the splatter screen, picking up the tongs again to turn the sizzling bacon.

"Good morning, sir. There's been a problem with the target."

The man finished turning his bacon and set the splatter screen back over the pan.

"I hope you plan on explaining."

The voice on the phone cleared his throat uncomfortably.

"Special Agent Walker is still alive."

The man's lips tightened and his face took on a decidedly unpleasant expression.

"I was under the impression that I made myself clear the last time we spoke," he said. "At what point did I lose you?"

"None, sir. I know she is a priority target. We're doing everything we can."

"Apparently not." The man lifted the frying pan off the burner and turned off the gas. He set the pan on a back burner. "What's the complication?"

"She had help, sir."

The man stilled. "What do you mean, she had help?"

"I sent a highly-skilled team in full gear and they were all killed. She had to have help. One person could not eliminate an entire team."

"How many were in the team?"

"Fourteen, sir."

"Oh, she had help all right," the man muttered, "and I know just who it was. Damn!" He was silent for a moment, his eyes fixed at a random spot on the wall. "Where is she now?"

"I don't know, but we're watching her apartment, and we've got ears on her office phone and her boss. I'll have something soon."

The man snorted.

"You'll forgive me if I'm not optimistic. This is not the result I paid for when I hired you."

"No, it's not, and I will make this right," the voice assured him. "You have my word."

"I'm not interested in your word. I'm interested in your results and, right now, they're very underwhelming. I've got desk jockeys that can do better than this."

"As I said, it will be rectified."

The man disconnected without another word and thoughtfully tapped his finger on the side of his phone. After a long moment, he set the phone down and turned to get eggs out of the fridge. He would finish making his breakfast, eat, and then get to work. Clearly he had to step in and do things himself. Who would think Agent Walker would turn into such an ordeal?

His lips thinned as he pulled out two eggs and cracked them into a waiting bowl. He hadn't expected such a fight from her, but he supposed he shouldn't be so surprised. After all, she was a childhood friend of Viper.

Viper. She was an even larger problem, and had been for a few weeks now. The woman simply refused to be a good soldier and die. He had known taking her down wouldn't be easy, and so far it was living up to his expectations. Although, he really *had* thought it would end in Atlantic City. Instead, she'd wiped out his entire senior team. Rather than risking any more seasoned specialists, he'd hired Marcel.

Marcel's reputation preceded him. He was a professional, and ran a firm of professionals, all ex-spec ops and mercenaries; these were people trained not to fail. And yet they had now failed twice with Agent Walker. Perhaps his reputation was a bit more inflated than he'd originally thought.

The man removed the splatter screen from the frying pan on the stove and transferred the bacon onto a plate. Turning the front burner on, he set the pan over the flame and waited a moment for it to heat up again. He was just pouring the eggs in when his phone emitted an alarm tone and he glanced at it with a faint frown. Now what?

Picking up the phone, he swiped the screen impatiently and glanced at the alert on the screen. His brows snapped together sharply and he sucked in his breath.

"It's not possible," he breathed in disbelief, touching the button to expand the alert.

The link sent him to a secure site and he logged in with his thumb print, unlocking the account. Fury, hot and fierce, swept through him as he stared at the digital proof that it was, indeed, possible. Someone had found the account in Singapore, the account that he had spent years carefully burying.

The same account that was the only remainder of what had happened twelve years ago in Iraq.

Chapter Six

Alina pulled a mug of steaming coffee out from under the coffee spout and sipped it. Turning, she left the kitchen and walked over to the sliding door where Buddy was waiting, his tail wagging. She slid it open, and he bounded outside and across the deck. She followed at a more moderate pace, watching as he went down the steps and onto the grass. After smelling the air for a moment, he trotted over to the tree line and lowered his nose, sniffing around for the perfect place to do his business.

Lifting her eyes, Alina watched as Raven glided across the lawn and came to rest on the roof of the garage. The sun was beginning to make its way through the trees now, casting pale streams of light across the grass and dispelling the remaining shadows. A gentle breeze promised a beautiful day, and she inhaled deeply, lifting her mug to her lips.

A moment later her phone vibrated in her pocket and she pulled it out, glancing at the screen. It was a secured message, and Alina frowned when she saw the blinking icon. And it wasn't from Charlie.

Turning, she went over to one of the Adirondack chairs and sank into it. After checking to make sure Buddy was still on the lawn, she lowered her gaze back to the screen in her hand. Swiping the alert, she opened a secure browser and started an antivirus scan. While it ran, she watched as Buddy finally found a perfect spot and crouched down.

Once the scan had completed, Alina tapped the screen and opened the secure message. Her brows snapped together in a scowl. There was a single line before an icon to connect to another message.

How well do you know your friends?

Viper tapped the link and watched as an image opened on the screen. Whatever she had been expecting, it wasn't what she was looking at. Her fingers tightened around the phone as she stared at an excerpt from a journal. Only one person she knew kept a journal going back well over 12 years. The entry was handwritten, and she recognized Angela's precise and flowing script.

Next Exit, No Outlet

June 15, 2005

Came back from the shore today. The sun was strong, but the water is still cold. I fried, as usual. It drives me crazy that Lina goes a gorgeous tan while I end up looking like an over-ripe tomato. So not fair. Aside from that, we had fun. Got totally wasted last night, and Lina ended up dancing on a table. Stephanie went up to get her down and they both fell off and broke a chair. Good times.

It's good to see Lina laughing again. She still misses Dave. He graduates from Parris Island next week and then he's going to Camp Pendleton. She's afraid he'll get sent to Iraq, but Steph and I don't think he will. We think she's worrying over nothing.

Lina still doesn't know anything about Dave and Stephanie. I keep telling Steph she has to tell her, but she won't. She says it's over and all it will do is upset Lina. I guess I can see her point. Lina would flip out if she found out her brother was banging her best friend and no one told her. On the other hand, I don't think friends should keep secrets from each other. We're like family. We should be able to tell each other the truth.

Confusion swept through Alina as she stared at the screen in disbelief. Emotions she hadn't felt in years clamored for attention, but Viper wouldn't let them take hold. Instead, she took a deep breath and her heart fell into a steady rhythm that she knew very well. Slowly, she raised her eyes and gazed blindly across the back lawn. Sitting very still, her heartbeat steady, she absorbed the sudden realization that she did not know Stephanie as well as she'd always thought she did. Not only that, but apparently she didn't know Angela as well as she thought she did either. Angela had known a pretty significant secret and had kept it to herself, even after all these years.

The door behind her slid open and she felt rather than saw Damon step out onto the deck. Buddy lifted his head from where he was sniffing around the tree line, spotting Damon on the deck. With a joyful bark, he bounded across the grass and up the steps, heading straight for him. Damon chuckled as Buddy reared up on his back legs and planted his front paws on his chest, tail wagging furiously as he attempted to lick Damon's face.

"Whoa, boy," he laughed. "Easy there."

He lifted Buddy's paws from his shoulders and dropped him back down onto the deck, glancing at Alina as he did so. She wasn't paying him any attention, her gaze fixed across the lawn, her mind years away.

"Hey," he said, walking over to the railing and glancing down at her. "What's going on?"

Viper raised her eyes to his, her lips pressed together in a thin line.

"What makes you think something's going on?"

Damon raised his eyebrow. "You look like you're ready to kill someone."

Viper's lips twisted sardonically. "I'm always ready to kill someone."

Damon studied her face silently as Buddy plopped down at their feet.

"What happened?"

Alina was silent for a long moment, never taking her eyes off Damon's. Even though she had just received an unexpected blow, the look in his eyes seemed to soothe the fury inside her.

"I just received a secure message," she said. "It was sent encrypted, with no traceable IP."

Damon looked at her steadily. "What was in it?"

Without a word, Viper held her phone out to him. Damon frowned and took the phone, lowering his eyes to the screen. He read swiftly, a frown gathering on his brows he did so. When he was finished, he handed her the phone.

"He's playing mind games," he said. "That's all this is. He's trying to get inside your head. You know that."

"I know, but it doesn't change the fact that this could be true. In fact, I'm sure it *is* true. This isn't something Angela would have made up years ago just to have in her journal. And actually, it does explain a few things," she added thoughtfully.

"Like what?"

"When Dave went to boot camp, Stephanie was very upset. At the time, I thought it was because we were all so close. But Angela wasn't that upset and, if anything, she and Dave were closer than he

Next Exit, No Outlet

and Stephanie, or so I thought. I was with John at the time thought, and I clearly didn't notice anything going on between Stephanie and Dave."

"What does it matter?" Damon asked after a moment.

"Normally it wouldn't."

"Normally?"

"This is just another example of something I don't know about Stephanie. What else don't I know?"

"Seriously? He's trying to get inside your head." Damon placed a hand on either arm of her chair and leaned down, his face inches from hers. "So she had a relationship with your brother years ago. So what? How does this affect anything today?"

Alina looked at him, her lips pressed together. He was right, of course. It didn't matter. Whatever happened all those years ago was in the past. It did not affect today.

"Why?" she asked softly. "Why the mind games?"

Damon straightened and backed up to lean against the railing, crossing his arms over his chest. He looked at her for a long moment, and then shook his head.

"You know why. He can't get to you any other way. Every attempt he's made to come after you has failed. Every person that he sent, you sent back in a body bag. The only other way he can get to you is through your head. Remember, this is what he's good at. He's always been able to push your buttons, especially where your brother's concerned. He did it in training, and he's *still* doing it."

Vipers lips tightened. "Yes, he did."

"Remember our final training mission? You were sent to Rio, where the CIA asset on the ground looked just like Dave. That was a test. He's always tested you with your brother."

"And I always failed," she said, her voice a whisper. "He doesn't know that I've changed. I've become the weapon they trained me to be. In the process, I've learned not to react the same way."

"You don't think with your heart anymore. We can't afford to, especially now."

She nodded slowly. He was right. The person who wanted her dead couldn't get to her physically, and so he was reaching for the one thing he thought would work. Divide and conquer. If he could sow doubt in her regarding everything she thought she knew about the people she loved most, then she would make a mistake. Even so...Viper shook her head and looked out over the back lawn.

"I already can't trust Stephanie," she said. "This only reaffirms that."

"This has nothing to do with that," Damon told her. "It's apples and oranges. You can't trust Stephanie because she's been spying on you. That has nothing to do with your brother, or any kind of relationship they had when they were kids."

Viper raised her eyes to his. "That's not my point."

Damon stared at her. "Then what is?"

"What else didn't I know? Not just about Stephanie, but about John? This whole time we've been wondering why Dave sent all these emails to him. John wasn't anything at the time. He wasn't even an investigator with the FBI yet. He was still bartending, for God's sake. So why did Dave send classified information from Iraq to him?"

Damon sucked in his breath. "You're wondering if John was something more than you knew."

Viper nodded slowly. "Maybe this isn't just about Stephanie."

Damon was silent for a long moment, staring at the ground thoughtfully. Finally, he raised his head.

"It could very well be that Dave sent him the information simply to keep it safe. He had no one he could trust there and, as it turns out, the one person he thought would help was the one who blew his brains out. Pardon my bluntness."

Vipers lips curved faintly and she waved one hand absently.

"Didn't we just talk about this last night? Stop apologizing for stating facts. He did get his brains blown out."

"I think it would be a mistake to read more into this than what might be there," Damon continued. "He's trying to get inside your head. That's it. In the long run, it doesn't matter why Dave sent those emails to John, only that he did. And if he hadn't, we wouldn't be where we are now."

"And where are we?" Viper asked, her face grim.

Damon shrugged.

"A hell of a lot closer than we would've been without those attachments. So let's just focus on that, and forget the mind games."

Alina sighed and lifted her coffee cup to her lips, draining the mug. Setting it down on the arm of the chair, she nodded slowly.

"You're right. That's a rabbit hole I don't need to go down."

Damon studied her for a minute. "Good. Am I still bringing Stephanie and Blake here?"

"Yes. As much as I don't like it, there really is no other choice."

"I think it's the lesser of the evils. We can keep an eye on all of them if they're together."

"I know." Alina stood up and picked up her coffee mug.

Next Exit, No Outlet

Turning, she began to move toward the sliding doors. "I have somewhere I have to go," she said over her shoulder. "Can you handle getting them here on your own?"

"Did you really just ask me that?" Damon demanded, following her.

Buddy waited for him to pass before getting up and stretching, then plodding after them, his paws sweeping across the deck.

"Just checking," Alina said, opening the door and stepping into the house. "I should be back by late afternoon."

Damon followed her into the house, Buddy close behind.

"I'll get Stephanie here safely," he said, closing the door behind them. "You just make sure you keep yourself alive, and get back as soon as possible."

Michael glanced in his rear view mirror as he pulled through the E-ZPass lane and out of the toll plaza, picking out the black sedan easily in the moderately heavy traffic. After getting a late start out of the house this morning, he hadn't gone two blocks before he noticed his tail. He'd lost that first one only to pick up another on his way out of the city. Since then, he'd lost and gained at least four.

His phone rang and he pressed the hands-free button on the steering wheel of his truck.

"Hello?"

"You don't sound happy," Blake said, his voice filling the cab.

"I'm not. Things aren't going according to plan today." He switched into the left lane and lowered the gas pedal. "I'm running behind."

"But you have left, right?" Blake pressed.

Michael frowned. "Yes. Everything ok?"

"I wouldn't define everything as ok, no."

"Care to explain?"

"There was a snafu when we tried to leave the hospital last night. They came after Stephanie again."

"What happened?"

"What happened? Your girlfriend happened, and thank God she did. They sent a full wet team."

"What?!"

"I gotta tell you, Mike, I felt like I was back on active duty, only without my gear. These people are serious. They were in full body armor and armed out the ass."

Michael rubbed the back of his neck and glanced in his mirror again at the sedan.

"And Viper?"

"She was waiting for them. She had a guy with her. His name is—"

"Damon."

"Oh, you've met?"

"Yeah."

"Well, between them, they took care of the whole team. I've never seen anything like it. I never want to be on the receiving end of either of them on a bad day, I'll tell you that much. I'm starting to see why she's such a threat."

Michael tamped down an irrational flash of irritation.

"She's not a threat, she's a target. Where are you now?"

"In one of her safe houses, but we're not staying. That's why I called. It seems Damon managed to talk some sense into her. He's coming to take Stephanie to her house in an hour."

"Why didn't she take her there to begin with?"

"They said there was no time. They wanted to get her hidden quickly. Then Stephanie went and complicated the issue by saying she didn't want to put your girlfriend in even more danger by bringing more trouble to her."

Michael frowned.

"There has to be more to it than that," he muttered. "I mean, she's right in one aspect. Someone *is* trying to kill Alina. She's a target herself, and has a lot on her plate trying to find the bastard before they succeed. But I can guarantee Lina doesn't care about that. If anyone is more qualified to protect Stephanie at the same time as herself, I have yet to meet them."

"Oh, there's definitely more to it. We had a big discussion about it last night and when they left, I thought something more was going on than she was letting on. Granted, I don't know Viper well, but I got the impression she was holding a full hand of cards to her chest last night."

"Sounds about right. That's usually the impression she gives, and it's often accurate." Michael was quiet for a moment. "Where are you going to go?"

"I'm not sure yet. Steph's apartment is out. They'll be watching it. They'll just latch on to me when they can't find her. I could stay here, but the email Alina sent this morning made it clear she didn't think this place would be safe for much longer."

"Did she say why?"

"Of course not. Hell, I'm not even supposed to be using my phone, but I wanted to get in touch with you and tell you what kind of storm you're walking into."

Michael bit back a short laugh.

"Welcome to her non-transparency. I'll see what I can find out when I get up there. Where's Buddy?"

"With her in Neverland."

Michael raised his eyebrows in surprise. "What?"

"It's better this way. I'll probably end up in a cheap motel where I can pay cash. He'll be happier in a house with Stephanie."

"What a mess." Michael glanced in his mirror at the sedan again. "I already got a hint as to the storm ahead. I'm passing through Delaware now, but it's going to take a little longer to get there than I thought. I've got a tail."

"What?!"

"Yeah. They've been following me since I left the house. This is the fifth one, if not more. They keep switching out. I lose one and then another comes along."

"Mike, that's not good. Who's after you? And how the hell do they know where you are?"

"I'm assuming it's the same people after Stephanie," Michael said. "Either they have access to the traffic cams or they've stuck a tracker on my truck. I'm not shaking them. I think I'll park the truck somewhere and try something else. I can't risk leading them straight to Viper."

Blake let out a long, frustrated growl.

"What the hell is going on, Mike?" he demanded. "Who are these people?"

"I wish I could tell you, Blake. All I can say is get yourself gone and keep your phone on you. You said Damon's coming to get Stephanie?"

"Yeah. Soon."

"When he gets there, ask him for the number to my other phone. It's safer than this one."

"And he has it?"

Michael glanced in the rear view mirror again. When Viper gave him the clean phone, she made him promise to use it only for herself and Damon, but the game had changed. The stakes had changed. Damon would have to pass the number on to Blake.

"It's a long story. It's a clean phone. I'll call you when I get to the house."

"For God's sake, get there in one piece."

Chapter Seven

Viper stood at the window and looked out over the city. The streets of the nation's capital were clogged with mid-day traffic, but the noise didn't penetrate the hotel room. She watched absently as a bicycle weaved its way through the bumper to bumper traffic, wondering why she was here.

She had just been falling asleep last night when her watch vibrated, alerting her that Charlie wanted to speak with her. She booked a ticket under the name Raven Woods from 30th Street Station to DC an hour later. Damon hadn't stirred when she got out of bed, but she knew he was aware she'd got up. This morning when she mentioned she had somewhere to go, he hadn't even raised an eyebrow. No one else could ever understand why she frequently took off at all hours of the day and night in response to a message from her watch, but Hawk did. He wore the same watch.

The air shifted around her and she smiled faintly. Turning, she watched as Charlie closed the door silently and flipped the lock.

"You're late."

"My apologies." Charlie looked across the en-suite sitting area and smiled. "You look well, all things considering."

Viper was surprised into a short laugh. "Well, that's something at least."

Charlie studied her for a moment, then glanced around the suite.

"The last time we were here the Vice President was trying to kill you," he murmured almost to himself. "Now, it's someone much more dangerous."

"I'm not exactly a teddy bear myself."

His gray eyes met hers and he cracked an amused smile. "No, you're not. That's why I recruited you."

Viper looked at him for a moment.

"Is that why you recruited Dave as well?" she asked, her voice soft.

Charlie raised an eyebrow and moved to sit in an overstuffed arm chair.

"Ah. You know, then." She didn't respond and he sighed softly. "Viper, sit down. There's a lot to go over and we don't have much time."

Alina responded to the steel threaded through his voice and moved to sit opposite him. Once she was settled, he regarded her soberly.

"I did recruit your brother," he began. "He came up on my radar when he made a damn near impossible shot at over two thousand yards in Iraq. He was in a position to help gather information for me while he was still serving in the Marines, and he agreed to do so. At the end of the deployment, he was scheduled to come to the Organization. His enlistment was almost up, and I talked him into leaving the Marines and coming to us. I'd already arranged for his transfer. Unfortunately, he never made it."

Alina swallowed, uneasily aware of dark gray eyes watching her closely.

"You had him investigating the missing artillery," she said flatly, her voice unemotional.

"Investigate is a strong word. He was supposed to see what he could put together, not start sending classified information stateside."

Alina raised an eyebrow. "Did you know he was sending information stateside?"

"If I had known, I would've had the information twelve years ago," Charlie said dryly. "As it stands, the first I heard about it was when you told me."

Alina looked at him thoughtfully for a moment, then shook her head.

"Why didn't he send the information to you? He was as good as working for you already."

"I wish I knew." Charlie shrugged and met her gaze. "What I'm about to tell you is classified. No one else knows this."

"Not even Harry?"

"Especially not Harry. When your brother popped up on my radar twelve years ago, I had an asset in Kabul who swore that the insurgents were getting weapons from our own troops. Before he could find out more, his head showed up in a ditch. They never found the rest of him. After that, I took a personal interest in monitoring the manifests. Over the course of four months, I saw the proof of what that asset had said. The problem was, I had no one on the ground."

"And that's where Dave came in," Viper stated, rather than asked.

Next Exit, No Outlet

Charlie nodded.

"The last I heard from your brother, he was gathering information and would send it all along together. He was killed a few days later. Once he died, I realized that more people knew about what was going on out there than I'd originally thought. It wasn't as simple as a couple of soldiers jumping into the black market. I can't tell you everything, but I *will* tell you that there are many more bodies involved in this thing than you're aware of. Many good, and not so good, men and women have lost their lives over this. Your brother's death, while tragic, did have one benefit. It convinced me that the problem wasn't necessarily on the ground in Iraq, but right here in Washington with me. Unfortunately, with your brother's death, the trail went cold."

"You didn't know anything?" Viper asked disbelievingly. "Forgive me if I find it hard to believe that you had no inkling of what my brother was sending to John. You know I'm going to sneeze before I ever get the cold! How did you not know?"

Charlie considered her thoughtfully for a long moment.

"I knew your brother had found something. However, he was very good at hiding his tracks. I personally went through every transmission he sent out of Iraq for the last month before his death. There was no indication that he ever sent any information to John. I had no idea that any information had gone out."

Alina pursed her lips and stared at him, her mind churning.

"He must've sent them from a different station each time," she said almost to herself, "blocking the IP with each email and re-routing it. It's what I would have done with such limited resources."

Charlie smiled faintly.

"That's the conclusion I came to after you told me about the emails." He shook his head. "It takes a lot to get something by me, even back then, but he did it."

Alina couldn't stop the smile that crossed her face. "Dave always was full of surprises."

"Why John?" Charlie asked.

"Trust me, I've been trying to figure that one out for the past two months. I have no idea why he sent the files to him."

They fell silent for a moment. Alina was still trying to come to terms with the fact that Dave had been working for Charlie, and this conversation was simply creating more and more questions. Why didn't he trust Charlie enough to send the files to him? It made no sense. Unless...Alina exhaled.

"What?"

She looked up in surprise to find Charlie's gray eyes studying her closely. Her lips twisted into a rueful smile.

"I think I know why Dave sent the information to John and not you," she said.

Charlie raised his eyebrows. "Oh?"

"A few times in the emails, he said he didn't know who to trust. At first, I thought he meant you, but that didn't really make sense. Now I think it wasn't that he didn't trust *you*, per se, but rather he didn't trust the people the information might go through before it reached you."

Charlie was silent for a long moment, and when she looked at him, his eyes were like great chips of ice.

"So he sent the information to someone he trusted to keep it safe until he could pass it directly to me from this side of the ocean."

"It's what I would do if I were in his position. At least, what I would have done if I hadn't been trained by the Organization yet," she qualified with a slight smile.

Charlie pursed his lips. "Dave would have made one hell of an asset."

"Dave was one hell of a person."

"After our troops pulled out of Iraq, I lost the trail altogether. Not only was the equipment and artillery missing, but there was no corresponding money trail to follow. After some time, I shelved the whole project and moved on."

Viper regarded him steadily. "What opened it up again?"

"You."

Viper stared him. "Me?"

"Well, more specifically, you and Johann Topamari. Do you remember when I told you that as far as I was concerned, Cairo was a success?"

"Yes, and I said that I hoped one day you would explain that."

"Johann was the first time I got a clue to what happened in Iraq all those years ago. I won't go into details, and I can't even if I wanted to, but suffice it to say something popped up in his financials that indicated he received some of the missing artillery. After the past few weeks, I'm sure you understand what that means."

Viper felt stunned, but she kept her face emotionless.

"When you sent me to Cairo, did you know we would end up here? Did you know I would end up following a trail right back to Iraq? Did you know about all of this?"

Charlie met her gaze solemnly. "In all honesty, no. But, I did hope."

"You have to explain that."

Next Exit, No Outlet

"When you joined the Navy, I watched your progress through training camp with great interest. With every record that you broke, I became more convinced that you could take your brother's place. When you requested military intelligence, I ensured your placement."

"Are you telling me that you manipulated my entire military career just to get me into the Organization?" she demanded in disbelief.

The look on Charlie's face was impassive. He didn't answer her, nor did she think he would.

"When you got to the training facility, Harry didn't think you'd make it through the first phase. I knew better. You're so much like your brother, especially with the rifle." Something close to a smile crossed Charlie's face. "When you passed phase one, I told Harry to push you harder than the others. I knew that one day, I would need you to be a weapon unlike any other. And that's what we created. We did our job so well that, as you worked over the years, I began to question if I had created too much of a weapon. When I told you that Cairo was a success in my eyes, it was because you failed."

Viper felt her mouth fall open. "You wanted me to fail?"

"No. I wanted you to prove to me that there was still some humanity left inside you. I knew Johann surrounded himself with innocents, and that the likelihood of you catching him alone was slim. When I read the report, I realized that the weapon we created could still think for herself."

"I don't see how that's a benefit," she said dryly. "My job is to follow orders, not think for myself."

Charlie smiled faintly. "And yet, isn't that what you've been doing for the past year?"

Her brown eyes met his gray ones, and she bit her lip. He was right. Ever since she'd gone back to New Jersey, she hadn't just been following orders. In fact, once Damon came into the picture again, her isolated and sterile existence had ended. Suddenly, following orders wasn't enough. She wanted more. She wanted to know that what she did, she did for a reason other than because Charlie had deemed it so. After a moment, she nodded ruefully.

"I suppose I have."

"And that is why Cairo was a success. You retired for two years and lived in a commune in South America. In that time, you found yourself again. You discovered your humanity again. We wouldn't be sitting here having this conversation right now if you hadn't done that."

"Forgive me if I'm being dense, but I don't see what any of this has to do with my brother or the bastard in Washington who's trying to kill me and every other asset you've created."

"I needed someone I could trust. You proved to me that you still believe in what's right and are willing to fight for your country, regardless of the cost. I have no doubt that you will give up your life for the greater good, and believe me, there are not many who would."

"Let me get this straight," Viper said after staring at him for a moment. "You've been grooming me for six years to kill a traitor so well hidden in Washington, DC that no one could find him?"

"Well, that's a much more simplistic view of the situation, but essentially yes."

Alina stared at him, her eyes hard and penetrating.

"Were you ever going to tell me about my brother?"

"Not unless it became necessary. You don't have a good track record when it comes to Dave. You tend to get emotional where he's concerned, and it has been known to affect your judgment. However, since that choice was taken out of my hands, I have to say that I've been quite impressed with your self-restraint. You proved me wrong, and I appreciate that."

"Tell me about Johann," she said after a long, silent moment.

"After Cairo, he went underground, and so did my lead. When the Vice President brought him into the country to create a terrorist attack, I knew we were back in business."

Viper gaped at him in disbelief.

"You mean to tell me this has all been in play since last year?" she demanded. "It started with Three Mile Island?"

"Yes."

"Son of a bitch!"

He let out a short laugh.

"Precisely. He's been playing you since you came out of retirement. He's been playing all of us. He used Regina Cunningham and the Vice President as pawns, and then used me to move you into position, just where he wanted you. I knew it was happening, but I didn't know who was playing puppet-master. So I waited, and watched."

"Why me? He was in the clear. After all those years, no one had a clue about him. What changed to make him come out in the open again? And why come after me? Why has he been targeting me for the past year?"

"I'm still working on that. I think Al-Jibad played a big role in that, to be honest. Whether or not he was blackmailing him, or just calling in some old favors, that's when I think it began. When I sent you after Al-Jibad, it may have been the straw that broke camel's back.

I don't know."

"You saw the photo in the attachment," she stated rather than asked.

Charlie nodded. "I'll do you one better. One of those financials from Johann connected back to him."

Viper shook her head, anger welling up inside her. She tamped it down and met Charlie's gaze.

"The Vice President wasn't the one who brought Johann into the country, was he?"

Charlie shook his head. "I don't believe so, no."

"Did he know about it? Or was he just an innocent pawn?"

"I think he knew about it," he said. "He had his own agenda and his own ends he wanted to meet. Of course, with both he and Regina dead, there's no way to confirm."

Viper let out a short laugh.

"Convenient how everyone who knows anything about this dies. And here, this whole time, I thought you'd arranged for the Vice President's death."

"Quite the contrary," Charlie said grimly. "The President and I had come up with a different resolution. Before I could implement it, the Vice President died."

She was silent for a long moment as she absorbed everything that she had learned in the past twenty minutes. Sorting the stunning amount of information into priorities, Viper focused on the most pressing.

"When he failed with Johann, he tried again with Moon and the bank virus," she said slowly. "When that didn't work, he turned to Asad. By that time, Al-Jibad was already dead. Even if Al-Jibad was behind it in the beginning, he wasn't any longer. The bastard was just going after the country for his own sake then. He couldn't have the banking virus, so he tried for a deadly one instead."

"Yes. Although, he did try to get the banking virus again. I pulled it from the FBI after a security breach when it was almost stolen."

Viper looked at him in surprise. "Where is it now?"

"Safe," Charlie said shortly. "Tell me about Kasim and Tarek."

"It was all in our debriefings," she said, dropping the subject of the traitorous leak for the time being. "Hawk and I were able to neutralize them without any collateral damage. We went old school to keep the risks low."

"It's much appreciated," he told her. "There were over six hundred school kids there that day. If even one of those bombs had detonated, the loss of life would have been devastating."

Vipers lips twisted. "Tell that to the media."

Charlie chuckled. "Ah, so you've seen the news."

"Hard to miss it."

"If you wanted thanks and recognition, you should have joined the Girl Scouts."

"I'm happy where I am, thanks," she said, then she paused. "Although, I'm waiting for the news of Kasim and Tarek to go public. When it does, it won't be pretty."

Charlie's eyes darkened.

"It's already not pretty," he muttered. "I assume you're referring to the open letter circulating with your location and photo?"

Viper nodded, unsurprised that Charlie knew about the letter.

"It was released the day before we killed them," she said. "Once news of their death gets out, and it will, I'm going to have every member of Al-Jibad's group and most of the ISIS cells across the globe looking for me."

"I've already pulled the letter and our cyber-team is working on damage control. They're circulating several other letters to make that one look like a fake, but it will take time. You've changed your appearance, so that will help. But there's no way around the fact that your identity is compromised and your cover blown. You know what that means."

Viper nodded, her face impassive.

Charlie studied her for a long moment in silence.

"What are your current views on running ops for me?" he finally asked. "That offer is still viable."

Viper's lips twisted and her dark eyes met his.

"I have to finish this first," she said flatly. "You trained me to take on Goliath, and that's what I'll do. If I make it to the other side, then we'll talk."

Charlie nodded and stood.

"I'm working on getting the information you requested," he told her. "It's taking a bit more time than I anticipated. I should have something for you by Monday, at the latest. Are you sure about this?"

Viper stood and the smile on her face was chilling.

"You asked me that once before" she said. "I'm always sure."

He nodded. "And the other arrangements?"

"I'll take care of everything. I just need you to keep the skies clear."

"Of course." Charlie turned to go towards the door, but paused before reaching it and turned to face her. "I probably won't see

Next Exit, No Outlet

you again until this is all over. Do me a favor? Stay alive."

Viper smiled slowly.

"I'll do my best."

Chapter Eight

Hawk eased the front door open and slipped into the apartment, closing it softly behind him. The murky light from the partly sunny day outside couldn't penetrate the closed mini blinds on the front windows, and the apartment was filled with gloom. He reached out and flipped the light switch on the wall, then froze.

Stephanie's apartment was trashed. Furniture was upended, pictures were off the wall and laying discarded on the carpet, and the contents of her entertainment center were strewn around the living room. Hawk reached behind him to pull his Beretta from the holster at his back and, making his way through the mess to the dining room, he let out a low whistle. All the neat piles on the dining room table had been thrown across the table and onto the floor, and two of the chairs were on their sides. Glancing into the kitchen, he found more of the same.

After making sure no one lurked in the kitchen or outside the sliding back door, Hawk turned to go down the small hallway towards the bedrooms. He held his Beretta up near his shoulder, listening for even the slightest sound. There was none. He poked his head into the spare room on the left. Storage boxes had been ripped open, the contents gone through and dumped out onto the floor. The closet stood open, empty. He shook his head and left the spare room. Someone had been very thorough.

After checking the small bathroom, Damon went into Stephanie's bedroom. He'd been in here before, when he'd searched the apartment and found John's safe deposit box contents. He was no stranger to the safe in the closet, and he went there first. The safe stood open and he bent down to peer inside. After studying it for moment, he straightened up and turned around slowly, surveying the disaster.

Whoever had done this knew exactly what they were looking for. All of Stephanie's spare weapons and cash were still in the safe. They didn't even try to make it look like a robbery. They were sending a message.

Next Exit, No Outlet

Confident that he was alone in the apartment, Damon tucked his gun back into its holster and left the bedroom. He went into the bathroom and opened the drawer under the cabinet to the right. There, just as Alina had promised, was a plastic box filled with pill bottles, lotion, powders and tampons. He grabbed it and went to the shower. After pulling out the shampoo and conditioner, he added them to the box and turned to leave the bathroom.

Before she left this morning, Alina asked him to stop at the apartment on his way to get Stephanie and Blake. As she said, the least they could do was make sure Stephanie had her meds. Hawk glanced into the box as he carried it to the dining room. So far as he could see, none of the meds were crucial to survival, but far be it from him to stop Special Agent Stephanie Walker from taking her birth control.

He set the box on the dining room table and looked around in the mess on the floor until he found a Kindle Paperwhite, partially hidden under a side table. Bending, he swiped it up and added it to the box. That was it. Alina hadn't said anything about clothes, and he wasn't about to guess. Stephanie could make do. As far as he was concerned, she should just be happy that she was still alive.

After gazing at the destruction around him for a moment, Damon grabbed one of the kitchen chairs and pulled it over to the far wall. Standing on it, he reached for the vent above the doorway leading into the short hallway. He lifted off the grate and reached inside, extracting the small wireless camera that Viper had placed when they came to get Buddy. He touched the button on the side of the camera and replaced the grate, tucking the camera into his cargo pocket.

Getting off the chair, he pulled it back to the table and picked up the box again. When Viper had placed the camera in the vent, he'd thought she was being overly cautious. Evidently, it turned out to be the right move. At the very least, they'd know who trashed Stephanie's apartment.

After one last look around, Hawk strode to the front door, letting himself out as quickly and as silently as he had entered.

Stephanie walked out of the bedroom into the living room where Blake was sitting on the couch with his feet propped up on the coffee table. He was glowering at the TV and she frowned.

"What's wrong?" she asked, moving forward.

"The news."

She made a face and went over to sit on the chair.

"I don't know how you can watch it," she said, glancing at the flat screen. It was a commercial break and white bears wearing tropical shirts were checking into a hotel. "They're so full of crap half the time. What's going on now?"

"They're talking about yesterday. They're saying the shooting at the FBI building is connected to the stabbings in Independence Park."

Stephanie stared at him. "What? How is that possible?"

He shook his head.

"I don't think it is," he said, stretching. "Not unless you're leading some kind of secret life I don't know about."

"Do we know anything about what happened in the park?" Stephanie asked after a moment.

"Only that two men were stabbed to death. I'm waiting to hear the latest on that. It's coming up after these commercials."

Stephanie watched the commercial absently in silence. With all the events of the previous evening, she had completely forgotten about the attack at Independence Hall. The last she'd heard about it was before she left the city yesterday, and that information was sketchy at best. All anyone seemed to know was that two men had been stabbed while touring the Liberty Bell and Independence Hall.

The commercial break ended and a female reporter dressed in a red jacket with a white blouse took over the screen.

"Yesterday, in South Philadelphia, two men were brutally stabbed to death in the birthplace of our nation's freedom," she told the camera solemnly, her glossy red lips enunciating each word with trained precision. "Although their identities have not been released, more information is coming to light regarding the vicious attack. Speaking on the condition of anonymity, a source close to the investigation says that they are not ruling out the possibility that this was a hate crime. Both victims were of Middle Eastern descent and, while their nationality is still being determined, there is strong evidence that suggests they were members of the Islamic faith. There doesn't appear to have been any reason for the attacks, and no threats were made on the security of the park. Anthony Corvero reports."

The camera switched from inside the studio to a tall reporter standing on the grass outside Independence Hall.

"I'm standing here in Center City where, just yesterday, two men were brutally murdered while they were touring the Liberty Bell and Independence Hall," he told the camera. "It was a normal spring day here, and the birthplace of our nation's freedom was filled with

Next Exit, No Outlet

tourists and school children on class trips. The afternoon ended in terror when two of those tourists were found stabbed to death in the middle of the crowds. One was killed inside the Liberty Bell building, while the other was found dead inside Independence Hall behind me. Both attacks occurred within minutes of each other, leading investigators to believe this was a coordinated assault. Nothing seems to connect the two victims aside from their ethnic origin, which points to the very real possibility that this was, indeed, a hate crime."

The alarm pad inside the door beeped as the front door to the condo opened silently and Blake was off the couch in an instant, his Beretta in his hands. Damon raised an eyebrow and closed the door.

"At ease, gunny," he said humorously.

Blake's shoulders relaxed and he slid the weapon back into his side holster.

"You could at least have knocked," he muttered, returning to the sofa.

Damon strode into the living room, his eyes going to the TV.

"...in light of the vicious attack, several area mosques are organizing a vigil for the unknown men," the reporter said.

The scene on the screen changed again to a clip from a man dressed in a white robe. The caption on the bottom of the screen identified him as a local imam.

"There are no words to describe the sorrow at this terrible tragedy. Two men, visiting an iconic, historical monument, were killed like animals in the midst of children. Those responsible must be caught and brought to justice. This violence against my people must stop! We want to live in peace, and not fear to go out in our own city."

Damon's lips tightened and the scene changed back to the reporter outside Independence Hall.

"The leaders of several area places of worship, including Catholic and Protestant churches, are joining with the Muslim community to condemn these attacks. A vigil is being organized and will take place right here, at the scene of the senseless and unwarranted murders that have divided our city."

"Watching this garbage will rot your brain," Damon said, his voice even. "Are you ready to go?"

Stephanie nodded and stood up.

"How are we going to do this?" she asked as Blake aimed the remote at the TV and switched it off. "Is Blake going to come with us part way, or will we drop him near a subway? He doesn't have his car to get anywhere."

"Blake's going with you." Hawk turned to look at him. "It's

safer for you to stay with her."

Blake nodded. "Good. I won't pretend that I was happy about leaving her alone."

Stephanie rolled her eyes.

"I'll hardly be alone. It's going to be a full house. Besides, you'll see when you get there: the place is Fort Knox. There would have been nothing for you to worry about."

Hawk turned to move toward the door.

"Let's move," he said. "You can discuss it on the way."

Blake and Stephanie followed him to the door, watching as he set the security alarm before opening the door. They moved out to the hallway and he followed, closing the door firmly behind him. He nodded to the far end of the hallway.

"We're taking the stairs."

Blake raised his eyebrows and glanced at Stephanie.

"Is that really necessary? With her leg, the elevator would be better."

Hawk didn't even glance over his shoulder as he moved towards the stairwell door at the far end of the hallway.

"Would you rather be safe, or sorry?"

Blake glowered at the back of his head, but followed obediently. Stephanie hooked her arm through his and leaned on her cane as they followed Damon.

"I'll be fine."

Damon reached the door and opened it, then stood aside for them to pass through. Once they entered the stairwell, he sent one last searching glance toward the door of Viper's safe house. Was the stairwell really necessary? Probably not, but he was not about to find out for sure. He followed them through the door, all his senses alert. Viper was expecting him to get Stephanie and Blake safely to Medford, and that was just what he was going to do.

The door to the stairwell had just clicked closed when the elevator doors slid silently open. Four men stepped out and considered both doors in the hallway. One of them glanced down at his phone before nodding to the door on the left.

"It's that one," he said softly.

"Are we sure about this?" another asked, his voice just as soft.

Next Exit, No Outlet

The first man shrugged and reached behind him. He pulled a Sig Sauer from the holster at his back with one hand and reached into his jacket pocket to pull out a silencer with his other.

"Alpha has camera footage showing them entering this building. This is the only condo in the whole building whose owner we can't trace. I'd say the odds are pretty high they're in here, wouldn't you?"

The second man shook his head and reached for his own weapon.

"Let's hope you're right."

The first man shot him a small grin. "If we're wrong, then it's empty. No harm, no foul."

He motioned with his hand and the two men behind them moved forward. One of them pulled a small box out of the bag over his shoulder. Moving to the side of the door, he moved the box along the wall parallel with the door. He started at the top of the door jamb and steadily moved the box down. About a third of the way down the wall, the box vibrated in his hand and a light flashed. He nodded to his companion and pulled the box away from the wall.

The other man reached into his pocket and pulled out another box that resembled a scrambler. He moved to the side as the first man bent over the door handle. A moment later, there was a soft click, and the door swung open. The fourth man slipped inside and the others followed, waiting while he attached the scrambler box to the alarm pad inside the door. Five seconds later, the alarm switched off.

By the time he pulled the box off the alarm pad, the first two had already moved down the hallway into the living room. They moved swiftly and silently, their weapons ready. At the end of the hallway, the first one went into the galley kitchen while the second turned right and moved toward the bedroom. The other two followed, watching as their companions cleared the condo.

"They were here," the one called from the bedroom. "The shower's still wet, and there are damp towels on the rack."

A moment later they all converged in the living room, looking at each other. The first one out of the elevator holstered his weapon and pulled out his phone. After dialing, he held the phone to his ear. It connected after the second ring.

"The nest is empty," he told the person on the phone. "They were here, but now they're gone."

There was a short silence on the line.

"What makes you think she was there?"

"Someone had a shower, and it was recent."

The man on the other end of the line let out a soft curse.

"Keep an eye on the place in case they return," he instructed. "I'll let Alpha know."

The man disconnected and slid the phone back into his pocket. He looked at his companions and motioned them to the door.

A minute later, the alarm was set again, and the condo was empty.

Viper slipped through the door and closed it behind her silently. The automatic lock clicked back into place and she glanced around the tiny alcove she found herself in. The entryway was little more than a five-by-five square, with a narrow stairwell leading straight up into the condo above. She moved up the steps silently, her ears tuned for any noise, taking the stairs two at a time.

Cresting the top, she stepped into a large living room. The alarm box was on the wall next to the stairs, and she glanced at it to ensure that the light was green. It had taken just over an hour to break through the security and disable the alarm, but in the end, it was easier than she'd expected. She would have thought the traitor would have a more advanced alarm system than he did.

Looking around the sparsely furnished living room, she took a moment to study all the vents and cracks visible to her. The security system indicated cameras, and she had disposed of them appropriately. However, Mr. X was no fool. He would have backups that were closed-circuit and not looped into his security. After scanning the large room, her eyes lit upon a single vent above the door leading into the hallway. Her lips curved faintly.

Moving across the living room, she went into the dining room and grabbed one of the chairs flanking the messy dining room table. With one hand, she picked it up and carried it over to place it beneath the vent. A moment later she had it open and was extracting a wireless camera. She pressed the button on the side, powering it down, and tucked it into her jacket pocket before replacing the vent grid. Then she got off the chair and turned to survey the condo.

The living room was spacious but contained only a recliner, a side table, and a loveseat. A large, flat screen TV hung on the wall above the mantle, and on the far side of the living room a console took up half the wall. Laid out on the console were variety of bottles and glasses, along with an empty ice bucket. Viper picked up the chair and

Next Exit, No Outlet

carried it back into the dining room, looking at the table. It reminded her of Stephanie's dining room table, or even Michael's. It seemed like she was the only one who didn't use her dining room table as an office.

Viper went through the stacks of files on the table quickly and silently, replacing them in exactly the same spot that she had found them. None of them were sensitive, and none of them would help her. When she'd gone through the lot, she turned and made her way down the short hallway to the master bedroom.

She only had a certain amount of time. There was no guarantee that Mr. X wouldn't come back while she was still there. According to his PA, he was at a congressional luncheon right now, but Viper knew how quickly plans could change. One call from someone in his office and he would leave.

Entering the bedroom, she glanced around and shook her head. This room was also sparsely furnished. With the exception of the queen-sized bed against one wall and a matching dresser on the other, the master bedroom was as empty as the living room. Clearly, Mr. X had never taken the time to settle in. He probably never thought he would stay that long, or at least, he probably hoped he wouldn't stay that long. At least it made it easy to search, she reflected dryly as she moved towards the closet.

There had to be a safe somewhere, and most people seemed to prefer the closet as the place to house it. Herself? With the exception of an apartment in Sorrento, she tended to hide her safes where no one could find them. However, Viper admitted that she was more cynical than most.

She stepped into the walk-in closet and looked around. Suits and dress shirts hung on one side while the other contained more casual wear. The back wall was lined with shelves holding neatly labeled boxes. Some were file boxes labeled accounts, financials, and taxes. Others were plastic storage bins and clearly held off-season clothing. And there, on the floor under all the shelves, was the safe.

How predictable, she thought as she went forward and crouched down before it. She reached into the inside pocket of her jacket and extracted a small box which she affixed to the outside of the digital pad. She pressed a button, and a moment later there was a click. Opening the safe, Viper peered inside. It was small and half of it was taken up with stacks of file folders. In addition to the folders and paperwork, there were a few jewelry boxes, a few large stacks of cash, neatly bound and labeled with the increments, and one external hard drive. Viper raised an eyebrow and reached for the hard drive.

She opened the messenger bag that hung across her body and

pulled out a Surface Pro. Moving quickly, she attached one end of a cable into her laptop and the other end into the external hard drive. In less than a minute, she was copying the encrypted contents. While the laptop worked, she reached for the top folders in the stack of paperwork.

Flipping one open, she sorted through several passports, all under different aliases. After noting the various countries, she closed the folder and reached for the next one. When she opened it, a single envelope fell out. She raised an eyebrow and opened it unceremoniously. Inside was a printed out confirmation from an airline. Her lips tightened.

It was a one-way ticket to Montenegro with an open departure date. The confirmation was dated three days ago.

Three days ago, she and Hawk had killed sixteen of Mr. X's men in Atlantic City. Obviously, he'd decided then that things were not going his way.

The laptop beeped and Viper glanced at the screen. The copy was complete. She replaced the ticket in the envelope, and then put the folders back where they had been. Her fingers rapidly disconnected the cabling and she placed the external hard drive in the safe at the precise angle at which she had found it. Closing the safe, she stood up and left the bedroom swiftly.

As she moved through the silent condo, Viper took one last look around the place Dave and John's killer called home. Fury washed through her, catching her by surprise, and Alina felt her hands begin to shake. It would be so easy to wait for him to come home and end this all right now.

Viper took a deep, calming breath and exhaled slowly. No. It wasn't time yet. There was more to do. She had a plan, and her plans always worked.

And in the end, when it was all said and done, he would die while she watched.

Chapter Nine

Damon looked up as a loud tone sliced through the silence in the living room. Stephanie had taken herself upstairs to the spare room to lay down, and Blake was stretched out in the recliner. Both men looked at the plasma screen above the mantelpiece at the sharp noise. One of the quadrants was flashing. Hawk was out of his seat on the couch and headed towards the sliding doors before Blake had even grasped what he was looking at.

"What the hell is that?" Blake demanded, swinging his legs down from the recliner and standing up.

"That is Viper's security system," Hawk replied over his shoulder. "Someone's breached the perimeter at the back of the property."

Blake scowled and looked up at the screen again.

"It's a guy," he said. "I can't see his face."

Footsteps came stumbling down the stairs at the front of the house and Stephanie flew down the hallway as fast as her limping leg would go.

"Already?!" she cried. "I just got here!"

Despite himself, Damon felt a chuckle escape.

"Stay here," he said shortly. "I'll be back."

With that, he disappeared out the sliding door, leaving Blake and Stephanie to stare at each other.

"What the hell is he doing?" Stephanie demanded, looking up at the screen on the wall. "Is it just one person?"

"That's all I see, but I don't know if we're seeing the whole system."

Stephanie rubbed the back of her neck and sank onto the sofa. Staring at the quadrants displayed on the screen, she watched as the tall intruder moved through the trees swiftly.

"What if he's not alone?"

Blake looked grim. "Then we'll handle it."

Hawk strode through the trees, moving steadily in the direction of the man who had breached the perimeter. He moved swiftly and silently, at home among the trees. He had a pretty good idea who the intruder was, but he didn't know why he had chosen to come through the back of the property. He paused, listening intently, then continued to the left. A sharp breeze blew through the trees above his head, rustling young, spring leaves. The woods had grown silent, the wildlife still and invisible, leery of the sudden and foreign movement in their midst. A few minutes later, Damon rounded the trunk of a pine tree, and came face-to-face with Michael.

"You're living dangerously, gunny," he told him, tucking his gun back into the holster at his back.

Michael held out his hand. "Good to see you, too."

Damon grasped his hand in greeting.

"This is a good way to get yourself killed. What the hell are you doing?"

"Viper asked me to come," Michael said, falling into step beside him. "Something about babysitting Angela."

Damon glanced at him, his blue eyes amused.

"So that's what she meant about a babysitter," he murmured. "Good luck with that."

Michael grimaced. "Thanks."

"That doesn't answer why you're coming through the back," Damon said. "Where's the truck?"

"I parked it at short-term parking at the airport. I was followed out of DC this morning."

Damon looked at him sharply. "How many?"

"Honestly, I lost count. I picked up the first one as soon as I left the house, and I lost him immediately. Then he was replaced with another, who I also lost, and then another one showed up. They kept switching out all the way up 95. I gave up keeping count after about the sixth."

Damon pressed his lips together and was silent for a moment. "Did they see you leave the airport?"

"No. I lost them, parked the truck, and then caught a cab at the terminal. I've been clear since."

"Where did you have the cab drop you?"

"About four blocks from the nature reserve at the back of the property."

Damon nodded.

"Good. If they were able to keep tabs on you all the way from DC, they either have your truck tagged or they knew where you were going."

"No one knew where I was going, not even my boss. My bet is on the truck being tagged, but I didn't have time to go over it at the airport. I just wanted to get moving while I had the chance."

"If they're going off the tracking device on the truck, then their trail ended at the airport. If the cab dropped you four blocks from the nature reserve, that's well within Viper's five-mile security perimeter. Even if they weren't going off a tracking device and somehow managed to follow the cab, you should be safe."

"It's not me I'm worried about," Michael said. "Is she here?"

"No. She should be back soon."

Michael glanced at him and shifted his duffel bag from one shoulder to the other. Hawk caught the grimace on his face and grinned.

"You're not getting soft on me, are you?"

Michael glowered at him.

"I wasn't expecting a two-mile hike today," he retorted. "How's Stephanie? I spoke to Blake this morning and he told me what happened at the hospital last night."

"She's fine. They're at the house now."

Michael looked at him, surprised. "They?"

"I convinced Lina to allow Blake to come with her," he said. "It's safer that way."

Michael let out a soft whistle. "I was going to try to convince her myself, but I wasn't holding out much hope."

Damon glanced at him but was silent. After moment, Michael up.

"How bad is it? What are we looking at?"

"Nothing good. I hope you came ready to fight. Chances are good you'll be thrown right into the ring. We all will be."

"And Viper?"

Damon hesitated for the briefest of seconds, then sighed imperceptibly.

"She's on a warpath, but for the first time, I think she's actually ahead."

Michael nodded. "About damn time. Whatever I can do to help, I'm here."

Blue eyes met brown.

"I appreciate that, gunny. I never thought I'd say this, but I'm glad to have you here."

Michael grinned. "Things must be worse than I thought.'"

"Oh, I have a feeling they're going to get even worse before they get better."

The man sat behind the steering wheel and watched as the woman opened her trunk. The silver BMW was parked fairly close to the store and in a well-trafficked part of the parking lot. As he watched, the woman began loading bags from a red cart into her trunk. He hoped this was the last stop. He was getting tired of watching her shop; she'd been at it most of the day.

He'd got the call from Alpha telling him to stick to Angela Bolan early this morning. He'd been watching her for days, but he hadn't been told to maintain continuous surveillance, and so he hadn't. He learned her routine and kept watch from afar. All that changed this morning.

Alpha had lost the FBI agent.

The man shook his head, his lips tightening. How Stephanie Walker had turned into such a nightmare was anyone's guess. All he knew was that if it had been him, Stephanie Walker would be dead. He should have had her in the parking garage, but she dropped her keys at the same second he pulled the trigger. That was freak accident and it would not have happened again. He could have finished the job if Alpha had allowed him to. But he hadn't and, as a result, the FBI agent was still very much alive. Why Alpha had switched to mercenaries was a mystery to him. He didn't care how good they were supposed to be, they had done nothing but fail since they came onboard. Now it was up to him to try to salvage everything. Alpha expected Angela Bolan to lead him to Agent Walker, and so here he was, watching her marathon shop through her Saturday.

The man watched as she lifted two cases of soda into the trunk. She really had a thing for soda. Yesterday, she'd gone food shopping and bought two cases there. Now here she was with more. Didn't the woman know how bad for her the stuff was?

Angela finally finished emptying the cart and slammed the trunk closed. The man watched as she walked the cart to the cart return, then turned and headed back to her car, pulling her keys out of

Next Exit, No Outlet

her purse. He glanced at his watch. The sun was starting to fade, and he was getting hungry, but if she didn't go straight home, there would be no dinner in his foreseeable future.

He watched as she started the car and backed out of her parking spot, waiting until she got to the end of the row before starting his own engine. She rolled to the stop sign at the edge of the parking lot, and then turned right onto the busy street. Once she'd merged into traffic, he pulled out to follow. He maintained a very safe distance, keeping her about eight cars ahead. At the next light, she would turn left if she were headed home.

The man frowned when she instead turned right. He glanced at the GPS tracker on his dash and watched as the flashing red dot that represented her vehicle moved along the line on the map toward Route 70. She was going in the opposite direction from where she lived. He bit back a sigh. She wasn't done yet.

A few minutes later, they turned onto Route 70, heading east. The frown grew as she drove away from the shopping areas. Where the hell was she going? The man glanced at his GPS again, expanding the map. As far as he could tell, there was nothing in this direction except residential areas and trees. Lots of trees.

He returned his gaze to the silver BMW ahead. As they drove, the traffic diminished and he held back even further. He didn't think she would notice a tail, but there was no point in being careless. He was hacked into the onboard GPS of her BMW. He couldn't lose her. Wherever she went, he would know.

After what seemed like forever, she pulled off the highway and wound her way through a small, sleepy suburban town. They rolled through the center of town, passing little strip malls interspersed with old, colonial houses. After going through four traffic lights, they approached a fifth one. The light was yellow when Angela turned right and turned red before he reached it. The man slowed down and rolled to a stop, glancing to the right. He could just see her taillights disappearing down a tree covered road. Looking to his left and seeing no oncoming traffic, he turned.

He hadn't gone half a block when red and blue lights lit up the street behind him and a brief wail sounded from a siren. The man looked in his rear view mirror, cursing softly at the sight of the patrol car with flashing lights. He took his foot off the gas and pressed the brake, pulling to the side of the road. In the distance, Angela's taillights disappeared into the growing dusk.

Irritation washed through him as he shut the engine off. The police car rolled up behind him, lights still flashing, and an officer got out. The man shook his head and reached into his glove box to extract the rental car paperwork. Angela was long gone now, but he wasn't worried. The GPS would tell him where she went, and he'd find her again soon enough.

The police officer walked up to the driver side door and the man lowered the window with the press of a button.

"Good evening, officer."

"How's it going?" The officer responded. "Do you know why I pulled you over?"

"Not the faintest."

"You turned right on a red light back there," the officer told him. "It's a no turn on red."

"Is it? I'm sorry. I'm not from around here, and I didn't know."

"Where're you from?"

"California," the man answered readily. "I'm visiting my brother."

"Okay. Well, let me see your license and registration."

The man handed over the rental car paperwork along with his license. After examining them briefly, he nodded.

"Sit tight, and I'll be right back. Is there anything on your license I should know about?"

"Nope."

The police officer nodded again and walked back to his patrol car. The man watched him go in the rear view mirror and the congenial smile left his face. Seriously? A no turn on red? The man rested his head back against the headrest.

This was going to be a long night.

Alina pulled the Range Rover next to Damon's Audi and killed the engine. The sun had sunk below the tree line, casting the backyard into deep shadows. She opened the door and got out of the rental SUV as flood lights flashed on, washing the area with white light. She looked towards the deck as the back door slid open and Damon moved onto the deck, closing the door behind him. Alina felt a rush of warmth go through her. It had been a long day, and she had never been much of a fan of trains. Seeing Hawk move across the deck and down the steps filled her with a sense of homecoming, and she frowned faintly in response.

"New Range Rover?" Damon asked, moving across the grass with his lethal, jungle cat stride.

"Just a rental," she replied with a faint smile. "Everything go okay today?"

Damon nodded, his face inscrutable.

"The gang's all here," he said. "You have a full house."

Alina fell into step beside him as they walked towards the deck. There was a whoosh of wings and a large black shadow swooped down from the roof of the garage. She turned her head to look and held out her arm. With a whisper, Raven landed on her outstretched arm and bobbed his head in greeting. A smile spread across her face and she stroked under his chin affectionately.

"I haven't heard from Michael," she said, glancing at Damon. "He should have been here by now."

"He's here."

She raised a questioning eyebrow.

"He got here earlier this afternoon. He was followed out of DC, so he left his truck at the airport and took a cab in."

Alina frowned. "Dammit."

Raven shook his head, disturbed by the harshness in her voice, and launched off her arm, heading for the deck. Damon looked at her sharply.

"You know who followed him," he stated, rather than asked.

"Yes. I was hoping he wouldn't get caught, but I guess that was wishful thinking."

"You think it was him? Mr. X?"

"Michael's been poking around into every aspect of his life for the past 30 years," she said. "I'd say it's pretty obvious."

Damon's lips tightened and he shook his head.

"I forgot about that," he admitted. "Well, that explains why they were so persistent."

They moved up the steps and across the deck to the sliding door. Before Alina could reach for the handle, Damon reached out a hand to stop her.

"How was your trip?" he asked softly, his eyes probing hers. "Anything I should know about?"

She met his gaze squarely. "You'll find out soon enough."

He considered her silently for a long moment, then nodded slowly.

"Before we go in, you should know Stephanie's apartment was tossed."

Alina turned to face him, her eyes narrowing. "What happened?"

"I stopped there on my way to get her. The place was trashed and the safe was open. All the cash and weapons were still there, so it wasn't a robbery."

"And the camera?"

"In your command center."

She nodded and looked through the glass sliding door into the living room. Stephanie was in the recliner with her injured leg elevated and Michael was settled at the dining room table with his laptop. There was no sign of Blake.

"Does she know?"

"No. I figured you'd watch the camera first, and then we'll know exactly what happened."

Alina shot him a look filled with amusement. "Coward."

Damon grinned, unrepentant. "Guilty."

She looked around the deck, watching as Raven settled himself on the railing with his back to them, facing the dark backyard.

"What about the security perimeter?" she asked, returning her gaze to Damon's face.

"It's secure. Before you, the last one to breach it was Michael. Everything's been quiet."

She nodded and reached for the door again.

"For now," she said quietly. "Let's hope it lasts."

Chapter Ten

Alina stepped through the sliding doors into the living room, nodding in greeting to Michael then glancing into the living room where Stephanie was in the recliner.

"I see you two got here ok," she said, moving toward the bar. She reached behind her and pulled the .45 from her back holster, setting it down with her keys. "Are you both all settled in?"

"For the most part," Stephanie said. "Thank you for getting Buddy last night. Blake just took him for a walk. He said he would stay in the woods where we could keep an eye on him with the security cameras."

"Smart man," Alina murmured, moving into the kitchen and heading for the coffee maker. "As for Buddy, it was no trouble," she said over her shoulder. "He's a good dog."

Damon perched on a stool at the bar and watched as Alina turned the coffee machine on.

"If you're making coffee, I'll take some," he said.

She nodded in acknowledgment as Stephanie hobbled across the living room with her cane.

"Thank you for letting Blake come with me," she said, pausing near the bar and glancing at the Ruger SR45. She seemed uncomfortable with the sight of it and quickly shifted her gaze to look across the kitchen at Alina. "I know how you feel about letting people know where you live. I appreciate you letting him in."

Alina met her gaze impassively. "Thank Damon. He's the one behind it."

"Yes, but it's your house," Stephanie persisted, a frown creasing her brow. "You could have said no."

Alina turned to the cabinet to get a couple of coffee mugs.

"I'm not happy about it, but Damon's right. This is the lesser of all the evils."

"Am I the lesser of all the evils too?" Michael called from the dining room.

"Hardly," Alina said with a short laugh. "You're a welcome necessity right now. I heard you had some trouble earlier."

He sat back in his chair and stretched, then stood and walked over to the bar.

"I was followed up from DC," he said, pulling out a stool and motioning Stephanie into it. "Get off that leg, Walker. You shouldn't be standing on it like that."

Stephanie made a face, but sank onto the stool with a sigh.

"I feel like an old woman," she muttered.

"Well, you're not. You've been shot."

Michael moved into the kitchen and opened the cabinet to pull another mug out.

"Any idea who followed you?" Alina asked him, taking the mug from him and adding it to the collection next to the coffee machine.

"No, but I'm guessing you do," he said, leaning against the kitchen island and crossing his arms over his chest. His hazel green eyes bore into hers. "So?"

Her lips twitched and she placed a mug under the coffee spout, pressing the button to brew espresso into the mug.

"You found something on Mr. X, didn't you?"

He nodded.

"Then you know who had you followed."

Stephanie watched the two in the kitchen and looked at Damon beside her at the bar.

"Do you know what they're talking about?"

"Yes."

She frowned and looked back at Alina and Michael.

"You were followed all the way from DC?" she asked. "Why? What's going on?"

"He poked a bear," Alina said, "and the bear poked back."

"You really think he's the one behind all this?" Michael asked, his brows drawn together.

"I don't think, I know." The coffee finished brewing and she turned to pull it out from under the spout, handing it to him. "Here. For fortitude."

He took it with a short laugh.

"If you're right, I'm going to need something stronger than coffee."

"I know you all love to talk in riddles amongst yourselves," Stephanie interjected loudly from the bar, "but will someone please fill me in? What happened? How do you know you were followed?"

Next Exit, No Outlet

Michael turned to face her. "I saw them. They weren't interested in keeping a low profile."

Stephanie frowned in consternation.

"I don't understand. Why would someone follow you?"

"Why would someone try to kill you?" Michael retorted.

"I have no idea. That's what Blake's trying to find out." Stephanie paused and looked around at the sudden silence in the room. After looking at Damon and Alina's impassive faces, she gasped in sudden understanding. "You all know already! You know who's trying to kill me!"

Michael glanced behind him at Alina, then turned and carried his coffee out of the kitchen.

"I'm not getting in the middle of this," he said, heading back to his laptop at the dining room table.

"Chicken," Damon murmured as he passed.

"Nope. Just know better than to get in the middle of two women."

"Lina?" Stephanie prompted, an edge to her voice. "Do you know who's trying to kill me?"

Alina pressed the button on the coffee machine and turned to face her. With one glance, Damon knew she was finished playing games.

"Yes."

The word was said shortly and matter-of-factly, without an ounce of apology.

Stephanie stared at her, storm clouds gathering on her face when nothing more was forthcoming.

"That's it?!" she exclaimed. "Just yes?"

Alina's expression never changed.

"What more would you like?" she asked, her voice dangerously soft.

"Oh, I don't know, maybe the name of the bastard?"

Before Alina could answer, the door to the deck slid open and Buddy bounded inside ahead of his master. He stopped and shook himself vigorously, then galloped joyfully past the bar and into the kitchen. Rearing up on his back legs, the pit bull planted his front paws on Alina's shoulders and tried to get her face with his tongue.

"Buddy! Have some manners!" Blake exclaimed in exasperation. "She doesn't want your tongue all over her face."

Alina rubbed Buddy's neck and behind his ears, dodging his tongue, then dropped him back onto the floor.

"It's fine," she said, turning to pull the mug from the coffee machine. She carried it over to the bar and set it in front of Damon. "Coffee?"

"Sure," Blake agreed, glancing at the two seated at the bar. "Thanks."

He took the last stool and Buddy padded over to sit on the floor next to him. Reaching down, Blake petted his head while his eyes went from Stephanie's stony face to Alina's emotionless one.

"What's going on?" he asked after a moment.

"Alina was just going to tell me who the hell is trying to kill me," Stephanie said tightly.

Blake's eyebrows soared into his forehead and he looked at Alina.

"Come again?"

"It seems we're the only two in the room who don't know. Considering I'm the one who's been through hell the past two days, I think that's pretty crappy."

"Ok, clearly I missed something. Let's start at the beginning."

Alina turned to put another mug under the coffee spout, pressing the button to start it. Stephanie glowered at her back, then turned to look at Blake.

"I don't know much more than you do," she said. "Michael was followed up from DC this morning. He lost them, but Alina knows who it was. Just like she apparently knows who's trying to kill me."

Blake frowned and glanced at Damon's impassive face.

"I'm sure there's more to it than that." He turned to look at Michael. "Mike? If you knew something about the people following you, why didn't you tell me?"

Michael glanced up from his laptop.

"I'm not sure we *do* know," he said. "Until I have proof, I'm not saying one way or the other."

"Then how about you just tell me what you know?" Blake suggested, an edge to his voice.

Michael shrugged and sat back in his chair, reaching for his coffee.

"All I can tell you is that last night I was doing some research and came across some financial information. This morning I had a tail. Alina thinks the two are connected, but I'm willing to wait for proof of that before jumping to conclusions."

Blake turned his attention back to the blonde woman in the kitchen.

"Why do you think these financials are connected to Mike getting followed out of DC?"

Next Exit, No Outlet

Alina's lips curved into a smile that didn't quite reach her eyes.

"Let's just say I was waiting for Michael to find something," she replied, "and now he has. The rest is about what I was expecting."

"And you think this same person is the one trying to kill me?" Stephanie demanded. "I don't even know what Michael's working on! What do I have to do with anything?"

"Apparently, you have a lot more to do with all of this than any of us knew," Damon said in a low voice.

Blake looked at him sharply. "What's that supposed to mean?"

"Just what I said."

The coffee maker chose that moment to finish grinding beans, making the resulting silence seem much more ominous. Damon was completely unconcerned with the hard looks he was receiving from both Stephanie and Blake. He sipped his coffee calmly, his eyes watching Alina over the rim of the mug. She pulled the cup of fresh brewed coffee out of the machine and carried it over to set it before Blake.

"Do you need milk or sugar?"

He shook his head and reached for the mug.

"I'm good, thanks. So what are we looking at, and why is Stephanie in the hot seat?"

Alina went back to the cabinet to pull down one last mug, turning to place it under the coffee spout. She pressed the brew button and turned to face the others once again.

"I'm sure there are a couple of different reasons," she said. "However, I'd say the main ones are probably because: A, she was John's partner; and B, they think she knows something she doesn't."

Stephanie and Blake looked at her for a moment, then at each other.

"What do they think I know?"

"What does John have to do with it?"

They both spoke at the same time.

Michael sighed from the dining room and closed his laptop.

"John knew something that was way above his pay grade," he said, standing and carrying his coffee back over to the bar. He set it down and crossed his arms over his chest, leaning against the granite top next to Blake. "That's what you're referring to, right?"

Alina met his gaze from across the kitchen. "Yes."

"Wait a minute," Stephanie exclaimed, waving her hands. "Hold on. What do you mean, *John* knew something? I thought John was killed because of the Casa Reinos Cartel and the bombs being moved up the East coast?"

"'Oh, what a web we weave...'" Damon murmured under his breath.

Alina shot him an exasperated look, her lips tightening ever so slightly.

"That was simply a means to an end. They used the street racers as a decoy, and John played right into their hands. But this is much larger than Asad, and it goes way back to long before that terrorist attack."

The coffee finished brewing behind her, and she turned back to the coffee machine, pulling the mug out from under the spout. She sipped it appreciatively and moved over to lean against the kitchen island.

"Why do you think John knew something that went above and beyond the cartel?" Blake asked.

"Because he left something behind."

Stephanie and Blake frowned at her in consternation.

"What?" Stephanie asked, sitting very still.

Alina never took her eyes off Stephanie's face. "You already know about it. He left an external hard drive in his safe deposit box."

Stephanie gasped, her eyes widening.

"Oh my God! I completely forgot about that," she exclaimed. "It was stolen out of my car."

"You found it?" Blake asked, watching Alina's face.

"Let's just say someone arranged for me to find it."

"You have it?" Stephanie asked. "What's on it?"

"Something worth killing over, obviously," Blake said, "and I'm guessing it's something to do with those financials you found," he added, glancing at Michael.

He shrugged.

"I wouldn't have thought so," he said. "At least, not if you'd asked me yesterday. After being followed all the way here, though, it's seeming more and more plausible."

Stephanie ran her hand through her hair and shook her head before getting off her stool and hobbling into the kitchen.

"The man in my apartment," she said, heading for the refrigerator. "That's what he was looking for?"

"I think so." Alina watched as she opened the door and pulled out a bottle of water. "When he didn't find it, he copied your laptop in the hope that the information was there."

"Well, that explains one thing at least," Stephanie muttered, opening the bottle and taking a long drink. "It still doesn't explain why they decided to kill me two days later."

Next Exit, No Outlet

"You're now a liability," Damon said, and finished his coffee. "They can't find the hard drive and, as far as they know, you were the last one to have it. That means you must know what's on it."

"What *is* on it?" Blake asked.

Damon and Michael looked at Alina and were silent. Stephanie followed their gaze and her eyes narrowed.

"Lina?"

Alina met Damon's eyes and read the warning there. She was quiet for a moment, then she looked at Stephanie.

"Why don't you move into the living room and sit on the recliner?" she suggested.

Stephanie frowned. "Why won't you answer the question?"

Alina shrugged, her lips curving faintly.

"When I went through John's laptop, I found a hidden, partitioned hard drive." Out of the corner of her eye, she saw Damon lower his gaze into his empty coffee mug, his lips tightening. Ignoring him, she continued, "Turns out John wasn't the technophobe everyone thought he was. He partitioned off information he didn't want anyone to see."

"What was it?" Stephanie asked apprehensively.

"Letters from Dave."

Whatever Stephanie had been expecting to hear, it clearly wasn't that. Her mouth dropped open and she stared at Alina, flabbergasted.

"Letters from Dave? *Your* Dave?"

Alina nodded and calmly sipped her coffee.

"He sent them before he died. It turns out his death wasn't quite as straight-forward as it seemed."

Chapter Eleven

The color drained out of Stephanie's face and she leaned heavily against the kitchen island.

"What do you mean?" she whispered. "How was his death not what it seemed?"

Blake got up from his seat and came into the kitchen swiftly, taking hold of Stephanie's arm.

"You'd better come sit down before you fall down," he said, leading her out of the kitchen and into the living room.

Alina watched in some amusement.

"I did try," she said. She shifted her gaze to Michael and Damon. "I told her to go sit down."

Michael shook his head a reluctant grin pulling at his lips.

"Maybe you should've led with the fact that she would need to sit down," he said.

Alina shrugged.

"I thought that was implied," she said, following Blake and Stephanie into the living room.

Michael looked at Damon and Damon shrugged, as much as to say 'women.' Shaking his head again, Michael turned to go into the living room as Damon stood and picked up the stool, carrying it with him as he followed the others. Stephanie settled herself back in the recliner while Blake leaned on the mantle next to her. Michael dropped onto the couch as Alina settled herself in the opposite corner.

"Okay. I'm sitting down now. Tell me what the hell you mean about Dave's death," Stephanie said.

"Before he died, Dave sent John six emails from Iraq. Someone was selling weapons and ammunition to the insurgents, and Dave was trying to figure out what was going on. When he was killed, it wasn't just a normal shot from an insurgent."

"You think he was killed because of what was going on?" Stephanie asked slowly, a puzzled frown on her face. "Why? Who would do that?"

"Someone who had a lot to lose if they were caught."

Next Exit, No Outlet

"But he was shot by the enemy in hostile territory. Why would you think he wasn't?"

Alina sipped her coffee. "Because the shot that killed him was fired from over 500 meters away."

Blake whistled softly. "That's not your average insurgent."

Alina glanced up at him with a faint nod.

"No, it's not. After reading Dave's letters, it's very clear what happened. He was able to gather some pretty damning evidence about the person or persons selling artillery to the enemy. In doing so, he managed to throw up quite a few red flags. In the last letter he sent, he said he met with someone who he thought could help him. He told him everything. The next day, he was killed with a shot that very few people can make."

Stephanie exhaled and leaned her head back, staring at the ceiling, stunned.

"I can barely wrap my head around this," she said. "My God, we all thought...well, I guess it doesn't matter now."

Alina's lips thinned into a line and the look on her face was decidedly unpleasant.

"Oh, it matters."

"If these emails were on John's laptop, what was on the hard drive?" Blake asked.

"Dave sent attachments with the emails," Alina explained. "The attachments weren't on the laptop."

He nodded slowly.

"John kept them separate," he said. "Smart man. What was in them?"

"Enough evidence to build a chain," Alina said shortly, "a chain that Michael is adding links to."

Stephanie looked at Michael. "That's why you were followed!"

He shrugged. "That certainly seems to be the popular theory."

"And that's why Stephanie's become a target," Blake said. "And you think this is all connected? Something that happened how many years ago?"

"I don't think, I know."

Alina drained her mug and leaned forward to set the mug on the coffee table. She glanced at Damon, sitting on a barstool a few feet away. His face looked as if it had been chiseled from rock and he was watching her steadily, the look in his eyes unfathomable.

"And you didn't tell me any of this?" Stephanie's voice was sharp. "You should have told me all of this before now. Hell, I could've been ready for this!"

Alina crooked one eyebrow. "Steph, you would never have been ready for this."

Stephanie looked at her, affronted.

"How do you know? You don't know that. You insist on keeping everything secret and trying to handle it all yourself, and you won't trust anyone else."

"I didn't keep it secret. I just didn't tell you."

Michael winced and Blake lowered his head in pained resignation.

"Obviously! Why not?!"

"You don't want to have this conversation right now."

Stephanie scowled.

"Oh yes I do! I've known you since we were six, Alina Renee Maschik, and there has never been a day that I didn't trust you. Why do you suddenly not trust me?"

Damon crossed his arms over his chest and watched Alina's face. She felt not only his eyes, but the eyes of everyone else in the room on her. Well, she'd tried to warn her, Alina thought dispassionately. If she wanted to have this discussion now, so be it.

"Let's start with the fact that you never told me John had a safe deposit box, or that there was a hard drive in it."

Stephanie waved her hand in the air, brushing the comment away.

"I forgot all about it," she said. "John was dead and someone was trying to launch a massive Ebola attack on the East coast. I didn't think it was a priority. If you had told me about Dave's emails, I would have told you about the hard drive."

Alina's lips tightened imperceptibly.

"Then let's discuss the tracking devices you put on both my cars," she said, her voice even.

Stephanie stared at her speechlessly, her eyes wide, and the color once again drained out of her face. Blake looked at her sharply and Michael sucked in his breath.

"Did you just say tracking devices?" he demanded.

Alina didn't answer, her gaze steady on Stephanie's face. Stephanie gulped.

"I can explain," she said, her voice strained.

Alina raised an eyebrow. "Oh, I know you can."

Her voice was soft and deadly and Stephanie visibly shivered.

"There's no need to sound like that," Blake said with a frown. "You've known her all your life. I'm sure she had a good reason for…what did she do, exactly?"

Next Exit, No Outlet

Viper's dark eyes flicked to his face briefly.

"Remember those tracking devices the two of you used to follow Tito and Ricardo the day all the bombs were set to go off up the coast?"

He nodded.

"She got them from me. I loaned her the devices and the software to track them. They're virtually unhackable and completely untraceable. She returned the favor by installing them on both my vehicles and monitoring my movements."

Blake glanced down at Stephanie. "Is that true?"

"Well yes, but it's not what it sounds like."

Michael stared across the room at her, his face darkening.

"Really? Because it sounds suspiciously like you're spying on your best friend," he pointed out tightly, "and there's only reason I can think of to do that."

Damon's lips trembled and he shifted his gaze from Michael's outraged face to Stephanie's pale one. His amusement faded as he looked at the woman responsible for leaking Viper's whereabouts to teams of assassins with orders to kill.

"Mike, give her a chance to explain," Blake suggested. "No point in jumping to conclusions before you know the facts."

"I can tell you the facts," Viper said coldly. "The trackers transmitted my location every time I crossed over the five-mile security perimeter around this house, and Stephanie forwarded that information to someone each time."

"How do you know that?" Blake demanded.

"Because I had highly-trained killers waiting for me when no one knew where I was," she replied flatly, her eyes on Stephanie's face.

The words fell heavily and a stunned silence followed.

"What?!" Michael finally roared.

Alina glanced at him.

"They've tried multiple times," she said. "Each time, no one knew where I was, not even Damon. One of the times, *I* didn't even know where I was going until I was enroute."

"Why didn't you tell me this?" Michael demanded and she shrugged.

"You were already overwhelmed with Dave," she said shortly. "There was no reason to add to it."

"No reason..." Michael stuttered incredulously. "You nearly had my head on a platter for wanting to stay here and help you, and the whole time you were aware that Mr. X knew where you were going?!"

Her lips twisted humorlessly. "You being here or not being

here wouldn't have changed anything."

Michael got up angrily and strode away from the sofa, pacing to the sliding doors restlessly.

"That wasn't your decision to make," he shot over his shoulder before turning and pacing back. "What happened? When did they come after you?"

Viper returned her gaze to Stephanie's face.

"Once while I was in New York City," she said deliberately, "and again when I was in Pittsburgh. The last time I can directly attribute it to the trackers was while I was in Atlantic City."

"Three times?" Blake sucked in his breath. "You were attacked three times?!"

For the first time that evening, genuine amusement lit Alina's eyes and her lips curved.

"Trust me, Hanover, I've seen worse."

"Lina, I had no idea," Stephanie broke her silence, her lips trembling. "You have to believe me. I didn't know!"

"You said those were the times you could directly link it to the trackers," Michael said, stopping his pacing next to Blake. He pinned Alina with a probing look. "There were others?"

"Yes."

"How do you know they weren't because of the tracking devices?" he pressed.

"Because I reprogrammed the devices so they weren't reflecting my true location," she said calmly. "They still aren't."

"Well, at least that's something," he muttered, resuming pacing.

"How many?" Blake asked. "How many came after you?"

"I don't know how many were in New York, but there were four in Pittsburgh." She glanced at Damon. "How many would you say in Atlantic City? Twelve? Fourteen?"

His lips twitched and were repressed. She knew exactly how many they had killed in Frankie's penthouse. Viper was just making a point now.

"Sixteen," he replied, his voice even.

The act had precisely the effect Viper was looking for. Stephanie sucked in her breath sharply and Michael let out a low curse. Blake stared at her hard.

"Sixteen?" he repeated. "A full team?"

"Sound familiar?" she asked softly.

"The hospital last night," Blake said, glancing at Stephanie. "Steph, what the hell have you done?"

Next Exit, No Outlet

"I didn't know this was going to happen!" she exclaimed, looking at him. "I swear, I had no idea any of this was happening!"

"Why the hell did you put trackers on her cars in the first place?" he demanded. "You know what she does! You knew someone tried to kill her at John's funeral! What the hell were you thinking?"

"I was trying to protect her!"

Michael stopped pacing at that and gaped at her incredulously.

"By giving away her location?"

Stephanie ran her hands through her hair in distress and gazed across the coffee table at Alina.

"When I was in the hospital after John's funeral, someone came to visit me," she said, her eyes meeting Viper's. "You'd already told me about Damon taking a bullet meant for you, and about the leak in Washington. Before he showed up, I thought there was no way I could help you. You saved my life on Three Mile Island, and again in Baltimore, and I've never been able to repay you. He offered a way for me to do that. All I had to do was keep an eye on you. If you left the safety of Jersey, where no one knew where to find you, then I would let him know. The plan was that he would have counter-measures in place ahead of you so that if someone tried to kill you again, they wouldn't succeed. Except then his whole system got compromised and he never got any of my messages. Someone else did. I didn't find out until the night before last when he called me to see why he hadn't heard from me."

"So when you sent her location, you thought it was going to one person, but it was really going to someone else?" Blake asked.

She nodded tiredly. "Yes. I had no idea, and I certainly didn't know that assassins were being dispatched each time."

"And when you found out the messages went somewhere else?" Damon asked, his voice soft and dangerous.

Stephanie looked into his arctic blue eyes and her gaze fell away quickly.

"I took the tablet and my phone to Matt, at work, and asked him to find out where the messages went," she told them. "I thought he might be able to trace them."

"And was he?"

"No. He got as far as Mexico, but then he lost them."

"Mexico?" Viper asked sharply, her head snapping up. "Where in Mexico?"

Stephanie frowned. "I don't remember. It was somewhere in the south. It might have started with a G?"

"Guerrero?"

"Yes!" Stephanie's face lit up. "That was it!"

Alina and Damon exchanged a grim look and Stephanie looked from one to the other.

"What's in Guerrero?"

"A military base," Damon said shortly. "That's why your forensic guru lost the trail. He ran into military servers."

Michael stopped pacing again and stared at Damon.

"Are you saying the Mexican Army is involved in this?" he demanded.

"No, I'm saying someone used their servers to conceal their digital trail."

"If that's the case, we'll never find out where those messages went," Michael said disgustedly. "Another dead end."

Blake was watching Alina's face and he shook his head slowly.

"I don't think Alina agrees with you," he said.

Her lips curved faintly. "No."

"Why not?" Stephanie asked. "If there was a way past it, Matt would have found it. You know how he is."

"He can only find what he knows to look for," Alina replied. "I already know where the messages ultimately ended up. That's not my concern right now. My question is why you."

Stephanie's eyes flashed briefly.

"I told you, I was trying to help protect you!" she exclaimed, throwing her hands up in the air.

"Who went to see you in the hospital?" Michael asked, stopping behind the sofa and bracing his hands on the back next to Alina's shoulder.

"There's no reason to look at me like that, Michael," Stephanie said angrily. "Stop looking at me like I'm some kind of traitor. Do you really think I would have spied on my best friend for someone she didn't know and trust?"

"So far, you haven't convinced me otherwise," he shot back.

Alina reached up and placed a calm hand over one of his, her eyes never leaving Stephanie's face as she glared across the room at Michael.

"I don't have to convince *you* of anything," she snapped. "It's Alina who's been compromised by me, not you."

"Then convince *me*."

Viper's voice sliced across the room, making Stephanie start and Blake scowl.

"For God's sake, it was someone you know and trust," Stephanie repeated. "He made me swear to him not to tell you. He said

Next Exit, No Outlet

you would be angry if you knew he was getting involved."

The look on Viper's face was decidedly ugly. "And your loyalty is to him now?"

"We all owe our loyalty to him in one way or another," she retorted. "For God's sake, the man helped train you and turn you into the...weapon you are now."

There was only the slightest hesitation in her voice to indicate that weapon was not her first choice of words and Alina's lips tightened imperceptibly.

"You'll have to break your promise, Steph," Blake said quietly, looking down at her. His mouth was pulled into a grim line. "We need to know who it was that talked you into this."

She met his gaze and hesitated, then sighed.

"Colonel Harry Shore," she said reluctantly. "He said he trained Viper for the Organization."

Michael and Blake both sucked in their breaths.

"Harry Shore?" Blake repeated, stunned.

Michael glanced at Damon's unsurprised face and looked down at Alina.

"Colonel Shore trained you?" he asked. "No wonder you're so...holy...I had no idea."

Viper glanced at him, clearly unimpressed.

"He's just a man," she replied shortly. "He helped train all of us. He's very good at what he does."

"He's not just a man," Blake objected, shaking his head. "He's a legend. My God, the things that man did in the Army are beyond belief."

"Clearly not," Damon said dryly. "Obviously you both believe them."

Blake's eyebrows drew together in a frown.

"If the Colonel was the one who was supposed to get the messages, how the hell did they not get there? That man is one of this nation's top intelligence officers! Security is his thing. There's no way his system simply got hacked."

"Not easily," Michael agreed.

"Now do you see why I did it?" Stephanie asked Alina, ignoring them. "He's been doing everything he can to try to help you. Hell, the man's a war hero!"

"I see why you thought it was good idea. Harry can be very persuasive."

She glanced at Damon and saw the anger lurking in the blue depths of his eyes. Standing, she turned and paced slowly away from the reflection of her own feelings.

"Of course it was a good idea," Stephanie said. "It was a fool-proof way to help keep you safe when you were clearly hell-bent on throwing yourself into the line fire at every opportunity."

"Not quite fool-proof," Damon said, his voice hard.

Stephanie looked at him in surprise.

"What do you mean? Of course it was! It's not his fault someone got to his secure server and was able to pick off the messages before he got them."

Silence greeted that statement and Blake suddenly grew still, his eyes going from Damon to Alina. He pressed his lips together and looked at Michael's stony face.

"Oh my God," he breathed in sudden understanding.

Stephanie looked at him, then at Michael. "Now what?"

"Oh Steph, you really know how to make bad situations even worse, don't you?" Blake said, running a hand through his hair. "Holy crap."

"How is this my fault again?" Stephanie exclaimed, her temper flaring. "For God's sake, I just told you! I was giving her location to someone who was protecting her!"

Viper stopped mid-stride and looked at her, her eyes dark, bottomless pools.

"You gave my location to the very man trying to kill me."

Chapter Twelve

The loud tone from the security system sliced through the house, shattering the stunned silence. Stephanie visibly jumped and Viper strode over to the coffee table to pick up the remote to the TV. Pointing it at the screen, she turned it on, revealing her property split into four security quadrants. The first one was flashing and she hit a button, zooming in. A silver BMW was pulling into the drive from the road.

"The rest of this conversation will have to wait," she said, dropping the remote onto the table. "I don't want Angela knowing any of this."

Michael nodded briskly in agreement, but Stephanie frowned.

"I don't see how you'll be able to keep it from her," she objected. "She already knows someone's trying to kill me, just as she already knows someone tried to kill you."

"The more she knows, the more of a liability she becomes," Viper said shortly.

"She's right," Michael said. "She can suspect all she wants, but if she doesn't know anything, she can't tell anyone anything."

Stephanie gasped furiously.

"This is ridiculous!" she exclaimed. "You can't distrust Angela simply because I showed what turns out to be poor judgment."

Damon stood.

"Right now, we don't have a choice. Anyone who learns anything or gets anywhere near Harry ends up dead. Is that what you want to happen to Angie?"

Stephanie swallowed and shook her head.

"What are you going to tell her?" she asked, resigned. "Lina, you know her. She can sniff out bullshit a mile away."

Alina smiled faintly. "Let me handle Angela."

The floodlights at the back of the house switched on, and a moment later they heard a car door slam. Alina strode over to the sliding door and opened it, stepping onto the deck. Angela was making her way across the grass, two brown shopping bags encased in plastic bags in either hand. Alina raised her eyebrows. The trunk to the BMW was open and she could see that it was filled with more shopping bags.

"I brought food," Angela called, raising the bags in her hands. "I hope you're hungry."

Alina watched as she came up the steps onto the deck. The distinct aroma of Chinese food reached her nose and her stomach growled in reaction.

"I hadn't given it much thought," she admitted as Angela passed her to go into the house.

Angela laughed. "I knew it! I bet none of you have eaten yet."

Alina followed her into the house and slid the door closed.

"I can't speak for anyone else, but I haven't."

"Is that Chinese food?" Michael asked, walking over to take two of the bags from Angela.

"Yes. I figured with everything going on, you'd all forgotten to eat. Turns out I was right."

"Angela, you're a saint," Blake announced, striding across the living room to take the other two bags from her. "I completely forgot about food, but now that I smell it, I'm starving."

She laughed and turned back to the sliding doors.

"Where you going?" Alina asked.

"I have more bags to carry in," Angie said over her shoulder, sliding the door open once again. "I brought provisions for Stephanie."

Alina's eyebrows soared into her for head and she looked at Stephanie, who was making her way towards the dining room where Michael and Blake were ripping open the Chinese bags.

"Provisions?"

Stephanie had the grace to look rueful.

"Just a few things," she said. "Things that I know you don't have in the house."

"Like what?"

"Oh, I don't know," she said evasively, not meeting Alina's gaze. "You know, things like soda."

Damon winked at Alina as he moved into the dining room.

"I'm willing to bet there's white bread out there somewhere," he murmured as he passed her.

Alina made a face at his back.

"I'm sorry if I refuse to pay for cancer in a loaf," she said, joining everyone at the table.

Michael and Blake had emptied the bags already, spreading what seemed like at least twenty Chinese food containers across the dining room table. Michael unplugged his laptop and moved it over to

Next Exit, No Outlet

the bar to make more room while Blake and Damon began opening the variety of containers.

Alina looked at all the food then turned to go into the kitchen for plates. She was opening the cabinet door when she sensed someone behind her. Turning her head, she glanced at Stephanie.

"I'll help," she offered, holding out her hands.

Alina pulled out six plates and handed them to her. "Can you handle those?"

Stephanie nodded.

"I've got them," she said, balancing them in one arm while she leaned on her cane with the other. "Lina…" she began, but Alina cut her off.

"Later," she said shortly as Angela came back into the house, her arms filled with shopping bags.

Stephanie's lips tightened, but she turned to make her way into the dining room with the plates. Angela headed straight into the kitchen and dropped all the bags onto the kitchen island before turning to head back towards the door. Michael raised an eyebrow as she passed by again.

"How many bags are there?" he asked.

"Just a few more," Angela said, continuing on her way.

Michael sighed and turned to follow her.

"If there's shrimp lo mein there, save me some," he said over his shoulder.

"You got it," Blake said, taking a plate from the stack that Stephanie had set on the table.

Damon went into the kitchen where Alina was investigating the bags on the kitchen island. Walking up behind her, he lifted her shirt at the back and Viper felt the familiar weight of her .45 settle into her back holster.

"I don't think you want Angela seeing that sitting on the bar," he murmured in her ear.

She turned her head and met his eyes. "Thank you."

He nodded, his eyes not leaving hers.

"I hope you know what you're doing."

"Trust me. It was only a matter of time before they found out, and it needed to be done."

"And if Stephanie's part of it?"

"She's not," she said shortly. "She was horrified when she realized what she'd done."

Damon shook his head and turned towards the refrigerator.

"You know her best, so you would know if that was an act. I

just hope you're right."

He opened the refrigerator door and reached in to pull out some beers.

"Stephanie, are you drinking beer?" he called over the door of the fridge.

Stephanie looked up from the dining room table where she was filling a plate with rice.

"I'll have wine if Alina's opening a bottle," she answered.

Alina turned back to the cabinets and took out three wine glasses. She carried them into the dining room, setting them on the table as Michael and Angela re-entered the house, laden with more bags and cases of soda.

"Are you opening a bottle of wine?" Angela asked, spying the wineglasses. "Fantastic! I've had a long day."

Alina blinked while Stephanie looked up, dumbfounded.

"She's had a long day?" she said under her breath, drawing a short laugh from Alina.

"Clearly," she replied in a low voice. "She was shopping all day."

After depositing the bags in the kitchen, Michael and Angela joined them at the dining room table. While everyone began filling their plates with food, Alina opened the wine cabinet and pulled out a bottle of Pinot Noir. Before she could take it into the kitchen to open it, Damon took it out of her hand and motioned her to the table.

"I'll take care of it."

Alina looked at him in surprise, then she nodded and reached for a plate while he took the bottle into the kitchen.

"I got a pretty good selection, I think," Angela announced, reaching for a quart of General Tso's chicken. "I didn't know exactly what everybody liked, so I got the basics."

"I didn't realize how hungry I was until I smelled all this food," Stephanie said. "Thank you for doing this."

Angela waved her hand, brushing the thanks aside.

"With everything that happened to you, I knew you wouldn't have eaten. I know you better than you know yourself, Stephanie Walker."

Damon came back with the open bottle of wine and began pouring it into the three glasses.

"Just make sure you save me some of that chicken," he told her, handing her a glass of wine.

"Oh, there's more here somewhere," she assured him. "I got two orders of it."

Next Exit, No Outlet

Alina scooped some chicken and broccoli onto her plate, foregoing the rice. Damon handed her a glass of wine and she smiled in thanks, setting it down next to her plate. Conversation stopped then as everyone dug in. It wasn't an easy silence, and after a few moments, Angela sent a questioning look around the table.

"Why is everyone so quiet?"

"Are we?" Michael asked when it became apparent that no one else was going to answer.

"It certainly seems like it," Angie said. She looked at Stephanie. "What's wrong? Are you okay?"

Stephanie looked like a deer in headlights.

"I'm fine," she said quickly. "Just tired."

"I'm not surprised," Angela exclaimed. "You should've stayed in the hospital. I still can't believe you signed yourself out. You could have brain damage!"

"I don't have brain damage," Stephanie said in exasperation. "I'll be fine. I just need to sleep."

"You know, if you have another concussion, the last thing you should do is sleep," Angela said. "Someone needs to keep an eye on you."

"She'll be fine," Alina said, looking up from her chicken and broccoli.

Stephanie's eyes narrowed and Blake shot Alina an unreadable look.

"You don't know that," Angela argued. "She left the hospital before they did any of the tests."

Alina looked like she was about to say something, then changed her mind, reaching for her wine instead.

Silence fell over the table again, and Alina suppressed a sigh. The tension was so thick she could cut it with a knife, and Angela wasn't stupid. She had to know she'd walked into something, and knowing Angela, she wasn't going to ignore it. This whole nightmare had just gotten even more complicated.

Damon met her glance and, for once, there was no laughter lurking in his eyes. Any other time, she knew he would be thoroughly amused at the collection of characters from her past acting like any other normal friends. Tonight, it was different. Tonight, everything was different.

"Michael, when did you get in?" Angela asked after a few more moments of silence.

"This afternoon," he answered, glancing at Alina.

"Are you staying here too?"

He nodded.

"At least for tonight," he said vaguely. "I'm not sure what my plans are beyond that."

Angela looked around the table again, then suddenly frowned.

"Where's Buddy?" she asked. "Isn't he here?"

Blake glanced around, then bent down to peer under the table. He chuckled.

"He's under the table," he said, straightening up again. "Hoping for something to drop."

"I already dropped something," Michael said with an unrepentant grin. "Sorry."

"Me too," Stephanie admitted. Blake looked at her and she shrugged. "He looked hungry."

"He always looks hungry," he said in exasperation. "It's his specialty."

"A few treats won't hurt him."

"It will when he gets fat."

Stephanie shrugged and silence fell again. Angela reached for an egg roll and Alina could almost see her squirming at the lack of conversation.

"What did everyone do today?" Angela finally asked, breaking the silence once again. She looked around expectantly, a determined gleam in her eyes. "Damon? What did you do?"

Alina almost choked on her food and shot a swift glance under her lashes at the man seated beside her.

"Went and got Stephanie and Blake to bring them here," he answered blandly.

"Is that why your car isn't here?" Angela asked Blake before biting into her egg roll.

"Yes. It's...hey, where *is* my car?" he asked, looking at Damon. "You said you were going to take care of it."

"I did. I removed the tracker and bugs and it's somewhere safe," Damon answered calmly. "When it's things have calmed down, I'll tell you where it is."

Blake frowned. "Are you sure it's safe?"

"Yes."

"For your sake, I hope you're right," Michael said, re-filling his plate with lo mein. "That car is Blake's baby."

"It's a nice car," Alina said, glancing up, "for a Chrysler."

"So is yours, for a Ford," Blake replied, drawing a smile from her.

"Why did Damon take your car?" Angela asked. "I don't

Next Exit, No Outlet

understand."

There was an awkward silence as Blake looked to Alina for guidance.

"The people who tried to kill Stephanie put tracking software on Blake's car," she told Angela calmly. "Damon had to remove it."

Angela looked from Alina to Blake, a frown creasing her lips.

"What's being done to find them?" she demanded. "How long is Stephanie going to have to stay here?"

The frown grew when no one answered and Angela set her fork down impatiently.

"Something *is* being done, right?"

"Yes," Alina said, her voice even.

Stephanie's lips tightened, but she remained silent.

"Good." Angela reached for her wine. "I don't know why things are getting so crazy around here all of a sudden. First John, then you, and now Stephanie is being attacked. It's making me see killers lurking around every corner now!"

Alina looked up sharply. "What?"

Angela looked at her. "What?"

"What do you mean you're seeing killers lurking around corners?"

Angela shrugged. "Just that all of this is making me paranoid."

"Paranoid how?" Michael asked, glancing at Alina's face. She was frowning, her eyes on Angela.

"I've had this strange feeling that someone is following me," Angela told him readily. "It's absurd. No one would have any reason to follow me. Trent is dead, and it's not like I have a dangerous job like Stephanie."

"How long have you felt like someone is following you?" Alina asked.

Angela frowned thoughtfully.

"I don't know. A couple of days, maybe? It doesn't matter. The whole idea is nonsense. No one's following me. I'm just shaken up because of everything that's been going on lately."

"They say if you feel something's wrong, it probably is," Stephanie said, her eyes darting from Alina's face to Angela's. "Did you see anyone? Any strange cars? Any new construction around your house?"

Angela shook her head.

"No, nothing like that. You know that feeling you get sometimes when someone's watching you? It's like all your hairs on your arm stand up?" she asked. "It's like that, only instead of my hair standing up, I just feel…uneasy. I'm sure it's nothing."

Alina glanced at Michael and he nodded almost imperceptibly.

"You're probably right," she said, turning her attention back to Angela, "but Michael's going to keep an eye on you just to be safe."

Angela stared at her as if she'd suddenly sprouted a second head.

"Are you crazy?" she demanded. "Stephanie's the one who needs protecting, not me!"

"We don't know that," Alina replied. Steel laced her voice, discouraging any argument. "Stephanie is here, where Damon and I can keep an eye on her. You're not. If someone *is* following you, Michael can protect you."

"No one is! I told you, I'm just being paranoid!"

"Then Michael won't have much to do, will he?" Damon said reasonably.

Angela gaped at them, then looked at Stephanie.

"What the hell is going on?" she demanded. "What did you get yourself into?"

Stephanie looked startled. "I didn't get myself into anything!"

"Well, you obviously did, and now I'm getting dragged into it!" Angela exclaimed. "Why do they think I'm being followed?"

"Because you just said you were!" Stephanie cried, throwing her hands up in the air. "Why is everything suddenly my fault?"

Alina reached for her wine glass and drained it. Damon's shoulders shook silently beside her and he took the empty glass from her hand, reaching for the bottle to refill it.

"I didn't say I was being followed!" Angela protested. "I've been saying I'm not!"

"Is this real life right now?" Blake asked, reaching for his beer.

"'Fraid so," Damon replied, his voice trembling.

"I don't see what the big deal is," Michael said. "You spend all your time working and plugged into your phone. You won't even know I'm around."

Angela shot him a look disbelief.

"How can I miss you?" she demanded. "You're six feet tall and as big as a barn!"

Michael blinked, unsure how to respond to that accusation. Alina felt her lips tugging upwards as a laugh built inside her and she sternly repressed them.

"Angela, don't be ridiculous," Stephanie said tiredly. "You were just saying the other day that Michael should come visit more often. Well, he's here."

Next Exit, No Outlet

Angela's cheeks flushed.

"I don't need a babysitter," she said defiantly. "I'm not the one who's got people trying to kill me!"

"This isn't up for discussion," Alina said firmly. "Until I'm convinced you're right and no one's following you, Michael is going to stick by you. End of discussion."

"Or what?" Angela demanded. "What will you do?"

In an instant, the friend Angela had known for years disappeared and the terrifying stranger she'd glimpsed a few days before took her place.

"You'd rather not find out."

Chapter Thirteen

Harry glanced at his watch as he climbed out from the backseat of the black SUV. He nodded to the Secret Service agent holding the door and glanced up at the large building in front of him. It was just past eight, and the gala was in full throttle. He buttoned the jacket of his black tux and started up the shallow steps, moving towards the wide double doors at the top. He was halfway up the steps when his cell phone vibrated from the inside pocket of his jacket. He frowned, pulling it out impatiently. This was a big night for the intelligence community, and Harry wanted to enjoy it. Everyone at the office knew not to bother him this evening unless it was an emergency.

"Hello?"

"I received your message, my friend," a heavily accented voice greeted him. "All is well. There is no need to fret."

Harry glanced around and moved to the side of the steps, out from the flow of people ascending to enter the gala.

"Martese?" Harry lowered his head and his voice. "Is that you?"

"None other," said Martese Salcedo, the head of the Casa Reinos Cartel. "Tell me, what is so urgent that you bypassed our security arrangement and contacted me directly?"

Harry rubbed a hand over his bald head, watching absently as a black limousine pulled up to the curb.

"I've had to move my plans forward," he said. "I'm running out of time."

There was a brief silence on the line, then Harry heard a soft sigh.

"I've heard that you've run into a few, how do you say it, snags?" Martese said. "Will everything still be as discussed?"

"Yes, yes," Harry said impatiently. "It's all been arranged. The problem is that I'll need to move sooner than expected."

"Is that all? Never fear, my friend. La Cabeza is a man of his word. The *Sea Queen* is already on her way. She will be in place at

Next Exit, No Outlet

whatever time I tell them."

He sighed in relief. "That's good news, Martese. And the crew?"

"All my own trusted people, led by Roberto, my second-in-command. Stop worrying! You'll give yourself a heart attack. There's no reason for all this bother. The crew will be at your command once you arrive. They will get you where you need to go."

"How soon can they be in place?"

"The *Sea Queen* is the fastest yacht in Mexico," Martese boasted. "When do you need her?"

"As soon as they can get there," Harry said. "Tell Roberto to contact me when he reaches Miami, and I'll direct him to the rendezvous from there."

"Already done, my friend. And your side of the arrangement?"

Harry's lips twisted into a cold smile.

"Don't worry," he said. "Not only will the Casa Reinos Cartel have exclusive run up the East coast, but you'll have Special Agent Blake Hanover to do with what you will."

"And his new partner? Agent Walker?"

"You won't have to worry about her. I'm in the process of taking care of her."

"Fantastic! It's a pleasure doing business with you, amigo. When you board the *Sea Queen*, Roberto will assist you with the wire transfer."

Harry nodded in greeting to a couple walking up the steps, smiling congenially.

"Of course. I look forward to hearing from you."

He disconnected and slid the phone back into his pocket, turning to continue up the steps to the doors. The last arrangements were made. By this time next week, he would be sipping whiskey in his villa in Montenegro, beyond the reach of extradition. With just a little luck, Viper and Hawk would be dead and he would be free to live out his days in luxurious obscurity. It was what he'd worked towards for twelve years.

And no one was going to stop him.

Angela's face went white, then the color rushed back and stained her cheeks pink as her temper flared.

"I don't know what you do, Alina Maschik, and I don't care. What I do know is that you're turning into a real bully! First my journal, now this. You can't just snap your fingers and expect me to do whatever you say. I won't! I don't need a bodyguard, and I'm certainly not going to take a Federal Agent away from Stephanie when *she* does!"

Stephanie pinched the bridge of her nose and shot Alina a look of reproach.

"She has a point," she said. "She doesn't have to allow Michael to keep an eye on her."

Viper turned that cold gaze on her and Stephanie shivered.

"No, she doesn't. But if she *is* being watched, how long do you think it will take them to realize that she knows where you are?" Alina asked, her voice clipped. "And then, what do you think they'll do?"

Stephanie's gaze wavered. "Do you think that's possible?"

"Hello?!" Angela waved her hands above her head. "I'm right here! You don't have to talk over me like I'm a child."

"You're certainly acting like one," Michael muttered just loud enough for everyone to hear.

Angela gasped and Alina felt a laugh building inside her again.

"I am not!" Angela cried. "You should be on my side! You can't honestly want to follow me around all day."

"You're right," he agreed. "I don't. But I also don't want to have your death on my conscience, so here we are. You're stuck with me."

"Like hell I am."

"Angie, maybe you should consider this for a minute," Stephanie said, turning to face Angela. "If you felt like you were being watched, you can't just discount that gut feeling. What if you are? What if Lina's right, and the person who tried to kill me is watching you? Not only are you in danger, but you could also lead them right to me."

Angela waved a hand impatiently.

"Don't be silly. This place might as well be the White House for all the security she has going on. You're safer here than anywhere. Even if someone did follow me, which is unlikely, Alina would see them coming a mile away!"

"Five miles away, to be exact," Alina murmured, reaching for her wine glass again, "if I know what I'm looking for."

Damon shot her a look of amusement, his eyes dancing. She glowered at him. He was enjoying this debacle way too much. It was easy for him to laugh; he had no idea how stubborn Angela could be, or how miserable she could make all their lives. Her lips tightened. Even so, she would be damned if she would have Angie's safety on her conscience as well. She had enough to worry about already without adding Angela to it.

"See?" Angela didn't miss a beat. "There's no way anyone can sneak up on you here."

"You're right," Stephanie agreed. Her gaze met Alina's and Alina recognized the glint in her old friend's eyes. "Why doesn't she stay here with me?"

Alina raised an eyebrow. "You'd have to share a room."

"That's fine. Michael and Blake are doing it. The rooms are big enough."

"Wait a minute!" Angela protested. "I can't stay here again. I just got back into my own house!"

Everyone looked at her.

"So?" Blake prompted. "It's only for a few days at most and, as you just pointed out, you've stayed here before. It's not like you're not used to it."

Angela sputtered and Alina saw Damon's shoulders shaking out of the corner of her eye.

"That's not the point! I don't want to stay here again. I didn't bring enough provisions!"

There was a long silence as they all stared at her. She looked around the table. "What? I didn't! I bought all the stuff for Stephanie, not me. I can't stay here."

"What, exactly, are you talking about?" Alina finally asked as one of her eyelids began to twitch.

"All those bags in the kitchen! It's food and snacks for Steph and Blake," Angela explained. "Lina, I love you, but your kitchen is severely lacking in anything that makes life worth living."

Alina sat back in her chair and looked at the ceiling, counting to ten.

"She has beer now," Damon said. Only the faintest tremor in his voice conveyed how much he was enjoying himself. "That's progress."

Angela snorted. "Does she have bagels?"

"No."

"Then it's not enough progress."

"Well, you have two options," Alina said, irritation pushing her amusement aside. "You can either stay here, or Michael can stay with you. Choose one."

She stood and picked up her empty plate, turning to go into the kitchen while Angela scowled.

"Ang, just stay here," Stephanie said. "It won't be for long."

"You keep saying that. How do you know? If you don't even know who's trying to kill you, then we don't know how long it will be!" Angela pointed out. "It could be weeks!"

Stephanie shook her head.

"It won't be weeks. It will be a couple of days, at most, and then you'll be back home with Anabelle."

Angela gasped.

"That's another thing!" she exclaimed. "I would have to go get my cat! This is ridiculous. I'm not upending everything all over again just because you guys think there might be a possibility that I'm being followed, which I'm not. It's not fair to Annabelle. Cats don't like being moved around."

"Then I'll come to your house," Michael said, resigned.

Alina strode out of the kitchen and headed for the sliding doors.

"Hey! Where are you going?" Angela demanded, swiveling in her chair. "We're having a discussion here!"

"No, you're arguing. That's not a discussion," Damon said, pushing his chair back and following Alina.

Angela's mouth dropped open and she watched as the pair disappeared out the door into the night.

"What just happened?" she demanded, spinning around again and looking at Stephanie. "Where did they go?"

Stephanie rolled her eyes and reached for some more fried rice. "How should I know?"

"They're probably running away," Blake muttered under his breath.

Stephanie shot him a look filled with amused sympathy. "Welcome to Jersey."

"Is there anymore lo mein?" Angela asked, peering around the table.

Michael handed her a carton and stood up.

"I'll go see what we're going to do about my truck," he said, turning toward the sliding doors.

Angela watched him go and then looked at Stephanie.

"Where *is* his truck?" she asked, forking shrimp lo mein onto her plate.

"At the airport."

"Why?"

Stephanie hesitated, then glanced at Blake. He offered no inspiration as he piled more rice and General Tso's onto his plate.

"He left the truck there when he realized he was being

Next Exit, No Outlet

followed," she said reluctantly.

"What do you mean, 'he was followed?'" she demanded. "By whom? What the hell is going on around here?!"

Stephanie sighed.

"It's a long story. Now do you see why we're so worried about you? Everyone is getting dragged into this mess, and Lina's right. It's only a matter of time before they come after you."

"I don't understand. What does Michael have to do with you and the cartel?"

Blake got up to go into the kitchen for another beer.

"It's complicated," he said over his shoulder.

Angela made a face at his back.

"Why is everything always complicated anymore? This is all because of Lina's job, isn't it?"

Stephanie stared at her like a deer in headlights. "What?"

This time it was Angela's turn to roll her eyes.

"Oh come on, Steph. I'm not an idiot. Ever since she came back, everything's been getting more and more 'complicated,' as you all like to say. Somehow, you and John got sucked in, and now Michael has too. What the hell is happening?"

Blake came back to the table with a bottle of Yuengling and gave Angela a considering look.

"What do you think is going on?" he asked, seating himself again and picking up his fork.

"I have no idea," Angela replied. "All I know is that someone is trying to kill both of my best friends, and no one will tell me anything. You're all treating me like a toddler."

"Well, I agree that Alina is acting like a warden, but she's trying to protect us," Stephanie said, finishing her wine. "She could be a little more tactful, though. Ordering us around isn't helpful."

"Exactly!"

"At least now she can't go anywhere, either," Stephanie continued, getting up and going over to the wine cabinet. She opened it and surveyed their options. "So, we're all in this together. Cabernet?" she asked, turning to look at Angela.

She nodded. "Sure."

Stephanie pulled the bottle out and carried it to the table. Setting it down, she turned to go into the kitchen to get the wine opener.

"Why can't she go anywhere?"

"Because the same person trying to kill me is also trying to kill her. Until they're caught, nowhere is safe."

Blake lifted his head from his food, looked like he was going to say something, then changed his mind.

"So you're saying we're all stuck here together?" Angela demanded. "Oh, she'd better have a lot of alcohol in this house or this will not end well."

Michael stepped outside and frowned. The deck was empty. Looking around, he spotted Damon standing near Angela's BMW. The garage door was open and Alina's Jeep and the Shelby were inside, but there was no sign of Alina.

He went down the steps and across the grass. A large black shadow sat perched on top of the garage, and he eyed the hawk warily as he walked toward Damon.

"What's going on?"

"Lina's checking Angela's car," Damon answered.

Michael looked in the garage and saw Alina in the back, rummaging through a box.

"You think she's got a tracking device too?"

"That's what we're going to find out."

"You really think the colonel will target her?" Michael asked, leaning against Angela's car.

"At this point, I think anything's possible," Damon said grimly. "He's tried to kill Stephanie three times now. Alina was right. It's only a matter of time before he goes after Angela, hoping that she will lead him to Stephanie. He's already hacked her online journal. He probably knows more about her at this point than either Alina or Stephanie."

"Wait, what? What journal?"

Damon glanced at him.

"You don't know about that? Where've you been?"

"Busy digging up the information we needed on Harry," Alina said, coming out of the garage with a rectangular box in her hand. "He wasn't around for the journal debacle."

"Lucky you," Damon told him.

Michael raised an eyebrow and looked from one to the other. "So are you going to fill me in?"

Alina pressed a button on the side of the box in her hand and walked to the front of the BMW. Holding it close to the car, she began to walk slowly around the front bumper.

Next Exit, No Outlet

"Angela had the bright idea of keeping her diary online," she said over her shoulder. "She enjoyed it so much that she decided to scan in all her old journals from years past. Harry tracked them down and hacked into them."

Michael frowned. "How do you know it was Harry?"

"I'd tell you, but I know how much you hate hearing what I do for a living now."

Damon raised his eyebrows and looked at Michael quizzically. Michael ignored him, and turned to look at Alina over the roof of the car.

"Just tell me."

Alina shrugged.

"Before I severed Asad's trachea, we had a little chat. He knew things about me that no one else knew, aside from the people who were there. I can count on one hand the number of people who knew some of those things, and one of them was my brother. Well, I know Dave wasn't talking from the grave."

"Maybe it was Asad who hacked her journal," Michael suggested.

Alina shook her head.

"Asad was wearing an earbud," she said. "I took it out of his ear myself."

Michael sucked in his breath. "So you think Harry was coaching him in real time?"

"Yes."

"I don't know," Michael said slowly, shaking his head. "That seems far-fetched, even for your world."

"Unfortunately, it's not," Damon said. "One thing you should understand about Harry right now is that psychology is his specialty. He's built his whole career on the ability to get inside the enemy's head and make them do whatever he wants. He's very good at it, and he incorporated that into our training. Trust me. Coaching Asad in real time to get inside Viper's head is SOP 101 for Harry."

Michael was silent for a long moment. Alina rounded the back of the BMW, the box still held an inch away from the car. Michael moved out of her way, watching as she completed her sweep of Angela's car. When she was done, she looked at Damon and shook her head.

"Nothing."

"Maybe she's not being followed," Damon said. "If they put a tracker on Blake's car, they would definitely put one on Angela's. They seem to be overly fond of the damn things."

Alina switched off her detector and tapped her chin with it thoughtfully.

"The people who put the tracker on Blake's car weren't Harry's people," she said slowly. "If Harry's using one of his own people to follow Angie, they might not have used a tracking device."

Damon considered her thoughtfully.

"You're thinking it might be the shooter from the Rittenhouse?"

"It's possible. I lost him yesterday after Philly. It's entirely possible that he doubled back to New Jersey. Hell, he could have been here all along."

"Okay, you've lost me again. What the hell are you talking about?" Michael demanded.

Damon flicked him an amused look. "Come on, gunny. Keep up. Are we talking too fast for you?"

"Remember I said there was a third shooter at the hotel in Rittenhouse Square when Stephanie went after Lowell and the virus?" Alina said, looking at Michael.

"Yes."

"Well, I saw him again yesterday. He was in Philadelphia."

Michael raised his eyebrows.

"Philadelphia?" He repeated. He began to frown then his eyes widened in sudden understanding. "The shooter at the FBI building!"

Alina nodded.

"I was on my way out of the city when I saw him a block away from Stephanie's building. He was walking up the street with a bag on his back. I followed him out of Philly, but lost him around Conshohocken."

"Well that explains who fired at Stephanie," he said. "Have you told them? Blake would want to know that."

"I haven't really had much time," she said dryly. "It's been kinda nonstop."

Michael smiled sheepishly. "Good point."

"If you're right, and it *is* one of Harry's protégés, then we need to look further than basic tracking devices," Damon said, returning to the original conversation. "If you weren't using a tracking device, how would you keep tabs on someone?"

"I would tap into their GPS," Alina answered immediately.

Damon nodded slowly. "Same."

As one, they turned and looked at Angela's BMW.

"If he hacked into her onboard GPS, there would be an outgoing signal, correct?" Michael asked, following their gaze.

Next Exit, No Outlet

"I wish it were that simple," Damon said. "If he was trained by the Organization, and we have to assume that he was, then no."

Michael stared at them.

"There has to be a way to find out, right? Come on. Do some of that magic assassin crap that you do all the time."

Damon grinned and Alina chuckled reluctantly.

"Magic assassin crap?"

"You mean to tell me that you can rig my truck, my phone, my laptop, and even my smart watch to conceal my location once I pass a five-mile perimeter around your property, but you can't see if someone hacked a BMW's GPS?" Michael asked incredulously.

"Sorry. I've lost Harry Potter's wand."

"Actually, there could be a way," Damon said after a moment of thought. "Unfortunately, it would involve time and equipment that we don't have."

"So, what? We're just going to let Angela drive off and hope that her GPS isn't compromised?"

Alina shook her head.

"No. We're not. Angela's car will have to stay here. If they're linked into her GPS, they're not reading anything while the car's here."

Michael ran a hand through his hair.

"This is getting more and more complicated by the second," he said. "My truck is at the airport, probably with a tracking device on it, and now her car has been compromised as well. What are we supposed to do now?"

"Well, your truck is out, for the time being," Damon said. "Even if we got to it and removed any tracking devices, Harry has eyes through the CCTV cameras all up and down the East Coast. Honestly, that's probably how he always knew where you were on the way here. Until this is over, the truck will have to stay at the airport."

"The Jeep and Shelby are also compromised," Alina said, "as is Blake's car. That just leaves Damon's Audi and my rental Range Rover."

"If we can't keep Angela here, you can take the Audi," Damon told Michael. "If needed, I can pick up another vehicle."

"You say that like it's just a matter of going to the store and grabbing a new pair of shoes," he said. "Who *are* you people? Do you have a running assassin's tab with the rental agencies? Or do you just steal them all?"

Alina winked at him. "Trade secret."

She turned to take the detector back into the garage. When she was out of earshot, Michael looked at Damon.

"I'm assuming you two have a plan?" he asked in a low voice. "If the colonel *is* the one behind everything, including Dave's death, I want in."

Damon considered him thoughtfully for a long moment, his face impassive.

"This can't get personal," he finally said.

Michael held his gaze steadily.

"Oh, this is personal all right," he said, his voice like steel. "He made it personal. There's no getting around that. But if you're worried that I'll let emotion get in the way, don't be. I'll be fine."

"That's what everyone says, right before it all goes to hell."

Alina came out of the garage, pressing a button inside the door. The automatic door slid shut and she looked at Michael as she walked up.

"You're good with keeping an eye on Angela?"

"I'll take care of her," he assured her. "With any luck, we can convince her to stay here. If not, I'll do what I can."

"I can't ask for more than that."

"What about you?" Michael asked.

The look that crossed over Viper's face sent a chill down his spine.

"I've got a target to prep."

Chapter Fourteen

When they re-entered the house, the dining room table had been cleared of the Chinese food and plates. Blake was loading the dishwasher while Stephanie and Angela were in the process of finding homes for the assortment of snacks, frozen dinners, bagels and lunch meat.

Alina took one look at the crowd in her kitchen and picked up the open bottle of Cabernet on the dining room table.

"I don't blame you," Damon murmured in her ear as she poured wine into her glass. He glanced at Michael. "Beer?"

"Please."

Damon nodded and strode into the kitchen.

"Lina, I opened another bottle of wine," Stephanie called. "I hope you don't mind."

"It's fine."

Alina picked up her wine glass and walked over to sit at the bar. She watched as Blake finished loading the dishwasher and closed it.

"You didn't have to take care of the dishes," she said.

Blake grinned. "I have to earn my keep somehow."

"You've already earned your keep as far as I'm concerned."

Blake picked up his half-empty beer from the counter and walked over to sit next to her at the bar.

"How's that?"

"You're helping to keep Stephanie alive. You would have taken a bullet for her in the parking garage last night."

"Thanks to you that wasn't required," he said.

Alina shrugged dismissively.

"The fact remains that you would." She hesitated, then looked at him. "I know you don't understand why I was so reluctant to let you come here," she said, her voice low so the others wouldn't overhear. "It's nothing personal."

Blake's brown eyes met hers.

"I understand more than you think I do," he replied, his voice just as low. "The more people who know about you and know where you are, the more people are at risk. What you need to understand is that I'm a Marine. You're not responsible for me. I'm responsible for me. No matter what happens here, I'll take care of myself."

Alina smiled faintly. "You Marines. You always think you're so invincible."

Blake grinned. "Maybe we're just too stubborn to die."

Damon came out of the kitchen with two beers in his hand.

"Or too dumb," he said as he passed.

"Or that," Blake admitted.

Damon walked over to where Michael had retrieved his laptop and set it on the table in the dining room. He handed him one of the beers.

"Working again?"

"I'm just checking my email," Michael said, opening the laptop.

"Don't get too comfortable," Angela called from the kitchen. "When I finish helping Stephanie, I'll be ready to go."

Alina suppressed a sigh and looked across the bar at Angela.

"You can't go anywhere tonight," she said. "We have to figure out the vehicle situation."

Angela stared at her, pausing in the act of stowing a box of cheese crackers in one of the cabinets.

"What vehicle situation?" she asked. "My car's right outside."

"You can't take your car."

Stephanie looked up sharply while Angela gaped.

"What you mean I can't use my car?" Angela demanded. "Why not?"

"If you're being followed, that car is like a beacon," Alina said calmly. "I'm not saying you can't leave, but you'll have to wait until tomorrow when we can sort out a different vehicle for you to use."

Angela closed the cabinet door and turned to face her, setting her hands on her hips.

"This is ridiculous," she said. "You're being completely paranoid. You can't just keep me here!"

"Angie, calm down," Stephanie said, putting the last of the groceries into the refrigerator. She closed the door and turned to gather up the empty plastic bags from the kitchen island. "She didn't say you couldn't leave, just that you can't leave tonight. If I've learned anything over the past two days, it's that it's better to be safe than sorry. Just stay here tonight and tomorrow we'll figure out something."

"What about my cat?" Angela demanded. "I can't leave her all night."

"Your cat will be fine," Alina said. "It's only for one night."

Next Exit, No Outlet

"Easy for you to say. Your pet goes and hunts for his own food."

"Missing one meal is not going to hurt Annabelle," Stephanie said with a laugh. "That cat has enough fat on it to last a few days."

"And you!" Angela spun around to glare at Stephanie. "You're supposed to be on my side!"

Stephanie blinked.

"I am on your side! But I can see why it makes more sense for you to stay here tonight. It's already after nine o'clock, and there's no way to get a rental car all the way out here this late. It makes sense to wait until the morning."

Angela threw her hands up in the air and stomped out of the kitchen into the dining room. Picking up the wine bottle, she refilled her glass.

"This is all so unnecessary," she complained. "All of this just because I thought I might be being watched. Why can't I take my car?"

"Use your head, Angie," Alina said. "Blake's car had a tracking device on it, Stephanie's car must have had a tracking device for them to pinpoint exactly when she would be crossing an intersection, and Michael was followed up from DC. Are you seeing a pattern yet?"

"And it's not entirely just because you thought you might be being watched," Stephanie added, hobbling out of the kitchen and into the dining room. She picked up her half-empty glass and took a sip of the red wine. "There's a lot more to it than just paranoia, Angie."

"Well, I wouldn't know anything about that, would I? No one tells me anything!"

Alina pinched the bridge of her nose and Blake glanced at her sympathetically.

"Did you know this was what you were getting yourself into when you agreed to have Stephanie come here?" he asked.

Alina nodded tiredly. "Unfortunately."

Stephanie picked up her wine glass and turned to carry it into the living room, heading for her spot in the recliner. Angela watched her go then looked at Blake and Alina.

"So what now?" she asked. "We all just hunker down here and hope for the best?"

"Well, I don't know about anyone else, but I'm in the middle of a case. I'll be working," Blake said, getting up and following Stephanie into the living room. As she settled herself in the recliner, he sat on one end of the sofa. "I'll call Rob in the morning and let him know we're safe. Then I'll get back to work."

Angela looked at Michael.

"Tomorrow is Sunday," she said, "but come Monday morning, what are you going to do? Come with me to work?"

"You'll have to work from home," Alina said, standing up. "You can't go into work right now."

Angela swung around to glare at her.

"And just what am I supposed to tell my boss?" she demanded. "I'm sorry. I have to work from home today because my best friend has lost her mind and thinks I'm in danger? Please."

"I'm sure you'll think of something," Alina said, turning to walk into the living room.

Michael closed his laptop and looked at Angela.

"We'll figure it out. You can always tell them something happened to the car."

Angela brightened. "That's true. I could say it has to go into the dealership."

She turned to go into the living room and Michael stood, picked up his chair, and followed.

"If you're going to keep having full houses like this, you'll need more furniture," he told Alina, carrying the chair into the living room and setting it between the recliner and the sofa. He straddled the seat and draped his arms over the back.

Alina glanced up from where she was settling herself in the opposite corner of the sofa from Blake.

"There's always the floor."

Angela dropped onto the sofa between Blake and Alina and looked around.

"It's not that bad," she said. "You could probably fit another recliner in here and that would take care of it."

"Or I could just stop letting you all invade my house."

"Hey, this is all your fault," Angela retorted as Damon perched on the arm next to Alina. "You're the one who won't let me leave."

"What about you?" Stephanie asked Alina, pointedly going back to the original topic. "With all of us here, what will you do?"

Alina shrugged.

"I've got work to do," she said flatly. "I'll be gone most of the day tomorrow, so I'll set the security system so that you can go on the deck and into the back yard to take Buddy out, but no further."

Stephanie stared at her. "You're leaving?"

Alina raised an eyebrow in question and Stephanie frowned.

"Out of all of us, you're the one most in danger," she said. "This whole thing started because someone tried to kill you!"

"And they failed."

Next Exit, No Outlet

"You won't let me leave here because someone's trying to kill me. Guess what? They failed too. So what's the difference?"

"The difference is that it's me."

"Do you have any idea how dumb that sounds?" Angela asked, looking at Alina. "Because it's you? What, are you bulletproof?"

Alina opened her mouth to reply, then paused. There was no good response to give Angela without giving her too much information. If Angela knew even a fraction of what Viper was capable of, she'd have a heart attack.

"No, she's not," Stephanie said grimly. "Lina, you can't have one rule for the rest of us, and one rule for yourself. If we have to stay cooped up, so do you."

"This isn't a democracy. It's not up for debate."

"That might be the most arrogant and egotistical thing you've said yet. And it's utter BS. You should have to stay put too."

Alina felt her patience wearing thin and she looked across the living room at Stephanie, her eyes narrowing.

"Do you want this bastard caught?"

"Not if it means putting you in the cross-hairs," Stephanie shot back. "You've spent the past twenty-four hours making security decisions for everyone in this room, everyone except you."

"I'm hardly a priority right now."

Angela gasped.

"You should be your first priority," she exclaimed. "Lina, you need to take some self-care classes. You know, I took one last year and it really opened my eyes. I didn't even realize that I was abusing myself so badly until I took that class. You need to take time for you, and make yourself a priority. After all, if you don't take care of yourself, how can you take care of anyone else?"

Alina felt her other eye begin to twitch.

"I'll keep that in mind next time I have a free weekend," she murmured, aware of Damon's silence beside her. She didn't dare look at him, knowing if she did, she would find him laughing.

"Angela's right about one thing," Stephanie said. "You can hardly help us if you're dead, now can you?"

Alina rolled her eyes.

"And I can't help you from here. At least, not entirely," she qualified.

Stephanie's face flushed red with anger and she glared across the room at her.

"You know what? You're being selfish and reckless, Alina. Look around you! Everyone in this room has been affected by your decisions. John's dead, I took a bullet in my leg, and Angela got pegged with pieces of the Virgin Mary! Hell, Damon almost died when a bullet that was meant for you hit him instead! Now they're coming after me and, more than likely, Angela too. Now is not the time to think you're invincible. After everything that's happened, you owe it to us to stay hidden and safe until this gets sorted out!"

As she spoke, Stephanie's voice got louder until she was almost yelling. Alina watched her, her mask sliding into place as she spoke. Her whole body stiffened and she was unaware that one of her hands had closed into a fist until she felt Damon's calming hand on her shoulder. Taking a deep breath, Viper relaxed her hand and forced the onslaught of anger and frustration back down.

"Wait, Damon's gunshot was meant for you?!" Angela shrieked, turning to face Alina. "What the hell? No one told me that! What happened?"

"Damon got shot, that's what happened," Stephanie told her. "We didn't tell you because we didn't want to alarm you, but I think we're beyond that now. The shooter was aiming for Alina."

"It's really not as dramatic as it sounds," Damon told Angela over Alina's head. "They weren't a very experienced shooter."

Alina pictured him laying a pool of blood on the flagged stones of the balcony in Singapore and her lips tightened. They were experienced enough. It was only through quick thinking on her part and the skill of a local surgeon that she was able to stabilize Damon and get him back to the States, saving his life. It was every bit as dramatic as it sounded, but she knew he was trying to de-escalate the conversation, not make it worse.

"You could have been killed!" Angela exclaimed. "How is that not dramatic?"

So much for de-escalation.

"But I wasn't."

"That's not the point!" Stephanie said. "The point is that every time she goes out of this house, she's in more danger than we are! She needs to stay put until this guy is caught."

"I've never backed down from a fight, and I'm sure as hell not starting now," Alina said grimly, standing up and moving restlessly away from the sofa. She began to pace the length of the living room.

"Yes, and how has that worked out for you recently?" Stephanie demanded. "Oh wait, that's right. You've been shot at and attacked more in the past two months than probably ever happened while you were on active duty with the Navy!"

Alina glanced at her from near the sliding doors.

Next Exit, No Outlet

"That's hardly a fair comparison. I was parked at a desk for most of my time with the Navy."

Stephanie made a strangled noise and threw her hands up in the air.

"And you say Angie's stubborn!" she exclaimed. "You're being ten times worse than her right now. My point is that you owe it to me, Damon, Angela, and Michael to take your own security into account and stay safe! You owe it to John! He's the one who kept all those emails safe all these years. You're just going to toss all that away by throwing yourself into the front line and getting yourself killed? And what about Dave? How do you think he'd feel about that?"

At the mention of Dave, Viper's lips tightened and her whole body stiffened as a wave of anger surged from deep inside her. Taking a deep breath, she forced the emotion down again before it led her to do or say something she would regret.

"Are you done?" Michael's voice sliced through the suddenly charged silence.

Stephanie looked at him and nodded, seeming to realize that perhaps she had gone too far.

"I think you're forgetting something," Michael said, his voice cold and hard. "If it weren't for Alina, both you and Blake would be in the morgue. If she'd been hiding here and playing it safe, and hadn't been throwing herself into that front line you're so opposed to, you wouldn't have made it out of the hospital."

"Gunny, you don't need to defend me," Alina said, her lips twisting.

Michael shot her an unreadable look and turned his attention back to Stephanie.

"She doesn't owe us anything," he continued. "Hell, we all owe her more than any of us can repay. How many times has she saved us individually in the past year? How many terrorist attacks has she prevented right here in New Jersey? None of that was her job. None of it was her responsibility, but she did it because it was the right thing to do. Now fighting is the right, the only thing to do, and she's the only one who can do it. As for Dave, I can tell you this much, he would be damn proud of what she's done, and if she backed down now, he would kick her ass. Maschiks don't run, they fight. And I'll be damned if I'm going to sit here and listen to you whine about her doing her job. The fact is she's trying to fix mistakes that all of us have made. She's going to war for us. The least you can do is show a little gratitude, and a little respect."

Michael finally finished and a heavy, uncomfortably charged

silence fell over the living room.

"Ok, I think we all need to calm down and take a breath." Blake was the one to finally break it. "Stephanie's not attacking her, she's just voicing her opinion."

"That was more than just an opinion," Damon murmured.

Blake grimaced. "Probably should have left the brother out of it," he told Stephanie.

She scowled. "I stand by what I said."

"And so do I," Michael retorted. "You're being a bitch."

Stephanie gasped and Angela's mouth dropped open. Alina felt an unruly laugh bubble up inside her and she turned away to pace toward the hallway, biting her bottom lip.

"That was uncalled for," Angela said, glaring at Michael. "Granted Stephanie can be a little outspoken, but she's got a concussion. She's been through a lot in the past couple days."

"And Alina hasn't?" Michael demanded incredulously.

Angela shrugged.

"I don't know anything about what Lina has been through because everyone seems to think I'm not able to handle the truth, but I know about Stephanie. She was shot in the leg, for God's sake!"

"Mike, calm down. Getting into a fight over this isn't going to help anyone." Blake tried again to defuse the brewing fight. "Steph shouldn't have brought up Dave, I'll give you that, but let the rest go."

"Why shouldn't I bring up Dave?" Stephanie demanded contrarily. "I happen to disagree with Michael. I think Dave would be appalled that Alina is going to continue to take reckless and unnecessary risks while she makes me and Angela stay out of sight. It's a double-standard, and Dave hated double-standards."

Michael glared at her.

"I hate to break it to you, sweetheart, but you obviously didn't know Dave very well," he said. "It's not a double standard. She's protecting you while she finds the bastard responsible for all of this. Dave would have done the same thing."

"He absolutely would not!"

Blake dropped his head into his hands in defeat.

"Steph, you just can't help yourself, can you?" he muttered.

"Well, I knew Dave pretty well," she said belligerently, "and I don't appreciate being told that I didn't."

"Oh, I'm aware you knew my brother a lot better than you ever let on," Alina said coldly, stopping behind the sofa and pinning Stephanie with a steely glance. "But in this case, Michael's right."

A pregnant silence fell over the group and Stephanie's face

Next Exit, No Outlet

paled.

"What are you talking about?" Her voice was soft but it sounded like it boomed across the room. "What do you mean?"

Viper's gaze never wavered.

"Michael's right. Dave would have done the same thing I am. He was a fighter. You may have been sleeping with him, but you clearly didn't know what made him tick."

Chapter Fifteen

Stephanie stared across the room at Alina, the blood draining out of her face.

"How do you know that?" she whispered, her lips white.

"It wasn't me!" Angela said quickly, throwing her hands up in the air. "I didn't say a word!"

Damon got up and went over to remove Stephanie's empty wine glass from her hand before she dropped it. Turning, he glanced at Angela questioningly and she wordlessly held out her glass. He took it and turned toward the dining room. His eyes met Alina's and he shook his head faintly. Alina wanted to shrug and make a face, but she refrained. Instead, she glanced at Angela.

"Actually, it *was* you," she said calmly. "Or rather, your journal."

Angela gaped.

"My journal?" she repeated. "How the hell did you see that? God, that must have been from…"

"June 15, 2005."

Angela's face darkened. "You'd better explain how you know that."

"It was sent to me by an anonymous source."

"Look, Lina, I don't know how you saw that, but…" Angela began, but Stephanie cut her off.

"When?" she asked sharply.

"This morning."

Angela looked from one to the other.

"Wait," she said slowly. "It really *was* sent to you?"

"Yes."

"By whom?!"

"I told you, it was an anonymous source."

"It was him, wasn't it?" Stephanie asked. "You said he likes to get inside people's heads. He sent it to you."

Alina didn't answer but resumed pacing.

"Who's him? What are you talking about?" Angela demanded.

Next Exit, No Outlet

"This is *my* journal we're talking about! I'd like to know who has it!"

"The person who hacked it," Alina said shortly. "It's the same person who's trying to kill Stephanie...and me."

Angela's mouth dropped open. "The cyber-geek from the basement in Russia?"

Alina's lips quivered despite herself. "You're the only one who ever thought it was some guy in a basement in Russia."

"Lina, I...I don't know what to say," Stephanie said miserably. "I should have told you years ago, but Dave didn't want you to know at first, and then when he died..."

"You must be the girl!" Michael exclaimed suddenly. "When we first met, Dave mentioned a girl back home. Then I never heard about her again. When I asked about it halfway through the Iraq tour, he said it was over."

"It was," Stephanie said earnestly. "It was a stupid fling, and when he went to Iraq, it was over. He just didn't want Alina to know because he didn't think she'd understand."

Alina's lips tightened briefly and something akin to anger flashed through her before it was replaced with the hollow feeling of loss that always accompanied thoughts of Dave.

Damon walked out of the kitchen and handed her a glass of wine as she passed before he continued to the sofa to pass a second one to Angela. Without a word, he turned to go back into the kitchen to get a third glass for Stephanie. Alina sipped the wine gratefully.

"And you never told her?" Blake asked incredulously. "Since 2005?"

Stephanie shook her head.

"There never seemed to be a good time, and then she joined the Navy and was gone for ten years." Stephanie looked up as Damon walked into the living room and handed her the wine. "Thanks."

He nodded and turned to go back to the kitchen.

"Hey Damon, can you..." Blake began, holding up his empty beer bottle.

"Already on it," Damon replied without turning his head.

Blake grinned and set the bottle back on the coffee table.

"That's messed up, Steph," Blake said, shaking his head. "He was her brother."

"Yes, and he was dead," Stephanie retorted hotly. "It was a moot point."

"Did John know?" Alina asked, pausing near Blake.

Stephanie looked guilty and that was all the answer she needed. Her eyes narrowed and she resumed pacing without a word.

"Lina, I think you're looking at this all wrong," Angela said, twisting on the couch to look at her as she passed behind them. "It was years ago, and they were just kids. We all were!"

Alina looked at her, her expression neutral.

"The only way I'm looking at it is as the weapon it was meant to be," she said flatly. "That journal entry was supposed to get into my head and make me question Stephanie, you, and everything I thought I knew about my family and my closest friends. What he didn't realize is that he picked an area that I laid to rest long ago. I won't question something that doesn't matter to me anymore."

Angela's eyes widened.

"Now we don't matter anymore?!" she exclaimed. "Lina, that's some coldness, even from you!"

Alina rolled her eyes. "That's not what I meant," she muttered.

Damon walked past her and his blue eyes met hers solemnly. He passed Blake a beer over the back of the sofa, then walked around to hand one to Michael.

"Well, that's certainly what it sounded like," Stephanie said, her color rising again. "If that's the case, then I don't know why you even care about Dave and I!"

Alina's jaw clenched and she felt her right eye twitch.

"If I didn't care, neither you nor Angie would be here right now. What I meant is that it doesn't matter to me who you slept with, or who Dave slept with, or why no one told me about any of it. It doesn't matter. The past is over. It's the present that concerns me."

"Agreed," Stephanie said unexpectedly after a long moment of thoughtful silence. "We need to come up with a plan of action."

"I have a plan of action," Alina said shortly.

Stephanie glared at her.

"A plan of action that includes all of us," she snapped. "You can't pull your Lone Ranger act on this one."

"Sure she can," Damon said, sipping his beer, "but she won't be alone. She has me."

Stephanie looked at him in exasperation.

"That doesn't make it any better," she said. "The two of you can't take—" She stopped herself abruptly before saying Harry's name in front of Angela. "What I mean is, the two of you won't be enough," she finished lamely.

"We always have been before," Damon replied, a thread of steel in his voice. He regarded Stephanie dispassionately for a moment, his blue eyes suddenly shifting from cobalt to ice blue. "This is what we do. You seem determined to forget that."

Next Exit, No Outlet

Stephanie gulped.

"You two work together, don't you?" Angela demanded, drawing his attention. "I knew it! Does she work for Homeland Security as well?"

"Homeland Security?" Blake repeated, looking from Angela to Stephanie in confusion. "Where did you get that idea?"

The question came out before he noticed Stephanie frantically trying to get his attention and her head fell in resignation.

"That's who Damon works for," Angela said, glancing at Blake. "You didn't know that?"

Blake looked at Stephanie helplessly.

"When we met Damon, he was with the DHS," she said. "He came in to help with a case John and I were working: the one that led us to Johann Topamari."

Michael choked on his beer and Damon glanced at him, amused. Alina paused in her pacing to whack him on the back helpfully.

"Oh. I see," was all Blake could muster.

Angela looked around the room, her eyes slowly narrowing. At last they came to land on Damon, and there they stayed.

"You *do* work for Homeland Security, don't you?" she asked him, her body still.

Damon hesitated, then shook his head. "No."

"Damon," Viper said warningly, all traces of amusement wiped from her face. His eyes met hers and her she frowned. What the hell was he up to?

"What do you mean, no?" Angela demanded. "Then where do you work? Does Lina work with you?"

"We don't work together, no, but we do the same job."

Angela frowned. "What do you do?"

"We do the jobs no one else can, and that's all you need to know."

"Well, that's rude!" Angela huffed. "I don't know why you're getting all snarky with me. If anyone should be crabby, it should be me! I've been thinking all this time that you work for Homeland Security and now that turns out to not be the case."

"Don't feel so bad, Ang," Alina murmured as she passed the couch. "At least you know his real name. Not many do."

"And you?" Angela twisted to peer up at her. "Do not many people know *your* real name either?"

"No."

Alina resumed pacing and Angela turned back around with a

pout.

"Well, at least now I know why you two are so perfect for each other," she muttered, lifting her glass to her lips.

"You two really think you can take on...this guy? On your own?" Blake asked after a moment of silence. "I mean, I understand that you two probably know him best, but this is...well, *him* we're talking about!"

"I guess not many people know *his* name either?" Angela asked snidely.

"We've faced worse," Alina said, ignoring her.

"Not at home, you haven't," Stephanie said. "This is insane. What you're talking about is suicide!"

Alina rolled her eyes and sipped her wine, tamping down her impatience. Stephanie didn't understand, and never *would* understand. Every day was suicide for them. That's why they did what no one else could.

"What we're talking about is making it possible for you to go back to work, and for Angela to go home," Damon said.

"Why do *you* have to get involved?" Angela asked suddenly, looking at him. "I mean, I get that you're invested in Alina's well-being and all, but why do you have to go charging out there with her?"

"There seems to be some opposition in this room to Alina doing it alone," he replied dryly. "Or did you miss that argument?"

"But that was about her leaving the house tomorrow," Angela objected. "What does that have to do with taking on the guy trying to kill Steph?"

The silence that followed that statement was deafening and Damon stared at her blankly, clearly at a loss. A giggle erupted from Stephanie. All eyes flew to her face and she chuckled again.

"Oh Angie," she gasped. "Please don't ever change!"

"Even if you two could take him down on your own," Blake said slowly, "and that's a big if, how are you going to get to him?"

Viper's smile was deadly.

"Oh, don't worry about that," she said from near the sliding doors. "We'll get to him. That's what we do."

Stephanie shook her head, frowning.

"I don't care what you both say, I don't like it," she said. "There has to be a way to do this together and minimize the risk."

"There probably is, but we're not doing it," Alina said shortly. "I've already got a plan, and it doesn't include any of you. Just sit tight and relax."

"And let the adults take care of it?" Blake demanded, looking

Next Exit, No Outlet

up. "That's dangerously close to being insulting."

"I'm pretty sure she didn't mean that for us," Michael said in a stage whisper. "She knows Marines don't just sit tight and relax."

"Neither do FBI agents!" Stephanie exclaimed.

"I'm perfectly happy to sit tight and relax," Angela announced cheerfully. "I just want to do it from my own house."

"Well, I'm not, and I won't," Stephanie said stubbornly, a martial light glinting in her eyes. "I'm not going to sit and twiddle my thumbs while they do all the work!"

"I hate to point this out, but you're not exactly in any condition to much of anything else," Michael said gently. "You're not thinking clearly. You can barely walk, and your head must feel like the Road Runner dropped an anvil on it."

"They're not exactly one hundred percent, either!" Stephanie retorted. "Damon had a rifle bullet go through him two weeks ago, and Alina's been shot herself."

Alina raised her eyebrows, surprised. While it was true, she had gone through great lengths to ensure that Stephanie had no idea.

"I have?" she asked.

Stephanie glanced at her impatiently.

"Yes. I saw the bandage on your arm when I came to tell you John died. You didn't tell me what happened, but I'm not stupid."

Alina looked down into her wine glass. She'd almost forgotten about the shot that went through her arm in West Virginia when she was saving Dr. Krupp. So much had happened since then that the minor flesh wound had been relegated to the past without a further thought.

"They aren't showing any signs of decreased mobility," Michael pointed out. "You are. All I'm saying is that, while your willingness is commendable, physically, you can't help."

"There are things I can do to help that don't require running a marathon," Stephanie said. "And you and Blake are perfectly healthy. There's absolutely no reason for her to take all the risk alone."

"As I said before: this isn't a democracy, and it's not up for debate," Alina said. "Case closed."

Anger flared in Stephanie's eyes.

"Case reopened," she snapped. "I'm not letting you do this. How many ways do I have to say it? You'll get yourself killed, and for what?"

"The short answer? For you," Damon said coldly. "Michael was right. You all seem to have forgotten that, if it weren't for Alina, none of you would be here right now. I've just spent the better part of two hours listening to you all argue and bicker over who's responsible for what and who owes who imaginary debts."

He turned his arctic blue eyes on Angela.

"You've done nothing but complain about the inconvenience of having to stay in a house overnight where you're protected by three Federal agents, a security system superior to the one that's in the White House - sorry, gunny, but it's true - and a bird of prey that takes the term 'guard dog' to a whole new level. Instead of thanking Lina, you've told her she's paranoid, ridiculous, and being unnecessary. Do the names Lowell Kwan and Trent Whitfield ring any bells? Was she being ridiculous and paranoid then?"

Angela sputtered and began to speak, but he cut her off ruthlessly, turning his attention back to Stephanie.

"You're talking about the dangers of Alina being visible outside this security perimeter and how exposed and at risk she'll be, but you're conveniently ignoring that you're the one who's exposed her the most. Whether you thought you were helping or not, you were the one who led teams of assassins straight to her. It was you who put the tracking devices on her cars, and you who sent the information straight to the enemy."

Damon's voice was even and void of emotion as he spoke, the words falling heavily in the silence. Viper sipped her wine, her eyes on his face. At least now she knew what he was up to.

"But I didn't know—" Stephanie began to protest.

"It doesn't matter what you knew," Damon cut her off. "What matters is what you did, and you led several teams of killers to her. Forgive me if I find it ironic that you're now pitching a fit because she might run into some more."

"Hear, hear," Michael muttered under his breath, drawing an amused look from Alina.

"You were quick to throw John's name out there, but his death is probably the only thing in this whole situation that couldn't have been prevented. Why? Because he didn't tell a soul what he had on his laptop! Instead of bringing Dave's letters to Alina when she came back last year, he sat on them, and tried to play the hero by investigating and figuring out the mystery himself. It got him killed. Not only did it get him killed, but it started the ball rolling that led us all directly here."

Alina pursed her lips thoughtfully and stopped pacing, leaning against the wall next to the sliding doors.

"The plain truth is that, for all your finger-pointing and moralizing, every last one of you is to blame for some part of this."

"I haven't done anything except complain, apparently," Angela said, tossing her head defiantly.

Damon turned his ice blue eyes on her.

"No? Then you didn't post your private journal online where it was then hacked by the very person trying to kill Alina?" he asked ruthlessly. "Because that same journal is now being used to get inside her head and force her to make a mistake. He knows he can't win straight-up; he trained us too well for that. So he's using *your* journal as a psychological weapon to try to weaken Alina to the point that she'll expose herself, and then he can take the kill shot."

By the time he was finished, Angela's face was white and her empty wine glass was trembling in her hand.

"I know that you all had good intentions, but you know what they say about those," Damon said slowly. "Good intentions aside, the damage was done. As far as I'm concerned, you all helped build this monster. You all created a threat that you aren't capable of defeating, and now Alina and I have to clean up your mess and take it down. That's fine. That's what we do and we've been trained to handle it. But next time you want to whine about her calling the shots or being high-handed, take a moment and remember exactly why you're here, and acknowledge that the only person you have to blame is yourself."

Silence fell heavily. Stephanie's face alternated between red and white as anger warred with guilt, and Angela sulked on the sofa. Alina watched Stephanie's face, absently wondering which emotion would gain the upper hand.

"Well, I'm glad to see you've mastered the art of sugar-coating," Michael said, breaking the silence at last. "I guess the SEALs aren't big on diplomacy? Funny. I thought all the politicians came from the Navy."

A laugh leapt into Damon's eyes, transforming the color back to the warm, cobalt blue.

"You're the one who ended up in Washington," he retorted.

Michael raised his beer in a silent toast, acknowledging the hit.

"Are you serious right now?" Stephanie demanded, her face bright red.

Alina's lips twitched. The anger had won.

"Are you seriously cracking jokes?"

Michael looked at her in surprise. "What?"

Stephanie made a furious noise in the back of her throat.

"First of all," she said, glaring at Damon, "who are you to start pointing out everything we've done wrong?"

"Here we go," Alina murmured under her breath, raising her glass to her lips to finish her wine.

"Yes, we've clearly made some bad judgment calls and some mistakes, but guess what? We're human. Humans make mistakes. We're not robots like you, working on some kind of ingrained algorithm that only spits out emotion in short bursts. I suppose you've never made a bad judgment call? Or trusted the wrong person? Or did something you thought was for the best? Don't judge us for doing what we thought was best at the time."

"I'm not judging you for doing what you thought was best," Damon said calmly, his even tone a direct contrast with her heated and emotional tirade. "I'm judging you for then twisting it around and trying to make Alina responsible for it."

Stephanie sucked in her breath.

"You've got some serious nerve," she sputtered. "You sit there all night and keep quiet, not getting involved in anything. Then, when you finally do open your mouth, you unleash this attack against me and Angela, and even John! He's not even here anymore to defend himself!"

"He doesn't need to defend himself. I didn't say anything that wasn't true, or anything that was disrespectful to the dead. I simply stated facts."

"But we don't have all the facts! We don't know why he didn't tell anyone about the letters. He may have had a valid reason to keep it to himself."

Damon shrugged.

"Maybe," he said in a tone guaranteed to feed the flames of her anger, "but if he had told Lina about them, we wouldn't be here now. It would never have come to this."

"You keep saying 'we' like you're working with Lina," Angela pointed out. "If you don't work together, I still don't understand why you're jumping into this. I mean, Blake and Michael aren't getting involved. Why are you?"

"Yes, why *are* you?" Stephanie demanded, her temper goaded beyond reason. "Dave didn't even know you, and you have no responsibility to me or Angela. What does any of this have to do with you? Alina's the one who should be having this conversation, not you. Why are you suddenly so involved in Jersey drama? From what I've seen over the past year, you all work alone and take care of yourselves. So why are you suddenly so determined to go to bat for Lina?"

Damon looked across the room calmly.

"Because she's my wife."

Next Exit, No Outlet

Chapter Sixteen

Frankie Solitto poured whiskey into two cut glasses and set the decanter down, replacing the glass topper. Turning, he carried them across the room and handed one to the man sitting in an armchair in his study.

"It's been a long time," he said. "I'm glad you agreed to come tonight."

The man took the glass, a diamond ring on his middle finger flashing in the lamplight.

"It *has* been a long time," he agreed, sipping the whiskey appreciatively. "Business has been challenging in the past months, and I was grateful for this chance to get away for a few hours."

The head of the Jersey Family glanced over his shoulder as he moved to the other armchair.

"That doesn't sound good," he murmured, seating himself and crossing one leg over the other. "I've never known you to stress over business, Bobby. Is it something I can help with?"

Bobby Reyes considered Frankie thoughtfully for a moment.

"Actually, I was going to contact you when you reached out to me," he said slowly. "I believe you may have some knowledge that might help."

Frankie sipped his whiskey, studying Bobby over the rim of the glass. He'd known Bobby for years and, at one point in time, they were competitors and rivals. Twenty years ago, after more bloodshed than either of them cared to admit to, they came to a truce. Bobby Reyes would have exclusive control over the arms distribution from New Jersey down to Washington DC. In return, the Solitto family businesses would remain untouched by Bobby, and Frankie received a yearly stipend to stay out of Bobby's business. As part of that agreement, Frankie negotiated a pact with the New York family, allowing Bobby Reyes a thirty percent margin on the arms deals in New York.

The arrangement had worked out to be very lucrative to all parties concerned, and over the past twenty years, Bobby and Frankie had become friends. In that time, Frankie had never known Bobby to come to him for counsel.

"What seems to be the problem?" he asked, lowering his glass.

"Last fall, there were rumors that you had a challenger for some of your business endeavors in New Jersey."

Frankie raised his eyebrows. "And what did those rumors say?"

"That the Casa Reinos Cartel was trying to move into the area. If that had happened, at a conservative estimate, over fifty percent of your revenue would have been taken out from under you."

"I wouldn't call that a conservative estimate," Frankie said with a faint smile. "However, the rest of the evaluation may be accurate. Luckily, it was taken care of."

Bobby nodded. "So I heard, and that's why I'm here. I'm facing a similar problem now."

Frankie frowned sharply. "The cartel?"

"Four months ago, they began moving weapons up the coast. Instead of using my network, they're using their own people. They've established connections with the gangs in Philadelphia, Newark, Trenton and Atlantic City. In doing so, they're undercutting my own agreements."

"By how much?"

"Forty-five percent," Bobby said grimly.

Frankie's lips twisted unpleasantly.

"That is unacceptable," he said. "What are you doing to correct the situation?"

"One of my senior boys is in Newark. He's the one who tipped me off four months ago. It was his gang that first started dealing with the cartel. When he told me, I told him to stay put and learn what he could. Two months ago, three cartel members moved into the gang. My boy has since become very tight with them."

Frankie nodded in approval. "That's good. What has he learned?"

Bobby sipped his whiskey and shook his head with a frown.

"The Casa Reinos expect to have full control from Miami to Boston within the year, including the drug stream."

"And just how do they plan on doing that?"

"They have someone in Washington."

Frankie waved his hand impatiently.

"So do we," he said briskly. "They'll need more than that to take on the Three Families."

"Unfortunately, they may have it," Bobby said. "From what my boy has been able to put together, it seems the cartel has managed to amass an army within the gangs. Some will side with us, if it comes

Next Exit, No Outlet

down to it, but the general consensus is that the majority of the Hispanic and Mexican demographic won't go against the cartel. There is, however, a weak spot that we can exploit if we move quickly."

Frankie raised his eyebrows in interest. "Oh?"

Bobby nodded. "Last fall, Jenaro Gomez, the cartel's second-in-command, was killed here in Jersey. His head was FedEx'd to La Cabeza, the head of the cartel."

"I believe I heard something to that effect," Frankie murmured, a faint smile on his lips.

Bobby looked at him and chuckled.

"I have to tell you, Frankie, I laughed when I heard the news. I never would have pegged you as having such a dramatic flair."

"And you would be right," Frankie told him after a short pause. "I had nothing to do with Jenaro."

Bobby stared at him in surprise. "What? Then who did?"

Frankie was silent for a long moment, his lips pressed together thoughtfully. Then, coming to a decision, he raised his eyes to Bobby's.

"Someone who is far more dangerous than the cartel," he said softly.

Bobby frowned and studied Frankie intently.

"Is there a new player I should be aware of?" he finally asked, his voice hard.

Frankie finished his whiskey and stood up to go refill his glass.

"No," he said over his shoulder. "Not a new player, per se. More of an...ally, if you will."

"Well, this ally has a target on their back," Bobby told him. "Some of the members of the cartel have become convinced that the person who killed their lieutenant is still in the Philadelphia area."

Frankie poured the amber liquid into his glass and set the decanter down gently.

"Is that a fact?" he said softly, turning to face Bobby. "And do you believe this information?"

Bobby shrugged.

"I didn't pay much attention to it, to be honest, until yesterday," he said. "You saw what happened in Center City?"

Frankie went back to his seat and sat down, nodding.

"Two men were stabbed in Independence Park," he said. "Not worth all the fuss, in my opinion. People are stabbed every day."

"Agreed, but it raises a serious question."

"In what way?"

"In light of what you just told me, what the cartel members are saying is beginning to make more sense," Bobby said, leaning forward.

"When I first heard about their contract on the person who killed Jenaro, I assumed that person was you or your enforcer, Stefan. If you had nothing to do with it, we're looking at a whole different situation."

"And what situation is that?"

"I know you don't pay much attention to what goes on out in cyberspace, but in this instance, you may want to. A few days ago, an open letter was released onto the dark web. That letter named an American assassin, along with her recent targets. Jenaro Gomez was on that list."

Frankie's face was impassive as he sipped his whiskey.

"And what was the point to this open letter?"

"As far as I can tell, it was simply to motivate someone to whack her. It gave her last known locations and even included a surveillance photo. When this was brought to my attention, it had nothing to do with me, but now I'm starting to think that it might. If this assassin truly *is* the one who killed Jenaro Gomez, then it isn't too much of a stretch to assume that she's also responsible for the two stabbings in Philadelphia yesterday."

"What makes you think the attack in Independence Park was a professional hit?"

Bobby shrugged. "Two men of Middle Eastern descent, killed at the same time in two different buildings, and no one saw a thing? It certainly wasn't a crime of passion."

Frankie smiled despite himself.

"Fair enough," he murmured. "So if we assume it was this assassin from the open letter, and I'm not convinced it was, what does this have to do with your situation with the cartel?"

Bobby sat back and crossed his legs.

"If the cartel is busy focusing on Jenaro's killer, they won't be looking over their shoulder."

"Presenting us with an opportunity."

Bobby nodded. "Exactly."

Frankie sipped his whiskey and was silent, deep in thought. The open letter was a surprise, but he supposed it shouldn't have been. This was not the first time his mysterious assassin-associate had been targeted. He pressed his lips together thoughtfully. Right now he owed the woman a debt. While they had agreed that she could call in a favor to erase that debt at an unspecified time in the future, Frankie was a practical man. If he was able to eliminate this latest complication for her, then he would have one of the most dangerous people he had ever met in his debt. That could come in very handy.

He set his glass down on the table beside his chair and reached

Next Exit, No Outlet

into his pocket to pull out his cell phone. He swiped the screen and pressed a button, sending a quick text.

"I think it's time for Stefan to join us," he said.

"I agree. How do you want to handle this?"

"It's past time for the Casa Reinos to be sent a message," Frankie said firmly. "I thought, after last fall, the message would have been clear. Obviously, they need a reminder of who they're dealing with. When Stefan comes in, give him a list of the cartel names. We'll start with them."

"Is Stefan up to it? These aren't little punks from the Bronx."

"Stefan is my chief enforcer for good reason," Frankie said evenly. "He'll handle them."

"If you focus on the cartel members, I can focus on the gang members most likely to oppose us," Bobby said. "Once we make an example of the cartel and their most loyal supporters, it won't take much to get the gangs in line again."

Frankie nodded in approval.

"This is a situation that's been brewing for months," he said. "As soon as New Jersey became a sanctuary state, this was bound to happen. It's created an internal competition between us and these young outsiders who don't understand how business is conducted here. It's time they learn."

"And the assassin?"

"There's no need to concern yourself with that. Once we take care of the cartel and their allies, the assassin won't be an issue."

Alina stood at the window, staring into the night thoughtfully. The moon was high, peeping through the clouds above and casting a pale glow over the back yard. As she stood there, the shower in the bathroom turned off, and she lifted a bottle to her lips, sipping the cool water.

Damon's announcement, delivered as it was, had caused nothing short of an uproar. At first, Stephanie and Angela had refused to believe it. Alina supposed she couldn't blame them. After all, there had been no warning and no indication that the relationship between herself and Damon was anything serious, at least, as far as they were aware. It was only after Alina confirmed that they had been married last month by a judge in Washington, DC that they began to accept the truth.

Alina capped her water bottle and set it on the sill, staring blindly out the window. They didn't understand the secrecy, or the rush, and she couldn't fault them for that. They didn't know, and could never understand, just how complicated it was. For that matter, Alina wasn't sure she fully comprehended it herself. While Asad was planning his Ebola attack, and Viper was patiently waiting for the traitor in Washington to reveal his hand, Hawk had convinced her that what they had between them was worth risking everything over. In a moment of pure insanity next to a remote lake in the Pine Barrens, he'd proposed that they secure their future and their assets in the most fool-proof way available to them. To her own surprise, she'd agreed.

It wasn't a marriage based on undying love, although Alina was beginning to suspect that that was a very real possibility. Rather, it was a union based on the undeniable fact that they both needed a legal safety net, and marriage provided that. Most of their work for the Organization could be considered a federal offense, and if a Congressional committee ever got hold of either of them, they could conceivably force them to testify against other assets, including each other. If, in the more likely scenario, one of them was killed, then the other would have access to their combined assets. In that case, the surviving spouse would be able to retire and disappear without a trace.

In its basic form, their marriage was a business arrangement.

In its non-basic form, it was far more complicated than that, Alina admitted ruefully. That night next to the lake, she had let Damon into a part of her life that she had kept isolated and to herself for years. In doing so, she thought there might be no going back. Less than twenty-four hours later, she was his wife, and she knew the truth. They were bound together for life, and not simply because it was the financially and politically safe course of action, but because neither of them could deny their connection any longer. They were two halves of the same person, and that was something they couldn't ignore. From the time she'd signed the legal form making her his wife, Alina had known it was much more than a business arrangement. The weeks that followed had only confirmed it.

The bathroom door opened behind her and light flooded into the dark room. Damon came out, dressed in an old pair of Navy sweatpants and nothing else. He went over to the bedside table and laid his Beretta down before walking over to stand behind her at the window.

"On a scale of one to ten, how mad at me are you right now?" he asked, his voice low as he looked over the top of her head into the

Next Exit, No Outlet

darkness.

Alina glanced over her shoulder at him. "Ten being the highest?"

His eyes dropped to hers and he nodded, his lips twisting ruefully.

"Yes."

She turned her head back to look out the window and shrugged.

"Less than two," she replied. "It had to come out sooner or later. At least you made it interesting."

A low chuckle went through him. "Yes I did."

Alina felt herself smile. "I don't think I'll ever forget the look on Stephanie's face when she finally realized it was true."

Damon slipped his arms around her waist, resting his chin on top of her head. She leaned back against him and they stood quietly for a long moment, staring out over the dark trees.

"How are you feeling about it?" Damon finally asked, lifting his chin but keeping his arms around her. "Tonight is the first time I've actually heard you acknowledge it."

Alina was quiet for a moment, then she sighed softly.

"I'm surprisingly comfortable with it," she admitted. "I've had time to adjust to the idea. And let's face it, you've hardly been crowding me since it happened. Getting it out into the open tonight just seemed like the next logical step."

"I'm sorry I announced it without discussing it with you first," Damon said slowly. "I didn't plan for that to happen."

"I understand." Alina hesitated, then turned in his arms and looked up into his handsome face. "Stephanie was being unreasonable, but she was right about one thing. This isn't your fight."

Damon's eyes met hers and his expression was unreadable in the moonlight.

"Harry isn't just after you. He's targeting all the Organization's assets, all over the globe. This is all of our fight."

Alina lifted her hand to touch his jaw.

"Yes, but I'm the one he wants. Go somewhere away from this and let me join you when I'm done." She pressed her fingers against his lips when he opened them to speak. "Listen to me. When you proposed this marriage, you said that if anything happened to one of us, the other would be taken care of. If we're both killed in this mess, then what was the point? The government will get everything, and this will all have been for nothing. Be smart about this, Hawk. We may be stronger together, but you'll be safer apart from me right now."

145

Damon removed her hand from his mouth, entwining his fingers with hers. He raised his other hand and slid a long finger under the edge of her shirt, lifting out the necklace hanging around her neck. A mangled lump of metal rested in his palm and he looked down into her eyes.

"I told you when you showed me this that it was a promise," he said quietly. "A promise that I will always put your life before my own, *until death do us part.* Nothing changes that. I'm all in on us, Lina, and that includes the impossible times. This isn't Peru, and I'm not leaving. We'll face it together and, if it comes down to it, we'll die together. But we're doing it together. That's what this means."

He dropped the bullet, leaving it to hang against her shirt as he took her other hand in his, entwining their fingers.

"You have a plan, and I've never known your plans to fail. We have a better chance together than you do alone. Right now Harry doesn't know I'm here. Charlie's been feeding him misinformation. I've been leaving breadcrumbs all over the Ukraine, and as a result, Harry believes I'm still in Russia. He's not expecting me. Face it, Viper, I'm your element of surprise."

Alina shook her head.

"If he has an ounce of sense, he'll realize that I couldn't kill both Kasim and Tarek at the same time in two different buildings," she told him. "Even if he believed you were in Russia before, yesterday would have convinced him otherwise."

Damon grinned slowly.

"Which is why it's a good thing that he received a secure message from me, sent from Kursk an hour after they were killed."

Alina stared at him in surprise. "What?"

He shrugged.

"I set it up and had one of my contacts send it. Harry answered it. As far as he's concerned, I'm in Russia."

A smile of approval curved her lips. "Well done."

"Thank you. Now, will you forget about getting rid of me? I'm not going anywhere."

"I'm not trying to get rid of you." A mischievous gleam came into her eye. "I'm actually getting used to having you around." She pulled one of her hands away from his and trailed her fingers across his chest teasingly. "I'm starting to see some of the benefits of having you here all night."

Damon's laugh was low and washed over her, filling her with warmth and comfort.

"Good, because so am I, on all counts."

Next Exit, No Outlet

He lowered his lips to hers and Alina leaned into him. As her arms went around him and he pulled her close, there was a scraping noise above them. Damon lifted his head and they both looked up, watching as the hinged door in the skylight swung inward and Raven dropped onto his perch in the corner. The hawk considered them with his black eyes for a moment before taking a few steps to his right along the wooden perch and settling down comfortably.

"I'll have to make arrangements for Raven," Alina said thoughtfully, almost to herself.

Damon looked at her and raised an eyebrow. "What do you mean?"

"Once this is over, I won't be coming back here," she said, her voice quiet and even. "He followed me here, but he doesn't belong this far north. I need to find somewhere that's more suited to him, and then hope he's willing to stay."

Damon studied her for a minute. The very lack of emotion in her voice told him just how deeply she felt about the hawk.

"It's that important to you?"

She nodded.

"He trusted me enough to follow me here, and absolutely refused to stay in the mountains in South America where he belonged. I tried. He's my responsibility now. I can't have him on my conscience along with John."

Damon pulled her close and rested his chin on the top of her head.

"What about my ranch?" he asked thoughtfully after a moment. "It's warmer there, and closer to what he's used to. Mount Scott isn't too far from me, at least not for him. It's not exactly South America, but it's better than the Northeast."

Alina pursed her lips. "It's a thought."

"I know we don't tend to look too far into the future, but my ranch is still secure. I know you're an East coast girl, but no one knows about it, not even Charlie."

Alina pulled away and looked up into his face.

"Hawk, are you asking me to become a redneck cowgirl?" she demanded. "Cuz it's not happening."

He grinned.

"I'm just pointing out the benefits of having a piece of property available to us," he told her, rubbing his nose against hers. "I think the possibility of you becoming a redneck cowgirl is sufficiently remote enough to risk it."

His lips covered hers and she smiled against them. His arms

tightened around her as passion ignited between them and Alina felt something close to hope flutter inside her. It was a foreign sensation, and almost unrecognizable. The day she'd walked into the training facility for the Organization, she had set hope aside. Over the intervening years, thoughts of the future and hope for a different life there became more and more remote. Her reality was that the only future she had was to survive the next twenty-four hours. That had become her mission, her constant goal. Hope was a luxury Viper could not afford. Now, here was Hawk, offering a glimpse at something beyond the next twenty-four hours.

They just had to get through the next few days. Maybe then, just perhaps, they had a chance to be free.

Next Exit, No Outlet

Chapter Seventeen

Alina sipped her coffee and leaned against the railing, looking out over the backyard. The sun was already high in the sky and she had been up for over three hours. Damon had left the house an hour ago to find a clean vehicle. She looked at the driveway and Angela's BMW, pursing her lips thoughtfully. If they had the time and the equipment, none of this would be necessary. They could find out if the GPS had been hacked and block the access. Unfortunately, they had neither.

The sliding door behind her opened, and she turned her head to watch as Michael stepped onto the deck, a steaming mug of coffee in his hand. He walked over to join her at the railing, sipping his coffee.

"Good morning," he said. "How long have you been up?"

"Since before dawn," she answered, glancing at him. "I knew once the others got up, my chance to work would be lost."

Michael grinned.

"They're something else," he said. "I'm beginning to see why you prefer to be alone."

Alina smiled faintly and turned to sit in one of the Adirondack chairs.

"I knew what I was getting myself into. So far, they haven't disappointed."

Michael turned to face her, leaning back against the railing. "How serious do you think the threat to Angela is?"

"Very."

"Have you considered the possibility that she could be a red herring?" he asked slowly.

Alina looked at him for a moment, then smiled.

"You mean as a ploy to divide and conquer?"

Michael grinned. "So you have."

"Yes, and I'm prepared for that. But I'll be surprised if that turns out to be the case."

"Why?"

"If Harry was going to do that, he would have done it already.

I don't think he had any intention of going after Angela again. I think he was expecting Stephanie's death to be the prompt he needed to get me out of hiding. Unfortunately for him, Stephanie didn't cooperate."

"Again? When did he go after Angela before?"

Alina sipped her coffee, silent for a moment, then raised her eyes to his face.

"Trent Whitfield," she said simply.

"I forgot about him," Michael said, making a face. "At least, I forgot about his connection to Trasker."

"Speaking of, have you been able to find a connection between Harry and Trasker yet?"

"No, but I'm sure there is one. If I can get Angela to stay in one place for more than five minutes today, I can get back to work."

Alina let out a short laugh. "Good luck with that. It's Sunday. This is her gym day."

"Gym day?"

"Every Sunday morning she goes to the gym for two hours, like clockwork. So keep your eyes open. If someone's watching her, they'll know that."

Michael nodded. "Roger that. Is there anything else I should know about her routine?"

"Actually, I think Sundays are her light days," Alina said thoughtfully. "After the gym, I think she takes the rest of the day for her. So you may get lucky and she'll stay in one spot."

"And you?"

"Once Damon gets back, I've got some things to take care of. I should be back later today."

"Where is your other half?"

Alina's eyes flickered briefly at his not so subtle reference to their new status.

"He went to find a clean vehicle for you to use," she said. "He should be back soon."

Michael studied her in silence for a moment. "Are you happy?"

The look he received was hooded and non-committal.

"I'll be happy when this is all over and I can lay Dave and John to rest."

Michael frowned.

"That's not what I meant," he said. "Why the sudden rush to take the plunge?"

Alina was uncomfortably aware that Michael's green eyes saw more than he let on. She shrugged and kept her expression neutral.

"Nothing in our life is guaranteed, especially tomorrow. This

Next Exit, No Outlet

way things are simplified should something happen to one of us."

"Simplified?"

"Let's just say that between the two of us, we've accumulated substantial assets."

Michael stared at her in disbelief.

"Are you saying this was a business arrangement?" he demanded. "Because I don't buy it."

"Not entirely," she admitted. "But you asked what the rush was, and that's it."

Michael was silent for a long moment, then he moved to sit in the chair next to her.

"You don't expect to make it through this, do you?" he asked softly.

Alina glanced at him, her gaze guarded.

"I'm going to do my best, but statistically my odds aren't that great. Harry trained me. He knows exactly what I'll do, how I'll do it, and where I'll come from. He knows my methods. He knows how I think. Hell, half the time I think he knows what I'm thinking before I do. If I'm realistic, the conservative estimate for rate of success probably sits around forty-five percent."

Michael swallowed some coffee and gazed across the lawn. "It's a chess game now."

She nodded.

"I do have a few surprises, and a few support personnel that he won't be expecting," she added, sending him a small smile. "If I keep him surprised, that success rate will go up."

"Dave would be proud of you," Michael told her. "I hope you know that."

Alina was silent for a long time, sipping her coffee. Dave probably would be proud of her, but he would also know at what cost this came.

"I'm sorry that you got dragged into all of this," she finally said, turning her gaze to his. "If I had known what I know now, I never would have left that bottle of Jameson on your doorstep last summer."

"Lina, I wouldn't have it any other way," he told her earnestly. "You're Dave's kid sister, but in the past year, you've become my friend. You've brought Dave back to me in a way that no photo or memory ever could. You're family now, and family sticks by each other."

Alina felt her throat tighten and her mask slid into place in reaction. She turned her attention back to the trees at the bottom of the yard. A second later, she felt his fingers close around hers and she squeezed gently.

"No matter what happens, you take care of yourself, gunny," she said, not looking at him. "Too many good men have died because of this bastard already."

Michael nodded and was silent. A moment later, her phone vibrated against her leg and she pulled it out, glancing at the screen.

"Damon's on his way," she said, tucking the phone back into her pocket. "Are the others up yet?"

"Yes. Blake is on his laptop in the dining room and Stephanie was in the kitchen when I came out."

"Good." She stood up and turned toward the door. "Time to lay down some ground rules."

Michael got up and followed her, his lips twisting in amusement.

"Oh, this should be interesting."

"Good morning." Stephanie greeted Alina from her seat at the bar as she walked into the kitchen. "You look like you've been up a while."

"I have." Alina rinsed her coffee mug in the sink and set it on the counter. "How did you sleep?"

Stephanie shrugged and sipped her coffee.

"Better than I expected," she said. "I thought Angela was going to keep waking me up, but she didn't."

Alina glanced around. "Is she up yet?"

"She's in the shower."

Alina turned to the refrigerator and pulled out a bottle of water.

"Good. I want to talk to you before she comes down." She took the cap off the bottle and drank, then walked over to the bar. "She already knows too much, but I want to keep it to a minimum. There's no need for her to be more freaked out than she already is."

"Agreed."

Alina glanced over to the dining table where Michael and Blake were at opposite ends, both on their laptops.

"Michael, she'll try to get information out of you," she warned. "Be prepared."

He glanced up with a quick grin. "Don't worry, I'll be ready.

Next Exit, No Outlet

She won't get much out of me."

Alina sipped her water, returning her gaze to Stephanie.

"How's the head?"

"The headache comes and goes," she said with a shrug. "I'll be fine. Where's Damon?"

"He went to get a car. He's on his way back now."

Stephanie raised her eyebrows.

"I don't suppose you want to share your secret on where you guys get all these cars from?" she asked.

Alina smiled faintly and was silent.

"I didn't think so. Well, if you won't tell me that, why don't you tell me about when the hell you got married?"

Michael and Blake looked up from their respective computers and Alina was suddenly very aware of three sets of eyes staring at her intently. She raised the water bottle to her lips, taking a sip calmly.

"About a month ago," she finally said, lowering the bottle, "in the middle of the Ebola fiasco. We went to DC and saw a judge he knows."

Stephanie stared at her.

"And you didn't tell me?" she demanded. "Why? Hell, Lina, I'm your best friend! I've known you all your life!"

Alina considered her for a moment, then sighed.

"I know. I'm sorry. But it's really not that big of a deal."

Stephanie's mouth dropped open.

"Not that big of a deal?!" she exclaimed in disbelief. "You got married!"

"Maybe she's been married before," Blake suggested, an unholy gleam in his eyes. "Maybe she really *is* a Black Widow."

Alina glanced at him, her lips pulling at the corners.

"If I am, you can be assured that none of the bodies will ever be found."

"Will you be serious?" Stephanie pushed her empty mug aside and glared at Alina. "How is getting hitched not a big deal? And don't give me any crap about it just being a piece of paper. I know you better than that. You would never take vows lightly."

The look on Stephanie's face made Alina inwardly cringe. She was right. She did know her too well, and knew that she would never get married on a whim, even if it *was* the perfect business arrangement. But Alina wasn't ready to admit to anything right now, not to herself and especially not in front of Michael and Blake. Her emotions were still too new for her to even understand, let alone verbalize.

"It's complicated."

She fell back on the vague answer that she knew drove Stephanie crazy, and she wasn't disappointed. Stephanie let out a sound that was a cross between a snort and a snarl.

"I hate it when you say that!" she cried, throwing her hands up. "Everything with you is complicated. Well, guess what? Marriage isn't complicated. At least, not at first. You fall in love and you decide to spend the rest of your lives together. See? Not complicated."

Alina looked at her for a moment, then her lips twisted humorlessly.

"Everything's always so simple and black and white for you," she told her. "I don't live in black and white. I live in gray, and that's where my marriage is."

Stephanie frowned, staring at her hard. "Do you love him?"

Alina waved a hand impatiently and turned to move around the bar.

"I can tolerate him better than most," she said, heading for the sliding doors.

Stephanie swiveled on her stool as the security system alerted them to a breach in the perimeter.

"Oh well, that's a good reason to tie the knot," she said sarcastically, glancing up at the plasma above the fireplace. "Is that him?"

"Yes."

"Don't you walk away from me, Lina Maschik!" Stephanie got up and followed her to the door, reaching out to grab her arm. "If you don't love him, why the hell did you marry him, for God's sake?!"

Alina glanced down at the hand on her arm and Stephanie released her quickly.

"I told you," she said softly, "it's complicated."

With that, she opened the door and stepped out onto the deck, closing it firmly behind her.

Stephanie swung around to look at Blake and Michael.

"Can you believe this?" she demanded, her voice rising an octave. "What the hell is going on?"

Blake shrugged.

"How are we supposed to know?" he asked, going back to his screen. "We know just as much as you do."

Stephanie made a face at his bent head and looked at Michael. A frown had pulled his eyebrows together and his eyes met hers. He shook his head.

"I don't know," he said, "but I can tell you this much: I don't think Alina will allow herself to think about anything remotely connected to love until this is all over. She's got blinders on. It seems to me that, as far as her marriage goes, it's just something in the background for now."

Stephanie huffed and hobbled back over to the bar, reaching for her walking cane.

"Sometimes I just want to beat her with this," she muttered, turning to make her way back to the door. "There's got to be more to it than she's telling us. No one just gets up one day and decides to get married. I don't care how long they've known each other."

Michael hesitated, considering whether or not to tell her what Alina had told him outside. After a second of thought, he turned his attention back to his laptop, remaining silent. It would only upset Stephanie to think that her best friend had no expectation of living to see the end of the week, let alone the rest of her marriage.

"If I were you, I'd leave it alone," Blake said, not looking up from his laptop. "Let them work it out themselves. When she's ready to talk about it, she will."

Stephanie glanced at him.

"Easy for you to say," she retorted. "How would you feel if Michael suddenly told you one day that he'd been married for a month?"

Blake looked up at that, his face breaking into a grin.

"I'd thank him for not making me wear a monkey suit in a church."

Stephanie turned her attention back out the door, watching as Alina went down the steps of the deck.

"Men," she muttered. "You don't get it."

"Oh, we get it," Michael retorted. "We just don't get involved."

Viper watched a gleaming black Porsche 911 roll down the gravel drive and stop behind the Range Rover. She shook her head, her lips curving, and moved across the grass towards the sports car.

"That's not conspicuous at all," she said as the door opened and Damon climbed out.

"No one will be looking for a Porsche," he replied with a grin, closing the door, "and it will outrun most things chasing us."

"That's true," she admitted. "They *are* quick. I don't want to hear what Stephanie and Angie have to say about it, though. They're already convinced we have a stash of cars somewhere. Now what will they think?"

Damon grinned and bent to kiss her swiftly.

"I can guarantee it won't be the truth."

Alina chuckled.

"No, it won't." She put a hand on his arm when he would have turned toward the house. "I have to go get supplies. I'll be gone most of the day."

His blue eyes met hers. "Ok…"

She hesitated, then sighed softly. "If anything should happen, you need to get Stephanie somewhere safe."

Hawk studied her for a long moment.

"I will," he said softly. "Where are you going for these supplies?"

"There's a storage unit in Baltimore where I keep some specialized things. The problem is that it's near my old safe house."

He raised an eyebrow.

"The safe house that was compromised last year when an assassin tried to kill Stephanie? *That* safe house?"

She nodded.

"I haven't been to the unit since then, and it's under a different name from the condo, but you know there's always a risk."

Hawk scowled. "I don't like it. Let me come with you."

She shook her head.

"I need you here to keep an eye on all of them," she said, jerking her head toward the house. "I've been thinking about it all morning, and I've come up with a way to get in without being seen, in case someone's watching. I just want you to be aware of what's going on. If you don't hear from me, get Stephanie somewhere safe."

Damon was silent for a long moment, then he nodded slowly.

"Take the Porsche," he said, handing her the keys. "It's faster, and there's no chance of it having been flagged yet. I'll use the Range Rover if I need to move. Just make sure you get back here in one piece."

Next Exit, No Outlet

Chapter Eighteen

Blake watched as the sliding door closed behind Michael and Angela.

"I wonder how long before Mike wants to strangle her," he said, glancing at Stephanie.

She shook her head and pushed back on the recliner, elevating her legs. She sighed in relief as the pain eased a bit.

"Not long," she predicted. "At least I talked her into staying here. That will help. Once she's done at the gym, they'll go get her stuff and then they'll come back. Not as much time for her to drive him insane."

"Long enough," Damon said under his breath, turning to head down the hall towards Alina's den at the front of the house. "I'll be in the den if you need me."

Stephanie waited until he'd disappeared then looked across the living room at Blake.

"I'll tell you this much, I wouldn't turn down a husband that came home and handed me the keys to a brand new Porsche," she said. "Lina doesn't know how she good she has it."

"I'm more curious about where they get these cars from," he said, stretching and getting up from his seat at the dining room table. "I mean, there's a Range Rover sitting out there, Damon let Michael take his Audi, and in the garage is a Shelby GT500 and a Jeep Rubicon. These aren't cheap cars."

"Nope." Stephanie watched as he went into the kitchen and opened the fridge, then leaned her head back and stared up at the ceiling. "I don't think we really want to know, do you?"

Blake emerged from the kitchen a moment later with two sodas in his hand. He walked across the living room to hand one to her.

"Probably not. Where did Alina go?"

"Who knows!" She took the soda and popped it open. "She doesn't tell me anything anymore, even when she's getting married."

"Steph, you gotta let that go," he told her, amused.

"No I don't." She sipped her soda and looked up at him. "I'm still pissed off that she went anywhere. It's just as dangerous out there for her as it is for me, but look where I am."

"Don't start that again." Blake turned to go back to his laptop in the dining room. "We've been down that road and you lost by a huge margin. She's a big girl. She's proven she can take care of herself."

Stephanie frowned as he went back to work and swiped her tablet, lowering her gaze to the screen. That was the problem. Alina was so used to taking care of herself that she'd forgotten that she was still human. Her fearlessness the other night in the parking garage was proof enough of that. She had walked right into the line of fire without flinching, almost as if she was daring Death to come for her.

Stephanie shivered, picturing the deadly stranger that she never wanted to see again. She knew what Viper did for a living, but seeing her in action was terrifying.

The first time she'd seen it was last summer in a clearing in Virginia, when Viper had coldly and methodically baited Regina Cunningham into thinking she had the upper hand. The transformation from the friend she'd known all her life into the government-trained assassin she had become was shocking, and Stephanie had never quite got over it.

Since then, Alina had been very careful to keep that side of herself away from Stephanie, sensing that it upset her. There were times when she glimpsed the deadly stranger, but Stephanie had been spared the full view of the killer until the other night. And it was even more horrifying the second time around, showing her clearly that what she had witnessed in Virginia last summer was nothing but a glimpse of the assassin called Viper.

Taking a deep breath, Stephanie raised her eyes and gazed absently across the room. Blake said that Viper did what she had to do to survive every day and that it wasn't necessarily a reflection of herself. He said that when he was in war zones, he did it as well. It was the only way to stay sane and stay alive. Viper lived and breathed in a war zone every day. Even so, after the other night, Stephanie wondered how much was coping mechanism and how much was actually what her friend had become.

Realizing that she wasn't going to be able to focus on the book on her tablet, Stephanie set it down and sipped her soda. She glanced over at Blake again.

"How's the case?" she asked. "Anything I can do to help?"

Blake glanced at her.

"Maybe," he said slowly. "I got a message from the guys down in Miami. I'm just opening it now."

Next Exit, No Outlet

Stephanie raised her eyebrow. "Those are the ones with connections inside the cartel, right?"

"Yes. If the Casa Reinos starts moving anything, they'll find out about it."

She chewed her bottom lip thoughtfully and watched as he focused on the screen. Blake had been working a joint case with the DEA for over a year now, trying to bring down the notoriously vicious Mexican cartel in the states. He'd come close last fall, when the cartel's second-in-command ended up in Jersey. He'd lost him, but had gone back to DC with the lieutenant's half-brother instead. Unfortunately, Blake hadn't got anywhere with him and the man was currently rotting in a prison in Virginia.

"What the..." Blake muttered, scowling at the screen.

"What's up?"

"I don't know, but something is definitely wrong," he said, looking at her. "The *Sea Queen* has left its port in Veracruz, Mexico."

Stephanie frowned.

"Isn't that Martese Salcedo's yacht?" she asked, furrowing her brows. "The head of the cartel?"

"Yes. The strange part is that he's not on it."

"What do you mean? How do you know?"

"I got an update from our man in Mexico earlier. Salcedo is still at his compound outside Mexico City." Blake sat back with a frown. "So where the hell is he sending his yacht? And why?"

Stephanie lowered her legs and reached for her cane. She got up and hobbled over to stand next to him, looking over his shoulder.

"Do we know which direction it's heading?" she asked.

"It was going east and was spotted passing Cuba."

"When was that?"

"Eight hours ago." Blake reached for his can of soda. "Hell, they could be heading anywhere. That's an ocean-going yacht. They could be crossing the Atlantic for all we know!"

Stephanie pulled out a chair and sank into it.

"I highly doubt that," she said, casting him an amused glance. "Maybe they're going to the Bahamas?"

Blake scoffed. "On vacation?"

She shrugged. "What else is there? Pull up a map. My geography is crap."

Blake pulled up a map and turned the laptop so she could see.

"If they were going south to Columbia, they wouldn't have passed north of Cuba," he said, looking at the map.

"The Dominican Republic?" Stephanie suggested. "Don't they

have suppliers in both DR and Puerto Rico?"

"That could be it," he said slowly, reaching for his phone. "I'll call down to Paul in Miami and see what he can find out. Maybe it's just a supply run."

Stephanie studied the map while he dialed. A moment later, he was talking to another agent in Miami. She sat back and sipped her soda. The only direction that made any sense was south. The only thing west was the Bahamas and Nassau and, as Blake had pointed out, there was no reason for them to go there except on vacation. Somehow, she didn't see Martese Salcedo loaning out his private yacht for someone else to take a vacation.

"What? Are you sure?"

The sharp question caught her attention and she looked at Blake in apprehension. He was scowling fiercely.

"Yeah, ok. Send it over to me. Thanks, Paul." Blake hung up and looked at Stephanie. "So much for a supply run. The *Sea Queen* passed the Florida Keys. Paul said he just got confirmation from a satellite. He's sending to me."

Stephanie frowned and looked at the map again.

"Where the hell is it going?" she wondered. "And why now?"

Blake shook his head. "Maybe they really are crossing the Atlantic," he muttered. "This makes no sense. Why would La Cabeza send his yacht east and stay behind? At least one of his Lieutenants must be on board. I can't see him letting the *Sea Queen* go without one of his senior men on it, so why? Where's it going?"

"And why now?" Stephanie wondered. "All our information indicates that they're in the middle of re-building their empire after the upheaval last year. Not only that, but we know they're in the middle of something big again. Why move men around now? You'd think he would want them with him."

"Unless what he's been working on has begun," Blake said grimly.

"And we have no idea what that is."

Alina pulled the overhead door down and turned around, drawing a Maglite from her duffel bag. She switched it on and shone it around the inside of the storage unit. Everything was just as she had left it last summer. Nothing had been touched.

Next Exit, No Outlet

She walked across the small, ten by ten area to a folding table opened along the back wall and dropped the empty duffel bag onto it. She turned to one of the four tall tool cabinets lined up along the other wall. Pulling out her keys, she unlocked it and opened the lid. Reaching inside, her fingers slid along under the rim until she felt a cold, round bump. Alina pressed it and heard a series of clicks as all the hidden locks on the drawers released.

Opening the top drawer, Alina surveyed her options. It was divided into several narrow compartments, each one containing bundles of wiring in various sizes. After a moment she reached for two different bundles before sliding the door closed. She moved on to the next drawer, opening it to reveal neatly folded tactical gear. She selected two leg holsters, two different pairs of gloves, and an arm sleeve with a magnetic brace inserted beneath the black fabric. Turning, she dropped the items into the duffel bag before returning to the cabinet.

Alina bent down and opened the bottom drawer. It was much deeper than the others and contained more tactical gear. She pulled out a black vest and set it on the floor beside her before reaching back in for a pair of tactical pants. Adding them to the vest, she carried them over to put them in the bag.

Long ago, on the advice of Hawk, Viper had begun to make use of storage units in strategically placed cities throughout the world. Usually close to one of her safe houses, the storage units housed emergency gear. Since implementing her the backup stashes, she had to admit that they had come in handy on more than one occasion. She never honestly thought she would have to use this one, though. This was a little too close to home.

Viper returned to the storage cabinet and closed all the doors locking them again. She moved to the next cabinet and, a moment later, was sorting through ammunition and weapons. While her armory beneath the kitchen of her house was well-stocked, there were a few things that she didn't keep on hand. She pulled out a thin six-inch blade and looked at it thoughtfully for a moment. It was a blade that she'd received at the training facility. They were standard issue once they passed a certain point in their training. Thin and narrow, the deadly blade was easily concealed and even easier to wield. In fact, it was this very blade that had tipped her off to Harry.

Alina's lips tightened as she kept the blade out and reached for another, smaller tactical knife. Earlier that week, when she and Hawk were on their way to Atlantic City, Michael called to fill her in on an autopsy report from Washington, DC. The terrorist that floated up in the Potomac had been stabbed in the neck with a blade matching these very dimensions. At the time, both she and Hawk realized the very distinct probability that the leak in Washington was a member of their own Organization. While they had suspected it for weeks, that one detail from Michael's report was the thing that convinced them they were right.

The reason they were all issued this knife was because it was Harry's knife of choice. He had carried it with him ever since his Army days, no matter the function.

Alina finished gathering what she needed from the drawers and returned to the table. It was while she was in the process of packing it that her cell phone rang.

"Yes?"

"How's it going?" Damon asked. "Any trouble yet?"

"Not so far. I'm in the storage unit now and should be leaving shortly. What's up?"

"Gunny junior found something you might be interested in."

"Gunny junior?" Alina repeated, diverted. "You mean Hanover?"

"Yes. You know he's still working on the cartel, right?"

"Yes."

"He found out this morning that the yacht owned by Salcedo left Veracruz yesterday. It was spotted passing Cuba eight hours ago."

Alina frowned. "Is it making a supply run?"

"That's what he thought, but it doesn't look like it. He spoke to one of his contacts in Florida and they have satellite footage of the yacht passing Miami."

Alina's brows snapped together and she was silent for a long moment.

"That's very interesting," she finally said. "Where the hell is he going?"

"That's the other thing," he said. "Salcedo's not on the yacht. He's still at his compound outside Mexico City."

"And his lieutenant?" she asked sharply.

"No one knows. It's unlikely he would send out his yacht without his own crew, though. My bet is that his second-in-command is on that yacht."

"And I can guarantee La Cabeza's not sending his lieutenant across the Atlantic," Alina said grimly.

"Nope."

They were both silent for a moment and Alina stared across the small space, deep in thought.

"Gunny junior seems to think the cartel is on the brink of

Next Exit, No Outlet

something big," Damon finally broke the silence. "If he's right, this could be the start of it."

Alina shook her head. "If it is, it's not our problem," she replied. "Not unless they get in our way."

Despite himself, Damon chuckled.

"You realize we're probably the only two people on this side of the Atlantic that aren't afraid of the Casa Reinos Cartel, right?"

"We know better," she said, a smile pulling at her lips. "We've both faced worse. Hell, you're the one who killed the previous head of the cartel."

"I have no idea what you're talking about."

Alina grinned. "Uh-huh. Just like I know nothing about Al-Jibad's death."

"And if they do get in our way?" Hawk asked, sobering.

"Then Salcedo will lose another second-in-command."

Harry stepped out of the store and onto the crowded city sidewalk. Holding a shopping bag in one hand, he pulled his cell phone from his pocket with the other.

"I hope you have good news for me," he answered, turning to stride up the street.

"Unfortunately no," a voice said. "Agent Walker has disappeared."

"I find that highly unlikely," Harry said. "She's not a ghost. What about the other one? Agent Hanover? Where is he?"

"We're also unable to locate him."

He scowled. "And the safe house?"

"It was empty when we got there."

Harry swore softly. "What about the security video? I'm sure the building has one."

"They do, and I went through it. Nothing."

"What you mean, nothing? There had to be something. We know they were there. The cameras in the street showed them going into the parking lot."

"And that's where it ends," the voice told him. "The Mustang went into the parking lot, but never shows up in any of the security footage from the building. It's like it disappeared."

Harry's back teeth clamped together and the scowl on his face grew. "Or was erased."

"The surveillance wasn't tampered with so I can't explain it."

"Oh, it was tampered with all right. You just couldn't tell." Harry came to a corner and paused, waiting for a break in traffic so that he could cross the road.

"With all due respect, sir, I find that unlikely. If the video feed had been altered, there would've been some indication."

"How many times do I have to tell you that you're dealing with a professional?" Harry snapped. "Hell, I trained her! Trust me, if she didn't want you to see something on that video feed, you won't see it."

"Well, I'm doing everything I can to—"

"Not anymore you're not. I'll take care of it from here. I've had enough of your incompetence."

Harry disconnected the call and crossed the street. He was about halfway up the next block when he dialed another number in his phone. It rang twice, and then a male voice picked up.

"Yes?"

"Do you still have eyes on Angela Bolan?"

"I do."

"The operation is a go," Harry said grimly. "I'll transfer the money to your account. Once you have her, I'll send coordinates."

"Understood."

Harry disconnected and slid his phone back into his pocket. This wasn't ideal, but it would have to do.

It was time to take care of Viper once and for all.

Next Exit, No Outlet

Chapter Nineteen

While Angela waited for Michael to finish signing in as a guest, she surveyed the main floor of her gym. It was fairly busy for a Sunday morning, but she'd seen it far worse. Today there were available treadmills and elliptical machines, and that was really all she cared about. Normally she would also do one of the yoga or aerobic classes, but she wasn't about to do that with Michael in tow. No way, no how.

Michael finished signing in and got his guest badge, turning away from the desk.

"I'm going to run to the locker room and store my bag," she told him as he joined her. "Where are you heading?"

"Wherever you're going."

Angela frowned. "Well, you're not coming into the women's locker room with me."

He stared back at her, his face impassive. "Then you're not going into the women's locker room."

"Don't be ridiculous, Michael!" Angela sputtered. "You're a man! You can't come with me."

"I can, and I will. Who knows? Maybe I identify as a woman these days."

Angela glared at him.

"Don't be snarky," she snapped. "I don't *want* you to come into the locker room with me."

"I'm not really concerned with what you want," he retorted evenly. "Are you going into the locker room?"

Angela stared at him. The set of his jaw told her that he had every intention of following her, regardless of her wishes. Her lips tightened as frustration rolled through her.

"I guess not," she said irritably. "I don't know what I'm going to do with my bag. What if I was going to take a class?"

"Then I would keep your bag with me."

She huffed and turned toward the elliptical machines. Neither of them noticed the tall figure standing near the front desk, listening to every word.

"This is stupid," she muttered, stalking toward the row of machines. "Are you going to watch me workout?"

"No, but I'm not leaving your side," he said, keeping pace with her easily. "So pick two empty machines together."

Angela sighed and headed for two vacant elliptical machines at the far end of the row.

"Have you even ever been on an elliptical machine?" she asked.

Michael shot her an amused look. "Yes."

"Well, that's something, at least. I thought you'd be more into the weight room. Isn't that what all you Marines do?"

"No. We prefer to lift cars instead."

Angela was surprised into a chuckle. She dropped her gym bag onto the floor next to a machine and bent down to pull out a towel. After glancing at Michael, she pulled out a second one and handed it to him.

"Since you didn't grab one in the front," she offered.

Michael took it with a nod of thanks and got onto the machine next to hers.

"I usually do thirty minutes here and then thirty minutes on the treadmill," she said, getting onto her machine. "Sound good?"

"Fine."

Angela suppressed a sigh and started the machine. She looked up at the TV's mounted from the ceiling and wrinkled her nose. The ones closest to them were broadcasting a news channel. She lowered her gaze and scanned the gym restlessly. This was supposed to be her 'me' time, reserved for her to relax and decompress after a long week. The tall Marine next to her was making that impossible.

"When we're done here, I have to go back to my house and get some things," she said, glancing at him. "I need to grab some clothes and get Annabelle into her cat carrier."

Michael lowered his eyes from the news and turned them to her.

"Oh? Did you change your mind?"

Angela nodded.

"Stephanie talked me into it last night," she admitted. "I still think everyone is being paranoid, but I can see why now. If it will make Stephanie and Alina happy, I'll stay there until you all determine that it's safe to leave again. Besides, Steph can use some moral support. She's a wreck."

"She is?" Michael asked, surprised. "I thought she was

handling it all pretty well."

"Of course you do. That's what she wants you to think. She's shaken up, though. I mean, who wouldn't be? Someone's trying to kill her, and they've almost succeeded twice!"

"Three times," he said automatically.

Angela glared at him. "Whatever. It doesn't make it any better."

"No, it makes it worse. So I'm glad you've come to your senses. I'm happier having you both in one place where Blake and I can work together."

"What are you going to do?" Angela asked after a minute. "I mean, the way Alina made it sound, all of you already know who the culprit is. Why not just got after him?"

Michael glanced at her. "It's not that easy."

"I don't see what's so complicated about it. You work for the Secret Service, and Blake and Stephanie are with the FBI. Between the two agencies, you should be able to catch one psycho."

Michael didn't answer, turning his attention back to the news pointedly. Angela's eyes narrowed and another wave of frustration rolled through her. Good intentions or not, everyone was purposely keeping her out of the loop, and she really didn't appreciate it.

"Have you been shot yet?"

That got his attention back to her and Angela raised her eyebrows questioningly.

"What?"

"Well, everyone else seems to have taken a bullet recently," she pointed out. "Stephanie took one in her leg, Damon took one in his gut, and apparently Lina got one in her arm. So what about you?"

"No, but don't worry. There's still plenty of time."

She shot him a reproachful look.

"Don't even joke about it. Three people getting shot is already three too many. I don't understand why all this is happening. Why is someone trying to kill Alina and Stephanie? And why am I getting dragged into everything? None of this makes sense."

"I know it doesn't," Michael said after a long silence, "but you have to trust us and let us take care of it."

"And Alina and Damon? Are they going to take care of it too? What do they do, exactly? I mean, Damon says they were trained together."

Michael's jaw tightened and he was silent. Angela watched him for a minute, then tossed her head.

"Fine. Don't tell me. I'll find out eventually. I always do."

Michael glanced at her.

"This might be one time that you should consider leaving it alone," he said. "You might not like what you find."

Angela shrugged.

"It's Lina. She's one of my best friends and I've known her forever. I've seen her at her worst. I've held her hair while she puked in an alley behind a dive bar. Seriously, how bad can it be?"

Stefan Delgado, Frankie's main enforcer, watched from behind dark glasses as a member of the Casa Reinos Cartel pushed open the door of the convenience store and stepped onto the sidewalk, a pack of cigarettes in his hand. He'd been following him since he left his house. He was the third name on the list.

The young gang member stopped and lit a cigarette, then sauntered down the street toward Stefan. He paid no attention to the stranger built like a boxer leaning against the building with a phone to his ear. Stefan spoke into the phone as his mark passed him, talking to dead air. The young man exhaled, blowing smoke into Stefan's face as he passed, completely unaware of his rudeness. If he had bothered to spare a glance for the man on the phone, he would have realized the man was staring at him. However, just like the first two names on the list, his arrogance was too great for him.

Stefan waited until he had passed, then lowered his phone and slid it into his pocket, turning to follow him. For such a large man, Stefan moved with a speed and silence that was disconcerting as the young man crossed the entrance of a narrow alley. In an instant, Stefan had him in the alley, pushed up against the side of a building with a meaty hand around his throat.

The cartel thug gawked at him for a split second, but before he could let out even one obscenity, a knife had penetrated his solar plexus. His eyes widened and he flailed in pain before Stefan pulled the knife out. Blood seeped over his teeshirt and he gasped. Before he could do anything else, Stefan's blade sliced across the front of his throat, cutting it wide open. Stepping back quickly to avoid the blood, Stefan watched emotionlessly as the Casa Reinos Cartel soldier slid down the cement side of the building until he was sprawled on the ground, bleeding out.

Stefan pulled out his phone and sent the text, turning to leave

Next Exit, No Outlet

the alley. He stepped back onto the street and turned right. Three blocks away was the house that the victim had been walking to, and the fourth name on the list.

Michael glanced at his watch and looked up from his seat on the couch as Angela came down the stairs. They had arrived back at her townhouse over an hour before, and she left him in the living room while she went upstairs to gather her things.

"I think that's just about everything," she announced, setting two large travel bags down on the floor at the base of the stairs. "I just have to get my laptop and then put Annabelle in her carrier."

"Anything I can do to help?" Michael asked, picking up the remote to the TV and switching it off. While he was waiting for her, he had been watching the news, and he was more than happy to switch it off. There was nothing remotely hopeful on the news anymore these days. "I'm tired of just sitting here."

Angela glanced at him. "You can get the carrier while I try to find Annabelle," she said. "It's in the closet near the back door."

Michael nodded and got up, going down the short hallway that ran past her kitchen to the back door. Angela's townhouse had a basic two entrance set up, with the front door leading to the street and the back door leading to a tiny backyard adjacent to her single car driveway. By her own admission, Angela rarely used the driveway. The street that it ran into was narrow and usually clogged with her neighbor's cars. When he'd asked her earlier, she shrugged and said it was faster to get in and out of her neighborhood from the front.

"Bella-boo!" Angela called in the front of the house. "Where are you?"

Michael opened the only closet near the back door and found himself gazing into the smallest coat closet he had ever seen. On the floor, tucked into the corner, was a hard-topped cat carrier. He bent down and picked it up, glancing at the row of designer coats hanging above it. Shaking his head, he straightened up. Angela certainly enjoyed the finer things in life.

He was just closing the closet door when he thought he saw something move out of the corner of his eye. Michael turned toward the back door sharply. It was a solid wood door with narrow windows on either side running from the top of the door to the bottom. Long, pale colored sheer curtains hung over both windows, but they were thin and light enough to see through.

He moved to the window closest to him and move the curtain aside, peering out. The narrow window afforded him a very limited view to the road and part of the driveway. True to Angela's statements, cars and trucks were lined up along the curb out back. He switched to the other window and peered out to get another angle of the small backyard. It was empty and there was no movement on the sidewalk near the road.

Michael frowned and let the curtain fall back into place. There was nothing there. Turning, he went back to the living room with the cat carrier in hand.

"You weren't kidding about the parking outback," he said, setting the carrier down on the floor.

Angela glanced at him as she stood at the bottom of the stairs, waiting for Annabelle to make her way down the steps. The orange tabby cat paused halfway when she heard Michael's voice.

"I told you," she said. "Half the time some kid has blocked the driveway. It's just easier to park out front."

"I can see that." He watched as Angela went up a few steps and reached for her cat. "You should probably have thicker curtains on the windows back there, especially after what happened with Trent. You can see right through them, which means anyone outside can see in."

She turned to come down the steps with her fluffy tabby in her arms.

"If I put darker curtains on those windows that hallway will be like a cave," she said. "There already isn't enough light in this house to begin with."

Michael shrugged and bent to open the door to the carrier. As he did so, the cat in Angela's arms let out a hiss. He looked up in surprise to find two green eyes staring at him.

"Oh Bella, stop," Angela admonished. "I know you hate it, but it'll be fine."

Angela bent down to put the cat inside the carrier, but Annabelle had other ideas. As the front half of her went into the carrier, her back legs stretched out and she planted her feet on either side of the door. Michael let out a laugh as her toes spread and curled around the edges of the opening.

"She is not going to go in, is she?"

"Oh, she's going in," Angela muttered. Keeping one hand on her cat's rear end, she unhooked one foot from the edge of the opening before shoving Annabelle into the carrier. An angry hiss and snarl emanated from the box and she swiftly closed the grated door, snapping the hinge into place.

She straightened up and looked at Michael.

"I stand corrected," he said with a grin. Then he glanced at the rest of the bags piled a few feet away. "Is that it?"

Angela nodded. "Yes. The laptop is with the other bags."

"I'll take the cat out to the car," he said, bending down to grab the carrier. "Then we can carry the bags out."

Angela turned towards the short hallway to the back door.

"I'll just make sure the back door is locked," she said over her shoulder, "and grab Annabelle's food."

Michael grabbed one of the overnight bags as he passed, heading toward the front door.

"Okay."

He hooked the overnight bag over his shoulder and reached out to open the front door, stepping into the afternoon sun. The street in front of Angela's house was in direct contrast to the crowded lane behind. Aside from Damon's Audi sitting at the curb in front of him, there were only three other vehicles parked along the entire road.

He glanced up and down the street as he strode towards the Audi. The neighborhood was quiet on this Sunday afternoon, and Michael saw nothing out of the ordinary. The other three vehicles had been there when they pulled up over an hour ago and Angela had assured him that they were known to her. Apparently, a few of her other neighbors felt the same way she did about the parking situation.

Michael reached into his pocket and pulled out the keys, pressing the button to release the back hatch of the Audi. He dropped the overnight bag into the trunk and circled around to the back door behind the driver's seat. Opening it, he set the carrier on the backseat, angling it so that Annabelle would be able to see Angela from her spot in the back. As he set the carrier down, the box shifted as the cat turned inside. A low growl voiced her displeasure and he chuckled.

"Don't worry," he told the cat. "It's not for long."

He shut the door and turned to go back up the short sidewalk to the townhouse.

"That is one unhappy cat," he said, stepping back into the house.

Silence greeted him and Michael raised an eyebrow, glancing around. The living room was empty, and Angela's bags were still sitting at the base of the stairs.

"Angie?"

Again, only silence. A prickle of awareness went down his spine and Michael's gut tightened as he reached for the 9mm side arm that he carried everywhere. The silence was unnatural and deafening, and he unsnapped his holster, pulling out his weapon.

"Angie!"

Nothing.

He strode through the living room to the short hallway and drew up short, his heart pounding. The back door stood open and the floor lamp that had been next to the umbrella stand was overturned, laying across the short hallway. His skin grew cold and Michael ran to the back door and out onto the back step. The ground in two-foot stretch of lawn between the back step and the driveway was disturbed, as if something had been dragged across the grass.

"Angela!" Michael yelled, stepping off the back porch. He carefully skirted the drag marks in the grass and ran down the driveway to the sidewalk. He looked down the street just in time to see the black bumper of a pickup round the corner.

"Dammit!"

Michael looked down as he replaced his weapon in his holster. Something glinted in the gutter next to the curb and he bent down to take a closer look. His breath caught in his throat as he recognized the designer gold charm bracelet.

Angela had been wearing it when she put Annabelle into the carrier.

Chapter Twenty

Alina rolled up and stopped behind the Range Rover, killing the engine. It was just after four and the sun had already sunk below the tree line. She climbed out of the Porsche and turned to go across the grass to the deck, glancing at the black Audi parked beside her. Michael must have been able to convince Angela to come back to the house.

She had just reached the steps to the deck when the sliding door flew open and Stephanie charged out.

"Thank God you're here!" she cried. "She's gone! He took her!"

Alina stilled at the top of the steps, staring at Stephanie as a wave of dread washed over her.

"What?"

Her voice was sharp and carried into the living room. Michael appeared in the open doorway, his face grim. Without a word, he held out the gold charm bracelet. Alina's eyes dropped to it and her lips tightened in an unpleasant line.

"Where?" she demanded, moving past Stephanie and into the house.

Michael moved aside before she pushed him out of the way.

"Her house," he said. "They went in the back door while I was putting the cat into the car out front."

Alina strode to the bar, dropping the keys to the Porsche on the marble surface. When she turned, it was Viper that gazed around the living room. Hawk was leaning against the wall near the hallway, his arms crossed over his chest and his lips pressed together. Blake was pacing in front of the fireplace, his cell phone pressed to his ear. He looked up and caught her glance from across the room.

"I'm on the phone with Rob now," he told her. "He's mobilizing a task force. We'll find her."

Viper shook her head. "No, you won't. He's too good for that."

Stephanie stared at her, her eyes welling with tears.

"What do you mean?" she whispered, her voice cracking.

Viper turned her emotionless gaze to Stephanie.

"Harry knows better than to leave a trail. Angela won't be found until he's ready for her to be found."

"So we're not even supposed to try?" Stephanie asked incredulously.

"You can try, but it won't do any good." She turned to look at Michael. "Tell me exactly what happened."

Michael crossed the living room, sinking down onto the recliner.

"We left here and went to the gym," he said. "We were there for, I don't know, maybe an hour and a half. When we left there, we went straight to her house. She said she wanted to get some clothes together and get her cat, and then we were coming back here. She'd decided to stay until this is all over."

Viper glanced at Stephanie and her friend nodded, sinking down onto the couch.

"It's true," she said. "I talked Angie into staying last night. I told her it would be safer here. After what happened with Trent, I was able to convince her."

Viper nodded and turned her attention back to Michael. "Did you see anything when you got to her house?"

Michael shook his head. "Nothing. There were three cars already parked on the street in front of her house, but she knew them. They belonged to her neighbors."

"You said they went in from the back." Damon said, breaking his silence. "What about back there? Did you see anything unusual back there?"

"The street behind her house was lined with close to twenty cars and trucks. According to what Angela said, it's always crowded back there. She never uses her driveway because of it."

"He's right," Stephanie said. "Everyone in the neighborhood parks behind their houses there, and the street is very long and narrow. It makes it harder to get in and out from the back, so Angela always parks in the front. She said she doesn't have the patience to deal with a traffic jam at her own house."

Viper's eyes met Hawk's.

"No one would notice a strange vehicle back there," he said.

She nodded. "That's why he went in the back."

Michael scowled.

"He must have known I was with her," he said. "He waited until I was out of the house."

Next Exit, No Outlet

Alina looked across the room at him. For a moment, something resembling sympathy crossed her face. In a second, it was gone and her expression went back to the neutral, unemotional mask they were all getting used to.

"There's nothing you could have done," she said shortly. "This was a professional. They don't make mistakes."

"That doesn't make me feel any better," he muttered.

"Dwelling on it is counterproductive," Damon said briskly, unfolding his arms and walking over to sit on the couch. He propped his feet up on the coffee table and glanced at Alina. "You know what this means."

She nodded and perched on the arm of the couch next to him. "Yes, and he'll regret it."

Stephanie looked from one to the other, her brows furrowed. "What are you talking about?" she asked. "What does it mean? Why did they take Angela? I mean, I understand why he may want me dead, but what the hell does Angela have to do with any of this?"

Alina met her gaze. "Individually? Absolutely nothing."

Stephanie scowled. "Then why take her? And what are they going to do to her?"

"Right now? Nothing."

"I don't understand."

"Harry's using her. This isn't about Angela right now, and this isn't about you. This is about me. He's using Angela to get to me."

Stephanie's eyes widened in sudden understanding and she gasped.

"He knows you'll go after her!"

"Yes."

"Well, you can't do it," Stephanie said. "We'll let Rob handle this. Let him send a task force. If you work with us, you can tell them where to go."

Alina's lips twisted humorlessly. "I wish it were that simple."

"I don't see the complication," Blake said, lowering his phone. He glanced at Stephanie. "Rob's calling me back in five minutes," he told her. "They're running the GPS on her phone now."

Damon and Alina glanced at each other. Catching the look, Blake raised an eyebrow.

"What?"

"They won't get any hits on her GPS," Damon said. "I can guarantee it's been turned off, and the phone destroyed."

"That's if the phone ever left the house," Alina pointed out. "If it was me, I'd leave the phone in the house. It's less complicated that way, and no risk of inadvertently leaving a trail."

Stephanie frowned.

"But if Rob is running the GPS, that means he already has a signal," she said. "So it must not be turned off."

"Trust me," Alina said. "The GPS track will get them nowhere."

"Then what the hell are we supposed to do?" Stephanie demanded. "You can't expect me to just sit here and let our best friend be tortured…or worse!"

The look on Viper's face was frightening. "No, but I'll be the one to handle this."

"This is ridiculous," Blake said. "You can use all the help you can get, and the FBI is willing to help. Why won't you let us?"

"The short answer? I don't trust you."

Stephanie and Blake both sucked in their breath and their mouths dropped open.

"Excuse me? Care to explain that?" Blake demanded.

Alina shrugged.

"Don't take it personally. It's not you specifically I don't trust," she said. "It's your agency. Do you really, for one minute, believe that Harry doesn't have people inside your agency? Use your head. You know who Harry is, and you know what he's capable of. I can guarantee that he's aware of every single thing Rob is doing right this second, and he's made counter plans."

"Not only that," Damon said, "but he's probably already planned for every possible scenario, taken it into account, activated counter-measures, and planned around all of it. In fact, he probably did all of that before he even gave the order to have Angela taken."

Stephanie sat back and stared at the ceiling. "So what you're saying is, Angela is already dead."

"Steph, you can't think like that," Blake said, shooting Damon and Alina an exasperated look.

"That's not what I'm saying at all," Alina said. "In fact, I believe just the opposite. Harry won't kill her until he has me. He won't risk losing the only leverage he has to get me out into the open."

Stephanie looked at her and let out a strangled sound.

"Is that supposed to make me feel better? Because it doesn't. Far from it."

Alina shrugged. "I'm just stating facts."

"So where does that leave us?" Michael asked, lifting his head and looking at Alina. "Because, I gotta tell you, if anything happens to her, I'll take the bastard down myself."

Next Exit, No Outlet

Alina met Michael's green gaze and she smiled faintly. Instead of his usual friendly face, she was staring at the deadly Marine that she knew he could be. She nodded slowly.

"Fair enough," she murmured.

"That's all very touching," Stephanie muttered, "but it doesn't answer the question. What now?"

"Now, I go to work." Viper said, her voice like ice.

Stephanie looked up as Blake handed her a bottle of water. She was settled in the recliner, her feet up, and her Kindle in her lap.

"There's leftover Chinese food from last night," Blake said. "I'm going to reheat some. Are you hungry?"

"You really expect me to eat?" Stephanie asked miserably. "I can't, not knowing that Angela is terrified and going through God knows what."

"Not eating isn't going to help her."

"If I eat now, I'll throw it right back up," she said bluntly, opening the water bottle taking a sip. "I'll try to eat later," she added at the look on his face, "when I've calmed down."

Blake nodded and turned away. "Let me know if you change your mind."

Michael looked up from his laptop as Blake passed the dining room table. "What's left over?" he asked, sitting back in the chair and stretching.

"I think some of just about everything," Blake answered. "What do you want?"

Michael got up and followed him into the kitchen.

"Let's see what there is," he said.

Blake opened the refrigerator door and began pulling out Chinese food containers and handing them to Michael.

"Have you heard back from Rob?" Michael asked, setting the food containers on the island behind him.

"Yes. The Black Widow was right. GPS shows the phone is still at her house and, so far, nothing on the surveillance cameras or CCTV of the area is giving any clue as to who took her."

"So she just disappeared," Michael said.

Blake glanced at him, noting the tone in his voice. "Mike, this isn't your fault," he said in a low voice. "There's no way you could have prevented it."

Michael glanced at him. "I should never have left her alone. If I had been with her, she'd be here right now."

"That's illogical and you know it," Blake said, passing him two more containers. "She would have been alone at some point, even if it was just to go to the bathroom. You heard Viper. These guys are professionals. They would've found a way."

"Yeah, well so am I, and I shouldn't have left her. I'm trained to protect the President, for God's sake!"

Blake closed the refrigerator door and turned to join Michael, opening up food containers to see what they had.

"Well, if you want to beat yourself up about it, feel free, but for God's sake, don't let it affect what you do next. You know as well as I do, there's no room in battle for self-doubt."

Michael glanced at him in amusement. "Battle?"

Blake looked at him. "That's what this is."

"But it's not our battle to fight," Michael retorted. "You heard Lina. She's taking this one on herself."

"Yeah, I heard her, but I also know you. You're not going to let this go. All I'm saying is leave the emotion behind. We've been through too much for me to watch you get yourself killed because you were stupid."

Michael let out a choked laugh. "Understood."

Stephanie hobbled into the kitchen, leaning heavily on her cane. She looked at all the containers on the island and wrinkled her nose.

"I don't know how the two of you can eat at a time like this," she said. "I mean, even Alina's not in here eating."

Blake raised eyebrow. "What's that supposed to mean?"

Stephanie frowned and leaned against the island.

"Just that she doesn't seem to show any emotion anymore, so it wouldn't be surprising if she was in here stuffing her face."

Michael frowned. "You think she's not upset?"

"Well, she certainly wasn't acting upset,"

"I don't know that I would say that," Blake said, turning to get two plates from the cabinet. "From what I could tell, she looked furious."

"Yeah, she was probably furious at me for letting it happen," Michael said, taking the plate Blake handed him. He began piling it high with beef lo mein. "But you're right. I don't think Alina felt nothing."

Stephanie looked from one to the other.

"I've known Alina for almost all my life," she said, "but I can't

Next Exit, No Outlet

read her at all anymore. You two have only known her for a couple of months. How come you think you know what's going on in her head?"

"Maybe that's why," Blake said. "You're looking at her as the woman she always used to be. We're seeing the woman she is now."

She sighed.

"I don't know who she is anymore, but I know she'll get herself killed if she keeps trying to handle this whole thing on her own."

"She's not on her own."

Damon spoke behind them, his voice deep and even. All three spun around and stared at him guiltily. He walked over to the cabinet to get a plate then turned towards the food.

"Don't be so quick to judge Alina," he told Stephanie. "She *is* a different person now, but that doesn't mean she doesn't care."

Stephanie grimaced.

"You weren't supposed to hear that," she said, turning away. "Anyway, it's not that I think she doesn't care. It's just that there's no emotion left in her. I don't understand it. Angela could be anywhere, going through anything, and Alina doesn't seem fazed by any of."

"What Alina feels and what she lets you see are two different things," Damon said, scooping chicken and broccoli onto his plate.

Michael looked at Damon consideringly.

"What do you think the odds are that we get Angela back?" he asked softly.

Damon's blue eyes met his. "Oh, Viper will get her back."

"And Alina?"

Damon's gaze became hooded, and he took his plate to the microwave.

"Well, that's a different question," he said, "and one I can't answer. I'm not blessed enough to see the future."

"Do you think it's possible for her to come out of this alive?" Michael asked the question all three of them were thinking.

Damon glanced at them.

"Yes, but only if you guys let us do our job."

Chapter Twenty-one

Alina opened the bottom drawer of the desk and looked at the document safe inside. She was in the front den with the door closed while the others were in the living room. Until they went to bed, she and Hawk were unable to access the command center. While she acknowledged the necessity of telling them about Harry, she drew the line at revealing the existence of the secret rooms under her kitchen. For the time being, the den was the new command center.

She bent down and typed in the digital code to the safe. Opening it, she pulled out a folder with CLASSIFIED - FOR YOUR EYES ONLY stamped across the front. Alina closed the safe and pushed the drawer shut, setting the folder on the desk.

Last week she had ended up saving the head of MI6 again when assassins tried to kill him in his hotel room in New York. In return, he agreed to find everything he could on a certain bank account in Singapore. When she met Jack in Philadelphia a few days later, he had passed her the file with the warning that it was the sole copy of the information inside. Then all hell let loose and she didn't have time to look through it. Now she flipped it open and reached for her coffee. It was time to see what MI6 had been able to discover about Carmichael's bank account in Singapore.

If there was a small part of her that regretted having to ask Jack for assistance, Viper ignored it resolutely. He owed her, and this was a very small price to pay for her having saved his life twice now. The fact was that, while she could have found the information she needed herself, Jack had saved her not only time, but exposure. There was no way she could have got into the account without Harry suspecting it was her and, more importantly, tracing her location. MI6 would have led him to a dead end, and even if Harry was able to determine that England's Secret Service had been nosing around in one of his accounts in Singapore, he would never connect it with her. Her association with Jack was something no one knew about, and she had worked hard to keep it that way. Even though Charlie had been the one

Next Exit, No Outlet

to initially send her on the suicidal rescue mission that had introduced her to the head of MI6, as far as he knew, she had retrieved Jack and moved on to the next mission. Nothing more.

Alina scanned the first page in the file as she sipped her coffee, bringing her attention back to the information before her. The door opened behind her and she glanced up as Damon entered carrying a plate of reheated Chinese food and a beer. He closed the door behind him quietly and went over to the armchair in the corner where he had left his laptop.

"Are you going to eat?" he asked, moving the computer and sitting down.

"Maybe later," she replied absently, turning the page.

He nodded and fell silent, setting his plate on the small side table next to him and opening his laptop. A comfortable silence fell over the room, the only sound the occasional tapping of his keys.

Alina focused on the information before her, ignoring Damon for the moment. Her lips tightened as she turned the pages, scanning what Jack had been able to gather. The information was substantial, and she was impressed, even though she was expecting it. The frown on her face grew as she sorted through the pages of figures and data. When she had finished, Alina turned to her laptop and opened the attachments Dave had sent John all those years ago. A moment later, she broke the comfortable silence.

"Son of a bitch," she breathed, sitting back in her chair.

Damon looked up from his screen. "What?"

She swiveled around in her chair, her face carefully devoid of any emotion.

"It's one thing to know that your mentor, the man who trained you and made you the weapon that you are today, had your brother killed. It's something entirely different to see the proof in black-and-white."

Damon's eyebrows came together and he closed his laptop, giving her his full attention.

"What did you find?"

"Not me. I didn't find anything. Jack did."

Damon's eyes narrowed.

"Jack?" he asked softly. "Jack as in the head of MI6? That Jack?"

Viper looked at him ruefully. "Yes, that Jack."

"What the hell are you doing, Viper?" Hawk exploded. "You brought a foreign agency into this? Are you out of your mind?!"

"I didn't bring a foreign agency into it. Jack owed me a favor.

Actually, he owes me two, and I called one in."

Hawk set his laptop aside and stood up swiftly, turning to stalk across the room restlessly.

"How many times do I have to tell you that people that high on the food chain can't be trusted?" he demanded, turning his head and fixing her with the glare. "All you have to do is look at Harry to see that! As for Jack, hell, he has a direct line to the Prime Minister of England! That means, if he wants, he's also got the ear of the President. You know who else has the ear of the President? Oh yeah, that's right. Harry!"

Alina watched him pace back and forth, her lips pulling upwards and amusement.

"Trust me, Jack does not have the ear of the President," she said calmly, "and as far as Harry goes, there is no good reason for him to connect MI6 to us. Calm down."

Hawk stopped in the middle of the room and looked down at her, his lips pulled into a straight line.

"When did you get this information from Jack?"

Alina's eyes slid away from his. "Thursday."

A heavy silence fell between them, Damon glaring down at her as she avoided his gaze.

"I thought we agreed no more secrets? Or did I just imagine that whole conversation?"

"First of all, I met with Jack initially before that conversation," she said, snapping her eyes back to his with a flash of irritation. "Second, he gave me the information on Thursday and then we went after Kasim and Tarek. When was I supposed to tell you?"

Damon's scowl lightened somewhat and, after a moment, he exhaled.

"You might as well tell me the worst of it," he said. "What did you have him do?"

"I asked him to look into Senator Carmichael's bank account in Singapore."

Damon raised his eyebrows.

"And he just did it? No questions asked?" he asked incredulously. "What did you tell him?"

Viper shrugged. "Nothing. I told him it was probably nothing, but I needed to know everything I could about that bank account."

"And he didn't wonder why you couldn't do it yourself?"

"Oh, he did."

"And?"

"I told him he was my insurance."

Next Exit, No Outlet

Hawk stared at her for beat, then threw his head back and let out a laugh.

"You told the head of MI6 that you were using him as an insurance policy?" he chortled. "Oh God, that's priceless!"

"I don't know that I would exactly call it priceless," she said thoughtfully. "Nothing comes for free, and I'm sure there will be dues to pay. It was worth it, though. He got more information in a few days than I would've been able to find in a week."

Damon sobered.

"That's because he's not being hunted like a wild dog. It's hard to be efficient and gather information when you have to cover every digital track and keep looking over your shoulder for killers."

He went back to his chair and sat down, leaning forward and dangling his hands between his knees.

"Let's hear it."

"Carmichael's account was in his name, but he's not the one who opened it. It was done twelve years ago by a shell company, Menlo Data LLC. Jack's team was very thorough. They were able to trace the company back to its sole investor."

Damon watched her steadily. "Who?" he asked, already knowing the answer.

"Harry. The bank account was opened by Harry, as the sole investor in Menlo Data."

He exhaled and dropped his head, silent for a moment.

"And Carmichael?"

"Last year, the senator was added as a signer on the account. On the same day, $1.4 million was withdrawn, and Menlo Data dropped off the account altogether."

"How much was left in the account?"

"Close to $4 million."

"That's quite a hefty payment. I hope the senator was worth it. What's happening with the account now that Carmichael is dead?"

"Oh, that's the fun part," Alina said, reaching behind her for the bottle of water on her desk. "As soon Carmichael's death was released, all his accounts were frozen, pending probate."

"But not that one?"

"Oh that one was included. The remaining funds in the account have been duly frozen, just like all the rest."

Damon raised an eyebrow. "I feel a 'but' coming."

"The total amount of funds frozen amounts to $150,000."

Damon shook his head.

"Son of a bitch," he muttered. "How did he get it out?"

"When Menlo Data dropped off the account, one board member remained on as an emergency signer. Kind of a silent partner, if you will."

"And they cleaned the account out."

Alina nodded. "Once you factor in the time difference between here and Singapore, the account was cleaned out eight hours before Sen. Carmichael was killed. The funds were wired out."

"Well, that's perfect. That means we can trace where they went."

"Oh, I already know where they went," she said. "As I said, Jack was very thorough. They went through a few different banks before ending up in a bank in Mexico."

Damon's lips tightened unpleasantly.

"Mexico, huh? Well, I can only think of one reason for the funds to go to Mexico. How about you?"

"Only one comes to mind," she agreed. "I'm sure Blake will be able to confirm what holdings the Casa Reinos Cartel has in Mexico, including bank accounts."

"Why the hell would Harry give the cartel close to $4 million?" Damon wondered, getting up again. He resumed pacing around the small den. "I don't see Harry letting that much money walk out the door to anyone."

"Agreed, unless he has no intention of letting the money stay there."

He stopped and looked at her sharply. "You think he's setting up the cartel?"

Viper shrugged.

"I wouldn't be surprised," she said. "He set up Carmichael, then pulled the money out before the account could get frozen. What's to stop him from doing the same in Mexico?"

Damon exhaled sharply and looked up at the ceiling.

"Well, it's the Casa Reinos, for starters. You can't just walk up to the head of the cartel and stab him in his back yard."

Viper was silent for a long moment, then she looked up slowly.

"Yet Jenaro Gomez's head was mailed to La Cabeza," she said softly.

Hawk looked at her, pausing in midstride. "FedEx'd, actually," he corrected, his lips twisting humorously. Then he sobered again. "Are you thinking what I think you're thinking?"

Viper's dark eyes met his steadily.

"No one else has been able to get close to the cartel," she pointed out.

Next Exit, No Outlet

Hawk shook his head and resumed pacing.

"How the hell does Harry think he's going to get either one of us to go after La Cabeza?"

"I have no idea," she admitted, "but you have to admit that it seems like something Harry would do. Arrange it so that we do the heavy lifting for him, and he pulls the money right back out of the account."

"And this time, there would be no trail," Damon said. "If the head of the cartel was killed again, there'd be chaos. It would be weeks before anyone realized money was missing from an account, and by then the trail would be cold."

He stopped in front of her. "You said you had proof in black-and-white that Harry killed your brother. What proof?"

"Over the past 12 years, there have been regular deposits made into Carmichael's account. We're talking large amounts, all coming in and going out at regular intervals. On a hunch, I compared the manifests that Dave sent John from Iraq with the account statements."

"And?" His blue eyes bore into hers.

"The amounts from the manifests match deposits made at the same time that the shipments went missing or were destroyed."

"All that proves is that Harry was dealing arms on the black market and charging cost."

Alina cleared her throat. "On the day Dave died, ten grand was withdrawn from the account, in cash."

Hawks sucked in his breath. "Where?"

"Erbil. It's a city in Northern Iraq, not far from where Dave's company was operating."

Damon swore softly. "Alina, I'm so sorry."

Viper waved her hand in dismissal. "There's nothing for you to be sorry about," she said shortly. "Trust me, by the time I'm finished with him, he'll be the one who's sorry."

Before Damon could answer, there was a knock on the door, and Michael poked his head into the den.

"Hey," he said. "Not to interrupt, but there's something on the news I think you two should see."

Alina strode into the living room, Damon close behind. Blake had turned on the TV above the mantelpiece and the screen was paused. She raised an eyebrow and looked at Michael.

"Well?"

Michael went over to the coffee table and picked up the remote.

"We paused it so you could see the rest," he said, pointing the remote at the screen and hitting play.

Alina crossed her arms and leaned against the back of the couch, watching the commercial on the screen absently.

"I wanted to watch the news," Stephanie said from the recliner. "I wanted to see if they had anything more on the shooting at work. Instead, we got this."

The commercial had ended and Alina found herself looking at a female reporter, standing on a city street.

"I'm in Atlantic City tonight where yet another body has been found in plain sight. This is the fifth so far today in what appears to be a deliberate and targeted attack ranging from Vineland up to Newark." The camera panned to a section of boardwalk outside a casino, cordoned off with police tape and surrounded by a smattering of onlookers. "The body was discovered just half an hour ago by a couple walking their dog. While the identity of the victim is unknown at this time, the attack appears to have followed the same pattern as the other four victims found today. Authorities tell us that the victim is a young male between the ages of 18 and 24, and sustained multiple stab wounds. In the same manner as the other bodies, this one had been stabbed in the stomach before his throat was slit. Authorities are scrambling to unravel what appears to be a mass killing spree. All the victims share the same wounds, but all have been found in different locations throughout the state. Authorities are asking anyone with any information to contact them."

Alina glanced at Michael. "Why is this something you think I needed to see?"

"Just watch."

The camera went back to the studio where two reporters sat behind a desk, looking appropriately grim.

"And that makes the fifth death today in what can only be described as premeditated and deliberate attacks," the male anchor on the right said. "While none of the victims' identities have been released, there are preliminary indications that all the victims had close ties to the Casa Reinos, a notorious and deadly Mexican cartel."

Alina stilled, her gaze arrested, and she felt Hawk stiffen behind her.

"While the association is still officially unconfirmed, there have

Next Exit, No Outlet

been several indications in the past few months that the cartel has moved into the United States, and even as far north as Boston," the female anchor on the left continued. "If all the victims are, indeed, connected with the cartel, this could be an indication of a growing gang war taking over the streets of New Jersey."

"That's exactly right, Patty," the man agreed to soberly. "Wait. I have something here. This just in: another body has been found in Newark. I repeat, another body matching these same wounds has been found in Newark. That brings the body count up to six."

"Still no official word from the authorities as to possible suspects," Patty said, "but it certainly is starting to look as though this could be an inter-gang related killing spree."

The camera cut again to a commercial and Michael switched off the plasma, turning to look at Alina.

"Well?"

She shook her head slowly, her lips pressed together.

"If they *are* Casa Reinos, it's not good," she murmured.

"That's an understatement," Blake said, getting up from his seat on the couch and going to the dining room table. "If someone's killing off cartel members, things will get very ugly very fast."

"You're the expert," Damon said. "Have the cartel established themselves here?"

"It's more than likely," Blake replied, sitting down and opening up his laptop. "They're moving products pretty freely up and down the coast, and have been for the past six months or so. Traditionally, Salcedo doesn't trust outsiders, so that would indicate a permanent presence of his own people."

"That certainly didn't hold true with the bombs a few weeks ago," Alina pointed out. "He had no problems passing those onto outsiders."

Blake glanced up.

"Those weren't his own product. It was product he was moving for someone else. As far as we can tell, the drugs coming up the coast are direct revenue for the Casa Reinos."

"Who would be going around knocking off members of the cartel?" Michael asked with a frown. "Could it be a rival gang?"

"That would be a little too convenient," Alina said. "When have you ever known anything to be that cut and dry with us?"

"More to the point, why is someone going after the cartel now?" Blake wondered. "It seems to be very suspect timing."

"Why do you say that?" Damon asked, crossing his arms over his chest.

Blake gave him a puzzled look for moment before glancing at Michael.

"You didn't tell them?"

Michael shrugged. "I told Damon earlier."

"Then you know about the *Sea Queen*," Blake said. "She left port yesterday and was seen passing Miami earlier today. You don't think the timing is strange given what we just saw on the news?"

"I'm not sure why you think the two are connected," Damon answered. "It's apples and oranges. Salcedo moving his yacht to the East coast wouldn't have anything to do with a possible gang war going on in New Jersey. He's too smart to get involved in something like that this early in his tenure as La Cabeza. He's still trying to regain control of the factions down in Mexico."

Blake looked at him, surprised.

"How do you know so much about Salcedo and the cartel?"

The look on Damon's face was impassive. "I've had some dealings with the Casa Reinos."

Alina's lips twitched and were repressed sternly.

"If Salcedo isn't on the yacht, who is?" she asked.

Blake met her stare.

"That's just it," he said. "We don't know. We're assuming it's his second-in-command, Roberto, but no one's been able to get eyes on the actual crew. The team in Florida is trying to pull better satellite footage from when it passed Miami, but we're not hopeful."

"So earlier today the *Sea Queen* passed Miami, destination unknown, and now, possible cartel members are showing up dead in New Jersey," she said. "Oh no, that's not suspect at all. Sorry, Damon. I'm with Blake on this one. Something's going on."

Blake began typing on his laptop.

"I'll see what I can find out about these victims," he said. "We can't take what the news says as gospel. Hell, they could all be members of the same book club for all we know."

"Blake, I don't think they were part of a book club," Stephanie said slowly from the recliner, her eyes on the tablet in her lap.

Alina glanced at her sharply. She knew that tone. Stephanie knew something.

"Neither do I. It was just a figure of speech."

"No, you don't understand," Stephanie said, dropping her legs down and struggling to her feet. "Something bothered me about the description of the wounds on all the victims. It sounded familiar, so I just pulled up some old case files that John and I worked."

She hobbled across the room, leaning heavily on her cane, her

Next Exit, No Outlet

tablet in her hand.

"I've seen those types of wounds before," she explained, setting the tablet on the dining room table.

"Where?" Michael asked, walking over to glance down at the tablet screen. "Are they exactly the same?"

"Without seeing the bodies of the victims from today, I can't be sure," Stephanie answered. "But if we go off of what the news said, it matches the MO of Stefan Delgado, Frankie Solito's main enforcer."

Chapter Twenty-Two

Alina's lips tightened and she felt, rather than saw, Damon glance at her sharply.

"Frankie Solitto?" Blake repeated, sitting back in his chair and staring at Stephanie. "Old-school mob boss; head of the New Jersey Family; *that* Frankie Solitto?"

"Yes. John and I worked a lot of cases where we tried to get something on him, but nothing ever stuck. He's got people everywhere on his payroll. John believed he'd even got his hooks into Washington." Stephanie pulled out a chair and sat down. "Stefan Delgado is his main enforcer. He's a real piece of work, and these killings fit his MO. When he's not arranging convenient accidents, he likes to get up close and personal. He usually reserves it for the ones Frankie considers traitors, though."

Michael circled the dining room table to the other side where his laptop was plugged in and charging. He seated himself and opened the computer.

"You said the cartel was moving drugs up the coast?"

Blake nodded. "Among other things."

"What other things?"

"As far as we can piece together, all kinds of things," Blake said with a shrug. "Drugs, guns, cash. You name it, the cartel probably has their fingers in it."

"Guns?" Stephanie repeated, her eyebrows coming together. "Frankie doesn't deal in arms. That's one of the only businesses he doesn't have a finger in."

"Who does?" Michael asked.

"Bobby Reyes," Alina answered, uncrossing her arms and turning to go into the kitchen. "They came to an agreement years ago. Bobby controls the illegal arms trade from New York down to Washington, and Frankie gets a stipend from the business. In return, Frankie stays out of it, giving Reyes a monopoly."

Stephanie nodded in agreement.

"Exactly. So Frankie wouldn't be bothered about the cartel

Next Exit, No Outlet

moving guns around." She frowned thoughtfully. "The drugs are another issue. That *would* cut into Solitto's revenue stream, but I really don't see Frankie targeting a handful of cartel thugs. It doesn't seem like it would be worth it to him. He's very careful these days. We've gotten too close to him and he's been toning down all his operations recently. At least, he's been toning down the publicity."

"Who's keeping an eye on Solitto now?" Blake asked. "The agency must have assigned him to someone else when they moved you and John into anti-terrorism."

Stephanie shrugged.

"Last I heard, he was on Agent Ross's plate, but that was six months ago. Check with Rob. He'll know who's working him."

Blake nodded and leaned forward to begin typing on his laptop.

"If these killings are the work of Delgado, the agent assigned to him will know about it," he said. "That's the best way to confirm whether or not Frankie is going after the cartel."

"It's one way," Stephanie said, glancing into the kitchen where Alina was pulling a bottle of water out of the fridge. "There are others."

Blake glanced at her.

"What are you talking about? What others? It's not like we can call Frankie and ask him."

Damon followed Stephanie's gaze and his eyebrows rose in amusement. She was looking at Alina thoughtfully.

"*We* can't," Stephanie murmured.

"I wouldn't go down that road, if I were you. I'm not sure that will end well," Damon told her, turning to go into the kitchen. "Anyone want a beer?"

"I'll take one," Michael said, not raising his eyes from his screen.

"Same," Blake seconded, then he turned his eyes back to Stephanie. "What road is he talking about?"

"We have someone here who has a direct line to Frankie Solitto," she answered.

"I wouldn't call it a direct line," Alina said, carrying her water to the bar and sitting on a stool. She pivoted to face the crew at the dining room table. "Follow the safe route and go through your agency."

"Oh, come on, Lina! When we went to Atlantic City just before all hell let loose with that Ebola nightmare, Solitto called you to a meeting. I was there. I remember. You weren't even surprised when his goon came over to get you."

"I wasn't surprised because I saw Frankie while we were at the roulette table," Alina replied calmly, sipping her water. "That doesn't mean we're best friends."

"Wait a minute," Michael said, looking up. "You had a meeting with Frankie Solitto? Are you out of your mind? The man's a crime boss! He's dangerous!"

The look he encountered from Alina made him flush.

"I can't really say I lose sleep over that," she said dryly.

"Well, you should," he muttered, dropping his gaze back to this laptop. "Hell Lina, people who associate with him end up at the bottom of a river."

"I can assure you, I have no intention of going swimming."

"You never did tell me what he wanted," Stephanie said after a moment of silence. "Why did he want to talk to you, anyway?"

"I don't remember," Alina lied.

Damon walked into the dining room and set two bottles of Yuengling on the table, then turned to pull out a chair.

"What difference does it make if Solitto's behind these killings?" he asked, turning the chair with a flick of his wrist and straddling it. "Who cares?"

Stephanie stared at him.

"We should all care. If Frankie Solitto is going to war with the Casa Reinos, it'll tear Jersey apart! Do you have any idea what happened the last time Solitto went head to head with someone? The death toll was astronomical."

"Well, that's another issue."

"It *is* another issue," Michael agreed, glancing up. "Let's forget Solitto for a minute. I just pulled up some rough numbers. You said that the cartel has been moving products up the coast for the past six months?"

"Yes."

"According to the ATF, the amount of seized illegal firearms has gone up by around forty-five percent over the past four months. Before that, it was increasing in line with expected trends, given what they know of the gunrunning networks already in place. Then everything spiked."

Blake whistled and sat back in his chair.

"That's higher than our estimates," he said. "We had it at around twenty percent."

Stephanie frowned.

"Why are the ATF numbers not part of our information flow?" she demanded. "That's information we should know."

"Oh, trust me, I'll find out," Blake said grimly.

Next Exit, No Outlet

"If the cartel is undercutting Bobby Reyes by forty-five percent, that would be enough for him to start a war," Stephanie said slowly. "He'd be furious. That doesn't explain Stefan Delgado, though. Frankie would hardly go after the cartel for Reyes."

Damon glanced at Alina. Her face was impassive and not by the flicker of an eyelid did she display the slightest interest in the discussion, but he knew better. If Frankie was going after the cartel, Viper would want to know why.

"I'm still not seeing what this has to with us," he said, sipping his beer. "If they're starting a power grab, that doesn't affect Viper and I, or our ability to find Harry and get Angela back."

"Actually, it might," Alina said unexpectedly. "We know Harry has had dealings with the cartel in the past, and the *Sea Queen* is moving into the Atlantic without warning and without Salcedo onboard."

"You think Harry is working with them?" Michael asked, looking up in disbelief. "To what purpose?"

Alina shrugged. "No clue, but it's not outside the realm of possibility."

Damon watched her thoughtfully for a minute. She wasn't giving anything away to the others, but he knew that she had just realized exactly the same thing he had: if Harry wanted to ensure that either Viper or Hawk went after the Casa Reinos Cartel, one of the fastest ways would be to have them involved with Angela's disappearance.

"Oh my God!" Stephanie exclaimed, her eyes widening in horror. "If Harry's working with the cartel, then do you think it was one of them who took Angie?!"

A decidedly ugly look settled on Michael's face and Blake's lips thinned and pressed together.

"God, I hope not," he muttered.

As one, everyone at the table turned their eyes to Viper. She met Stephanie's gaze, her face an emotionless mask.

"It doesn't matter who took her," she said, her voice cold and flat. "Whoever it was is a dead man walking."

The bedroom was pitch black, the moon unable to penetrate the thick, black storm clouds that covered the sky. Raven lifted his beak from his shoulder, directing his steely gaze onto the bed. His mistress was stirring restlessly, something disturbing her sleep. He straightened and moved to the end of his perch, staring at her for a long moment before his gaze darted to the man beside her. When she jerked sharply to her side, the man sat up swiftly, casting a sharp glance around the dark room. Seeing it empty, he exhaled and slipped his weapon back under the pillow before turning to the writhing woman beside him.

After watching her for a moment, Damon shook his head and reached out to smooth a thick strand of bleached hair off her forehead.

"Hey," he said softly, dropping his hand to her shoulder. "Wake up."

Viper came awake suddenly, terror flowing through her, leftover from the vivid nightmare that had had her in its grip seconds before. Surrounded by darkness and completely disoriented, her heart surged into her throat. She reacted in the only way she knew how: she attacked.

Damon threw up his left arm in a defensive block as her right hook drove toward his head.

"Viper, it's me!" he exclaimed. "Wake up!"

The deep voice made it through the noise and chaos in her mind and Alina gasped, lowering the Ruger that she'd pulled from under her pillow with her left hand. In an instant, the remnants of her dream evaporated and she realized she was in her own bed, staring into Damon's face.

"Oh my God," she breathed, lifting a hand to his face. "I'm so sorry. Did I get you?"

He shook his head and turned his head to kiss her palm.

"No, but only because I had a feeling you'd wake up fighting," he told her. "Damn, you're quick."

Alina dropped back against the pillow, breathing heavily, and stared at the dark ceiling.

"Then so are you." She took a deep breath, willing her heart rate to slow, and rubbed her face. "I didn't know where I was for a second."

Damon looked down at her for a moment. "What happened? In your dream?"

Alina visibly shuddered and he frowned.

"It's just a dream," she said. "I've had it before, but this time it was...different."

He studied her and the frown grew when she didn't continue. He laid down on his side and propped his elbow on the mattress, his head in his hand.

"Tell me."

Next Exit, No Outlet

Alina looked at him and shook her head. "It's nothing. It's over. Don't worry about it."

"It's not nothing," he said bluntly. "You woke up in a blind panic."

Her gaze wavered then dropped away, and he sighed, sliding his other hand across her bare stomach and pulling her closer. He leaned down and pressed his lips softly against hers, kissing her until she finally relaxed against him.

The heat from his body and gentleness of his lips combined to ease the remaining tension from her body and Alina sighed into him. His arm was strong around her, his shoulders solid above her, and for the first time in her life, Alina actually felt that she wasn't alone. The night was no longer empty, and the nightmares seemed far away.

Damon lifted his lips and laid back, pulling her with him until her head was cushioned on his broad chest. She exhaled, his strong, steady heartbeat beneath her cheek, and a feeling of contentment washed over her. The fingers of one hand were playing with her short hair while his other hand covered her forearm where it lay across his abs. This was where she belonged, she realized with a start, right here in Damon's arms. This was where she had always belonged. He was her rock, and always had been.

"I dream about the night I killed Al-Jibad," she heard herself say after a few moments of silence. The fingers in her hair stilled, the only indication that he was listening. "I've had dreams about some of them before, the ones that were more…messy, but this is different. The dream is the same, but the target changes."

"Changes?"

Alina nodded, not lifting her head to look at him. She wasn't sure why she was telling him about the dreams, but it was easier to say it if she didn't have to see his face. Then she didn't have to see what a nutcase he thought she was.

"The first few times, it was Al-Jibad. It was the events as they happened, nothing more or less." She paused and pursed her lips thoughtfully. "Is a memory really a dream?" she wondered. "I mean, a dream is a subconscious manifestation, but a memory, well, it's real."

"You don't think you can have a subconscious manifestation of something that really happened?" he asked, a thread of amusement in his voice. "If you're asleep, it's a dream. Let's keep things simple."

Alina smiled and pressed a soft kiss against his chest. "Ok."

"You said the first few times the target was Al-Jibad. What about the next time?"

Alina's body stiffened and he squeezed her gently before his fingers resumed playing with her hair. She inhaled and forced herself to relax again.

"It started out as Al-Jibad," she said softly, "but when the head hit the floor, it was John's face that stared up at me."

Damon stilled and was silent for a long moment.

"You actually re-live cutting off Al-Jibad's head in the dream?" he finally asked. "The whole thing?"

She nodded.

"How messed up is that?" she demanded, sitting up and leaning on her elbow. "I remember it all, even the shock going up my arm as the blade hits the spinal column."

Damon looked up at her thoughtfully. "And tonight? Was it John again?"

The impassive, emotionless mask that she wore so well slid into place and she began to turn away. Damon frowned and pulled her back.

"Oh no, you don't," he murmured. "You can't keep me out now. Spit it out. Who was it?"

Alina bit her bottom lip and raised her dark eyes to his. "You."

Damon exhaled and pulled her down onto his chest again, holding her close.

"Baby, I'm not dead," he murmured soothingly, "and I don't plan on being dead for a long time."

"No one plans on being dead," Alina muttered against his chest. "John didn't plan on it, but look what happened to him."

"Trust me. I'm not going anywhere any time soon."

"It was bad enough when it was John's eyes staring up at me," Alina said in a low voice, "but seeing yours…"

Damon tightened his hold as a shudder went through her and lifted her hand to press a kiss on her palm.

"Like I said, I'm not going anywhere, and I'm sure as hell not getting beheaded."

They lapsed into silence, and she stared at her hand as her pointer finger traced random patterns across his pectoral muscle. It was solid and hard, a clear testament to his extremely active life. There wasn't an ounce of fat on the man.

"Why?" she asked, breaking the silence a few minutes later. "Why am I having these dreams?"

Damon was quiet for a long time, then he sighed.

"We deal in death," he said slowly, his thumb rubbing back and forth on her arm absently. "Quite literally, we're death dealers. We

Next Exit, No Outlet

have to keep all those emotions that normal people feel about dying buried and out of the way. That's how we work. It's the only way we can work. But you lost someone close to you, someone who was a big part of your life for a long time, and you're having a problem accepting it. You're not used to facing emotion like this now. I warned you to deal with it before it started to affect you. Maybe your mind is taking matters into its own hands and dealing with the emotions the only way it can: when you're asleep."

"I haven't had time to deal with it!" Alina protested, raising her head and glaring at him. "We've had just a little bit going on over the past couple of weeks."

"I know," he said, raising his hand to her cheek. "I'm not saying you could have done anything differently. I'm just saying that maybe that's why these dreams are happening."

"And you? Why am I now seeing *your* head hit the floor?" Alina shook her head and pulled away, sitting up and leaning against the headboard. "I better not be losing my mind. I don't have time for that right now."

Damon chuckled and sat up, propping his pillows up behind him.

"You're not losing your mind," he assured her. "You really want to know what I think?"

Alina glanced at him. "Yes."

"You might not like it."

"Just get it out."

"I think you blame yourself for John's death. There's nothing you could have done to prevent it. You didn't have the information needed to even suspect that he would be in danger. When he survived the crash, you thought he would pull through. When he didn't, and you found out about Dave's letters, you blamed yourself for not seeing it coming. There's no way you could have stopped it."

"I should have known something was going on. He tried to tell me in the hospital, but I wouldn't listen."

Damon looked at her. "What?"

"The last time I saw him, he kept trying to apologize," she said quietly, her eyes on some invisible spot across the room. She refused to look at him. "He was trying to tell me something, saying he was so sorry, and I thought he was just going over old ground again. I thought he was still trying to apologize for how things ended between us, and I wouldn't listen. It wasn't until afterwards that...well, that I realized he was trying to tell me about the emails from Dave."

Damon turned to face her, reaching out and cupping her chin

to gently force her to look at him.

"Lina, it's not your fault," he said firmly. "You didn't inject him with potassium chloride, Kyle did. John's death is not on you."

Alina felt her bottom lip quiver and she bit it sharply, sucking in a gulp of air and willing the unexpected feeling of grief to pass.

"And you know what?" Damon asked, softening his tone, his eyes probing hers. "I'm not your responsibility, either. We're going to take on Harry together, and that's my choice. If anything happens to me, that won't be your fault, either."

"I know."

"Really? Because your subconscious manifestations tell a different story."

Alina let out a choked laugh. "Ass."

She took a deep, calming breath and tried to push down the emotions clamoring for attention. Damon was right. John's death wasn't her fault, but it didn't seem to make any difference to her feeling of guilt. Deep inside, she felt that she should have listened when he'd tried to tell her that day in the hospital, but she didn't. If she had...

"Stop," Damon said, cupping her face in his hands. She looked at him in surprise and he smiled faintly. "I know what's going on in that head of yours. It's not your fault. It doesn't matter what you think he might have told you if you'd listened, it really doesn't. The fact is, an assassin was hired to kill him. You know as well as I do what that means. John was dead the second Harry made the call."

Alina gazed into his eyes, drawing strength from the bright blue depths. She felt her bottom lip tremble again despite her attempts to push the overwhelming feeling of sorrow down. Inhaling sharply, Viper focused on the only thing that would stop the onslaught of emotion.

"That's a call Harry's going to regret making," she said, her voice low and dangerous.

"Not if you don't let John go," Damon replied, his voice just as low. "Until you accept John's death and move on, Harry has a weapon to use against you. And you know he'll use it, just like he used Dave against you all through training."

He was right. She wasn't able to think clinically when it came to John. Instead, these debilitating emotions threatened to paralyze her. She stared at him helplessly.

"I don't know how," she said brokenly. "I'm not like Stephanie. I can't just cry every day and wait for it to get better; I don't have that luxury. I have to find Angela before Harry decides she's more trouble than she's worth. And unless he keeps her permanently gagged,

Next Exit, No Outlet

he *will* decide she's not worth it."

"*We* have to find Angela," he said, "and we will. But you have to face up to the fact that John is gone. It sucks, and it's not fair, but it's how it is and you have to let him go."

Alina had no idea what it was that pulled that final thread inside her, unraveling the weeks of pent-up grief she had carefully stored away. Perhaps it was the look of empathy in his eyes, or the fact that he acknowledged that it wasn't fair. Nothing in their life was fair, but she'd known this was how it would be when she'd agreed to this life. John had made no such agreement. He deserved a long, full life, not a shot of potassium chloride in an IV when he was too weak to defend himself.

Her bottom lip quivered again and this time she didn't push the feeling aside. Allowed to run free, grief welled up inside her, choking her and making it impossible to breathe. Alina sucked in some air and tried to turn away from Damon as panic at the raw emotion rolling through her set in. Instead of letting her go, Damon grabbed her arms and pulled her to him, holding her close as violent tremors went through her body.

"And here we go," he murmured to himself, resting his chin on top of her head as he held her tight.

Alina didn't hear him as another shudder ripped through her and her body released all the tension it had been holding onto for weeks. She took a deep, ragged breath and felt hot tears begin to burn a path down her face. The yawning, hollow feeling of emptiness that now accompanied thoughts of John engulfed her, and Alina could do nothing except bury her face in Damon's neck and surrender to the vacuum.

She closed her eyes in an attempt to stem the flow of tears, but it didn't make any difference. They kept coming, and Alina felt as if she was falling apart, getting sucked into a kind of void where nothing mattered except the grief ripping her into a thousand pieces.

John was gone. He was dead. He was never coming back. She would never see his pale blue eyes squinting in the sunlight before he put on his sunglasses again. His Ducati would never come roaring down the driveway again, and Raven would never again attack him when he crossed to the deck. The Firebird she loved so much had gone with him, along with all the memories, both good and bad, that they shared in it.

It was all gone.

The memories whirled through her mind like a tornado while waves of sorrow crashed over her. Alina tried to find something to hang on to, a thought to help her stem the flow of senseless grief, but they all kept spinning out of reach. Only one stayed constant: John was gone.

Through the storm, Damon was a solid, unmoving strength, his heartbeat steady and calm against hers, his arms strong around her. Alina clung to him as her world was torn apart, and the tears flowed unchecked, never once questioning why she drew such comfort and strength from him. It was enough that she did, and that he freely offered it. She wasn't alone anymore, and she didn't have to be strong. He would help her through this.

And then they would go after the bastard who started it all.

Next Exit, No Outlet

Chapter Twenty-Three

The air was thick and heavy with humidity when Angela slowly became aware of the darkness. She tried to hang on to the comfortable nothingness of sleep, but a persistent feeling of unease kept nagging her, pulling her back toward consciousness. Something wasn't right. The thought popped into her mind and she reluctantly came awake. Her arms and legs felt heavy, as if they were weighted down with something, but she knew that couldn't be right. She was on her back, laying on some kind of seat, surrounded by dark, filtered light. Angela tried to push herself up, and that's when she realized her arms were beneath her, and they wouldn't move.

Sheer panic tore through her as she tried to pull her arms from behind her and felt hard plastic cut into her wrists. The last vestiges of sleep evaporated and she gasped, turning her head and straining to see through the gloom. She was on the backseat of some kind of vehicle and it was dark outside. What time was it? Where was she?

Angela swallowed her panic and forced herself to think clearly. What was the last thing she remembered? She was at her house with Michael, gathering her things to go to Lina's. Michael took Anabelle out to the car and…then what? She went to make sure the back door was locked.

Memory rushed back and she gasped. Someone had grabbed her from behind and she felt a sharp prick in her arm. What happened next was a blur. She remembered being disoriented as she was guided from the back door across the back yard. The houses seemed to be triple their size around her, and everything was doubled. Her legs had felt heavy and she wasn't able to move them very well, but it hadn't made any difference. She had been pulled away from the house and when she tried to call out for Michael, her tongue wouldn't work and she couldn't seem to form any words. Her lips moved, but nothing came out, not even a sound. A pickup truck was at the curb, and that was the last thing she remembered.

Oh my God, I've been taken! Lina was right!

Terror washed through her and she sat up quickly, looking

around. She was in the backseat of the pickup and she leaned forward to peer out the side window. She couldn't see much. The truck was stopped in some kind of parking lot between what looked like two eighteen-wheelers. Was she at a truck stop? Where was her kidnapper?

Angela gingerly tested the bonds at her wrists. They were immovable. She moved her feet, relieved when they moved freely. Good, only her hands were bound. Turning her back to the door closest to her, she awkwardly pulled the handle with her fingers and pushed. The door didn't budge. Letting out half a sob, she moved to the other door and tried again, with the same result. Neither door would open.

Angela shifted to the middle of the bench seat and eyed the opening between the front seats. If child locks were keeping the back doors from opening, her only other choice was to try the front doors. The center console would be a problem, but she didn't see any other option.

Her heart began pounding as she turned sideways and shifted her hip onto the console. Pushing against the back seat with one foot, she moved awkwardly between the seats, gripping the back of the driver's seat with her bound hands to keep her balance. Coming to the end of the console, Angela paused and turned her head to gaze out of the windshield.

She was surrounded by trucks, all eighteen wheelers. She was in a rest stop and could see the bright lights of the gas and eating area in the distance. The pickup had been parked far away from the people, and Angela swallowed, her mouth painfully dry. If she was going to try to escape, she was going to have to do it through a sea of dark and silent tractor trailers. She wasn't stupid. She'd seen the police dramas on TV. She knew what happened in dark truck stops on the highway. Uncertainty and fear paralyzed her, and Angela stared out the window at the distant lights, longing for the relative safety of crowds.

A door slammed next to her and Angela gasped, looking out the passenger's door window and shrinking back against the side of the driver's seat fearfully. A large man walked away from the cab of the truck beside her, heading toward the lights in the distance. He never glanced at the pickup.

She exhaled, her heart beating a rapid tattoo against her chest, and twisted around to look out the driver side door. The truck parked on the other side was dark and appeared empty. Taking a deep breath, Angela pulled her legs from the backseat and managed to swing one around the back of the passenger's seat. Her foot landed on the seat, but the maneuver made her lose her tenuous grip on the seat behind

Next Exit, No Outlet

her and she fell backwards into the driver's seat. Unable to use her hands to steady herself, her head smacked the door, making her grunt and sending a sharp pain down her neck.

Ignoring the discomfort, Angela pulled her right leg through the gap between the seats and sat up, peering out the windshield. In the distance, she could see people moving between the parking lots and the building, but no one seemed to be heading in her direction.

Angela felt behind her for the door handle, exhaling when her questing fingers located it. With one last fearful glance towards the building in the distance, she took a deep breath and pulled the handle, opening the door. The silence in the parking area was broken immediately by the shrill wail of an anti-theft alarm.

Angela gasped and swung her legs out the door, sliding out of the truck and hitting the pavement. Her legs trembled and, as she moved to take a step, she realized that her muscles felt like jelly. The car alarm was blaring in her ears and she knew it was only a matter of seconds before someone looked to see what was going on. Gritting her teeth, Angela resolutely turned towards the back of the truck, ignoring the pins and needles shooting down her legs. While she admitted to herself that she hadn't really had a set plan in mind when she opened the door to escape, she was fully aware that the alarm complicated things. She couldn't head straight for the safety of people now. Her assailant would know she had managed to escape.

Stupid! I should have looked to see if there was an alarm, she thought disgustedly, forcing one foot in front of the other as fast as her weakened muscles would allow. *And what the hell did they do to me? Why won't my legs work?*

One question led to another and, before she knew it, fear was choking her and robbing her of breath. She forced herself to stop thinking. It didn't matter right now. All that mattered was that she reached the safety of crowds and enlisted help before her kidnapper caught her again.

The darkness between the tractor trailers enveloped her as she moved quickly away from the pickup and deeper into the rows of silent, looming trucks. As she got further away, the feeling in her legs slowly returned to normal and she picked up the pace, breaking into a run. If she could loop around to the end of the parking lot, she might be able to come up behind the rest stop building.

The sound of the car alarm lessened as she put distance between the pickup and herself, and Angela wound her way through the trucks, her heart pounding. They were all silent and still, the drivers either in the rest stop restaurant or asleep, and she was both grateful and terrified. On the one hand, she desperately needed help. On the other, she had no idea if she had simply jumped out of the pan and into the fire. Her mind shot back to one true crime episode that followed a serial killer truck driver and Angela gulped as she ran.

She had to make it to the safety of the rest area building. There was no other way.

The car alarm in the distance suddenly stopped, and so did her heart. Angela came to a halting stop beside a long eighteen wheeler, gasping for breath, and listened. The sudden silence was more terrifying than the shrieking alarm. He knew she was gone, and now he would come after her.

Catching her breath on a sob, Angela tried to hear over the sound of her own blood rushing in her ears and her heart pounding in her chest. He would know she hadn't gone straight for the rest area. If she had, he would have seen her. There were three directions she could have gone: to the woods behind the parking lot, to the highway, or the direction she had gone - into the trucks. Forcing herself to think, Angela took a deep breath and began moving. No matter what, she couldn't stay where she was.

She reached the front of the truck beside her and peered around it, searching in the darkness. She could only see as far as the next truck. Light from the occasional street lamp didn't penetrate this far, and the shadows seemed endless. Angela looked to her right, hesitating. Should she risk moving toward the rest area? Or should she continue to put distance between herself and the pickup before running for safety? Indecision paralyzed her for a few precious seconds before she decided to risk it. There were three trucks between her and the open expanse of parking lot leading to the building. Once she got to the edge of the last one, she would sprint across the parking lot. It wasn't a great plan, but it was all she had.

Sweat covered her face and trickled down her back. Wherever she was, the air was heavy and humid and the temperature had to be over seventy degrees. The high in Jersey that day was only fifty-eight. That could only mean she was somewhere south.

Angela frowned as she began moving swiftly toward the end of the line of trucks in front of her. She didn't even know where she was! How the hell was she going to get back to New Jersey? She had no money, no identification, nothing on her that would help get her home. Hell, she didn't even have her phone. All of that was in her purse, which had been in the house when she was taken.

A door slammed somewhere behind her and Angela gasped, spinning around to peer into the murky blackness behind her. She couldn't see anything and, her heart in her throat, she turned and began running toward that last truck. Screw being quiet. She had to get out of there.

Fear gave her speed and she flew toward the edge of the parking area, her eyes on the lights in the distance. She was just coming to the front of the second-to-last truck when her foot hit something laying across the tarmac. Angela gasped and had the terrifying sensation of falling without the use of her arms to aid her. Without thinking, she turned her shoulders to try to break her fall. Her left shoulder slammed into the pavement hard, sliding a few inches as her body weight carried her forward. Angela let out a muffled cry as searing pain shot through her and her head hit the ground.

She lay immobile for a few seconds, the wind knocked out of her and stars swimming behind her eyelids. Excruciating pain flowed down her left arm and she bit down hard on her bottom lip to keep from crying out. Tears blurred her vision as she rolled onto her stomach and tried to bring herself to her knees. Another rush of pain rolled through her as her arms automatically tried to help balance her, and she bit harder on her lip in agony. The pain shifted to her lip and Angela felt something thick and wet slide slowly down her chin. Looking down, she watched as a fat drop of blood splashed onto the pavement. With a soft gasp, she released her bottom lip and tasted blood. Spitting it out, she struggled to her feet, her heart slamming against her ribs as she heard footsteps on the other side of the truck. They were moving quickly to the front and, in another second, they would round the corner and see her.

Casting a frantic look around, Angela turned to run back into the darkness of the trucks and away from the footsteps. She didn't know who they belonged to, but she sure as hell wasn't taking a chance. The pain in her left arm was almost unbearable, but she resolutely ignored it, darting behind the next tractor trailer. Once she was out of sight, she leaned against the back of the truck, gasping for breath and trying to fight back sobs of pain and terror. She was never going to make it.

As soon as the thought entered her mind, her head snapped up and her spine stiffened. She had clawed her way to the top in a male-dominated career field and had faced down a serial killer in her own home. She wasn't about to give up now, stranded at a truck stop God-knows where, and wait for the bastard to find her. Pain or not, she had to keep going. She straightened, took a deep breath, and ran around the back of the truck.

And straight into the arms of a tall, solid figure. She was just opening her mouth to scream when a hand clamped over mouth and she felt a sharp prick in the side of her neck. Wrenching her head away, she sank her teeth into the hand hard and had the satisfaction of tasting blood and hearing a grunt of pain before everything began swimming before her. The shadow became a blur and suddenly the pain in her arm and lip faded away into numbness.

Angela tried to pull away from the solid mass before her, but instead she felt herself falling as darkness claimed her.

Damon jogged down the stairs and rounded the corner to stride down the hallway towards the back of the house. He'd heard Blake and Michael talking from the stairs, and it didn't sound good. He walked into the living room and raised an eyebrow. Michael was pacing near the sliding door to the deck, while Blake was seated at the dining room table with his laptop. Neither man looked happy.

As he walked into the room, Buddy got up from where he'd been basking in the morning sun inside the sliding doors. After stretching, he trotted over to Damon and shoved his muzzle against his hand demandingly. The two men grew quiet, watching as Damon greeted the dog. He glanced up at them.

"Don't stop on my account."

"It's not you, it's my dog," Blake said. "He doesn't like anyone. Or, at least, he never used to. We came up here and suddenly he loves everyone."

"Maybe he's a Jersey boy," Damon said with a grin, straightening up. "Where's Stephanie?"

"She's not up yet." Blake stretched. "Probably a good thing. She needs the rest."

"I haven't seen Alina yet either," Michael said, glancing at his watch. "She's usually up by now."

"She's been up and she's left," Damon said over his shoulder, heading into the kitchen.

"Where did she go?"

Damon didn't answer and Michael scowled. "I don't like her being out there when it seems like the entire population is trying to kill her."

"Join the club," Blake said. "You know Stephanie's going to have a fit when she comes down and finds out she's gone."

Next Exit, No Outlet

"You all need to stop worrying," Damon said. "This isn't Alina's first rodeo. She'll be fine."

"That's what I said about Angela and look how that ended up," Michael muttered. "Now she's going through God-knows what onboard a cartel yacht."

"We don't know she's on the damn ship!" Blake exclaimed. "Hell, we don't even know where the ship is. For all we know, it could be halfway across the Atlantic."

"Where else would she be?" Michael retorted, his face drawn into a scowl.

"She could be anywhere! Just because the *Sea Queen* sailed around Miami doesn't mean that that's where Angela was taken. In fact, it's a pretty big jump to assume that the cartel has anything to do with this."

"It's not that big of a jump," Damon said, opening a cabinet to pull out a coffee mug. "The cartel has been popping up left and right. Alina was right last night. It is too much of a coincidence. I'm starting to think they might be involved in this after all."

"You would really support seizing the cartel's yacht on a hunch that Angela might be on it?" Blake demanded incredulously.

Damon set his coffee mug under the coffee maker and pressed the button to brew. "No."

"See? Even the Navy SEAL thinks it's a bad idea," Blake said, turning back to his laptop.

"I didn't say it was a bad idea," Damon said. "I just said I wouldn't support it."

Michael looked across the bar at him. "I have to do something."

Damon met his gaze impassively.

"Jumping into the fight isn't going to help Angela," he told him. "Let's find out what we're dealing with first, and then we'll go from there."

His calm tone seemed to soothe Michael and the tension left his shoulders. He nodded once, then picked up an empty mug from the dining room table and carried it into the kitchen.

"I was up most of the night thinking about it," he said, setting his mug down on the counter. He leaned against the island while he waited for the coffee maker. "There's no sign of her or the truck on the surveillance cameras in the neighborhood. The footage must have been tampered with, which means that they'd already planned to take her yesterday."

Damon pulled his mug out from under the coffee spout and

moved out of the way so that Michael could get his mug under it.

"Yes."

"If he was watching her for any amount of time, then we're looking at the wrong day. We need to be looking at the footage from the past week."

Damon smiled faintly.

"The Marine can think after all," he murmured, sipping his coffee.

Michael shot him a disgruntled look.

"Hey, I wasn't thinking clearly last night," he protested. "She was taken while I was there! Give me a break."

"I've already put in the request with the Bureau," Blake said from the dining room. "Don't feel bad. It didn't occur to me until this morning. I think we're all a little off our game on this one."

Damon didn't answer, wisely choosing to keep silent. There was no point in telling either of them that Viper had already pulled footage from the past two weeks and had the license plate of the truck. Her server under the kitchen was already running it, waiting for a hit. For all he knew, they could have gotten one already, but until the two gunnies cleared out of the area, he couldn't go down and check.

"How long will it take?" Michael asked, pressing the button to brew coffee into his mug and turning to look out of the kitchen at Blake.

"I'll have it by mid-day. Rob said he'll forward it as soon as they get it."

"Where are you with the money trail?" Damon asked Michael.

"It's slow. I'm working around layers of bank encryption."

"I'll help. I know some shortcuts that you probably wouldn't agree with using," Damon said, turning to go set his coffee down on the bar. "Show me what you have so far and we can work together."

Michael looked at him, surprised. "You're going to help me?"

Damon's lips twisted in amusement.

"Don't look so shocked. Alina asked me to give you both a hand to speed up the process."

"That's great, but I don't see how you can help me," Blake said from the dining room table, sitting back in his chair and stretching. "I'm tapped into all my sources trying to get information about Salcedo's yacht and no one's talking."

"I have a contact in Guerrero," Damon said after a moment of silence. "I contacted them last night."

Blake stared at him. "What? The military base?"

Damon nodded. "That's where the messages Stephanie sent hit

Next Exit, No Outlet

a wall. That's where we need to start."

"But...that's...you can't just hack into the Mexican military!" Blake stammered. "God, relations are bad enough with Mexico as it is! You'll start a war!"

Amusement lit Damon's blue eyes and he grinned.

"That's a bit extreme, don't you think?" he asked. "Anyway, I'm not the one hacking into their military servers. My contact is doing it for me."

"That won't matter if they find out who was behind it," Blake shot back. "God, you guys really do run unchecked, don't you?"

"It's because we do that you're still alive, and the East Coast hasn't been thrown back to the dark ages with a death toll equivalent to the plague," Damon said. "Man up and accept it. The bad guys that go bump in the night don't play by the rules, so neither do we."

"Are you hearing this?" Blake demanded, looking at Michael.

Michael shrugged and carried his coffee over to his laptop on the other side of the dining room table.

"You're talking to a Secret Service agent who's in the process of hacking through bank security and breaking about twenty privacy laws in the process," he said with a shrug. "I'm telling myself the ends justify the means."

Blake grunted, showing his disagreement, and turned his scowl back to his laptop screen. Damon sipped his coffee and waited. A few moments later, after coming to terms with the fact that he was in the minority, Blake glanced at him.

"What are you looking for in Guerrero?" he asked reluctantly.

"A reason why those messages got bounced there," Damon said shortly. "It's not coincidence that Viper's location got routed through Mexico, not when the Casa Reinos has been so heavily involved through all of this."

Michael looked up with a frown. "You think the cartel hijacked those messages?"

"No. I think those messages went exactly where Harry wanted them to go."

"But he told Stephanie..." Blake began, then his voice trailed off as he realized the truth. "Damn. He was playing her right up until the end."

"Welcome to Harry's Playhouse," Damon said, his mouth twisting into a grim, non-humorous smile.

Michael sat back thoughtfully.

"If the cartel has people inside the military, that means Harry had the messages go through them," he said slowly. "Why? Why not just send them directly to himself?"

"Too much of a trail. His plan was for Viper to die, and if that happened, Stephanie would be asking questions, as would my organization. He was making sure that nothing could be traced back to him."

"He sent it through the cartel so they would take the hit," Blake breathed. "Everything would lead back to the Casa Reinos."

"And with you already on top of them, no one would look any further."

"So what do you think you'll find in Guerrero?" Michael asked.

Damon's eyes turned arctic.

"Something to hang him with."

Chapter Twenty-Four

Alina rolled slowly down the street, her eyes moving between the few parked vehicles and the townhouses lined on either side. The cars and trucks parked along the curb were empty, and the houses were still and silent. Reaching the end of the block, she turned left and rolled up to the stop sign. After pausing, she turned onto the next street and pulled to a stop at the curb near the corner.

Angela lived in a working neighborhood. The few homes owned by couples with families had both parents working, leaving the street quiet and deserted on a Monday morning. After having circled the neighborhood twice, looking for signs of surveillance, Alina shifted the Porsche into park and killed the engine. She was a block away from Angela's house. She would go on foot from here.

Opening the door, she got out and beeped the alarm before turning away from the sleek sports car. She was dressed in running clothes and, after a swift glance around, she broke into a run. Just because there were no obvious signs of surveillance on the street didn't mean that they weren't watching. Whoever took Angela knew Viper would go looking for her, and the place she'd start was here. Alina adjusted the Phillies cap on her head and scanned the street from behind the sports sunglasses covering half of her face. What Harry had forgotten was that he'd trained her for this. She lived for it. It was as second nature to her as breathing.

Alina crossed a side street and started up Angie's block. Everything was quiet and still. At the far end, a utility truck was parked at the corner. The technician climbed out of the truck and went up the sidewalk to the end house. Viper watched as he circled around to the meter and shifted her gaze back to the row of houses on her left. She passed Angela's, scanning the front windows with their curtains pulled tight against the morning sun. The house looked like any other on the street, quiet with its owner at work. Except Angela wasn't at work. She had been taken to be used as a pawn in a deadly game that she should never have known was taking place.

Her lips tightened as she ran past the house and continued down the street. Angela was safe from being killed for the time being. Harry needed her alive to draw Viper out. But depending on who took her, that didn't preclude bodily injury. If it *was* the cartel who had snatched her, Viper knew that every minute Angela was missing was another minute of pure hell that she would experience. If it was the nameless assassin from Rittenhouse, her chances were higher for a somewhat civil captivity. But which was it?

Alina turned the corner at the end of the block and continued to the street that ran behind the row of townhouses. Regardless of which one had taken her, Viper knew she had a very small window to find her.

Turning down the back street behind Angela's house, Alina scanned the windows of the houses opposite, searching for telltale gaps in curtains or shades. Not seeing anything suspicious, she headed for Angela's house, crossing the small patch of grass to the back door a few moments later.

Viper eased the door open and slipped silently into the house. She glanced around the small alcove as the door closed behind her. The silence in the house was deafening as she moved past the hall stand near the back door and down the short hallway toward the kitchen. The house was just as Michael had left it with nothing out of place. Her lips tightened when she saw Angela's purse sitting on the kitchen counter, right where she'd left it. Going over to the red designer bag, Alina opened it and looked inside. There, tucked into the inside pocket, was Angela's cell phone.

Turning from the counter, Alina paused just inside the living room, her eyes scanning the room slowly. Unlike Stephanie's apartment, all the air vents in Angela's townhouse were in the floors rather than near the ceilings. The walls and ceiling were solid, leaving no spot to conceal a hidden camera easily. Yet she was sure there was one here somewhere. Harry was too smart to send an agent in cold to take the target. His man, whether he was cartel or not, would have been instructed to start watching Angela days ago. He wouldn't leave anything up to chance this time.

After studying the room, her eyes came to rest on the front wall. Two floor-to-ceiling windows were separated by an expanse of wall, and a round mirror mounted on rattan hung between them. Alina pursed her lips and strode forward. That was the only place in the room where a camera would get a clear shot of both the living room and hallway, as well as the stairs leading to the second floor. It had to be there.

Next Exit, No Outlet

Reaching the far wall, she studied the mirror and the rattan. Her lips curved faintly when she detected a small hole in the rattan to the right of the mirror. She pulled a pair of latex gloves from her jacket pocket and slid them on. Carefully lifting the mirror off the wall, Alina turned it over. There, cunningly inserted into the backing of the mirror, was a dvr camera no larger than a chapstick. She set the mirror face-down on the sofa and bent over to slide the small camera out from the backing. She pressed a button on the side of the device, turning it off, and slid it into the inside pocket of her jacket.

After replacing the mirror, Alina turned and headed for the stairs. While she doubted there was a camera up there, it was better to be sure. She was halfway across the room when a shock of awareness snaked down her spine and she froze. A second later, she heard it. Someone was working the lock on the back door.

Her lips tightened and she looked around quickly. The living room offered nowhere to conceal herself, so she spun around and strode swiftly to the kitchen. She had just slipped inside when the back door opened and someone entered the house.

Viper moved silently to the walk-in pantry in the corner and opened the door, stepping inside and pulling the door closed behind her. She left it open a crack, watching the door to the kitchen. A moment later, a man passed the kitchen, glancing in. He was of medium build and dressed in a navy uniform with an alarm company logo on the shirt. Her eyes narrowed. The company on his shirt was not the company Angela used for her alarm service. She watched as he continued past the kitchen before she slipped out of the pantry and crossed the room to peer around the corner.

He was paused just inside the living room, looking around. As she watched, he moved forward, going toward the mirror on the front wall. Viper moved out of the kitchen, moving up behind him swiftly and silently. Her heart beat in a steady rhythm and her hands were perfectly steady as she pulled her .45 from the holster at her back. Sensing movement behind him, the man began to turn around, but froze as the muzzle of her gun pressed against his side.

"You don't belong here," she said coldly.

The man didn't answer. Instead, he reached behind him with his right hand, going for her gun. Anticipating the move to disarm her, Viper clamped her left hand around his wrist and wrenched his arm behind his back, pulling up sharply. He stilled as his arm strained at an unnatural angle behind him.

"Nice try," she said. "Who sent you?"

"Go to hell."

"Not today."

Viper shifted the hand holding her gun and squeezed the trigger, blowing out his knee. He let out a howl of pain and collapsed onto the floor, gripping his leg as blood poured out.

"Now that I have your attention," she said conversationally, looking down at him. "I'll ask once more. Who sent you?"

The man glared up at her, remaining silent. Viper studied him for a moment. He wasn't going to talk. She could see it in his eyes. He would die before giving up a name. Too bad for him.

"Ok. Let's try this instead," she suggested, crouching down beside him and pressing the muzzle of the .45 against his other knee. "What did you do with the woman who lives here?"

He looked startled. "What?"

She crooked her eyebrow. "The woman who lives here. Where is she?"

"How should I know?"

Viper studied him coldly.

"Why are you here?" she asked after a moment, keeping her gun pressed against his knee.

"I came to get the camera," he said, shifting with a groan of pain. "I don't know anything about anyone who lives here. I didn't put the camera in."

"Then why are you taking it out?"

"I was told to."

"And do you always do what you're told?" she asked, her lips twisting humorously. "What a good Boy Scout."

His lips thinned unpleasantly. "You have no idea," he snarled.

Too late, Viper saw something flash out of the corner of her eye. She ducked to the side as a long, deadly blade slashed forward, aimed for her throat. Her quick movement saved the front of her throat, but the sharp blade still found a target on the side of her neck. Searing pain went up her neck as the knife sliced into the soft skin below her ear and where her jaw began. She sucked in her breath and raised her gun, firing straight into his heart. Blood spread across his torso and the knife slipped from his fingers as he fell backwards, dead.

Viper exhaled and stood slowly, staring down at the body at her feet. His eyes were still open and she shifted her gaze away from his face and to the blood beginning to seep out beneath him. Angela's hardwood floor was going to be destroyed.

She slid the Ruger back into the holster at her back and lifted a hand to investigate the wetness streaming down her neck. Her fingers came away covered with more blood than she was expecting and she

Next Exit, No Outlet

scowled, spinning to stride down the hall towards the powder room near the back of the house.

She flipped on the light inside the door and stared at herself in the mirror. Blood was pouring from a deep gash that extended in an arc from below her ear and along her jawline.

"Son of a bitch," she breathed, reaching for a thick paper hand towel from the basket on the vanity.

Pressing the paper against her neck firmly, she turned and left the powder room, striding through the house to the stairs. Somewhere upstairs Angela had to have a first aid kit, or at least bandages. She went up the stairs swiftly, heading for the master bathroom and silently berating herself. She should have known he was being too amenable. There was no excuse for her injury. He should never have been able to get to the knife, wherever he had it, let alone make a move with it.

She was just finishing taping down a gauze bandage a few minutes later when her watch vibrated against her wrist. She glanced at it with a frown, took one last look at the sterile bandage taped to her neck, and pulled out her phone. She dialed into a secure line and walked out of the master bathroom as it rang. The line picked up and she entered her security code, then listened to dead air as the call was routed through several servers on its way to her boss.

Crossing the bedroom, Alina sank down onto the side Angela's bed and looked at the bedside table. The phone charger was empty, a stark reminder that her childhood friend was gone. Alina's lips tightened as she glanced at her watch. She'd been gone for twenty-one hours. While Harry wouldn't kill her until Viper showed up, time was ticking away. His plans to flee to Montenegro wouldn't wait forever.

"Viper?"

The call connected and Charlie's voice broke into her thoughts.

"Yes."

"Are you secure?"

"Yes, and I'm alone."

"Good. I know I said we wouldn't speak until this was over, but I got some new information today and I think we should meet. How soon can you get down here?"

Alina frowned.

"Do you really think that's a good idea?" she asked softly. "Things aren't exactly stable up here at the moment."

There was a slight pause, then Charlie spoke.

"They weren't stable before. What's happened now?"

"Nothing I can't handle," she told him. "I'm not sure that it's a good idea for me to leave, though."

"I wouldn't suggest it if I didn't think it was necessary. The more you move around, the more at risk you are, and I don't like that anymore than you do."

Alina pursed her lips and stared at the wall across the room thoughtfully, silent for a long moment.

"If I leave later this afternoon," she finally said reluctantly, "I can be there by nine."

"Perfect. Contact me when you're in the city and I'll tell you where to meet."

"Okay."

"Viper, be careful."

Alina's lips tightened and the look that crossed her face was deadly.

"Oh, don't worry about me."

Chapter Twenty-Five

Alina stepped into the small, family-owned Italian restaurant and looked around. The dining area was half-filled with patrons finishing up their lunch, and her dark eyes scanned the tables briefly, searching. Not seeing who she was looking for, she turned toward the desk near the front of the restaurant. Before she could open her mouth, a solidly built man in black slacks and a gray shirt that did little to conceal the firearm at his side emerged from a swinging door in the wall a few feet behind the hostess desk. He nodded to her as he strode forward, saying something in a low voice to the waiter behind the desk as he passed.

"Mr. Solitto's expecting you," he said, turning his attention back to Alina. "You can follow me."

She followed him through the dining area without a word and he led her to a set of double doors in the back corner. Opening one, he motioned for her to go in and Alina stepped through the door, keeping one eye on him as she did so.

She found herself in a private entertaining area capable of seating about thirty patrons. However, there were only four present. Frankie Solitto, the head of the New Jersey family, was seated at a table on the far side of the room with a man whom Viper immediately recognized as Stefan Delgado, his chief enforcer. Two bodyguards stood just inside the door and, as she entered, they turned toward her. The one on the right motioned for her to raise her hands and she sighed silently, raising them until they were level with her shoulders. Her eyes met Frankie's across the length of the room.

"Is this really necessary?" she asked, one eyebrow crooked.

He smiled faintly, the lines at the corners of his eyes deepening.

"Just a formality," he replied, watching as his guard began to pat her down. "I'm sure you understand."

Frankie Solitto was still an imposing personality, despite the fact that she had gotten to know him somewhat over the past year. He was on the taller side, with wide shoulders and graying hair along his temples. He still looked good for his age, and hadn't allowed himself to get soft around the middle as most older generation Italians did. He kept himself fit and solid, exuding an undeniable strength that would make anyone think twice before trying to take him on, physically or otherwise. His olive skin was beginning to show the lines of his age, but his deep-set eyes were still alert.

Alina never took her gaze from those eyes as her escort from the restaurant came in behind her and closed the door. The holster in the small of her back was empty, as was the one at her ankle that normally housed her combat knife. She had removed the weapons before entering the restaurant out of respect for Solitto. However, if the meathead running his hands all over her didn't stop his groping, her good intentions would go out the window.

The guard finally finished and looked over to Frankie with a nod, stepping back. Alina was just lowering her hands when she felt a hard, metal barrel press into her left kidney. Her eyes narrowed dangerously and there was a split second of deadly silence. She saw Frankie stiffen and Stefan reach for his weapon. That was all she needed to see.

Her left hand moved behind her as she spun swiftly to the left, grabbing the barrel of the 9mm and angling it upwards at the same time that her right leg hooked around the man's left leg. She pulled his leg out from under him and the pistol discharged, firing into the ceiling with a suppressed pop. Her attacker lost his balance, and she wrapped her arm around his neck as he began to fall, ripping the gun away from him with her other hand. Hauling him up against her as a shield, she turned to face the bodyguard who was groping her seconds before. He already had his weapon out, but before he could fire, Viper shot him in the forehead. He swayed, his eyes widening in shock, before he fell.

Viper felt rather than heard the other bodyguard move behind her. She kicked her human shield's knee, releasing her hold on his neck as he fell with a grunt. Presented with his head below her, she leveled a sharp blow to the back of his skull with the butt of her gun. Pivoting swiftly, she went low and swung her leg in an arc, sweeping the legs of the other bodyguard out from under him. He began to fall and, as he did so, she planted one hand on the floor and flipped herself into a one-handed hand-stand, hooking her other leg around his neck. With a quick movement, she used her leg to spin him around, snapping his neck. Following him down to the floor, she released her leg and landed easily on her feet in a crouch.

It was all over in seconds, and Viper raised her eyes to the two men at the table on the other side of the room. Her heart rate settled

Next Exit, No Outlet

again from the unexpected physical exertion and she straightened up from her crouched position slowly, her eyes on Frankie and Stefan. The low burning anger that was constantly present inside her these days tried to surface, but she tamped it down. Emotion had no place here.

Stefan had drawn his Glock and was just getting to his feet. As one, both he and Viper raised their weapons, pointing them at each other.

"You'd better start talking, Frankie," Viper advised, her voice icy.

Frankie reached out and pressed Stefan's arm down, lowering the Glock.

"That did *not* come from me," he said, pushing his chair back and standing. He came around the table and strode forward, his eyes on the three bodies on the floor. "I didn't authorize that."

Viper studied his face for a moment, then slowly lowered the gun, slipping her finger off the trigger. As soon as she lowered her weapon, Stefan slowly holstered his.

"Are they all dead?" he asked, his voice low and gravelly.

"Two are," she said. "The one who started it should be alive."

Frankie shot her a look under thick brows. "Why?"

"For information."

He grunted and nodded, then motioned to Stefan.

"Get him into a chair and secure him," he commanded, "and lock those doors."

Stefan nodded and came over to the group by the door. Alina watched as he bent down and pulled a leather belt off one of the corpses. He took it over to the double doors and looped it around the two handles, securing it tightly.

Frankie turned to Alina and held out his arm, motioning to the table.

"My apologies. Come sit down while Stefan takes care of Angelo," he said. "Keep the gun. In future, I'll understand if you prefer to come armed. That was inexcusable."

Alina glanced at Stefan, who had turned to the unconscious Angelo and was busy tying his wrists together with zip ties. Her lips trembled despite her wariness. Leave it to the mob to carry zip ties to lunch.

After a second of hesitation, she turned and walked with Frankie to the table across the room. Bowls of pasta and bread were in the center, along with a glass carafe of red wine and a pitcher of ice water. Frankie reached the table and pulled out the chair next to his for her to sit.

"Please."

Viper tucked the gun into her back holster before seating herself in the offered chair. He seated himself again, glancing at her.

"What happened to your neck?" he asked, motioning to the gauze bandage.

"This wasn't my first skirmish today," she replied, her voice even.

Frankie frowned.

"I don't like the sound of that," he said in a low voice, sitting back in his chair and studying her. "That sounds like things aren't going so well for you."

She smiled faintly. "Nothing I can't handle."

"That I don't doubt." He reached for his glass of water. "I heard about what happened to Agent Walker on Friday. Is she okay?"

Alina watched as Stefan hauled the unconscious Angelo into a chair and proceeded to tie his ankles to the chair legs.

"She's fine," she said shortly.

Frankie glanced at her. "And yet here you are, prepared to call in that favor I owe you."

Alina turned her dark eyes to his. "You see more than many would give you credit for."

He acknowledged that with a slight incline of his head, then motioned to the pasta and bread.

"Have you eaten? The penne vodka is particularly good."

"I'm fine, thank you."

Alina turned her head and watched as Stefan walked back to the table. Angelo was still out cold, but he had been tied securely into the chair. When he woke up, he wasn't going anywhere.

"I would introduce you to Stefan, but I don't think I've ever caught your name," Frankie said as his enforcer sat in the chair on the other side of him.

A swift, cold smile passed her lips. "You can call me Raven."

Frankie shot her a quick look under his eyebrows and then glanced at the man beside him.

"Stefan, meet Raven. Raven, Stefan."

Stefan nodded to her and she nodded back.

"Any idea why Angelo thought it would be a good idea to stick a gun in your back?" Frankie asked conversationally, reaching for a piece of garlic bread and going back to his lunch as if the interruption had never occurred.

"Aside from your ordering him to do so?"

Frankie frowned, glancing at her. "I already told you I had

Next Exit, No Outlet

nothing to do with that."

"Since when do your men do anything without your say so?" she asked softly, her gaze steady.

He set down his bread and sat back. "Since just now."

Stefan grunted.

"There's another possibility," he said gruffly, breaking his silence. "I heard something yesterday that might mean something."

Frankie and Viper looked at him and he shrugged. "Sorry, boss. I was gonna talk to you after your meeting with her."

Alina raised an eyebrow. "So talk now."

Stefan flicked her a look that would have made most men very nervous for their continued good health.

"It's Family business."

"It's my business now," she retorted coldly.

Frankie raised a hand placatingly.

"What did you hear?" he asked Stefan.

"It's the Casa Reinos Cartel, boss," he said reluctantly. "Some of the guys have been working with them."

Anger flared in Frankie's eyes and he stared at his enforcer in silence for a moment. When he finally broke the silence, his voice was soft and deadly.

"What?"

Stefan nodded and shifted uncomfortably in his seat.

"I think they've been bought. I've been putting together a list of names."

Alina turned her gaze to the two bodies near the door thoughtfully.

"And were they on it?" Frankie demanded, waving a hand toward the three inanimate figures.

"Yes."

"Then why the hell did you suggest they come today instead of Carlos and his brothers?"

Stefan looked at him steadily.

"Because I knew you'd want to take care of them. I figured after we were done talking, you wouldn't have to go far. I didn't know Angelo would try to clip her."

Alina turned her gaze to Stefan's face.

"Do you know who I am?" she asked softly.

Stefan shrugged.

"No, only that Frankie likes you," he replied. "And after what you just did, I can see why."

Frankie looked at her sharply.

"You know something," he stated, his eyes narrowing. "Does this have to do with that bandage on your neck and the trouble Ms. Walker seems to have gotten herself into?"

Alina's lips tightened. "If you had nothing to do with what just happened, then it would appear so."

Before he could reply, a low groan came from the chair across the room. Stefan looked at Frankie, who nodded before going back to his lunch. Stefan pushed his chair back and picked up one of the knives from the table.

"Are you sure about the penne?" Frankie asked her as Stefan walked over the chair. "I'd offer you something else, but the less people in here right now, the better."

Alina smiled in some amusement. "I'm not hungry."

Frankie picked up the carafe, pouring wine into two clean wine glasses. Across the room, Stefan stood behind Angelo's chair, waiting for him to open his eyes. Frankie pushed one of the glasses over to her.

"Then have a glass of wine," he said. "We can't have Angelo thinking you're not an honored guest."

Alina met his eyes and read the silent command in them. He wanted to present a united front, and a show of strength to his traitor. She nodded slowly and accepted the wine, setting it before her. Another groan emanated from the chair and Angelo's head rolled, then his eyes opened.

"What the…" he began, then stopped abruptly when he caught sight of Alina sitting next to Frankie. "You bitch!"

Angelo jerked on his arms as he tried to get up, then let out a string of curses as he realized his arms and legs were held securely against the chair. He jerked his arms, testing the strength of the zip ties, and cursed again when they held fast, cutting into his skin.

"What's going on?" he demanded angrily, glaring at Frankie. "What the hell, man?"

Frankie sipped his wine, setting the glass down purposefully before going back to his pasta. After a scooping a forkful of penne vodka into his mouth, he chewed while he considered Angelo in silence. Then, swallowing, he nodded to Stefan.

Stefan moved forward and looped a belt around Angelo's throat, pulling back sharply. He gasped for air and struggled against the unrelenting leather. His eyes began to bulge out of his head and his face was turning a peculiar shade of purple when Frankie finally made a movement with his hand. Stefan eased the pressure and Angelo gasped, sucking in deep gulps of air.

"You tell me, Angelo," Frankie said, reaching for another piece of garlic bread. "You're the one who pulled a gun on my guest and caused the deaths of two of my guards."

Angelo sputtered and tried to twist his head to look for the guards in question but Stefan tightened the belt again, preventing him from turning his head.

"I didn't kill anybody!" he yelped. "Yeah, I drew on her. So what? She's not one of us."

Frankie stared at him for a long moment, then slowly and deliberately put down his fork.

"I'll give you one chance," he said, holding up a long index finger. "One. Why?"

Angelo gaped at him, his eyes big, and sweat gathered on his forehead. Viper watched dispassionately as the man evaluated his options. It was clear that he was trying to determine how much Frankie already knew, and how much he could get away with saying. Unfortunately, he took too long and Frankie grew impatient. He nodded to Stefan and the belt was pulled tight around his neck again.

"How's the wine?" Frankie asked Viper, looking at her.

"Very good," she answered calmly, lifting the glass to her lips. "It's a novello, no?"

He raised his eyebrows and smiled slowly in surprise.

"You know your wines," he approved. "You're a woman after my own heart."

A choking sound pulled his attention back to the man in the chair and he watched as Angelo struggled, wrenching against the zip ties that bound him. Blood appeared at his wrists as the plastic cut through his skin, but it was doubtful if he realized it. Frankie nodded to Stefan and the pressure was eased again. As Angelo began gasping for air, Frankie pushed his chair back and stood, moving out from behind the table and walking toward the chair, the linen napkin from his lap still in his hand.

"Angelo, mio vecchio amico, you've been with me a long time," he said. "How long has it been now? Twelve years?"

"Fourteen," Angelo gasped out.

"Fourteen! And in all this time, haven't I taken care of you?" Frankie asked. "Didn't I see to it that your mother, God rest her soul, saw out her last years in relative comfort, with the best medical care money can buy?"

"Yes, boss."

"And didn't I step in when your son wanted to go to Brown? Didn't I make sure his application was accepted?"

"Yes, boss."

"Joey's a lawyer now, isn't he?" Frankie continued, his voice easy. "Works for a big firm in New York, isn't that right?"

"Boss, I..." Angelo began but Frankie waved him silent.

"You know why I did those things?" he asked, looking down at him. "Because loyalty deserves reward. You had been loyal to me, and you earned the right to be rewarded." Frankie looked at Stefan. "Take that belt away."

Stefan lifted the leather strap over Angelo's head and looked at his boss questioningly. While Angelo took deep breaths of free air, Frankie walked around the chair to join Stefan behind him. Without a word, he handed him the napkin and took the table knife, nodding to the back of Angelo's head. Stefan gave a barely perceptible nod and Frankie moved around to Angelo's other side.

"I don't like seeing you tied down like this," he said, laying his left hand on Angelo's shoulder. "We've known each other too long for this. We should be able to trust each other."

Angelo looked up at him, apprehension clear on his face.

"I do trust you," he stammered. "You're my Don."

Frankie nodded and clapped his shoulder.

"That's right," he agreed amenably. "I am. The problem is that I no longer trust you."

Stefan moved at the same time Frankie did, whipping the napkin around Angelo's head to pull it tight across his mouth as Frankie drove the knife through the center of Angelo's right hand. Angelo let out a scream that was muffled by the thick linen cloth pulled tightly across his lips.

Frankie turned to face him, placing a hand on either forearm and leaning down until he was inches from Angelo's face.

"That's for pulling a gun on my guest," he told him. "Now tell me why."

Angelo nodded and Stefan pulled the napkin away so he could speak.

"They're giving ten grand to whoever kills her," he gasped, sweat pouring down his face and mixing with the tears of pain streaming from his eyes. "She's got a bounty on her head. I was just trying to make some money."

Frankie straightened up and glanced over his shoulder at Alina. "You hear that?"

She nodded.

"Ten grand is a rip off," she told Angelo. "I've had ten times that placed on my head. You made a bad choice."

Frankie turned his gaze back to Angelo. "Who's paying this ten

Next Exit, No Outlet

grand?"

"The cartel," Angelo said. "They're offering it to anyone who gets to her."

Frankie studied him in silence for a long moment.

"Tell me when you started working with the Mexicans."

Angelo gulped. "I'm not—"

Stefan whacked him on the back of his head.

"No lies!" he snapped. "You tell your Don the truth."

Angelo let out a noise similar to a whimper.

"Six months ago," he gasped. "They said you're on your way out. Face it, Frankie, they're everywhere. They're taking over. The Family can't last much longer. Times change, and we have to change with them. They're already taking over Reyes' business. It's just a matter of time before we're next."

"How much did they pay you?"

"They didn't," Angelo said miserably. "They threatened my wife."

Frankie looked down at him, then shook his head.

"Angelo, you should have come to me first," he said sadly. "This was all so unnecessary. I'll always protect my Family."

"I know, boss. I should have come to you."

Frankie sighed again and bent down.

"Angelo, I'm going to pull this knife out of your hand now," he said. "Can you keep quiet? Or do we need the gag again?"

Angelo shook his head violently.

"I'll keep quiet."

Frankie nodded and gripped the hilt of the knife.

"Ready?" he asked.

Angelo nodded, clenching his jaw shut, and Frankie yanked the knife out.

"Good man," he said when Angelo let out only a muffled grunt. He leaned down again, his lips close to his ear. "Fourteen years, and it all comes down to this. Your loyalty is no longer to the Family, but mine will always be to yours."

With a swift movement, Frankie drove the knife deep into the side of Angelo's chest. Angelo's mouth opened, but no sound came out as the blade pierced one of his lungs, robbing him of breath.

"Your family will be taken care of," Frankie continued, pulling the knife out. "I see no reason for them to be punished with you."

With those words, Frankie plunged the knife into his heart and stepped back, leaving the knife in his chest. He watched as Angelo died, then held out a hand. Stefan handed him the napkin, and Frankie began wiping the blood off his hands.

"Make arrangements for the bodies," he told Stefan. "And make sure we know the names of everyone who's working with the cartel. We need to clean this up before it gets any worse."

Stefan nodded and pulled a cell phone out of his pocket. "On it."

Frankie finished wiping his hands and dropped the bloody napkin into Angelo's lap. Turning, he started back to the table where Alina waited.

"You knew about the bounty on your head?" he asked, circling to his chair.

"There are a lot of people coming after me," she replied. "It wasn't a surprise."

"I owe you an apology that it happened in my house." Frankie seated himself and looked at her. "There's no excuse I can offer. It should never have happened. You came unarmed into a trap."

Viper smiled faintly.

"I'm never unarmed. I don't need a weapon to kill. They're simply more expedient."

Frankie watched her thoughtfully for a second, then sat back. "Tell me how I can help."

She met his gaze. "You can repay that favor."

Next Exit, No Outlet

Chapter Twenty-Six

Alina walked up the steps to her deck, a rare smile breaking across her face as Buddy barked from the other side of the sliding door, his thick body wriggling in welcome. A sharp command from his master made him turn and trot over to stand beside the chair where Blake was working on his laptop. She stepped into the house and Stephanie looked up from her seat in the recliner. She took one look at Alina and gasped, swinging her legs down and grabbing her cane.

"What the hell happened?" she demanded, getting to her feet and hobbling as quickly as she could toward Alina.

At her words, Blake and Michael both look at her. Michael scowled and got to his feet.

"Nothing worth mentioning," Alina said, closing the door behind her.

"You have a bandage stuck to your neck!" Stephanie exclaimed. "That's not nothing."

"It's fine."

"What happened?" Michael asked, coming around the table and approaching from the other side.

Alina rolled her eyes and pushed them both away.

"It's nothing!" she exclaimed in exasperation. "Good Lord, you're worse than a pair of grandparents!"

Blake grinned from his chair.

"They've been antsy all day, waiting for you to come back," he told her as she passed him on her way to the bar.

"Do you blame us? Our numbers are dwindling, and *she's* the primary target," Stephanie snapped.

"I'm fine," Alina said with a sigh, dropping the keys to the Porsche onto the bar. "Where's Damon?"

"Locked in the den," Michael said, going back to his seat. "He's been in there for about two hours now."

Alina glanced around. Michael and Blake had taken over the dining room table, and Stephanie had claimed the recliner. She didn't blame Damon for hiding in the den. She would have done the same thing. She started for the hallway leading to the front of the house.

"Lina?"

Alina turned to glance at Stephanie. She was leaning on her cane, staring at her. Alina hesitated, then gave her a reassuring smile.

"I'm fine," she said before turning to go down the hall to the closed door at the end.

She opened the door and stepped into the small, closing the door behind her. Damon looked up from the desk where he had two laptops open and his eyes narrowed, going straight to the bandage on her neck.

"I thought you were just going to Angela's," he said, turning to face her and sitting back in the chair.

"You know things are never that simple," she muttered. "I'm starting to think I just have all round bad luck."

Damon frowned and stood up, coming towards her. "What happened?"

"Harry sent someone to her house to remove the surveillance camera," she told him tiredly. "I was there when he came in."

"Is that where you were all day?"

"It was big chunk of it," she said, lifting her face to accept the kiss he dropped on her lips. His arms went around her and she sighed, leaning against him briefly. "I made a mess and had to clean it up. Angela's going to need a new floor."

Damon pulled away and looked down into her face.

"You should have called me."

"I can clean up my own messes, thanks," she said with scoff. "Anyway, I want you here in case Harry manages to find this place. It was just an inconvenience."

Damon raised an eyebrow.

"That looks like more than an inconvenience," he said, motioning to her neck.

She waved a hand impatiently. "It's nothing. Just a scratch."

"Well, that scratch is bleeding through the bandage," he said bluntly.

Alina's eyes widened and her hand went to the gauze bandage. She frowned when her fingers came away damp with blood.

"No wonder Stephanie and Michael looked at me like I was dying," she said sheepishly. "It must have been aggravated when I had the fight with Solitto's goons."

It was Damon's turn to frown, and he did so fiercely, his eyebrows snapping together.

Next Exit, No Outlet

"Solitto!"

She shrugged. "I may have failed to mentioned that to you this morning."

"Damn right you did!"

They stared at each other in silence for a long moment, then Damon sighed.

"Come on. Let's go upstairs and get a new bandage on that."

Alina frowned.

"I can do it myself," she muttered, turning toward the door.

"I know you can, but I want to see it for myself," he retorted, close behind her. "Humor me."

Alina rolled her eyes and went out of the den. The stairs were across from the door and she went right to them without glancing down the hall to the living room. Climbing the steps with Damon behind her, she shook her head. This was turning into a farce. She felt like she was sneaking around her own house, for God's sake.

She reached the second floor and turned to stride down the hallway to the master bedroom. Angela's orange tabby cat peeked out from one of the spare rooms and slinked into the hallway as she passed. Anabelle let out a sound that was a cross between a chirp and a meow and Alina paused, glancing down. The cat strolled over to her and rubbed her face against Alina's calf, looking up at her.

"Oh Bella," she murmured, bending down to lift the tabby into her arms. "I forgot all about you."

She was rewarded with a rash of purring as Anabelle curled into her arms contentedly.

"She tried to get into your bedroom this morning," Damon said, his voice low in her ear. "I closed the door after that. The last thing we need is Raven making a meal out of Angela's cat."

Alina glanced at him with a smile.

"Thank you." She reached out and opened the door to the bedroom, setting the cat down in the hall. "Sorry, Bella. That's one fight you don't want to have."

She and Damon and went through the door and she closed it firmly in the cat's face. Anabelle voiced her displeasure with a loud yowl before pawing at the door.

"Why doesn't she go downstairs?" Damon asked, following Alina to the bathroom. "She's obviously missing Angela."

"Because Buddy's down there. She's not a fan of dogs."

Damon leaned against the vanity and watched as she bent down to pull the toolbox that housed her first aid kit out from under the sink.

"Did she tell you that?" he teased.

Alina shot him a look of amusement. "Very funny."

"Hey, you're the one who communicates with animals," he said with a grin. "I'm just trying to figure out how."

"Not by talking," she said, setting the toolbox next to him on the vanity and opening the lid. Then she turned to look in the mirror. "Holy cow!"

The exclamation came out unexpectedly as she stared at the blood-soaked bandage on her neck. It looked like something out of a horror movie.

"Exactly."

Alina carefully removed the useless gauze square and examined her neck. Blood was seeping steadily from the cut and she reached for the box of tissues on the vanity. Damon shook his head and reached around her to grab a clean washcloth.

"You're going to need more than a tissue," he said, turning on the faucet in the sink and holding the cloth under the stream of water.

He gently turned her chin so he could start cleaning the blood off the wound. Alina made a face but allowed him to carefully wipe away the excess blood from her neck so they could see what they were dealing with. She watched his face as he focused on the gash, his lips pressed together grimly. The set of his jaw showed his concern and a rush of warmth went through her.

"What did this?"

He finally broke the silence as he finished washing away the blood, turning to drop the wash cloth into the trash can.

"A knife," she said reluctantly. "I saw it just in time, or I wouldn't be here."

His eyes met hers briefly and his jaw clenched, then he tilted her head so he could get a better look at the cut. After a minute, he shook his head.

"This needs to be stitched. It's deep, and it's not showing any signs that it will stop bleeding. Do you have thread?"

Alina motioned to the toolbox reluctantly and Damon turned to rummage through it until he found the plastic container with packages of sterile nylon thread. He pulled out a needle and looked at her.

"Do you have a lighter I can use to sterilize the needle?"

Alina nodded and turned to go into the bedroom. A moment later, she was back and handing him a cigarette lighter.

"Hop up on the counter," he said, taking it.

She moved the toolbox down and jumped up to perch on the

Next Exit, No Outlet

edge of the vanity, watching as he carefully threaded the nylon through the needle.

"Tell me about Frankie," he said. He didn't even lift his eyes from his task and his tone made it clear that he'd brook no argument.

"I went to find out what the story was with the cartel," she said, shifting on the vanity counter to get more comfortable. "I also decided it's time to call in that favor he owes me."

Damon looked up at that.

"What do you have planned?" he demanded. "I thought you were never going to call that favor in."

"I wasn't, but the situation has changed. Things are more complicated than I thought they would be, and we're going to need manpower."

"You think?" he muttered, switching on the lighter and holding the prepped needle over the flame. "Are you sure about using him?"

"Yes. He's perfectly able to handle what I asked, and his boys won't talk. In fact, I think he's looking forward to it," she added thoughtfully.

"Are you going to tell me what the plan is, or am I just along for the ride?"

Alina smiled.

"We'll go over it when we're done here. I need to get into the command center, though, and I have no idea how we're going to do that with the Three Stooges down there."

"Buddy will need to be walked. I'll convince Michael and Blake to do a full perimeter check. That should buy us about half an hour, if not longer."

"And Stephanie?"

"How hard can it be to convince her to take a nap?" Damon turned off the flame and looked up. "You ready?"

"Would it matter if I wasn't?"

"Nope."

"Then let's get it done."

Something like a laugh lit his blue eyes and Damon stepped close to her, turning her head gently so that he had access to the wound.

"You said you had a fight with Frankie's bodyguards," he said, his voice low as he tried to distract her just before the needle pierced the tender flesh on her neck.

Searing pain through her neck and Alina sucked in her breath, then clenched her jaw.

"Yes. One of them pulled a gun on me."

"You were unarmed?"

"Not for long, once he did that," she said dryly, sucking in her breath again as another searing flash of pain shot through her. "Turns out some of Frankie's faithful have defected over to the cartel. He was one of them, along with the two other guards."

"And he went after you why?"

"The cartel has a bounty on my head. It's damned insulting, actually."

Damon's eyes flicked to her face before going back to her neck.

"Why? How much?"

"Only ten grand. Hell, it's not even worth putting bullets in the gun for that," Alina said disgustedly.

"It's certainly not worth getting killed over," Damon agreed. "I'm assuming they *are* dead?"

"Yes. I think Frankie's enforcer has a crush on me now. He was practically drooling."

Damon was surprised into a laugh. "He saw?"

"He and Frankie were both in the room when it happened. I'm not sure what they thought was going to happen. Stefan was reaching for his gun and Frankie was furious with them when I took matters into my own hands. The guards never had a chance. What the hell were they thinking?"

"About ten grand, apparently." Damon paused, then looked at her. "This will hurt, babe. I'm sorry. I'm at the middle and it's wide."

Alina met his gaze. "Thanks for the warning."

He lowered his eyes again and she braced for the pain she knew was coming. She'd stitched herself before without any pain killers, but it was never in a sensitive place like her neck. Most of her injuries ended up being torso hits, with a few notable exceptions.

Conversation stopped as blinding pain resonated through her neck and down her jaw. Clenching her hands around the edge of the counter, Alina concentrated on taking deep and even breaths, willing the pain away. It wasn't working, but it was keeping her occupied while Damon steadily made his way along the length of the gash. Just when she was convinced she couldn't take it anymore, he pulled the needle away and set it on the counter.

"You still with me?" he asked, glancing into her face.

"Of course," she muttered, annoyed when her voice sounded strained.

He grinned and tied off the thread. "Good."

Next Exit, No Outlet

He reached past her to the toolbox and pulled out a sealed gauze bandage.

"I'm not saying I have a future in the medical profession, but this isn't half bad."

"I don't look like Frankenstein?"

"Maybe just a little," he admitted, tearing open the package and pulling out the gauze square. "Don't worry. I didn't marry you for your looks," he added with a wink.

Alina shook her head and twisted on the counter to get a glimpse of her neck in the mirror. She grimaced at the line of black stitches, but it wasn't as bad it could have been.

"That should heal up pretty well," she decided after examining it for a moment. "Thank you."

She turned back to face him and Damon laid the bandage over the stitches. Lifting her hand to hold it in place while he reached for the tape, she sighed.

"I'm feeling more and more like the walking wounded," she muttered. "How's your side?"

"Muscles are still sore, but I'm almost there," he said, tearing off pieces of tape and sticking them along the edge of the counter. "The running in the morning is helping to build my strength back up. I feel almost back to normal."

Alina nodded and was silent for a moment, then she shook her head.

"I'll tell you this," she said, her voice controlled, "now I'm pissed. I've got the bastards coming from all directions."

Damon set the roll of tape down and picked up one of the strips, turning to her again. He replaced her hand with his on the bandage and taped one side down.

"What did Frankie have to say about the cartel?" he asked, reaching for another strip.

"He and Reyes are working together to get them out. Frankie's going after the cartel members, and Reyes is making sure the gangs they infiltrated are solidly back on the Family's side. Frankie seems to think they can contain it between them."

"And the ones in his own house?"

"You mean, aside from the three from today?" she shrugged. "He's taking care of it."

Damon finished taping the bandage down and turned to wash his hands.

"If Harry promised Salcedo an open market up the coast, then Solitto will have to deal with more than just the low-level players," he said, lathering his hands with soap. "Harry will have people helping in Washington and in local governments."

"Frankie's already identified two of them," Alina said with a grin. "He's got people in high places, too. I have to hand it to him, the man is a formidable force. I'm glad he's on my side."

Damon grunted. "Men like that switch sides in an instant. You know that."

A cold smiled crossed her lips.

"I also know that he's well aware of what I'm capable of."

Damon turned off the water and dried his hands, looking at her pensively for a long moment.

"I'm more concerned with keeping you alive long enough to get through this," he finally said in a low voice. Tossing the hand towel onto the counter, he moved to stand in front of her. "This was too close for comfort," he said, motioning to her neck.

Alina reached out and slipped her hands around his waist, pulling him closer.

"I have no intention of letting you off that easy," she murmured, her eyes twinkling mischievously as they met his. "I've got too much invested in this now. I'm not going anywhere."

Damon slid his arms around her and leaned his forehead against hers.

"We have no say in when our time comes. You know that."

"Then there's no point in worrying about it," she pointed out. "Let's just make the most of what time we have."

He smiled slowly and lowered his mouth to hers, his lips moving overs hers warmly.

"I won't argue with that," he murmured against her mouth, pulling her up against him firmly.

Alina's eyes slid closed and she relaxed against him, confident that she had successfully distracted him. It wouldn't last, she knew, but at least he wasn't worrying about her right this second. And neither was she.

The kiss began as a distraction, but quickly turned ravenous as desire exploded between them. Alina shifted against him and they both groaned. No matter what happened, this attraction between them was volatile and undeniable, and Alina was incapable of doing anything but surrender to it. All thoughts of their very uncertain future faded under the onslaught of pure, raw passion coursing through her.

Damon pressed her against him as if he couldn't get close enough and stars exploded behind her eyelids as she dropped her hands to his hips. She slid them under his shirt and her heart started pounding

Next Exit, No Outlet

as she touched his warm skin. He made a sound deep in his throat and was just reaching for his shirt when a sound made its way through the haze of desire.

Someone was knocking on the bedroom door.

He lifted his head, his breathing ragged, and glanced at the open bathroom door. Alina opened her eyes, trying to catch her breath as he brought his gaze back to her. His eyes were dark with desire and he exhaled loudly, leaning his forehead against hers. They both breathed deeply, then she sighed and gently pushed him away from her.

"Full house," she muttered, disgruntled. "I told you this would suck."

Despite his frustration, Damon chuckled and moved away from her. Alina slid off the vanity, landing on shaky legs, and turned to head out of the bathroom.

"Later," he promised, watching her go.

She glanced over her shoulder and the look on his face sent another wave of heat clear through her.

"I'll hold you to that."

Chapter Twenty-Seven

Alina moved out of the bathroom, striding around the corner and to the closed bedroom door. She took a deep, calming breath before opening it. Stephanie stood before her, holding Anabelle in her arms.

"Are you okay?" she asked, frowning in concern.

Alina stifled a frustrated laugh.

"I could be a lot better," she said dryly, turning to move back into the bedroom, "but I'm fine."

"I came up to get my pain killers and saw the door to the den open," Stephanie said, following her. "I figured I'd make sure everything was good. I see you changed the bandage. Are you sure you're all right?"

Alina shot her a sheepish look and sank onto the foot of the bed.

"Damon just finished stitching it up," she admitted. "It was deeper than I thought."

Stephanie gasped. "He did it? Why didn't you go to Urgent Care?"

"Why would I go to Urgent Care?"

"What do you mean why?" Stephanie scowled. "Because that's what you do when you need stitches. They have the right equipment."

"You mean a needle and thread?" Alina demanded, amused. "I have that."

"Oh, pardon me. Does it come in your pre-made assassin kit?"

"Yes. We keep it right next to the cyanide pill," Damon said, coming out of the bathroom.

Stephanie looked at him. "Very funny. How bad was it?"

"I've seen worse," he replied with a shrug. "It just needed some help closing up."

Stephanie shook her head and dropped onto the bed next to Alina, the orange tabby cat still in her arms.

"Do you see why Michael and I were worried now?" she demanded. "You were gushing blood!"

Next Exit, No Outlet

Alina raised an eyebrow. "Gushing is a bit of an exaggeration."

"Streaming, then."

"More like seeping," Damon said, amused. He glanced at Alina, desire still simmering deep in his eyes, then turned and headed for the door. "I'm going to get something to eat. I'm suddenly starving."

Alina felt a laugh bubbling inside her at the disgruntled note in his voice but tamped it down.

"How can he eat after sewing up your neck?" Stephanie demanded as he disappeared down the hall.

"He can always eat."

"Well, I'm glad he left. I want to talk to you." Stephanie bent down and set Anabelle on the floor. "We haven't had much of a chance the past two days."

Alina looked at her apprehensively. "Talk about what?"

"You."

She turned to face her and Alina inwardly grimaced. She knew that look. This wasn't going to be pleasant.

"More specifically, what you do for a living and what you've become. We've been avoiding the topic for almost a year. It's time to discuss it."

"To what purpose? It won't change anything."

"No, but I want to understand. I thought I could just pretend that that part of you didn't exist, and we could continue as we have been, but I can't. Especially not after the other night."

"I'm not sure what you're trying to understand. You know what I do. You've seen me do it. It's not a puzzle that you need to solve."

Stephanie sighed impatiently.

"This isn't about your work," she snapped. "It's about *you*. Last summer, when I watched you kill Regina, it was like watching a stranger. There wasn't any part of you that I recognized. You moved and spoke like someone who wasn't even a human being. Over the months since then, I managed to convince myself that you were angry at the time and so you were being reckless."

Alina looked at her, her face impassive. Stephanie continued, ignoring the unnerving stare.

"But the other night, I saw it again. You become this terrifying person who doesn't have any fear or regard for her own safety. You really *are* reckless, and I need to understand why. Why do you have this death wish?"

Alina raised an eyebrow, amused. "A death wish? Do I?"

"Yes! Last summer, you let Regina beat you to within an inch of your life—"

"Hardly," she interjected dryly.

"And then the other night, you showed up with a handgun to confront men with automatic rifles in full body armor," Stephanie continued relentlessly. "It was suicide. You weren't even wearing a vest!"

"I wasn't aware there was a dress code for saving my best friend from a hit team."

"Will you be serious?!" she snapped. "I'm trying to have a serious conversation."

"I'm still trying to figure out what you feel you need to understand," Alina replied. "I don't carry bulletproof vests in my car. I wasn't expecting to run into a full team on Friday. It's not like I had time to plan for it. I worked with what I had."

"You didn't even take cover behind the van," Stephanie retorted. "You walked down the middle of the aisle, in full firing range, without blinking. It's just plain luck mixed with pixie dust that you weren't shot point blank right there!"

"Mmmm…it was a little more than luck and pixie dust," Alina said, amused again. "I don't leave anything to chance."

"That's not what it looks like to me."

Alina studied her thoughtfully for a moment, then got up and walked aimlessly over to the dresser. Perhaps it would help Stephanie to learn a little about how she worked. It couldn't change anything, but it might help prepare her for what was coming.

"What happens when you fire an automatic weapon through a window from inside a car?" she asked, glancing at Stephanie.

Stephanie looked at her blankly. "What?"

"Humor me. What do you think happens?"

"The glass breaks."

"And the shooter?"

"I don't…what are you getting at?"

"Most people won't fire an automatic through a windshield from inside the vehicle," Alina said, turning and pacing back. "First, it's ungodly loud, and second, the barrel is typically too long to aim without hitting the glass, which is no good. The smarter choice is a handgun."

"Ok, but you didn't know he didn't have a handgun!"

"It wouldn't have mattered." Alina paused and looked down at her. "When you fire a 9mm handgun from inside the windshield, the bullet deflects up when it passes through the laminated glass. If he had managed to get the first round through, which isn't guaranteed, the

Next Exit, No Outlet

shot would have lost much of its velocity and would be off-target. If, in the more likely scenario, his first shot didn't make it through, the second would, and he would have presumably corrected his aim. It would also have better velocity because it would have gone through already weakened glass."

"All the more reason..." Stephanie stopped when Alina held up her hand.

"IF that's what he had done, I would have had a warning shot to dive out of the way," she said. "But that's all assuming that he was thinking fast enough to shoot through the windshield. Human nature is still human nature. When a heavily-armed and protected person sees someone coming towards them unprotected, and in an apparently suicidal move, instinct is to hesitate. At our core, we are all human, and humans have doubt. If you think someone is crazy, you pause to evaluate how best to proceed."

Stephanie stared at her, nonplussed. "You're saying you did that on purpose?"

"In that instance, yes." Alina shrugged. "But just in case you think I'm completely insane, there's a reason I carry a .45. Not much will slow down a .45 caliber round, even a windshield. If he had shot through the windshield, I can guarantee my shot would have gone through his head before his second round made it out."

"You couldn't have known all that in the couple seconds it took for that SUV to stop," Stephanie protested. "That's ridiculous!"

"No, that's how I was trained. I have to make judgment calls and decisions in seconds, not minutes, and usually under less than ideal conditions. If I make the wrong one, I die. Trust me when I say that I've gotten rather good at making the right decisions most of the time."

Stephanie shook her head, staring up at her wordlessly. Alina sighed and sat down next to her again.

"You think I'm crazy," she said. "You think I'm suicidal. I'm not. I've been trained to be highly focused and to anticipate how any given person will react to any situation. I evaluate everything, every likely attack and every possible outcome, and then adjust accordingly. I've learned to do it in seconds. That's why I'm one of the best at what I do."

"One of?" Stephanie asked, her voice cracking.

Alina smiled faintly. "Damon's the other. We're still alive because we can adapt and adjust."

Stephanie was silent for a long while, her lips pressed together in a thin line.

"And that's why you think you can go after Colonel Shore?"

she finally asked.

"I don't think I can. I will."

"If he's the one who trained you how to adapt, I don't see that your ninja skills will be much good."

"Oh, I'll have more than just my .45, don't worry."

"I still think it's suicide. Let's discuss other options. There has to be another way."

Alina exhaled loudly and got up impatiently.

"We've gone over this frontwards and backwards," she said, turning to go over to the window. "There's nothing more to say."

"I know you think I'm being naive and dramatic," Stephanie said after a moment, watching as Alina looked out the window and up into the sky.

"I don't think that at all," Alina said absently, scanning the tree tops.

"What are you doing?" Stephanie asked, distracted.

"Looking for Raven."

Stephanie gasped and looked around for the cat.

"Oh my God, I forgot about the hawk," she exclaimed. "Where's Anabelle? I'll put her outside the door."

"She went under the bed." Alina turned away from the window. "I'll get her out of the room when we're done. I don't see him out there, so I think we're safe for right now."

"Angela will kill me if anything happens to that cat, and I wouldn't blame her." Stephanie shifted on the bed. "You don't think I'm being dramatic?" she asked after a moment. "I mean, about Colonel Shore, not the cat. Obviously."

"No, I don't think you're being dramatic. You're worried. I understand."

"I'm flat out terrified. Blake was telling me some of the stories about Harry. The man's a legend, Lina, and for good reason! He's brilliant, and he never fails."

Alina's lips thinned unpleasantly. "Neither do I."

"But that's just it! You've never gone up against your instructor! He's dangerous. And yes, I know that everyone you face is dangerous, but this is the man who gets paid to know more than you. He taught you everything you know. You don't think he kept some things back for himself?"

"I'm sure he did," Alina said, turning to move restlessly across the room. "But I know I've picked up a lot since then, and he hasn't been active in the field for years. I have. That gives me an advantage."

Stephanie snorted.

Next Exit, No Outlet

"Don't let that cane of his fool you," she said. "Blake said he's just as deadly now as he was twenty years ago."

"Oh, the cane's just for show," Alina agreed. "I know for a fact that Harry still runs every morning and goes to the weight room three times a week."

"See? I rest my case."

"What case? You haven't presented one yet. So far all you've said is that Harry is dangerous, which I know better than most."

"Alina, remember that time we went to the Poconos for the weekend and I didn't want to go out on the lake in that sketchy boat?" Stephanie asked. "Remember how I had a bad feeling all night and in the morning I begged you not to go?"

Alina paused and looked at her, memories rushing back from the distant past. She nodded slowly.

"Yes."

"You gave in and we went to the pool instead. Do you remember what happened to the boat?"

Alina stood very still, staring at Stephanie. When she finally spoke, her voice was quiet and her shoulders were tight.

"The engine caught fire in the middle of the lake. Two of the passengers were killed."

"Well, I feel the same exact way now when I think of you going after the colonel," Stephanie told her earnestly. "Don't go. It's suicide. Let someone else handle it."

Alina was quiet for a moment, a chill going through her despite the warmth in the bedroom. Raising her eyes, she looked into her old friend's face and slowly shook her head.

"I can't."

"Why not?" Stephanie demanded, her eyes searching Alina's. "Help me understand. Why does it have to be you?"

Alina sighed and went over to sit next to her again.

"I have to do this, Steph," she said slowly, carefully. She turned to face her, meeting her gaze squarely. "I know it's hard, but try to understand. I don't live in the same world you do. My world is…very different. It has to be. I have to see and do things that you can't possibly imagine, and I do it so that you can live your life in relative freedom and peace. I went into this life with my eyes wide open, holding absolutely no illusions about how it would end. There are no happy endings for people like me and Damon; we don't get that luxury. There'll be no big funeral or parade when we go. No one will even know we're gone. As far as the world knows, as far as the majority of our *government* knows, we don't exist. So, you see, I never expected to live to a grand old age, watching my grandchildren play in the yard."

"So just because you don't think you'll survive, it's okay to take a suicide mission and speed it up?" Stephanie asked. "Lina, don't be an idiot."

"I'm not being an idiot, I'm being practical and trying to explain. If it's my time to go, I can't think of a better way to do it than while killing the man who killed my brother and John."

Stephanie stared at her, understanding breaking across her face.

"This is vengeance," she breathed. "You're talking about payback."

"And making amends." Alina got up again and took another restless turn around the room. "I brought all this back here and dragged you, Angie and John into my mess. John's dead now, and Angela is being held as bait to get to me. Your brain is scrambled egg right now, and you can't walk without a stick because a bullet that was meant for me hit you instead. I brought this down on all of you."

Alina stopped pacing in front of Stephanie and looked down at her.

"Let me make this right. I *have* to make this right: for John, for Angela, and for you. This is the only way."

Stephanie's eyes filled with tears.

"Even if it means we never see you again?" she whispered.

Alina's eyes slid away from hers. "Yes."

Silence fell in the bedroom and Alina turned to pace back to the window. She knew Stephanie didn't fully understand, but she couldn't explain it any other way. This had to end now, or none of them would ever be safe again. And Dave and John would never be avenged.

Alina's lips tightened and her spine stiffened. If Stephanie's sudden tears had made her question for a second if this was really necessary, the thought of Dave and John both being murdered in cold blood reinforced her resolve. The bastard was going to pay for both of them.

"Damon will be with you?" Stephanie asked from the bed, breaking the silence.

"Yes." Alina turned away from the window. "We make a good team, funnily enough. He'll watch my back."

Stephanie sniffled and nodded.

"Well, tell him if he lets you die, he'll have me to deal with."

Chapter Twenty-Eight

Hawk stared at her, his chiseled jaw clenched and lips pressed together in a grim line. "Absolutely not!" he exclaimed. "Are you out of your mind?"

Viper stared back at him steadily.

"It's the only way."

"It's suicide, and you know it!" He punctuated his statement by pointing at her, then turning to stride impatiently to the far end of the command center. "It's completely insane."

Alina watched him as he ran a hand through his hair before turning to face her again. He was still for a long moment, then he strode back towards her.

"I'm not opposed to taking risks," he said, his voice calmer but still hard, "but this is taking it too far. There are too many variables we can't control and too much that can go wrong. Hell, if our timing is off by even a second..."

His voice trailed off and he spun around to take another restless turn around the narrow room.

"I don't see another way," she said quietly. "I've had to adjust for the *Sea Queen*. The yacht complicates things. This is the only way I can guarantee that Harry doesn't get away."

Hawk shot her a look carved in stone. "But at what cost?"

She shrugged and turned her gaze back to the plasma screens on the wall, focusing on the one with a blueprint of the *Sea Queen*.

"Since when do we think of the cost?"

"Since we decided to try to make this work," he retorted, striding back. He grabbed her shoulders and turned her to face him, staring down into her face. "There's no way this ends with both of us walking away. You know that."

Alina looked into his blue eyes and, for the first time ever, saw fear lurking in their depths.

"Possibly not, but at least our job will be done," she said softly.

"Will it? *Is* this our job? Did Charlie actually make this an official op? Because last time I checked, our own personal vendettas weren't part of the mission statement."

"Yes, it's an official non-official op. I wouldn't be dragging so many people into it if it wasn't, especially Michael." Alina lifted her hands and rested them on his chest. "If you can think of another way, I'm all ears. This is the only fool-proof plan I can think of that will get me to Harry *and* get Angela back alive."

Damon tilted his head back and exhaled, dropping his hands from her shoulders. He turned to stare at the plasmas on the wall and crossed his arms, leaning back against the counter that stretched the length of the room. He was quiet for a long while, and she reached for her bottle of water. Her neck was throbbing painfully and her stomach rumbled, reminding her that she hadn't eaten anything since early this morning. Taking a long drink, she glanced at Hawk's profile, noting the set of his jaw. For the first time, she had a tremor of doubt. If he wouldn't get behind this and work with her, the plan was dead in the water. Harry would get away with everything, and Angela's chances slipped down to nothing. She needed Hawk.

"Do we even have confirmation that she's onboard?"

His voice jolted her out of her thoughts and she set the water down, turning to type on a keyboard.

"This is the truck from the camera footage behind Angie's house," she said, pulling up the surveillance footage.

Damon turned and looked at the monitor. "Ok."

"This is the entrance to a marina in Georgia at four-thirty this morning."

The image changed to footage of the same pickup truck pulling through the marina gates. Alina zoomed in on the cab, blowing the picture up until they could clearly see the profile of the driver.

"Is that him?" Damon asked, glancing at her.

She nodded. "That's the man from Rittenhouse."

He rubbed the back of neck, turning his eyes back to the image.

"I don't see another passenger."

"If I was transporting a kidnapped woman, I'd make sure she was drugged and out like a light. If she was lying in the backseat, we wouldn't see her."

Damon turned his head to the map on one of the plasmas on the wall.

"And this is in Georgia?"

"Yes. St. Simons Island. He entered, but hasn't left yet."

Hawk glanced at her.

Next Exit, No Outlet

"If he has a boat there, he won't leave in the truck," he said unnecessarily.

"Exactly."

"This doesn't prove Angela's on the *Sea Queen*. It just indicates that she was taken to a boat."

Alina smiled coldly. "Which is precisely why Charlie is pulling satellite footage."

He stared at her for a beat, then shook his head, a reluctant grin crossing his face.

"Of course he is."

"I contacted him this morning. Of course, that was before he contacted me."

Damon looked at her sharply. "What?"

"I have to go to DC."

His lips tightened briefly and his eyes probed hers. "Why?"

She shook her head.

"I don't know. He wouldn't say. He said he had something that I needed to see."

"I don't like it," Damon said, shaking his head. "Why call you down there? I thought you said you wouldn't see him now until it was over."

"I didn't think I would. Trust me. I don't like it any more than you do."

He was silent for a long moment, then turned to her.

"Be on your guard down there," he said in a low voice. "I don't like this at all. When will you be back?"

Her eyes met his. "That depends entirely on what he has for me."

Damon nodded. "When are you leaving?"

"Around six."

He glanced at his watch.

"That doesn't give us much time," he said, turning back to the plasmas on the wall. "Tell me what arrangements I can take care of here while you're gone. If Angela *is* on that yacht, we're running out of time."

Alina sighed silently in relief, aware of a load of tension leaving her shoulders.

Hawk was in.

245

Alina looked up when a plate containing a ham and cheese sandwich on whole grain sprouted bread was set next to her laptop. She looked at Damon in surprise.

"What's this?"

"You haven't eaten since this morning," he replied, sitting next to her at the bar with his own sandwich. "You need to eat, and I know you won't stop on your way to DC."

She stretched and glanced into the dining room. Michael was intently studying his computer screen, earbuds in, oblivious to everything around him. Stephanie was still upstairs, and Blake had disappeared as well.

"It's too risky to stop for food," she murmured, reaching for the sandwich. "You know that."

"That's why I made you a sandwich."

Alina took a bite and turned her eyes back to the laptop. "Anything new on your side?" she asked after swallowing.

"I'm still waiting to hear from my girl in Guerrero. I should hear tonight if she could dig anything up."

Alina glanced at him. "Do you think she'll find something?"

"I don't know, but I'll tell you this: if there's something to find, she'll sniff it out."

She nodded and took another bite of her sandwich, dismissing the unknown contact from her mind.

"How's it going with the camera footage from Angela's house?" he asked after a moment of silence.

"I just got in. I'm pulling up the footage from Stephanie's now."

He leaned over to look at her screen as she opened the footage from the wireless camera they'd left in Stephanie's apartment a few nights before. The camera position gave them a clear view of the living room, dining room and front and back doors.

Alina clicked a button and began forwarding through the footage, moving that screen to the side and pulling up the camera from Angela's house. They watched as the footage from Angela's began with a view of the living room partially obscured by what looked like a hand.

"I guess he didn't bother to set the camera remotely," Damon murmured.

"It probably never occurred to him that it would be found," she said, watching as the hand shifted and the whole first floor came into focus. "Sloppy, but not really surprising."

They watched as the camera shifted slightly, then stilled. A few seconds later, a tall man came into view. He looked straight at the camera and Alina paused the footage, freezing the full image of his face.

"Hawk, meet the third player from Rittenhouse."

Damon studied the face for a moment. "Send that photo to me," he said after a moment. "I'll run it and find out who he is."

She nodded and her fingers moved over the keys rapidly.

"See if you can get a hit before I meet Charlie," she said, glancing at him. "If he's one of us, I want to know before I walk into that meeting."

He nodded. "Agreed."

Alina turned her attention back to the camera from Stephanie's apartment and reached for her sandwich while she watched the hours roll by without movement. She was halfway through her ham and cheese when the back door slid open and a shadow fell across the wall in the dining room. Reaching out, she clicked play and the footage slowed down to real-time.

"Here we go."

She and Damon watched as a lone, tall figure moved into the dining room. He slid the door closed and paused, looking around slowly before moving through the dining room. He passed the table and turned to go down the hall towards the bedrooms, moving out of camera view.

"He's going for the safe," Damon said.

Alina nodded, finishing her sandwich while they waited for the intruder to come back into the living room.

"He's probably the one who hit Steph over the head," she said after a moment. "He didn't even look twice at all the papers on the table. He already knows what he's looking for isn't there."

Damon nodded, then glanced over his shoulder at the hallway leading to the front of the house.

"Here she comes," he said in a low voice. "Do you want her to see this?"

Alina shrugged. "It makes no difference."

Stephanie came down the hall slowly, leaning on her cane, as Alina and Damon continued to watch the footage.

"What are you watching?" she asked, hobbling up behind them. "Anything good?"

"Not especially, no," Alina said, glancing over her shoulder. "How do you feel?"

"About the same as when I laid down," she replied with a shrug. "At lease my headache is starting to ease up."

247

She looked over Alina's shoulder and let out a gasp. "That's my living room!"

Alina nodded. "Yes. When we went to get Buddy the other night, I put a wireless camera in your apartment as a precaution."

Stephanie gaped at her. "A precaution against what?!"

"Not against, in case of," Alina said. "In case someone came back."

"And did they?"

"Yes." Damon finished his sandwich and looked at Stephanie. "When I went to get your meds, your place was trashed."

"What?!" Stephanie looked from one to the other. "And you didn't tell me?!"

Alina looked at her and shrugged. "I haven't exactly had time."

Stephanie huffed and leaned her cane, watching the footage. "Well, it looks fine there," she pointed out.

"That's because the intruder is in your bedroom right now."

Stephanie let out another gasp. "You mean you saw someone go in?"

Damon picked up his empty plate and got up, grabbing Alina's plate as he did so.

"Why don't you sit down?" he suggested, moving into the kitchen.

Stephanie took his seat and stared at Alina's screen. "I don't understand. They were already there. Why go back?"

"To make sure they didn't miss anything," Alina replied, stretching. "Damon said the safe in your closet was open when he was there, but all the cash, ammunition and your backup weapons were still in it. He was looking for John's hard drive."

"And when he didn't find it, he trashed the place?" Stephanie demanded incredulously. "Why go through the trouble?"

"To make it look like a break-in that got interrupted," Damon said from the kitchen.

Stephanie scowled and watched the screen. The scowl grew when the tall man finally moved back into the camera frame.

"Is that him?"

Alina nodded silently, watching as he paused in the living room to look around slowly. After a moment, he went over to the dining room table and calmly and systematically began to pull everything off the table, throwing it on the floor. Stephanie sucked in her breath and they watched as he went through the dining room and living room, overturning furniture, pulling picture frames from the walls, and generally ransacking the rooms.

Next Exit, No Outlet

"Oh my God, is that really necessary?" Stephanie exclaimed. "What the hell?!"

Alina didn't reply, watching as the assassin moved into the kitchen and out of sight of the camera, presumably to do the same in there. So far, he hadn't looked once in the direction of the camera, denying her a full-face image. Based on the height and profile, she was certain it was the same man she had killed this morning at Angela's, but she wanted to be sure.

"Well?" Damon asked from the other side of the bar, his eyes on her face.

She shook her head, not looking up from the screen.

"It's not him," she said. "I think it's the one who came at me this morning, but he hasn't given the camera a full shot yet."

"Wait, what?" Stephanie looked at her. "This is the person who did that to your neck?"

Alina glanced at her. "I think so."

"Where were you?"

Alina didn't answer immediately, watching instead as the man emerged from the kitchen. He paused outside the kitchen, looking around at his handiwork, then he finally looked up and toward the vent above the hallway. Alina clicked pause to freeze the frame, then lifted her eyes to Damon's.

"It's the one from this morning," she told him.

Damon came around the bar and looked over her shoulder at the face on the screen.

"So this was the clean-up crew," he murmured. "That explains why he didn't kill Stephanie when he had the chance."

"What do you mean?" Stephanie asked, looking from one to the other.

"He wasn't authorized to do anything except search and retrieve," Alina explained. "When you came in, he didn't have orders to kill you, so he knocked you out and left."

"Where was he this morning when you had a run-in with him?"

Alina hesitated, then sighed. "Angela's."

Stephanie's mouth dropped open.

"What was he doing there? For that matter, what were you doing there?"

"As it turns out, the same thing he was." Alina stretched and restarted the video. "I was looking for evidence of surveillance, and he was there to retrieve that evidence."

"Evidence? What evidence?"

"A camera."

Stephanie shook her head and rubbed her forehead.

"What is it with you people and cameras?" she demanded. "What happened to it?"

"I have it."

Stephanie dropped her hand and looked at her expectantly. "And?"

"And I have a good, clear photo of the man who took her."

Stephanie gasped. "Let me see!"

"No." Alina watched as the man left Stephanie's apartment through the back door and then clicked the video off.

"What do you mean, no?"

"No. The opposite of yes. What you don't want to hear, but what I'm saying anyway."

Stephanie glared at her. "Why not?"

"Because the less you know, the better," Damon said. "We're handling it. Just relax and let us take care of it."

Stephanie looked from him to Alina.

"You know who it is," she said slowly.

Alina's eyes narrowed and she closed her laptop. "Not yet, but I will."

"And then what?"

"You don't want to know."

Chapter Twenty-Nine

"What are we looking at?" Blake asked, striding into the living room.

Both Michael and Stephanie were standing at the sliding doors to the deck, peering outside. When he entered, they turned to glance at him. He frowned when he saw the grim look on Michael's face.

"Alina's leaving," Michael said, turning his attention back out the door.

"And this calls for staring out the door like lost souls?" Blake asked, walking up behind them and looking out. "Where's she going?"

"Who the hell knows," Stephanie said disgustedly. "All she'd say was that she had somewhere she had to go."

Blake looked from her to Michael, then back again.

"Ok. So what's the big deal?"

"Damon is out there saying goodbye, and he doesn't look happy," Michael said. "Something's going on."

Blake raised an eyebrow and watched as Alina closed the trunk to the Porsche and walked over to the driver's door where Damon was waiting.

"Do you think she got a lead on Angela?" he finally asked as Damon opened the door for her. She didn't get behind the wheel immediately. Instead, she stood with one foot in the car and her right arm braced on the roof, talking to him.

"I don't know." Michael shook his head and turned away. "I don't know why she's suddenly taking off. She has a duffel bag with her, so she's going some distance. She obviously doesn't expect to be back tonight."

"She found something," Stephanie said. "She went to Angie's this morning and said she found a surveillance camera. The bastard was watching Angie."

Blake frowned and stepped back as Stephanie turned and followed Michael into the living room.

"And?"

"And she refused to show me," she said over her shoulder. "She said the less I knew the better. All I know is that she has a picture of the man she thinks took her."

Blake whistled and went over to perch on the arm of the couch.

"If she's got a match on him, she can get Angie back," he said. "This is good news! Why do you both look like you're going to a funeral?"

"Because we might be when this is all over!" she exclaimed, dropping into the recliner and elevating her feet. She laid her cane beside her and looked at Blake. "If she's going after Angie, she'll be walking right into Harry's trap."

"I doubt that's what's happening," Blake said. "Damon won't let her face Harry alone. He already made that clear."

"Why else would she go off all of a sudden, without warning?"

"She could be doing reconnaissance," Michael suggested. "Blake's right. Damon won't let her go after the colonel alone."

Stephanie leaned her head back.

"Even doing reconnaissance is dangerous anymore," she muttered. "She went to Angie's this morning and came back with her neck cut open."

"Do you know if Damon heard anything back from his contact in Mexico?" Blake asked after a long moment of silence.

Michael shook his head. "Nothing yet."

They all fell into a brooding silence, then Blake sighed and got up, turning toward the dining room.

"I'm going to check for any updates on the cartel, then I'm making some dinner," he said. "What do you guys want?"

"I can't eat," Stephanie said. "I'm too worked up."

"You have to eat something," he retorted. "Mike? What do you want?"

"What are our options?" Michael got up and followed him into the kitchen. "I can help."

Blake went over to the refrigerator and opened the freezer, peering inside.

"There's a frozen lasagna in here," he said. "Or it looks like there's frozen burgers."

"Lasagna works for me."

Blake pulled it out and flipped the box over to read the back. "Preheat oven to 375," he read. "You got it?"

Michael pressed the button on the oven, selecting the temperature. "Yep."

Next Exit, No Outlet

Blake glanced into the living room where Stephanie had picked up her Kindle and was reading, her head bent to the screen, not paying them any attention.

"Did she say anything to you before she left?" he asked Michael, lowering his voice.

Michael glanced at him, turning away from the oven. "What makes you ask?"

Blake rolled his eyes.

"I've known you long enough to know when you're not saying something. I also know that you wouldn't be worried just because she's heading out without warning. So spill it. What did she tell you?"

Michael looked at him reluctantly, his lips pressed together grimly.

"To be ready to move."

Alina dropped her bag into the trunk and closed it, circling around to where Damon was waiting near the driver's door. His face was impassive but the set of his jaw spoke volumes on how he felt about her going.

"Stop looking at me like that. You know I have no choice."

"It doesn't mean I have to like it," he said, opening the door for her. "If anything feels out of place, if anyone even looks at you funny, get the hell out of there."

She paused, searching his face intently.

"You don't trust Charlie," she said rather than asked.

"I don't trust anyone right now. Until we're certain Harry is acting alone, we have to consider the possibility that he's not. I don't think Charlie would be that reckless, but it's better to be on our guard."

"I think if Charlie wanted me dead, I'd be dead," she said, "but don't worry. I'll be careful. I've had enough excitement for one day."

That brought something close to a smile to his lips. "How's the neck?"

"Feels like it's been cut."

"Just don't go yanking those stitches out."

Her lips twisted dryly.

"I'll do my best." She started to get into the sports car, then straightened up again. "Just to be on the safe side, you'd better get started making the arrangements. If Charlie has something from the satellites, we need to be ready to move."

"I'm already working on it. The basics are no problem, but the pilot is going to be tricky."

"Hawk, I gave you the least tricky part of the whole operation," Alina said, her lips curving into a laugh. "If I can handle the hard the part, I think you can handle a lousy plane."

He grinned. "Do you want lousy, or do you want reliable and efficient?"

"If you get absolutely stuck, call Frankie. I'm sure he has one on speed dial who won't ask questions," she retorted wickedly, her eyes dancing.

"Hell no," he said cheerfully. "You'll get lousy before you get one of Solitto's goons."

She laughed outright at that.

"You know, for an assassin, you sure have a strange sense of ethical obligation."

"No, I just don't trust the mob."

Alina thought for a moment, then shrugged.

"I guess that's valid," she admitted. "They're definitely a different breed. Frankie's firmly on our side, though. Trust me. He doesn't want either of us coming for him in the night."

"Smart man." Damon glanced at his watch. "If you're going to get there by nine, you need to get going. As soon as I have something, I'll let you know. Did you tell the gunny he's going to get the chance to make amends for losing Angie?"

"No. If I can't get back here to brief him, you can have the honors. Keep going with the arrangements we discussed. I have a feeling this meeting is going to speed things up. Charlie wouldn't have called me down there unless he has something actionable we can use."

Damon nodded, his eyes meeting hers. "I'll take care of it. You just take care of yourself."

"I always do."

A comfortable silence had fallen over the living and dining rooms as Damon, Michael, and Blake sat engrossed in their laptops. Stephanie was settled in the recliner, with her feet up and her Kindle in her hands. The only sound was the hum from the refrigerator in the kitchen and the occasional huff as Buddy changed positions at Blake's

Next Exit, No Outlet

feet. The silence broke when Michael sat back in his chair, stretched his arms over his head and whistled softly. Damon looked over from his spot at the bar, raising an eyebrow.

"You okay gunny?"

Michael exhaled and shook his head.

"Okay? No. I wouldn't say I was okay," he said, lowering his arms and rubbing his face.

Blake glanced up from his laptop. "What's wrong?"

"I think I know how he did it," Michael said slowly. "I think I've found the colonel's money trail from the very beginning."

Damon looked at him for a moment then got up and walked over to stand beside him.

"Show me."

Michael shook his head.

"It would take too long," he said. "I'm still compiling all the data, but from what I can tell from using the interest rates over the years, Harry's been siphoning money between the two main accounts for over twelve years."

"Just the two accounts?"

"No. That's where it gets tricky. He has multiple offshore accounts where the money has been bouncing around, but it all ends up in those two main accounts."

Blake frowned. "How do you know?"

"I picked one transaction that we can confirm was made by Harry," Michael explained. "Then I backtracked that transaction and followed the interest rate pattern. I lucked out because the transaction I picked also happens to be one of only two transactions that Harry didn't reroute or try to conceal."

"What transaction was that?" Damon asked softly.

Michael met his look steadily. "The withdrawal in Erbil the day before Dave died."

He nodded slowly. "Good choice."

"I'm confused," Stephanie said from the recliner. She had laid the Kindle down in her lap when Michael began talking and now she was looking at them with a frown on her face. "How are you able to build a trail from just one transaction?"

"Very carefully," Michael said dryly. "Unfortunately, none of it will hold up in court. In order to get what I needed, I had to hack three different bank databases."

Blake stared at him in disbelief. "You did what?"

Michael shrugged.

"I had no choice," he said. "It was the only way to get

transactions and backtrack the money trail."

"But if we can't use it in court," Stephanie said, "then what good is it?"

"It would've taken too long to wait for subpoenas. However, now that I found the information, I can request the subpoenas."

"Then aren't we just back where we started?" Stephanie asked. "It'll take a long time for a judge to sign off on private bank records offshore, and that's time we don't have. It's time Angela doesn't have."

Damon crossed his arms over his chest and nodded thoughtfully.

"Request the subpoenas," he told Michael. "By the time they come through it will all be over, but it will give proof that can be presented in Washington. It will mean the difference between our pursuit of Harry being considered a terrorist attack, or it being considered lawfully attempted justice."

Blake's mouth dropped open.

"Lawfully attempted justice?" he repeated. "You've got to be kidding me. There's nothing lawful about this!"

"There was also nothing lawful about what Harry's done," Michael said slowly. "In this instance, I think the end will justify the means."

"I think you're insane," Stephanie announced. "You're assuming that the subpoenas will be granted. I don't know that I've ever heard of a judge signing off on an investigation into the private offshore accounts of a war hero so firmly established on Capitol Hill."

The smile that passed over Damon's face was downright terrifying.

"A judge will sign off on it," he said. "He'll have no choice."

Stephanie threw her hands up in the air in disgust.

"You can't just go around threatening federal judges!"

"She's right," Blake said. "It's not that easy to get a judge to agree to infringe upon basic human rights, especially in offshore accounts."

"Don't worry about the judge," Damon said. "Leave that to me." He turned his attention back to Michael. "How long will it take you to compile all of this into a file that I can securely transmit?"

Michael glanced at his watch and shrugged.

"It's complicated, but I should be able to have it ready to go sometime tomorrow. I'll have to plug it all into spreadsheets to make it easier to read, and add in tracking markers to the different accounts. Provided that the subpoenas *do* come through, financial experts will be going over the data. I can plug the information into the spreadsheets

Next Exit, No Outlet

and rely on them to decipher it into something usable."

Damon nodded and laid a brief hand on Michael shoulder.

"Get on it," he said, "and request those subpoenas. You have until noon tomorrow."

Michael looked at him, startled. "What do you mean, noon tomorrow?"

Damon turned to go back to his seat at the bar where his laptop was open.

"Just what I said, gunny. You have until noon tomorrow."

Chapter Thirty

Harry pulled the phone out of his pocket and glanced at the screen, swiping it to read the incoming text message. He smiled faintly in satisfaction.
Package sedated and secured.
At least one person knows how to do their job, he thought to himself, tucking his phone back into his pocket. Angela Bolan was now in play.

He turned to go back to his dresser, gathering together an armful of clothes and carrying them to the bed. He dropped them next to the open rolling-case and began to roll teeshirts into neat, space-saving tubes.

Neither Agent Walker nor Agent Hanover had surfaced yet, remaining well-hidden and out of sight. Harry's lips tightened. Not only were they not dead, as expected, but their whereabouts were a mystery. They had simply disappeared without a trace. The last known location was a condo in Center City, Philadelphia, and all efforts to track them from that location had proven futile. Only a handful of people were that good at covering their tracks, and he had trained them all. No doubt about it, Stephanie Walker and Blake Hanover had help.

His phone vibrated again and Harry sighed, pausing in his packing to pull it out again. He swiped the screen and a scowl settled on his lips. He stared at the message for a moment, then slowly lowered the phone. Another one of his agents had disappeared.

A few days ago, as a precaution, he tasked someone to keep an eye on Charlie. There was always the outside chance that he would meet with Viper, and Harry could settle this whole thing once and for all if the assassin showed up in Washington, DC. It was a longshot, but he believed in keeping all the bases covered, even if the play was a walk. To that end, he put one of the few agents he had left on the intelligence king. Now that agent had disappeared.

"Damn!"

Harry glared across the room ferociously. If Charlie knew he was being followed, he would take steps to lose his tail, not kill it. If, however, Viper was in town, she would have no such compunction. If

Next Exit, No Outlet

she thought for one second that her boss was being watched, she'd kill first and ask questions later, just as any good asset would.

Harry glanced at his watch. It was almost ten. Lifting his phone, he sent an answering text.

When was his last check-in?

He dropped his phone onto the bed next to his open case and began rolling the rest of the shirts quickly, abandoning neatness for speed. A few moments later, the phone vibrated and he looked at the message.

Three hours ago. All attempts to contact have failed. GPS offline.

Harry paused to pick up the phone.

And the mark?

Dropping it onto the bed again, he turned to stride to his walk-in closet. When he emerged a few minutes later with another armful of clothes, the phone was blinking. He laid the clothes on the bed and picked up the phone, swiping the screen impatiently.

Unable to locate.

Harry let out a low string of curses and slid the phone back into his pocket. Charlie could be anywhere. The man was notoriously slippery, moving in the shadows like a ghost. He could be eating dinner in the middle of a crowded, trendy Georgetown restaurant, or he could be standing in the street outside, watching him pack. Or he could be meeting with Viper right now.

Going back to rolling clothes, Harry pressed his lips together thoughtfully. He had no fear that Charlie had figured out the truth about him yet. Viper was a fool if she hadn't realized he was behind everything, but Charlie was a different story altogether. He had taken every care to ensure that Charlie would be left in the dark until he was long gone. He had to. It was the only way he could make it out of the country. If Charlie even got so much as an inkling that something was off, Harry knew his chances of getting away were non-existent. Charlie was ruthless. He wouldn't wait for formal proceedings. He would freeze all Harry's assets and then eliminate Harry himself.

Harry's lips pulled into a dry smile. That was why the majority of his assets were so well hidden that even Charlie couldn't find them. The smile faded abruptly at the thought of the breach of the account in Singapore. Perhaps not as well-hidden as he had planned. Michael O'Reilly had managed to find one of them.

The case was full now and Harry zipped it closed. While he had assured that there was no possibility of Charlie discovering anything before it was too late, Harry acknowledged a strange sense of relief that he was leaving tonight. In a few days, this would all be over. Angela was in place, Viper would come to rescue her, and both women would be killed. Without Viper to conceal and shield them, Agents Walker and Hanover would quickly follow. The only one left that could possibly threaten his retirement at that point would be Michael O'Reilly, and Harry had already taken the precaution of arranging an accident for the Secret Service agent when he came back into town after his vacation.

Yes. It was all arranged, and his plans never failed.

Viper stood deep in the shadows with her hands in her jacket pockets, watching as Charlie hailed a cab. A moment later a white taxi pulled to the curb and he got in, disappearing into the backseat. As she turned away to melt into the darkness, she wondered if she would ever see her boss again. The way things were shaping up, it didn't look promising.

She had arrived in the nation's capital over an hour ahead of schedule, courtesy of the 3 liter, 443 hp engine under the Porsche's hood. Using that time to her advantage, she'd scouted Charlie to make sure there were no surprises waiting for her. And that was when she saw him.

He was a slightly built man, completely unremarkable in every way except one: he was following Charlie. No small feat, given Charlie's experience in counter-espionage.

There was only one person who was arrogant enough to think he could get away with putting a tail on Charlie, and Viper was not in the mood to humor him. After disposing of Harry's spy, she called Charlie and told him she'd arrived. Less than forty minutes later, she was seated across from him in the dark corner of a dive bar on the outer edge of the city, choking down a domestic brewed beer from a bottle.

Alina pulled the hood of her jacket up over head now, covering the bleached hair, and strode up the city street. She kept her hands in her pockets as she walked, her senses alert to her surroundings. Like every city in the world, this one had its good sections and its not-so-good sections. The deeper the shadows got, the sketchier the people became, and Viper was right at home amongst them. She moved confidently and deliberately, passing unnoticed

Next Exit, No Outlet

through the night.

Charlie had been right to call her down. Not only did he have satellite footage of Angela being carried onto the *Sea Queen*, which was enough on its own to make the trip worthwhile, but he also had satellite images of the nameless assassin from Rittenhouse. He was no longer nameless, and he was someone Charlie knew well.

Viper's lips tightened as she walked and she pulled out her clean phone. At least now she knew exactly what they were dealing with, and she had full authority to handle it. Dialing, she held the phone to her ear and listened to it ring, glancing behind her as she came to a stop at a cross street.

"Hey," Damon answered, his voice a welcome sound in her ear. "What's up?"

"I just finished," she told him, jogging across the road and turning up a side street. "Are you alone?"

"I can be." There was short silence and she heard the sound of the sliding door in her living room through the phone. "Go ahead," he said a moment later.

"Angie's definitely on the *Sea Queen*."

"You have satellite confirmation?"

"Yes. And there's more. The guy from Rittenhouse? Turns out Charlie knows him. His name is Ryan Harrington, and he supposedly died in an accident two years ago."

"Well, that explains why I'm still searching for him." There was a brief silence, then, "Why does Charlie know him?"

"He was in the training program for the Organization, but never made it past phase two. He failed a pysch eval and his overall scores were below average for his class. Any of that sound familiar?"

"Kyle March was dropped from the training," he said after a moment.

"Yes, and for one of the same reasons; he failed a pysch evaluation as well."

"Are you telling me that Harry's been using ex-students with mental issues?" Hawk demanded.

"It certainly seems like it," she said, stopping at another side street and waiting for a line of cars to pass. "Charlie pulled all the files of the trainees who didn't make it and ran a check on the names. Fourteen of them are unaccounted for, either reported as deceased or just missing."

"I wonder how many of those are still alive. We made a serious dent in his people so far, certainly more than fourteen. So not all his puppets were Organization trained."

CW Browning

"Yes, but there's no way of knowing who was. We have to assume that anyone we run into was at least partially trained by the Organization." Alina glanced at her watch and turned to hail a cab. "How's it going on your end?"

"Michael's cracked through the money trail," he told her. "He's compiling it all into a file with the reference markers. I'll send it to Charlie when he's finished."

"And the other arrangements?" she asked as a cab pulled up next to her.

"I'm working on them. I did get a call from my foreman, though. The ranch is ready."

"Good." Alina opened the back door and got into the cab. "Chinatown," she told the driver. "Sixth Street."

"You got it."

"I'll be leaving in less than an hour," she told Damon, switching to Russian so the driver wouldn't understand. "I have to get some things together. We're running out of time. Harry cleaned out his account in DC and transferred everything offshore today. He's getting ready to move."

"And Charlie?"

"Gave us the green light. He's keeping the skies and sea clear."

"When?"

"We go tomorrow night."

The first thing Angela became aware of was pain. As the nothingness of sleep faded, excruciating agony replaced it, pulsing through her body. At the same time she became aware of the pain, she also became aware of voices. Memory flooded back to her in an instant and she just stopped herself from gasping in fear. Where was she? She was laying on something soft and comfortable, and there was a gentle rocking motion that she couldn't place. She wasn't in the truck anymore; of that she was certain.

The low voices seemed closer now and Angela realized that they hadn't moved. Rather, as she came awake, they became clearer. Fighting to remain still, she tried to focus enough to hear what they were saying. After a few moments of listening intently, she was unable to make out even one word. Was that Spanish? She thought it might be, but the tones were so low that she couldn't be certain.

Next Exit, No Outlet

Giving up, she tried to figure out where all this pain was coming from. Her entire left arm throbbed incessantly and when she tried to move her fingers, she couldn't tell if she succeeded. Tamping down a sudden surge of panic, Angela tried to think. What had happened to her arm? She didn't remember anything after being grabbed behind a truck at the rest stop.

The unmistakable sound of a door opening made her catch her breath, and the low voices suddenly stopped. There was a moment of complete silence and Angela knew someone else had entered the room. Resisting the urge to crack open one eye and peek, she lay perfectly still, listening.

"Wait outside," a deep voice commanded in English and Angela felt a wave of relief go through her at the sound of a language she understood.

There was the sound of movement and then the door closed, leaving her alone with the newcomer.

"Well?"

The same voice spoke again and Angela froze.

"She's fine," another voice answered, and Angela relaxed. He hadn't been talking to her. They didn't know she was awake yet. "I'm keeping her heavily sedated. Her shoulder is dislocated."

"What? How did that happen?"

"The man who brought her said she fell and popped it out when she tried to escape."

"Can you put it back in?"

"I looked at it, but it's been out for a long time. The swelling is extensive. It's beyond my skill now. She will need surgery to replace it."

"She must be in a lot of pain."

"Yes."

"Well, that will keep her from trying to escape again. Do you have enough sedative to keep her out of it?"

"Yes."

"Then make her as comfortable as possible. There's no need to keep her restrained any longer, not with a dislocated shoulder. Keep the door locked with two men outside at all times. No one in or out." The deep voice paused and Angela sensed a presence move to stand next to her. "Has she had anything to drink?"

"No."

"Get her some water. She's no good to me dead."

The presence moved away again.

"What about food?"

"Not yet. Let's keep her too weak to cause any trouble."

"Yes, sir."

The door opened then closed a moment later, and Angela remained still, waiting to see if she was really alone. After a few moments of silence, she cracked one eye open, peering in the direction the voices had come from. The door was there, closed, and she couldn't see anyone near it.

Moving her head cautiously, she opened both eyes. She was in a fairly spacious room, laying on a bed. Opposite the bed was a wall with a built-in closet and low dresser, both painted a glossy nautical blue. Above the dresser, a large flat-screen TV was mounted to the wall with a full entertainment center and a mini bar beneath it. To the right of the wall and in the corner, a door was ajar, giving her a glimpse into what looked like a bathroom. A long, matching nautical blue sofa was built into the wall to her right.

"What the hell?"

Angela shifted on the bed and pain surged through her arm again. She couldn't hold back a groan and she closed her eyes again in agony. At least now she knew where the pain was coming from. She had a dislocated shoulder! It happened when she tripped and fell in the parking lot. How long ago was that? Apparently long enough for her shoulder to become too swollen to get the joint back in.

Angela frowned and stared at the ceiling, trying to think. She had no idea how much time had passed, where she was, or even who she was with. The gentle, repetitive rocking motion made her think she was on a boat of some kind, but where? And why was she no good to someone dead?!

She was just working herself into a state of near hysteria when the door opened abruptly and a slim, dark man came in carrying a tall bottle of water in one hand and a black medical bag in the other.

"So you're awake," he said in heavily accented English, closing the door.

Angela recognized the second voice from earlier and eyed him warily. The man didn't say anything further, but brought the bottle of water over to set it on the small table beside the bed. He set the bag down and turned to her. When he leaned toward her, Angela gasped and tried to jerk away from him, letting out a cry of pain as she did so.

"I'm going to help you sit up so that you can drink," the man said calmly. "Come. You won't be able to lift yourself."

Angela bit her lip. He was right. She was in so much pain that the thought of trying to push herself up brought tears to her eyes. Even if she struggled, all she would accomplish was more pain with no result. She looked at the bottle of water. Her tongue felt swollen and her

Next Exit, No Outlet

mouth was like a desert. She was so thirsty! It would be stupid not to drink when she was offered the chance. Who knew when the next opportunity would come along.

The man leaned over her again and put his hands under her arms. When he lifted her to sit her up against the headboard, pain wracked through her with such ferocity that the room began to swim and she closed her eyes, breathing fast as she broke into a cold sweat. She gasped and waited for the sudden bout of nausea to pass. Leaning her head back and focusing on one spot across the room, Angela sat very still as her arm and shoulder throbbed unbearably. Slowly, the wave of sickness passed and the room stopped rotating around her.

She turned her head as the man held out a glass filled with water. Taking it with her right hand, she lifted it to her lips and drained it thirstily. When she was finished, he took the glass from her and set it on the bedside table before opening his case.

"I'm the ship medic. I'm going to give you something for the pain," he told her. "It will make you sleepy, but it will help give you some relief."

"Ship?" Her voice was hoarse and Angela cleared her throat. "What ship?"

The man didn't answer. He pulled a small glass bottle from the bag, then a needle and syringe. She averted her eyes from the needle quickly, memories of Stephanie's ordeal in the car fresh in her mind. Tamping down panic, she focused on what had been said when they thought she was still asleep. She was no good to them dead. Repeating it like a mantra inside her head, she took a deep, steadying breath. They wanted to keep her comfortable, and if it would take some of this god-awful pain away, she was more than willing for them do so.

The medic finished filling the syringe from the bottle and turned to her, depressing the plunger slightly and tapping the syringe to ensure there were no errant air bubbles. He reached for her arm.

"Wait!" Angela gasped. "What is it?"

"Morphine."

He took her arm and pushed up her sleeve. Angela turned her head away, biting her lip when she felt the sharp pinch as the needle went in. She inhaled deeply and then it was all over. He released her arm and turned back to his case, capping the needle and putting it away.

"You should start to feel some relief in a few minutes," he said, closing his bag. "Just rest."

He turned to go back toward the door and Angela watched him go with a mix of relief and frustration. He had given her good drugs for her pain, but she still had no idea where she was or who had taken her. In fact, the only thing she knew for sure was that her shoulder was dislocated and her arm was hanging at an awkward angle.

Shifting against the pillows, Angela tried to find a comfortable position before giving up and leaning her head back. She had to think. There had to be a way to get herself out of this room and off this ship. She just had to think. Staring up at the ceiling, she frowned as she tried to focus, but her thoughts were too scattered to come into any semblance of order. A comfortable numbness was stealing over her and Angela closed her eyes, exhaling in relief as the acute pain eased somewhat.

She would just close her eyes and enjoy the lack of excruciating pain for a brief minute, then get back to the business of trying to find a way out here.

Next Exit, No Outlet

Chapter Thirty-One

Alina slid open the door and stepped into the house silently. It was just past midnight and the first floor was dark, but she knew Hawk was still up. There was too much to do for him to have gone to bed yet.

She walked to the bar, setting her bag down on one of the high stools before continuing into the kitchen. Not bothering with the light, she went straight to the fridge and pulled out a bottle of water. The door was just closing when she heard footsteps on the stairs. Glancing at her watch with a frown, she moved out of the kitchen and looked down the dark hall just as Michael rounded the bottom of the stairs.

Her shoulders relaxed and she opened her water, lifting the bottle to her lips as he came towards her.

"When did you get back?" he asked in a low voice.

"Just now."

"Everything okay?"

"Fine." She watched as he went into the kitchen, heading for the fridge. "I heard you cracked the Singapore accounts."

He glanced at her as he opened the door and the light from the refrigerator illuminated his face. It was drawn and tired.

"Yes." He pulled out a bottle of water. "I'm moving all the information into spreadsheets to make it easier to pick out the trail. It's mind-blowing how much money he moved around over the years."

Alina's lips tightened, anger welling inside her at the thought of how many people had died so that Harry could accumulate his fortune, her brother included.

"And it's definitely him?"

The fridge door swung closed and darkness descended on the kitchen once more.

"Absolutely." He opened his water, took a sip, and came back to where she was standing near the hall. "He was sloppy with two transactions. That's all I needed to backtrack everything."

"How far back does it go?"

Michael met her gaze and in the dim light, she saw her own

anger reflected on his face.

"Iraq, about a year before Dave died."

She was silent for a long moment, then exhaled and straightened up away from the wall.

"That's good work, gunny," she said softly.

"I did my part," he told her in a low, hard voice. "Make sure you do yours. He doesn't get away with this."

"Oh, he won't," she assured him, "but your part's not completely over yet."

He raised an eyebrow. "Oh?"

"You know how you keep reminding me that you're a Marine? Well, now's your chance to show me what you've got."

He studied her for a long moment. "You're not talking about desk work, are you?"

She smiled faintly. "No."

"Thank God. I'm tired of staring at monitors all day. I need some exercise."

"Oh, you'll get it. Damon will brief you tomorrow." Alina turned to go over to the bar and pick up her duffel bag. "Be ready to roll tomorrow afternoon."

"And Blake and Stephanie?"

She turned to move toward the hall, glancing at him.

"It's too risky for them to leave this house," she said. "Just you."

Michael walked with her toward the stairs.

"That's not going to sit well with either of them. They won't want to stay behind."

"Oh, I know." Alina started up the steps. "And I've planned for that."

Alina came out of the bathroom wrapped in a towel to find Damon in the process of pulling his Beretta from the holster at the back of his jeans and setting it on the bedside table. He glanced up as she came out and his eyes swept over her quickly, causing her heart rate to quicken.

"You got back fast," he said, turning toward her. "Not that I'm complaining," he added, slipping his arms around her and dropping his lips to hers for a quick kiss.

Next Exit, No Outlet

"I took a leaf out of Dutch's racing book and ran up the interstate with night vision goggles and no lights," she said with a grin, pulling away and going towards the walk-in closet. "My speed hovered around 130 all the way up."

He chuckled. "Aren't you glad I got a Porsche now?"

"It's fun," she admitted from the closet. "I can see why they did it."

Damon walked over to lean against the door to the closet, watching as she pulled a large, rolling suitcase from the back corner.

"You're heading right back out?"

"I'll try to catch a couple hours of sleep, but I have a plane leaving from Philly Northeast at seven," she said. "How's it going here?"

"The command center is dismantled and everything's packed up." He moved out of the way as she carried the case out of the closet and over to the bed. "I'll move the servers and armory out in the morning before anyone's up. Are you sure about leaving the rest?"

"Yes. It will be taken care of. Just make sure everything sensitive is out. It can go to the address I gave you. It will be secure there until I can move it." She turned to the dresser and opened a drawer, pulling out a black pair of yoga pants and a tank top. "I talked to Michael. He went down for water when I came in."

"Did you tell him about tomorrow?"

"Only that you'd brief him," Alina said, pulling on the pants. "You'll need to get him gear. I didn't have time to do it while I was in DC. I ran into a small hiccup that ate into my buffer time."

Damon frowned and sat on the edge of the bed. "What kind of hiccup?"

The towel dropped to the floor as she pulled on the tank top.

"Harry had someone following Charlie," she said, her head emerging from inside the shirt. "I couldn't risk him seeing me, so he lost another agent tonight."

"Fantastic. Did you find out who he was?"

"No. I didn't take time for conversation. I wanted to make sure there weren't more."

"And?"

"There weren't." Alina glanced at him. "Charlie knew he was being followed. He said he would have lost him before our meeting."

Damon met her gaze steadily. "And Harry?"

"He was holed up in his house, packing." She smiled coldly. "He hasn't found the camera I left. He's getting sloppy."

"Or he just doesn't care," he said. "Don't underestimate him."

She nodded and opened a drawer to the dresser, lifting out a pile of shirts and carrying them over to the case on the bed. Damon watched her for a second, then sat back against the headboard.

"I heard back from my contact in Guerrero," he said as she began rolling the shirts to pack them. "She found something."

Alina shot him a quick look. "And?"

"On the surface, it didn't look like much," he said, pulling his phone out of his pocket and swiping the screen. "It was an old file from two years ago involving a couple of arrests the military made in connection with the Casa Reinos. One of the prisoners garnered some interest from our government."

She paused in the act of rolling up a tank top and looked at him. "Interest from whom?"

"Harry. He brokered a deal with the Mexican government to have the prisoner released into US custody on the basis that he was a US citizen and was wanted for questioning here."

Alina raised an eyebrow. "Who was the prisoner?"

"His name at the time was Marcus Rodriquez." Damon held out his phone with a photo on the screen. "Look familiar?"

Alina stared at the photo and her lips formed a silent whistle. "Well hello Kyle March."

"Exactly." Damon pulled the phone back and swiped the screen again. "He was released from the military prison where he was being held and, according to their records, taken over the border."

"But?"

"He never arrived on US soil. He dropped off the face of the earth until he showed up in Madrid using Jordan Murphy's name a year later."

Alina tucked the shirt into the case with a frown.

"Harry had dealings with the cartel even then," she murmured. "Somehow, I'm not surprised. Who were the others arrested with Kyle?"

"One of them was my old friend Jenaro Gomez. He was released not long after Kyle."

"What the hell was Kyle doing with the cartel?" she wondered, turning to go back to the dresser for more clothes. "What was Harry up to?"

"That's for Charlie to find out," Damon said, stretching and setting his phone next to his gun on the table. "I made a copy of the file and sent it to him. The only thing that concerns us is that it establishes firm contact with the cartel going back at least two years, probably more."

Next Exit, No Outlet

"Everything keeps circling back to them." Alina returned with a stack of pants. "Harry had the perfect set up. You realize the only reason any of this is coming out now is because La Cabeza made the decision to go after you last fall, right?"

Damon grinned. "You're saying this is all my fault?"

She shot him an amused look.

"No. I'm saying that if he hadn't tried to get revenge on you for killing his predecessor, we would probably never have known about Harry's connection to him. Why would we look at the cartel? And Blake certainly wouldn't have found it."

"No, and the connection from Dominic to the street racers was so removed that if Dutch hadn't been killed, and John wasn't close with him, no one would have ever connected the cartel with the terrorist attack."

"Exactly." Alina felt a wave of anger wash through her and tamped it down firmly. "Harry covered every angle and made sure that every connection couldn't lead back to him. He accounted for everything."

"Except us."

She looked at him thoughtfully for a long moment.

"I think he even accounted for us," she said slowly. "Think about it."

Damon raised his eyebrows. "I have thought about it. I don't see it."

"When I asked you for that clean phone so that we could communicate, you arranged it, but then you came here," she reminded him. "You didn't have to come. You knew I was perfectly capable of taking care of myself, but you came anyway."

Damon sucked in his breath sharply.

"Because Harry contacted me!" he exclaimed, his eyes meeting hers. "Holy hell, he's the one who told me you were in trouble."

"I think Harry wanted you here, with me, so that he could take us out together. At the very least, he had to have been hoping that you would lead him to me."

"But why? It makes no sense. He trained us!"

"I have absolutely no idea," she confessed, rolling a pair of black jeans into a tight cylinder and setting it in the bag. "It's not just us. Other Organization assets have been targeted overseas and those that are left are being forced into inactivity until we finish this. Charlie's shut all ops down until he knows it's safe for them to continue. We can't fail."

Damon was silent for a long moment, then he exhaled loudly.

"Does Charlie have any ideas as to why Harry would go on a rampage against the operatives he helped train?"

"If he does, he's not sharing. I'll tell you this much, before I kill Harry, I'll find out why. He'll be more than happy to tell me, I'm sure. You know he can never resist talking."

Damon made a face.

"That's true." He watched her pack in silence for a few minutes, then sighed again. "I'm going to grab a shower while you do that," he said, swinging his legs off the bed and heading for the bathroom. "I haven't seen Raven yet, so I'm not sure how you're going to get him squared away."

Alina glanced at the skylight and smiled.

"He's out there. He'll come home now that I'm back."

Damon paused at the bathroom door and looked at her curiously.

"Do you really think he'll stay at the ranch when you leave?"

Alina shrugged. "There's only one way to find out."

Alina came awake slowly in the pre-dawn hours. The room was still dark, and she was warm and comfortable with a strong arm wrapped around her. She laid for a moment, breathing in the fresh, woodsy scent of Damon and allowed herself to savor the feeling of safe contentment that washed through her. Her bag was packed and near the foot of the bed, the hidden safe was emptied of her stash of passports and cash, and a large plastic carrier was sitting near the window. Everything was ready for her to leave, but she wasn't quite ready to move and start the day. Perhaps she was simply delaying the inevitable. By this time tomorrow, it would all be over, and either Harry or herself, or both of them, would be dead.

Alina stared across the dark room. It wasn't fear or uncertainty that she felt as she contemplated the next twenty-four hours. She was far too experienced in her job to allow basic human emotions to cloud her thoughts. Rather, it was the simmering anger that bothered her. It had been there since John was killed, and had grown steadily worse over the intervening weeks. Now that she was close to bringing justice to the man who had caused the deaths of so many, the building pressure of rage was demanding to be released. Alina knew that that rage, fed by emotions she had tried to ignore, had the ability to defeat her more effectively than Harry or any of his cartel henchmen. She had to find a way to ignore or overcome it if she was going to have a chance at all.

Damon stirred against her and she exhaled silently. There was more at stake now than just herself. The game had changed drastically when she'd agreed to his insane idea of marriage. She wasn't alone anymore. It was a realization that filled her at once with both comfort and fear. Anything that happened to her now affected him, and vice versa. The days of walking into an op without any attachments were over.

The arm around her tightened briefly as he shifted behind her and Alina felt warm lips press against her bare shoulder.

"You awake?" he whispered.

"Mmm-hmm."

Alina stretched and rolled onto her back, looking up into his face. His eyes were still heavy with sleep and he nodded tiredly before stretching, yawning widely.

"Everything okay?" he asked when he was finished.

"Yes." She forced a smile and raised a hand to run a finger along his jaw. "I'm just procrastinating. I'm not ready to starting moving yet."

He caught her hand and turned his head to press a warm kiss on her palm. Lifting his head, he glanced at his watch.

"It's not even five yet," he said, his voice husky from sleep. "You have some time."

He turned onto his back and pulled her into his side, his arm around her shoulders. Alina laid her head on his shoulder and, after a few minutes, his even breathing told her he had gone back to sleep. She laid there, relishing the warmth of his skin and the feel of his arm wrapped around her. Sliding her hand across his flat stomach, she paused when her fingers touched the fresh scarring on his left side.

Alina let her hand rest over the healing skin where the bullet had torn into him, and her lips tightened. That shot should have killed them both. Instead, she had walked away with a scratch and he had been rushed stateside to undergo the surgery that, ultimately, saved his life; a life that he was now going to risk again on her behalf. It didn't matter that it was their job, or that they had been trained for situations just like this. The rules had changed. It wasn't just about the mission anymore. Now it was about survival.

And vengeance.

His chest moved steadily as he slept, and she felt a wave of something close to panic crash over her. All at once, Alina needed to feel his heart beating strong against her chest and his lips against hers. She needed to feel that they were both alive and together, even if it was only for a brief time. Propping herself up on her arm, she looked down at him and lowered her lips to trail them softly along his jaw. His even breathing shifted when she reached the side of his neck and Alina knew he was awake. His arm tightened around her and she smiled against his skin when he rolled her onto her back, his lips coming down to move over hers warmly.

Her arms went around him and her heart pounded against her chest as the feeling of panic was replaced with a more powerful surge of desire. No matter what happened today, and no matter how it ended, right this second they had each other. Damon's lips were demanding a response from her that she was more than willing to give and, at least for this moment, the reality of what the day would bring could be ignored. There would be time enough to focus on Harry later. Right now, she had this, and she was rapidly coming to accept that this was more important to her. Harry's time would come.

Right now was for the two of them.

Chapter Thirty-Two

Hawk turned away from the coffee maker with a full mug of steaming coffee and watched as Blake opened the back door to take Buddy out.

"You don't look like you got much sleep," Michael commented, opening the cabinet and taking out a mug.

Hawk glanced at him and shrugged. "There's a lot to do."

"Lina said you'd fill me in today," Michael said in a low voice. "Anything I can do, just let me know."

"Let you know what?" Stephanie asked, limping into the kitchen without her cane.

"Where's your cane?" Michael asked, watching as she limped toward the fridge.

"I can't keep coddling my leg," she said over her shoulder. "It won't get better if I don't force myself to use it."

"You also don't want to set it back," he said. "Are you doing your physical therapy exercises?"

She made a face as she pulled a box of frozen waffles out of the freezer. "Yes, Dad."

Michael grinned and pressed the button to start his coffee brewing.

"Hey, I'm just looking out for you."

"Has anyone heard from Lina?" she asked, looking from one to the other. "Is she okay?"

"She came back last night," Michael said, leaning against the counter and crossing his arms over his chest. "She seemed fine."

"She's here?"

"No." Damon moved over to the bar with his coffee. "She left early this morning."

Stephanie frowned and turned to put two waffles into the toaster oven on the counter.

"*Now* where did she go? I swear that woman never sits still for more than ten minutes." She opened a cabinet door and pulled out a plate, then went back for a mug. "When she gets back, I'm going to put another tracker on her, but this time I'll stick it in her shoe!"

"Somehow I don't think that will do much good," Michael murmured, pulling his coffee out from under the spout and taking a sip. "Remember what happened last time."

Stephanie made a face and moved past him to put her mug under the machine.

"Lord knows it's the only way I'll know what she's up to anymore," she said. "It's not like she's telling me anything."

Michael glanced at Damon and moved out of the kitchen, heading for the dining room table.

"I think that's for your own piece of mind," he said over his shoulder.

Stephanie snorted. "Nothing's going to make me feel better about any of this, so she might as well just lay it on me."

"You wouldn't like that," Damon murmured. "Trust me."

The sliding door opened then, and Buddy came bounding back into the house with Blake close behind.

"It's a great morning out there," he announced, closing the door. "I saw the Porsche in the driveway. Alina's back?"

"She was, but she's gone out again," Stephanie said. She looked at Damon. "If the Porsche is there, what did she take?"

"The Range Rover. We switched cars," he answered. He didn't tell her it was because Alina needed the space for a large bird of prey in a carrier. What Stephanie didn't know, she couldn't worry over. "The Porsche is better for me today."

"Where are you going?" Blake asked, heading into the kitchen to get a mug. "Need company?"

"You're not going anywhere," Stephanie said, pulling her mug out and moving aside so Blake could get to the coffee maker. "If I have to stay stuck in this house, so do you."

"She's right. You both have to stay hidden until Harry's taken care of," Damon said, finishing his coffee. "Sorry."

Blake pressed his lips together in displeasure, but remained silent as he set his mug under the coffee spout and pressed the button to brew.

"Any word on the *Sea Queen*?" Damon asked, standing and walking over to the dishwasher to put his mug in.

"She's off the coast of Georgia," Blake said, turning to look at him. "As far as anyone can tell, she's just coasting in international waters. I want to contact the Coast Guard and work with them to keep an eye on her, but without a good reason, that's not going to happen. And we don't have a good reason."

Next Exit, No Outlet

"We don't even have a not good reason," Stephanie muttered, pulling her waffles out of the toaster oven and dropping them onto her plate quickly. "We've got nothing except a bunch of circumstantial leads that really point to nothing."

"I did see something interesting last night before I went to bed," Blake said, grabbing the box of waffles off the kitchen island and pulling out the sleeve. "Something's going on in New York, New Jersey, and Pennsylvania."

Damon closed the dishwasher and looked at him, raising an eyebrow. "What?"

"It looks like war is breaking out in the gangs." Blake put two waffles in the toaster oven and closed the door, turning it on. "Over twenty gang members were killed yesterday alone."

"How is that interesting?" Michael asked from the dining room. "Gang members are killed all the time."

"All the ones killed had affiliations with the Casa Reinos," Blake said. "It's almost like they're being targeted, but we're not sure who would have the balls to do that. Certainly not the other gangs."

Damon's lips tightened slightly and he turned to leave the kitchen.

"My bet would be on Solitto's crew," he said, moving toward the back door.

"Frankie?" Stephanie repeated, carrying her waffles and coffee to the bar. "I don't know if he has that kind of reach anymore."

"He does if he's gotten the other Families involved," Blake said slowly. "Between the New York Family and Bobby Reyes', they have a pretty substantial army. And this wouldn't be the first time the cartel has threatened Solitto's business."

"That's true," Stephanie admitted, sipping her coffee before setting the mug down and turning back toward the fridge. "I'll bet Lina knows something about it. I don't care what she says, she's more involved with Frankie than she admits. The head of the Jersey Family doesn't just call you over for a meeting after he sees you on the casino floor for no reason."

"When she gets back, we'll ask her," Blake said with a shrug, pulling his mug out and lifting it to his lips. He paused in the act of taking a sip. "When *is* she coming back? And where did she go, anyway?"

Silence greeted that, and Stephanie paused with a container of spreadable butter in her hand, looking across the kitchen and bar at Damon. He had his hand on the back door, but he stopped at Blake's question. Michael looked up from his coffee and watched as he hesitated, then turned around reluctantly.

"She caught a flight out of Northeast Philly at seven."

"A flight?" Stephanie's mouth dropped open. "Is she insane?! Harry's got people everywhere looking for her and she went to an airport and *got on a plane?*"

Michael was staring at Damon and he slowly shook his head.

"She's too smart for that," he said. "She knows the security at airports will feed her location straight to Colonel Shore. What was it? A private plane?"

Damon's blue eyes met his and his lips curved faintly. "Well done, gunny," he murmured.

"A private plane out of Philly International?" Stephanie demanded. "Even so, it's still too big of a risk."

"Not Philly International," Damon corrected her. "Philly Northeast. It's a smaller airport."

Michael nodded. "Good choice."

"Why is she flying anywhere?" Stephanie carried the butter and a knife over to the bar and sank down on a stool. "How far away did she have to go that she couldn't drive? And when is she coming back?"

When Damon didn't answer, she turned on the stool to look at him in apprehension. He met her stare impassively and her lips parted on a silent gasp.

"Oh my God. She's not coming back, is she?"

"Don't be ridiculous," Blake said, looking from Stephanie to Damon. "Of course she's coming back. She wouldn't leave you alone here unless…"

He stopped abruptly and stared hard at Damon.

"Why are you still here if she's out there?" he demanded. "You swore to Stephanie that you would be with her."

"And I will."

"*That's* where you're going?!" Stephanie cried, throwing the butter knife down on the bar. "It's happening? She found Angela?"

Damon nodded. "She's on the *Sea Queen*."

Blake's eyebrows soared into his forehead and he slowly set his coffee down on the bar.

"How do you know?"

"We got satellite footage of her being carried aboard."

"Just like that? You pulled satellite footage that quickly?" Michael demanded. "Hell, *I* can't even pull satellite images that fast, and I'm Secret Service!"

Damon shot him an amused look. "We're a little higher up on the food chain."

Next Exit, No Outlet

Michael snorted. "You mean your mysterious boss is."

"Then we know Angie's on the yacht?" Stephanie asked, her voice raising an octave.

"Yes."

"Now we have a good reason to call the Coast Guard in," Blake pointed out. "We can get her back without risking Alina!"

Damon smiled faintly. "Oh, I wish it were that simple. There's a reason they're coasting in international waters."

Blake waved that away impatiently. "We can still pull jurisdiction. We do it all the time in the Caribbean."

"Trust me, it won't work this time," Damon told him, "not with Harry onboard. Besides, if anyone other than Viper approaches that yacht, Angela is as good as dead."

Stephanie's face paled. "What?"

"You don't know that," Blake argued.

Damon shrugged.

"If you want to risk it, by all means, go ahead," he told him. "Keep in mind, though, Harry doesn't like loose ends, especially ones like Angela."

Blake's jaw tightened and he glanced at Stephanie's white face. "Then what's the plan?" he asked after a moment of silence.

Damon looked from one to the other.

"You both stay here and stay out of it," he said bluntly. "That's the only plan you need to know."

Jack glanced at his watch and looked up as his assistant knocked once and then opened his office door.

"Sir?"

"Get Rear Admiral Jessup on the line," Jack told him briskly, sliding his laptop into a leather briefcase, "and call the car around. Do you keep an overnight bag with you here?"

"Yes, sir." His assistant glanced at the briefcase. "Where are we going?"

"Scotland." Jack looked up. "Faslane, to be exact."

"Yes, sir." He turned to leave. "I'll get the Admiral on the line now."

Jack nodded and watched as the door closed behind the younger man. Jones really was a saint. He didn't seem even remotely discomposed by the news that they were off to Scotland at a moment's notice.

Snapping the briefcase closed, he lifted it off his desk and set it on the floor before turning to stride across his office to the large filing cabinet on the opposite wall. He pulled a set of keys out from his pocket and unlocked the second drawer, opening it all the way to pull a file folder from the back.

"Sir, I have the Admiral on line two," Jones spoke through the intercom.

"Thank you." Jack closed the drawer and locked it again, carrying the folder back to his desk. He dropped it onto the surface and sat down, reaching for the phone. "Terry, is that you?"

"One and the same," a cheerful voice answered. "How are you, Jack?"

"Keeping busy. How's the weather up there?"

"Chilly, but clear and sunny." Terry paused. "Am I right in assuming that you're calling in regards to the directive I just received from London?"

"Yes," Jack said, sitting back in his chair. "This morning I took a call from Washington. They requested our assistance."

Terry snorted inelegantly. "Requested?"

Jack grinned. Terry's views on their allies across the pond were very well-known by anyone who had ever come into contact with him.

"Yes," he said. "I've extended my personal guarantee that it will be handled with the utmost speed. Will there be an issue with that?"

Terry sighed heavily.

"No. I have a boat that's already been alerted and sent the coordinates," he said. "They can be in position in six hours."

"Excellent. I'm leaving within the half hour. I'll be there by tea time."

"You're flying up?" Terry was surprised. "It's that important, then?"

"As a matter of fact, yes." Jack glanced at his watch again. "We'll talk when I get there."

"Well, my day just became significantly more interesting. Is Jones coming with you?"

"Yes."

"I'll make reservations for dinner. While you're here, you really must try this new restaurant that opened. The lamb is outstanding."

"That just might make up for Jones not having advance notice," Jack said with a short laugh. "We'll see you soon."

Next Exit, No Outlet

Jack hung up and flipped open the folder on his desk. He studied the neat columns of numbers in front of him and turned the pages in the file until he came to the last page of figures. Turning his eyes to the monitor on the desk, he reached for his mouse and clicked open the attachment Charlie had forwarded to him a few minutes before. While he had been expecting a call from Washington after his conversation with the enigmatic Maggie yesterday, he had been surprised when it came from a man whom, until today, he hadn't known existed. If it weren't for the other man on the call, whom Jack knew well, he would have been inclined to question the authority of the mysterious Charlie.

The conference call lasted a grand total of nine minutes, but that was ample time for him to realize that Charlie was no fly-by-night desk jockey. Suddenly, Jack had a better idea of just who Maggie worked for, and why her very existence had been impossible to trace since she pulled him out of the ground in Afghanistan last fall.

Staring at his monitor now, Jack skimmed over the excel spreadsheet before looking back to the file on his desk. His lips tightened and he looked more closely at the columns of figures, glancing back to the excel sheet after a moment. Finding the same amounts listed, he sat back in his chair and stared at the screen thoughtfully.

"Well, I'll be damned," he murmured to himself. "She was right."

"Sir, the car is downstairs." Jones interrupted his stunned reverie and Jack glanced at his watch swiftly.

"Thank you."

He pulled a flash drive from his desk drawer and plugged it into the USB port on his tower, copying the excel sheet onto the external drive before powering down his system. He reached for his briefcase again, sliding the folder and the flash drive into it.

Maggie had certainly delivered. Now, it was his turn to return the favor.

Viper glanced at her watch and took one last look around the nearly deserted cemetery. She was running out of time. There was no sign of surveillance and no indication of anything out of the ordinary. As risky as it was, if she was going to do it, now was the time.

She moved from behind an ancient oak tree and glanced at the park bench a few feet away. Her chest tightened as she remembered a man sitting on it in the rain. It had been a lifetime now, since John sat on that very bench and watched the parade of women come to pay their respects at her brother's tomb. Pressing her lips together, she moved along the path away from the vantage point overlooking Dave's final resting place. John had been looking for her, unwilling to let her walk out of their lives forever without a word. Now, he was dead, and she was about to do that very thing to Stephanie and Angela.

Alina made her way through the cemetery and towards Dave's grave, her eyes alert and watchful behind very large, dark glasses. She was dressed in trendy jeans, a Washington Redskins jacket and a baseball cap. The over-sized glasses covered most of her face and she walked with a faint swagger that decreased her height by a full inch. If she had missed anything in her preliminary sweep of the cemetery, she wasn't very worried. The likelihood of anyone but Harry himself recognizing her was nonexistent. And she knew he wasn't watching. He was already aboard the *Sea Queen*. He had flown out to the yacht on a chartered helicopter just after midnight.

She tucked her hands into her jacket pockets and lowered her head as she walked, her senses tuned for the slightest change in her surroundings that would indicate a threat. It was just past six, and she had landed two hours before. It had been a whirlwind of activity to get here. The private flight out of Philly left precisely at seven, and she was driving through the abandoned wilds of Oklahoma by ten-thirty with Raven's cage in the back of her rented SUV. After introducing him to his new home and making sure the skylight in Damon's bedroom was acceptable, Alina ate lunch in Damon's large and sunny kitchen, watching as Raven surveyed the area from atop one of the many smaller buildings on the ranch. When she walked out the back door with a cup of coffee in her hand, Raven flew down to land on the banister surrounding the porch. She spent the next twenty minutes with him before reluctantly getting back into the SUV. Her last sight of Raven was him soaring high above the ranch, surveying the new territory.

Landing in Washington, DC a few hours later, Viper went straight to the storage unit she kept in the heart of the city. Everything she needed was there, and it was half an hour later that she'd left and headed for Arlington. Her side trip was reckless, a fact that she acknowledged now as she strode toward the row of uniform grave stones where Dave's final resting place was located. She shouldn't be here. She shouldn't have taken the time or the risk to come here.

Next Exit, No Outlet

Stepping off the pavement and onto the perfectly manicured grass, Alina's lips tightened again. Logically, she shouldn't be here, but it was a trip she had to make for herself. Approaching Dave's headstone, she sighed silently, casting one last look around from behind her glasses. No one was in sight. Dropping her eyes to Dave's grave, she took a deep breath and bent down to crouch before it.

"Hey you," she murmured softly, staring at his name and rank etched into the marble. "I know it's been a while. I've been busy and haven't been able to get here. Remember that mess you got yourself tangled up with in Iraq? Now I'm tangled up in it, too. But don't worry. I'm going to finish it, once and for all."

Alina paused, then swallowed the lump in her throat.

"Michael will be helping, so rest easy knowing that he held up his end of the promise to you. He's been a huge help. He's good people, but I guess you knew that." She cleared her throat as her vision blurred, and she blinked the tears back impatiently. "A lot of good people have been dragged into this mess, and a lot of them haven't made it out alive. I know you had no idea what you were starting back then, but holy hell did you open a Pandora's box."

Alina paused again and cast a swift glance around once more. Seeing nothing, she turned her gaze back to the silent, cold stone before her. She took a deep, steadying breath and embraced the anger deep inside her, allowing it to force away the pain and sorrow.

"In case I don't make it back again, just know that I'm going to make the bastard pay for what he did. I can do now what you didn't have the means to do twelve years ago. You and John *will* be avenged. It's not without risk, though. Quite a lot, actually. So, if you could see your way to put in a good word with the Big Man up there, maybe you can ask Him to look out for us tonight. Lord knows Hawk and I could use the help."

She exhaled and swallowed again, reaching out to lay a hand on the cold marble. She stared down at the grave, wondering if she would ever see it again, or if she would see Dave in person instead. Lowering her head, she closed her eyes briefly, drawing strength from the memory of Dave's easy smile and warm brown eyes. She remembered him hugging her tight before he left for that last deployment, almost feeling his arms around her again. He had been so alive! Then Harry took that away from him, took it away from them all.

Fury, swift and strong, flowed through her. Alina drew a deep, ragged breath and opened cold, dark eyes. The memory dissolved and the cold, impersonal marble head marker stared back at her.

Viper slowly stood, looking down for a moment at the grave.

She pulled a stainless steel chain out of her jacket pocket, leaning down to hook it over the top corner of the head stone. It was time to leave the past behind.

She turned to walk away, her breathing steady, leaving the chain hanging on Dave's grave. Two dog tags rested against the marble and the fading evening light caught the stamped name in a streak of light. Alina Maschik, Petty Officer Second Class, had no need of her old identification tags. That woman was part of the past.

Viper would take care of the future.

Chapter Thirty-Three

Stephanie watched in stony silence as Michael carried a large duffel bag out the back door. She still couldn't believe that Michael was going with Damon, while she and Blake were expected to simply sit this one out and stay put in the house.

"It's not his fault."

Blake spoke from the sofa after the door closed behind Michael, his eyes on her face. She glanced at him.

"I know."

"Then why are you glaring at him every time he goes by?"

"I'm not."

Blake raised an eyebrow and shook his head. "Could have fooled me."

"You mean to tell me that you aren't even remotely bothered that we're being left behind?" Stephanie demanded after a moment of silence.

"Honestly? No, I'm not."

She stared at him in disbelief. "Are you serious?"

His eyes met hers steadily.

"Absolutely. You're in no condition to get involved. The only reason you're not in a hospital right now is because it was more dangerous for you to stay. Face it, Steph. You're more of a liability out there than you are a help."

She glowered at him, but before she could say anything, the door slid open and Michael and Damon came into the house.

"Blake, you want to come over and I'll give you a crash course on the security system?" Damon asked, moving over to the bar.

Blake nodded and got off the couch, circling around to join him. Michael glanced at Stephanie, then moved into the living room.

"You okay?" he asked, looking down at her.

She shrugged.

"As okay as I can be expected to be," she replied. "I'm not happy about any of this, but you already know that."

"I know." Michael leaned against the empty hearth and crossed his arms over his chest. "The whole situation sucks. I wouldn't want to be in your position, but to be honest, I'm not sure any of us are in a better one."

She considered him for a long moment. "Do you really think you can get Angela out?"

Michael raised an eyebrow.

"What makes you think that's why I'm going?" he asked, startled.

Stephanie rolled her eyes.

"I'm not an idiot, even if I did hit my head a couple of times," she muttered. "Angela got taken on your watch, and now you're going with Damon to get involved in something both Lina and Damon made very clear none of us would have anything to do with. It's not rocket science. If you focus on Angela, they can focus on the colonel."

Michael smiled ruefully. "Guilty as charged, on all counts."

Stephanie nodded and sighed, leaning her head back.

"I think what bothers me most is that she didn't even say good-bye."

"She left before any of us were up," he pointed out. "And you need to rest and give your body chance to recuperate. I'm sure it wasn't intentional."

Stephanie was silent for a minute, then she looked at him.

"You'll get Angela out safely?"

Michael met her gaze somberly. "Yes."

She nodded.

"Try to bring yourself back, too. Too many people have died because of this man already."

"I'll be fine."

"We all will," Damon said from the bar. "Stop worrying."

Stephanie looked across the living room in surprise to find both Damon and Blake looking at them.

"I thought you were showing him the security system," she said, flushing.

"He was. We're done," Blake said. "It's not as complicated as it looks."

"I'm leaving the keys to Alina's Jeep," Damon said, holding up a set of keys. "If anything happens and you have to leave the property, take that. I changed the plates, so that should buy you some protection if Harry still has people watching the traffic cams. Don't risk it, though, if you don't have to."

He set the keys on the bar next to the tablet that accessed the

Next Exit, No Outlet

security system, then looked at Michael.

"You ready, gunny?"

Michael straightened up, dropping his arms to his side. "Let's roll."

He nodded to Stephanie and walked toward the back door. Blake met him halfway there, gripping his hand.

"You take care of yourself," he said in a low voice, "and watch your six."

Michael nodded.

"It'll be a walk in the park," he said. "You just keep Stephanie safe until this is all over. I don't want to know what Alina will do if anything happens to her."

"I've got it."

"Remember," Damon said, opening the back door, "no traceable contact and keep the perimeter set twenty-four seven. If you have a breach, shoot first and ask questions later."

"Trust me, I won't stop to chat," Blake assured him. "Good luck."

"Luck has nothing to do with it, gunny."

On that cryptic statement, Damon disappeared out the door with Michael close behind. Blake slid the door closed after them and watched as they went across the lawn to the Porsche. Once the sports car had started and was turning around in the driveway, he flipped the lock on the door and turned to go back to the sofa.

"And this is where we wait," he said, sinking onto the cushions.

"For what? Michael can't even call us when it's over. We don't have phones anymore, thanks to Lina, and there's no land line here that I can see." Stephanie exhaled loudly and looked at Blake. "We won't even know if everything goes to hell and they end up getting their butts kicked."

"I know."

They were both silent for a long moment.

"You're as uncomfortable with this as I am," Stephanie finally said. "I know you are. You weren't built to sit by and do nothing either."

"No," he agreed unexpectedly, "but I'm not leaving you, and you can't fight. So here we are."

Silence fell again as they both stared at the coffee table, lost in thought.

"Who said anything about fighting?" she finally asked slowly.

Blake looked up. "What?"

287

"I know I'm not a hundred percent," she began, but Blake snorted and cut her off.

"You're not even twenty-five percent," he said ruthlessly.

She made a face at him and continued.

"So I can't help them get Angela back or go after the colonel. I get it. But what if Angela needs me when Michael gets her off that boat? We have no idea what's happened to her. Michael is a great guy and all, but he's a man. He's not a woman who's known her since she was five."

Blake blinked and she could see that he hadn't considered the possibility that Angela might need a female available.

"And as for Lina, she and Damon are going into this completely alone," she continued, pressing her advantage. "Michael will be extracting Angela. Who's to say that we can't have some backup waiting? We *are* the FBI. There's no reason we can't arrange to have a contingency plan in place in case things go south."

He considered her thoughtfully for a long moment.

"What kind of contingency plan?" he finally asked. "The *Sea Queen* is in international waters. We can't send in a team."

"No, but the Coast Guard can," she pointed out.

"You heard what they said when we suggested that before," he objected. "If Harry sees a boarding party, or even something that he thinks *might* be the Coast Guard, he's more likely to kill Angela, or worse."

"That's why it would be a contingency plan. It would only happen if the situation got out of control and things got dire."

"There's no way for us to know if the situation is under control or not."

"Not from here."

The words fell heavily between them and Blake pressed his lips together.

"Oh no," he said, shaking his head again. "You're not leaving this house. It's too dangerous."

"It's dangerous for Michael and Lina, too" Stephanie argued, "but they took precautions and they went. We can take precautions as well. Hell, Damon already switched the plates on the Jeep. He did half the work for us. Even if they're still looking for the Jeep, they're looking for a single female driving it."

Blake hesitated, wavering.

"What's your plan?" He held up a hand and looked across the coffee table sternly. "I'm not agreeing. Tell me your plan and then I'll decide."

Next Exit, No Outlet

Stephanie smiled slowly. "We contact the Coast Guard and wait."

"Wait? For what?"

"For Michael to get Angie off the boat."

Viper glanced at her watch and lowered the binoculars. The marina was dark and quiet. It was closed for the night, and the only sign of life was the security guard ensconced in his hut at the entrance to the docks. He had relieved the previous guard at nine and a quick check of the previous week's security logs showed that he would be the only guard on duty until seven in the morning. She wasn't worried about him. He could be easily taken care of. What *did* concern her was the lack of anyone else in the marina. It was too quiet. Harry knew she was coming. He would never leave the port unprotected, especially when he'd laid out the breadcrumbs to lead her straight here. So where were they?

The *Sea Queen* was drifting in international waters about two hundred and ten nautical miles off the coast of Georgia. The only way out to her was by water, and Harry would be expecting her to come alone. Everything else aside, he still believed Hawk was halfway around the world. Viper turned to move silently across the roof of the main building in the marina. In that respect, she still had the element of surprise.

Reaching the edge of the building, Viper stayed in the shadows and raised the binoculars to scan the other side of the marina. Everything was quiet, but she knew that wouldn't last long. They were out there somewhere.

She lowered the binoculars thoughtfully. They were waiting for orders to emerge, and if she knew Harry at all, he wouldn't give that order until she was already on the yacht. He wouldn't risk anything until he knew he had her, then he would cut off the escape routes. If, by some stroke of luck, she managed to get Angela off the yacht, he would have reinforcements waiting.

Her phone vibrated and she pulled it out, glancing at the screen quickly. Hawk was in position at the rendezvous two miles away. It was time to wrap this up.

She made her way through the shadows to the back corner of the building where the nylon rope she had used to come up was still hanging in the darkness. A few minutes later, she was on the ground and moving through the night, away from the docks. She moved swiftly and silently, staying in the shadows until she reached Marina Drive, the road leading from the causeway. The black rental was a few meters up, pulled onto the grass and hidden deep in the shadows of the brush lining the road. Protected from curious eyes traveling the causeway by those shadows, she opened the driver's door and slid behind the wheel, pulling her phone out again. She tapped the screen and dialed, starting the engine.

"Hey," Michael picked up on the second ring.

"I'm on my way," she said, pulling out and turning towards the causeway. "Everything is quiet here. Is the boat ready?"

"Not much to get ready, but it's fueled and checked out."

"I'm bringing your gear. I'll be there in fifteen minutes."

"And Damon?"

"He's in place." Despite herself, Alina felt her lips curving in faint amusement. "Is that worry I detect in your tone?"

"Just making sure we're on schedule," he retorted. "Timing is everything in this plan you've cooked up."

"This isn't my first mission, gunny. I'll see you in a few."

Viper hung up and pulled onto the causeway, pressing the gas. He was right. Timing *was* everything. If anything went wrong with the timing, the whole mission would go dangerously sideways. She glanced at the clock on the Nav system in the dash.

She wasn't about to let that happen.

Hawk watched as the twin-engine plane came in and touched down on the runway, the lights on the wings flashing in the darkness. He stood in the shadows outside the main airport hangar and waited as the aircraft turned and taxied towards him. The flight plan had been logged earlier in the day, and security at the small regional airport was negligible. As far as the airport was concerned, he was a rich playboy catching a late-night flight on his way to more exotic locations.

Glancing at his watch, he waited in the shadows as the King Air 90 came to a stop a few yards away, the engines shutting down. A few minutes later, a man appeared in the door behind the wing, jumping down onto the pavement. After studying him for a minute by the light from the hangar, Damon moved out of the darkness towards

Next Exit, No Outlet

him. Seeing him, the man lifted a hand in a wave.

"Miles?" he called.

Damon nodded and held out his hand. "You can call me Damon."

"Jon Parker." Jon gripped his hand firmly. "It's good to meet you. Matt sends his regards. He said to take good care of you."

Damon smiled easily and turned to walk with Jon towards the hangar.

"I appreciate you coming on such short notice," he said. "I know you had to move your schedule around. I appreciate the effort."

Jon shrugged and waved away the thanks.

"It was no trouble. The way I hear it, you've helped us out a few times. Matt's told me stories."

Damon glanced at him, amused.

"Take everything your brother says with a grain of salt. He likes to exaggerate. Of course, if they made me look good, then he speaks the truth."

John chuckled.

"It was all good stuff," he assured him as they entered the hangar. "He speaks very highly of you."

"He's a good man."

"Is it true that you hung onto the side of a chopper with your bare hands as it flew over part of Cartagena?" Jon asked, looking at him.

Damon smiled faintly. "He told you that one, huh?"

"He said you were crazy. You did it for a bet?"

"In my defense, I was very drunk at the time. We were on a forty-eight hour leave."

"Like I said, crazy!"

"Don't let Matt fool you. Your brother did his fair share of stupid things. Ask him about the admiral's daughter."

Jon's blue eyes lit up with interest. "Oh, I will."

"How's he doing? It sounds like you two have a nice little business set up down in Louisiana," Damon said, glancing at him. "He's doing all right?"

Jon shrugged.

"You know Matt," he said. "He gives his all every second of the day. It's not easy for him, but he makes it work. The prosthetics these days are amazing. Thanks to them, he can still fly and ride his bike, so he's content."

Damon nodded. Jon's brother had lost his leg when an IED detonated next to him in a marketplace in Uzbekistan. After months of agonizing therapy, Matt had finally admitted to Damon that he struggled daily with depression and PTSD. The last time Damon saw him, he was doing much better, but he knew that the struggle was something Matt would live with for the rest of his life.

"As long as he has his Fat Boy, I'm sure he's happy," he said now. "He'll be all right."

"The business helps a lot," Jon told him. "It gives him a purpose. It's doing well. We're thinking of getting a fourth plane, maybe in the fall. But enough about us. Let's get to business. When are we leaving?"

"Forty-five minutes."

"Perfect." Jon glanced at him. "Do you have gear?"

"Yes. I'll load it just before we leave." Damon looked behind them at the plane. "Mind if I do a pre-flight check myself before you go through yours?"

Jon raised his eyebrows. "Don't trust me?"

"Nothing personal."

Jon grinned. "Matt warned me you'd want to check everything. No worries. I'll let you know when we're fueled and ready."

Damon nodded and held out his hand again.

"I'll see you then," he said, shaking his hand and turning to leave the hangar. "I'll check back in thirty."

Next Exit, No Outlet

Chapter Thirty-Four

Charlie stood at the window and looked out over the city. Night had fallen, cloaking DC in shadows while lights flashed and traffic moved through the streets, illuminating sidewalks crowded with people on foot hurrying to their destinations. Like any other city, the nation's capital seemed to come alive at night, sparkling with a careless excitement that wasn't present during the daylight hours. This was what Charlie liked to call the twilight period: the few hours between when the sun went down and when the serious night-dwellers stirred and came out from their safe spaces. This was when the city enjoyed itself before settling down to the business conducted in shadows; the business and shadows Charlie lived and thrived off of.

He glanced at his watch before sliding his hands into his pockets, staring down at the glittering lights below. Both Viper and Hawk had gone offline over forty minutes ago. Now all he could do was wait. Charlie's face was impassive as the scenario Viper had outlined played in his mind once more. There were so many ways the operation could fail, and yet he recognized that this was the only way Viper could do it. He shook his head slowly.

If she succeeded, there would be one hell of a mess for him to clean up. Yet, if she failed, the Organization would be finished, and Harry would be free.

Harry.

Charlie's eyes narrowed into a wintry glare as his lips tightened. His old friend and closest partner over the years, the one who helped him build the Organization and train the elite assets who worked for it, had betrayed not only Charlie, but his country and his oaths. Over the past months, as it became more and more apparent that the traitor was still right here in Washington, Harry was the glaringly obvious candidate. Charlie exhausted all other avenues before reluctantly accepting that it had to be him. Every road he followed led to the Department of Homeland Security, and to Harry.

The final nail in Harry's coffin came when one of Charlie's

cyber spies intercepted classified names of assets being sent from inside the DHS firewall. Less than twenty-four hours later they traced the leak back to Harry's department. Armed with the knowledge that his best friend was most likely a traitor, Charlie had met with Harry and told him to turn his agency upside down and inside out until he found the source of the leak. Under pressure, Harry had no problem serving up two of his own men as scapegoats. When the two directors from DHS were found on the side of the mountain in Shenandoah, Charlie knew he was running out of time. Harry wasn't stupid. He knew his cover was close to being blown. He was going to run and disappear, and he'd amassed a large enough fortune to be able to do it.

The only things standing in his way were Viper and Hawk: the specialized weapons Harry had helped create.

Charlie turned from the window as the phone on his desk chirped. Crossing to the desk, he picked up the receiver.

"Yes?"

"I have Commander Frampton of the Coast Guard on the line, sir."

"Thank you."

He waited for his assistant to hang up. Before he could say anything, a deep, gruff voice barked into his ear.

"Charlie? Is that you?"

He grimaced faintly and put some distance between the phone and his ear.

"Hi Steve. Thanks for calling back. I know it's late."

There was a sound suspiciously like a harrumph on the line.

"You also know I play poker on Tuesday nights," Steve said. "What can I do for you, Charlie?"

"If you haven't already, you're going to get a call from a Rob Thornton with the FBI. He'll try to convince you to work with two of their agents."

"Already had the conversation," Steve told him. "They're on their way to the base. The Casa Reinos Cartel is hanging offshore. Since when are you interested in a domestic issue?"

"Since it ran headfirst into my operation," Charlie said calmly. "Steve, I have to tell you something and it stays between us for now. Do you understand?"

There was a short silence on the line, then a soft sigh.

"You've known me long enough to know I can keep my trap closed. What's going on?"

"It's not just the cartel on that boat. Colonel Harry Shore is aboard."

Next Exit, No Outlet

"Harry?" Steve repeated, surprised. "What's he doing on a yacht with the cartel? Are you two up to one of your tricks?"

"Not exactly," Charlie said dryly. "Let's just say that your crews are at a disadvantage."

"What are you saying? For us to stand down?"

"Not precisely. I'm asking you to keep your distance."

There was another short silence, then a heavy sigh.

"Charlie, you're going to have to be blunt. I don't speak spook. Thornton wants us to send a boarding crew along with his two agents out to the yacht."

"You absolutely cannot do that. The only thing you're authorized to send in is a single chopper with the two agents onboard."

"On whose authority?"

"The President of the United States."

Steve blew out a gust of air and grunted.

"I should have known," he muttered. "You really like to pull out the big guns, don't you?"

"Only when absolutely necessary."

"And that's now?"

"Unfortunately."

"A single helicopter, huh?" Steve was quiet for a long moment. "What's Harry doing on that yacht, Charlie?"

"You know I can't tell you that."

"Can the agents board the *Sea Queen* from the helicopter?"

"I wouldn't advise it."

"Then why the hell am I sending them out on a chopper?!"

Charlie couldn't stop the amused smile that crossed his lips.

"Because if you don't, I wouldn't put it past Agent Walker to commandeer a boat herself and go out the *Sea Queen*, putting herself, her partner, and a civilian at risk. Trust me. You don't want that shit-show on your hands."

"Somehow, I have the feeling I'm still going to end up with a shit-show on my hands," Steve muttered.

"I'll be the one cleaning it up," Charlie promised. "You just keep the area clear."

"I suppose you have a plan for me to do so?"

"Of course."

"How complicated is it?"

"The only thing complicated will be convincing the agents that everything the Coast Guard does for them is a result of their own design," Charlie replied. "Your people need to make them believe that they're the ones in control. Can they do that?"

Steve was quiet for a moment, then he grunted.

"I have a pilot who was a Marine," he said. "He'll follow orders to the letter. Tell me what the script is and we'll see it done."

Viper climbed out of the SUV and looked across the rocky sand to where Michael was standing near the water. She circled around to open the back, pulling out two large, black duffel bags. Setting them on the ground, she reached for a smaller bag and closed the back quietly.

The tiny beach was deserted this time of night, the waves lapping against it quietly as the moon shone brightly overhead. A stiff, balmy wind blew off the water and ruffled her short hair as she picked up the two larger bags and turned toward Michael. It was a perfectly calm night, with a clear forecast. She couldn't have asked for better weather.

"How're we doing?" she asked, walking up to Michael. He was dressed in black neoprene pants and dive jacket. "I see Damon got you outfitted ok."

"I have to admit that I didn't take you seriously when you said I'd need special gear," he told her. "I stand corrected."

She grinned and dropped the large bags on the ground at his feet.

"You're the one who wanted to do more," she said, crouching down and unzipping one of the bags. "Be careful what you wish for, gunny."

She pulled out a black tactical drysuit and handed it to him.

"What's this?"

"A drysuit. Put it on over your clothes. It keeps the water out. It also helps protect from hypothermia, but you don't need to worry about that tonight. These waters are pretty warm."

She turned to the other bag and unzipped it, glancing at the motorboat tied to a dock a few feet away.

"I'll get the boat ready," she said, picking up the bag and turning toward the short, private dock.

"Who owns this place?" Michael asked, shooting a quick look behind them at the large, dark and silent house that fronted the small beach.

"No idea."

Next Exit, No Outlet

His mouth dropped open and he stared after her. "What? You mean, they could come home any minute?"

Viper glanced over her shoulder with a grin.

"Now gunny, do you really think I'd take that risk? The house is closed up for the season. The dock is all ours for as long as we need it."

She walked along the weather-worn wooden boards to the boat bobbing in the waves next to the dock. She tossed the bag in and then followed it, dropping into the boat easily. The small craft shifted with her weight and the familiar sway of the water welcomed her as she bent to pull a package out of the bag. Breathing deeply, Viper felt a rush of contentment roll through her with the salt air. She loved the water, always had, and if tonight was going to be her last night on this earth, Viper couldn't think of anywhere better for her to go out.

With that thought flitting through her mind, she turned toward the back of the boat, seating herself on the bench seat. Pulling a thin Maglight from her jacket pocket, she bent over and shone it under the seat. After a cursory look, Viper put the flashlight down on the floor and set the square package on the bench beside her. She was just reaching into the bag again when her phone vibrated briefly against her thigh.

Frowning, she pulled it out and glanced at the screen. It was an incoming text message from a number she didn't recognize. Swiping the screen, she read the message quickly.

Marina is quiet. There's no one here. What's the plan?

The frown faded and she typed a quick reply back.

They're there. They're staying hidden. Hold your positions.

Setting the phone down, Viper went back to the bag. She didn't like using outside crews, but tonight she had no choice. She and Hawk had to secure the yacht, and that left Michael and Angela exposed when they returned to shore. She needed helping hands and, unfortunately, that meant using a crew she hadn't worked with before.

Shaking her head, she pulled some wiring out of the bag and picked up the package again. Five minutes later, it was secured under the seat against the back side near the outboard motor. Her phone vibrated again and she picked it up, glancing at the screen.

We're on schedule?

She glanced at her watch. Y*es.* ***Passengers will arrive in less than 2 hours, as arranged.***

Setting the phone down again, Viper turned back to the bag and used both hands to extract a large, rubber inflatable. She was just connecting a battery-powered pump to it when her phone went off again.

And if they don't?

She stifled an impatient sigh and glanced back at the shore where Michael was just finishing pulling on his drysuit.

They'll be there. But if not, wait for another half hour, then abort.

Viper slid the phone back into her pocket and connected the pump to the inflatable, then carefully laid it out on the boat bottom between the front and back seats. Then, picking up the empty duffel bag, she stood and climbed back onto the dock.

She turned to stride down the short pier, her boots making no sound on the wooden planks as she moved swiftly and silently.

"Need any help?" Michael asked as she joined him on the beach again.

"It's all done. Quick and clean." Viper dropped the empty bag to the ground and picked up the smaller one. Opening it, she motioned him closer. "It's very straight-forward. Everything's in here. Detonator, GPS, breathing mask and tank. The tank only has thirty minutes of air, so don't waste it. This is a homing beacon. Before you go in the drink, attach it to your suit. If things go sideways, that will transmit your location to the Coast Guard. You activate it by twisting the outer dial."

"How long does that last?" he asked, glancing at the small, round disc.

"Longer than you'd need it to," she assured him. Closing the bag, she handed it to him. "The inflatable is hooked up to the pump and ready to go. It takes about thirty seconds to fully inflate. Do you need a crash course on the boat?"

Michael looked at her in exasperation. "I *have* driven a boat before."

She grinned. "Hey, just checking."

"Are you sure the *Sea Queen* has a tender onboard?" he asked, watching as she bent down to open the bag she'd pulled his drysuit from.

"Yes. It's inside, at the stern." Viper pulled out a waterproof leg holster and handed it to him. "It's a drive-in garage. Once you open it, you can pull right out into the water. Here. Put that on. It will keep the gun dry."

"I already have my piece in here," Michael said, patting a pocket at his waist.

She looked up and smiled at him as she pulled a Ruger SR1911 out of the bag.

Next Exit, No Outlet

"The holster is for this," she said, handing him the weapon along with extra ammunition and a suppressor. "The accuracy is far better than what you carry. The night scope is already attached, and its mods give it an outstanding range. Use that when you absolutely have to hit your target."

"If I'm pulling the trigger, I already absolutely have to hit my target," he retorted, taking the gun from her. He pulled out the clip, familiarizing himself with the pistol. "You really do have the fun toys, don't you?"

Viper zipped the bag closed and stood up, her lips twisting in a self-deprecating smile.

"Not sure I would call them toys," she replied, glancing at her watch. "Any questions?"

Michael glanced up from the gun, his eyes meeting hers.

"Do you think this will work?"

"Which part?"

"The part where I get Angela off that boat and to shore."

"Yes."

Michael slid the gun into the holster and secured it, then strapped the holster around his thigh.

"And the part where you get the colonel?"

Viper's impenetrable mask slid into place. "I'll get back to you on that one."

Michael looked at her, his face grim.

"You might need help. Once I get Angela away, I can go back," he began, but she was already shaking her head.

"Your job is to take care of Angie," she said, cutting him off. "Get her to the marina. There'll be transport waiting. Take it and get her somewhere safe, and keep her safe. That's what I need from you."

"How will I know when it's all clear?"

"You'll know." She looked at her watch. "Transport will wait for half an hour in case you get held up, but then it leaves. Whatever happens, make sure you and Angie get there in time and are on it."

"I know. Timing is everything. What is our transport?"

"A car with a driver."

She hesitated for a brief a second and Michael raised his eyebrows.

"What's wrong?" he asked.

"Michael, when you get to the marina, you're not a Federal agent. Do you understand?" she asked softly. "As far as anyone knows, you're simply a business associate trying to get an innocent woman to safety. You're not law enforcement. You're not the good guy. Got it?"

Michael stared at her for a long moment, his brows pulled together in a frown, before he finally nodded reluctantly.

"No mention of who I am. Got it."

Viper nodded and looked at the boat, bobbing in the water next to the dock.

"Time to go, gunny," she said, looking back at his face. "You ready?"

"Oorah!"

She grinned and held out her hand. "I can't ask for more than that."

Michael gripped her hand and pulled her close to wrap his arms around her in a hug.

"You take care of yourself, Lina," he said softly, squeezing her gently.

Viper pulled away and her lips twisted faintly.

"I'll see you on the other side, gunny."

Chapter Thirty-Five

Viper draped a bag across her body and reached for the last black duffel in the back of the SUV. She had already wiped down the entire vehicle for any stray prints and the black gloves on her hands ensured that it remained clean. Hawk had taken care of the surveillance cameras in the small parking lot before she arrived, and she turned to walk away, confident in the knowledge that she was leaving no trace behind.

By tomorrow all this effort would be a moot point. They were extra steps that both she and Hawk were used to taking, but when this was over, they wouldn't really matter. Harry would be dealt with, and Charlie would clean up the rest. Their work would be done, and it would be as if they were never here. They would fade into the darkness and disappear.

Just as they always did.

For once, the prospect didn't sit well with her, and Viper felt an unfamiliar sense of disquiet. As many times as she'd walked away in the past, this time was different. She wasn't just leaving a town she had called home for a few weeks. She was leaving a life behind; one that she hadn't wanted to return to last year when she was forced back into the game.

The disquiet was pushed away by a rush of anger. Harry had been responsible for it all. She had been content on her mountain in South America, learning to accept herself again despite the things she had done, when he dragged her back into the world she had walked away from. Like a puppet, she had danced along on his string, not realizing that she was playing a part in an elaborate production.

The anger remained, simmering inside her as she strode across the small airport parking lot towards the single, large rectangular building. Not only had she been drawn back into the game, but she'd inadvertently dragged the only family she had left along with her. It had cost John his life, and nearly cost Stephanie and Angela theirs.

Reaching the doors to the airport, she went inside and glanced around. Her eyes lit on Hawk, sitting on the far side near a wall of windows overlooking the dark landing strip, and the anger intensified. The only reason he was still alive was because a random helicopter flew in front of an inexperienced shooter in Singapore.

All because of Harry.

Damon looked up then and his blue eyes met hers across the large room. The anger evaporated in an instant, replaced by a warm feeling of belonging. She felt a surge of warmth and all the tension in her shoulders eased when he smiled. At some point, when she wasn't paying attention, Damon had come to mean much more to her than she'd ever dreamed possible. When she saw him now, she felt like she was home.

Striding across the building toward him, Viper felt her lips curve in an answering smile. He stood and started toward her.

"You made it!" he said, his voice carrying to the two night employees behind the desk a few yards away. "I was beginning to think you changed your mind."

Aware of the curious eyes watching them, she tossed her head and laughed gaily.

"And miss Palm Beach?" she demanded. "As if!"

A genuine laugh leapt into Damon's eyes at her playful tone and he slid one arm around her waist while his other hand took the duffel bag from her.

"It'll be the time of your life," he told her, lowering his lips to hers. "I guarantee it."

He turned her towards the glass double doors leading outside to the tarmac, his arm still firmly around her waist.

"Don't I have to check in or something?" she protested, glancing over to the desk.

"All you have to do is relax and get ready to party. The pilot's just waiting on us. I told you I'd take care of everything!"

Hawk pushed open the door and ushered her outside, away from the watching eyes. As soon as the door closed behind them, Viper glanced at him.

"Get ready to party?" she repeated, her voice trembling. "Is that what you call it these days?"

He looked down at her and grinned. "It's got a better ring to it than let's go to work. Besides, you're one to talk. 'Don't I have to check in?' I almost choked."

He still had his arm around her and Viper didn't feel inclined to pull away as they walked along the sidewalk towards the large hangar. An airplane was outside on the tarmac, waiting.

"Everything's ready?" she asked. "The pilot's briefed?"

Next Exit, No Outlet

"Yep. I did a pre-flight check as well as the pilot. We're good to go. Did you get Michael squared away?"

"Yes." She glanced at her watch. "He should be getting into position now. He'll hold until he gets the word."

He looked at her. "You're sure he can handle it?"

She shrugged. "We'll find out."

They were silent for a moment, then Damon stopped walking and turned to face her, dropping the bag onto the pavement. She looked up at him questioningly and caught her breath at the grave look on his face.

"We need to discuss what happens if something goes wrong," he said quietly.

"We already have. It's plan B."

"No. *You* discussed plan B. I never agreed to it." Hawk stared down at her, his jaw twitching. "We don't do suicide missions, and that's what your plan B amounts to."

"Every mission is potentially a suicide mission. This is no different. If something goes wrong, Angela has to be a priority. You're the only other person who can get her to safety."

"Leaving you alone, outnumbered by Organization rejects and cartel thugs, on a yacht with Harry!"

She shrugged. "Then that's how it is. Angela has to get off that boat. You know what will happen if she stays."

"If Michael can't get it done, there is another option," he said slowly. "We get Angela out and let Harry go." Damon swiftly pressed his finger against her lips as she started to protest. "Listen to me. We know where he's heading. We can get him in Montenegro."

"And in the meantime, Stephanie, Blake and Angela are in hiding," she retorted. "No. This ends tonight."

"Agreed, but only if the gunny can execute his end. If not, I think we should abort." He slipped his other arm around her and pulled her close. "The odds are already very heavily on their side, even with both of us together. Take one of us out of the mix, and our odds are almost non-existent. I'd rather Stephanie and Company have a few uncomfortable weeks in a safe house somewhere than go through the rest of my life without you."

Something deep inside her tugged and Viper felt the bottom of her gut drop out as her breath caught in her throat.

"I don't know what I'm supposed to say to that," she whispered around the lump in her throat.

"Say we extract Angela and live to fight another day."

She let out a choked laugh and gazed into his deep blue eyes.

He was deadly serious, and she knew if she refused, he would simply find another way around it. Hawk was nothing if not stubborn.

"Michael will do it," she said after a long moment. "I think it will take something extreme to make him fail."

"You know as well as I do that the smallest thing can derail an operation. It may not happen, but we have to be on the same page if it does."

With a soft sigh, Viper capitulated.

"Fine. If things get fubar, we get Angie and get off the boat," she said grudgingly.

Damon wrapped her close and rested his chin on top of her, exhaling. "Good."

She smiled against his shoulder, feeling some of the tension leave him with her agreement. He really had been worried about plan B. Of all the things that could go wrong, he was worried about her. A wave of warmth rolled through her again and a strange feeling of being cherished engulfed her. She couldn't remember the last time someone had worried about her.

Damon lifted his head and pulled away slightly, looking down into her face. Bending his head, he brushed his lips against hers softly.

"Let's get this show on the road," he said, lifting his head and bending to pick up the bag again.

They turned to continue to the plane and as they drew closer, a man appeared in the open door behind the wing.

"You must be Raven!" he called, jumping down and striding towards them. "Damon said we were waiting on you. I'm Jon. Good to meet you."

Viper grasped his offered hand. "Thanks for helping us out. We appreciate it."

"No worries. You have your gear?"

"Yes."

"Then let's get this party started."

Jon turned back toward the plane and she glanced at Damon in some amusement. He winked and followed Jon to the open door of the plane, tossing her bag inside before climbing into the plane easily. He turned and reached out a hand to her, but she waved him away impatiently. He chuckled and backed up as she climbed into the belly of the plane.

Instead of rows of passenger seats, the back half of the plane was outfitted with a row of bench seats along each side. Damon's bags were already onboard and as Viper straightened up, she pulled her bag over her head and moved to one of the benches. She sat down and

Next Exit, No Outlet

opened it as Jon got in behind them and closed the door, latching it.

"Damon gave me the coordinates. Once we takeoff, you have about seventeen minutes to the run," he said, turning to look at them. "Your window is going to be very tight. When I say go, you'll have about sixty seconds before that window closes."

"Wind gusts over the target?" Viper asked, glancing up.

"About what we expected. It's a clear night with minimal wind. No surprises, which is just how I like it. It'll be a walk in the park for you two. Good luck."

Damon nodded. "Thanks."

Jon moved down the aisle toward the cockpit and Viper watched him go to the front seat thoughtfully. Once he was seated and going through his takeoff routine, she looked at Damon.

"Who is he?" she asked. "And why does he know your name?"

"I served with his brother," he answered, unzipping a large bag. "He's someone we can trust. His brother is a good man. He's the only one I kept in touch with." Damon looked up. "I trust him with my life."

She raised an eyebrow. "A SEAL?"

He nodded. "They run a small business out of Louisiana now."

"And Jon's done this before?"

Damon looked at her, amused. "Every day. This is what their business does."

She grinned and bent down to unzip the big black duffel bag as Jon started the engines.

"Just checking." She glanced at her watch. "Where's my pack?"

Damon nodded to the back of the plane where two black backpacks were on the floor. Viper followed his gaze as she reached into the open bag at her feet.

"Did you check them?"

"Yes." He pulled a phone out of the inside of his jacket and swiped the screen, typing something quickly. "I'll get the gunny moving."

She nodded and pulled a leg holster out of her bag, securing it around her right thigh. Reaching back into the bag, she extracted a second one for the left leg. Hawk slid the phone back into his jacket and reached for his bag, pulling out his own holsters. He glanced across at her as he strapped one on.

"You have the charges?"

"They're in the gray bag, inside the big one."

He nodded and finished securing his holsters, then reached for the large duffel bag.

"When you're ready, your bag with your tank is in that bag over there. It will have to hook on your opposite side from the weapons bag."

Viper nodded, waiting for him to pull out the gray bag before reaching for the big bag. She pulled out a long, slender black bag that could be worn across her body. Draping it over her shoulder, she secured it flush to her torso with straps and turned back to the bag. She unzipped another, smaller bag and pulled out a Ruger SR22. It was one of a pair, and she quickly checked the magazine before reaching for the other one. Hawk looked up from the open bag next to him as she checked the clip on the second one.

"Once these charges are set, you'll have five minutes," he told her. "I'll tell you when it's done and the countdown starts. Are you sure that's enough time?"

"Any longer and we might as well broadcast what we're doing," she replied, sliding the Rugers into the narrow weapons bag.

"It'll be fine. Just make sure you get off the yacht as soon as they're set."

"Is Trident in place?"

"It will be, if it's not already."

They fell silent then as they finished preparing their gear and getting it secured to their bodies. Viper glanced over to Hawk more than once as he worked quickly, his movements precise and efficient. It was strange to be preparing for this with someone else, especially him. They were both so used to working alone that it was surreal to now be working as one unit. Even so, she admitted to a tremendous feeling of relief not to be going into this alone.

Getting up, she moved down a bit to the bag Damon had motioned to earlier. She opened it and found two oblong bags. Pulling one out, she checked the small oxygen tank inside. It was nearly identical to the one she had handed Michael earlier.

"They'll last for an hour and a half," Hawk said, joining her. "That should be more than enough time."

She nodded and checked the mask, then closed the bag and strapped it on so that it was held tight against her left side.

"They just have to get us to Trident," she agreed.

Hawk strapped on his own tank and then turned to move to the back of the plane.

"Ten minutes to run!" Jon called from the cockpit.

Viper followed Hawk, glancing at her watch.

"We're right on schedule," he said, handing her one of the black packs as she joined him.

Next Exit, No Outlet

She nodded and took the pack, swinging it onto her back. While she tightened the straps around her torso, Hawk began to secure the straps around her legs.

"As soon as Michael and Angela are clear of the boat, I'll take out the satellite and electrical system," he said as he pulled them taut against her.

He finished getting her straps done and turned to reach for the other pack.

"Once the electrical goes out, we'll be blind. The night-vision will help, but get as many charges as you can set before you cut the power," Viper said, watching as he swung the bag onto his back. "With any luck, I'll get to Harry before he realizes there's two of us."

Hawk adjusted his straps, waving her away when she reached to help him with the bottom ones. She grinned and turned to make her way back to the bags.

"Stubborn bastard," she muttered under her breath.

"What was that?"

She looked over her shoulder. "Why do I need help with the leg straps, but you won't let me help you?"

He let out a bark of laughter.

"Seriously?" he demanded, finishing with the straps and turning to go over to her. "Are you honestly complaining because I helped you?"

"No. I'm just observing that you think you're above help."

"I don't need help. I've done this so many times it's like putting on shoes in the morning." He lowered his head to press his lips against hers swiftly. "You, on the other hand, have probably only done this a handful of times."

She shrugged. "Fair enough, but I still know how to work my own gear."

He winked. "Maybe I just wanted an excuse to get my hands between your legs."

It was her turn to let out a laugh.

"Oh honey, all you had to do was ask." She turned him around so she could check his pack. "At least let me make sure you're not going to plummet to your death."

He grunted and was silent while she went over the bag on his back, testing clips and straps.

"If I die, it won't because the gear was bad," he said when she'd finished. He turned her around to check hers. "Remember, the wind gusts coming off the water will make it tricky. Aim for the stern. That's the easiest landing point."

Viper turned to face him. "Now you're just being insulting."

He grinned and was lowering his head to kiss her again when Jon yelled the five-minute warning. He glanced at his watch and sighed.

"And it's time to go to work."

He turned towards the door and Viper braced herself for the rush of air as he unbolted the safety bar and opened the door. Cool salt air flooded in and she grabbed hold of the hand railing bolted into the side of the plane. Hawk moved beside her, grabbing the railing with one hand and bracing the other on the roof. They both looked out into the black void. Far below, the rough and choppy waves of the Atlantic waited for them.

As did Harry.

Viper shifted her weight, getting used to the balance of the gear. Everything was ready. Everything had been planned down to the second. The only thing left to do was jump.

Her eyes met Hawk's and she saw her own excitement reflected in them. It didn't matter what waited for them on the yacht. Right now, they were staring out the door of a plane and waiting for the word to dive. She felt a familiar rush of adrenaline go through her as her heart thumped once before settling down in a steady, strong rhythm.

"You ready?" he asked loudly over the howl of the wind and salt air.

"I'm always ready for this!"

Next Exit, No Outlet

Chapter Thirty-Six

"Tell me again how I let you talk me into this," Blake muttered as they strode through the doors of the airport and emerged into the heavy, humid evening air of Savannah, Georgia.

"I don't know why you're complaining," Stephanie said, stopping next to him and leaning on her cane tiredly. "We just got a ride on a private jet! Tell me you didn't enjoy that."

"I didn't enjoy it."

"You're full of crap."

"How could I enjoy it when I kept waiting for an assassin to walk through the cabin and put a bullet in our heads?" he demanded, raising a hand and flagging down a cab. "Talk about reckless!"

"You agreed that the risk was probably minimal as long as we were smart about moving around," she pointed out as a taxi pulled up to the curb.

Blake glanced at her incredulously.

"I was talking about driving back roads in a Jeep with new plates," he exclaimed. "Not flying between two major airports on the East coast!"

She shrugged and grinned.

"Rob got us through Philly without any issues, and now we're here without any signs of assassins lurking around the corner. Stop worrying. It's fine."

Blake opened the taxi door and waved her inside. "Uh huh. Just get in the car and out of sight, please."

Stephanie got into the cab and slid over on the seat as Blake got in beside her.

"Coast Guard Air Station," he told the driver, closing the door.

The driver nodded and flipped something on the dash before easing away from the curb.

Blake looked at her, then at the plastic box she'd set on the seat between them.

"I still can't believe you brought the cat."

Stephanie looked at him. "Well, I couldn't just leave her."

"She's a cat! She'd be fine!"

"I don't know how long we'll be here!" she shot back. "Do you have any idea what Angie will do to me if anything happens to this cat? Besides, after what she's been through, her cat will be much appreciated."

"I don't get it."

"Oh really? Then why did you leave Buddy with Rob? Why not just leave *him* at the house?"

He shrugged. "That's different. It's a dog."

Stephanie sputtered and glared at him.

"That doesn't even rate a response," she muttered, leaning down and slipping a finger through the grate in the front of the carrier. A soft nose nudged it, then Anabelle let out a sad meow.

Blake shook his head and looked out the window. She pulled her hand away from the carrier and sighed.

"Did Rob get hold of the Commander?" she asked after a few minutes of silence.

"Yes. He's got someone waiting for us." Blake looked at her. "You realize this hare-brained idea of yours can't possibly work, right?"

She looked at him. "Then why are we here?"

He grunted and turned his gaze out the window.

"Because I didn't have a better hare-brained idea."

"Then quit complaining. What's the name of the person meeting us?"

"Lieutenant Miller." Blake looked at his watch. "Rob said the Coast Guard will have a crew ready to go once Angela is off the yacht. Do you know how many things can wrong with this?"

"You need to have a little faith," she said with a frown. "Just because they aren't the Marines, it doesn't mean they don't know what they're doing."

Blake glanced at her but was silent, his lips pressed together in a grim line. Stephanie looked at him and sighed silently. It was clear that he wasn't happy about them being here, but what else was she supposed to do? Just let her two best friends die while she relaxed in a house in the woods?

She turned her gaze out the window and stared at the dark city speeding by. Who knew what Angela had gone through, or was currently going through! And as for Lina, Stephanie was determined that tonight would not be the night that her old friend met her fate. Alina might be of the opinion that this was how her life would most likely end, but Stephanie wasn't about to let fate have any say in what

Next Exit, No Outlet

happened on that yacht. As soon as Angela was safe, she was sending in the cavalry, whether Viper liked it or not.

"When Michael does get Angela off that boat, he's going to have to get her somewhere safe," Blake said, breaking the silence. "Until we know for sure that Harry has been…neutralized, she's going to need to be hidden."

"We'll take her back to Lina's," Stephanie said. "That's the only logical place. But to be honest, I don't think we'll have time to get her there. I've seen Lina work. It'll all be over tonight."

Waves lapped at the sides of the speed boat and Michael glanced at his watch, pressing the button on the side to illuminate the face. He was in position and letting the motor idle, waiting for the text that would tell him to proceed. If it didn't come in the next five minutes, he was to abort. Damon had been very clear about that when he briefed him earlier.

Michael's jaw tightened and he looked up into the night sky sparkling with a million stars. It was a cloudless, mild night and the breeze across the water was warm. He really couldn't ask for better weather to attempt his first covert ship boarding. He shook his head. Those were words he never would have dreamed he'd think. He was a Marine, not a sailor. Yet here he was in a boat, waiting for the signal to storm a yacht on the open seas.

All for a woman he promised to keep an eye on twelve years ago.

She certainly wasn't boring, he'd give her that. Michael lowered his gaze to the plastic dummy laying across the bottom of the boat and felt his lips pull up at the corners. Then he looked at the instrument panel again, focusing on the silently flashing dot that represented the *Sea Queen*. She was straight ahead, six nautical miles away in the darkness. When he got the signal from Damon, it would take the boat about ten minutes to reach the yacht. Once they saw him, there was no turning back. He was committed to risking his life to save a woman he barely knew.

He must be out of his mind.

As soon as the thought entered his head, Michael sighed. No. He wasn't out of his mind. He was doing the right thing. It wasn't Angela's fault that she was caught up in this, just as it wasn't Alina's fault that they were all where they were now. He knew she blamed herself, but in his mind that was ridiculous. She hadn't arranged for a terrorist to come into the United States and attack Three Mile Island, kicking off the series of events that had led them all here. That was solely the work of Colonel Harry Shore.

His brows drew together and Michael stared out over the moonlit black waves thoughtfully. Why had the colonel done all this? None of it made any sense. He was a war hero, who had committed his military career to doing what was best for the United States of America. What made him suddenly turn traitor twelve years ago? By then he was already well-established in Washington and, as it turned out, busy training men and women to lead the next wave of clandestine security to protect US interests across the globe. Why risk all of that and turn into one of the enemy?

The watch on his wrist vibrated and Michael's pulse leapt. He pulled his phone out from a pocket on his arm and glanced at the screen.

Go.

He tucked his phone back inside the pocket and secured it again. He touched the leg holster to ensure it was closed and then patted the other pocket at his hip. Satisfied that the suit was sealed properly, he pushed the throttle and the boat leapt forward over the waves. Once he had the speed at a steady forty-five knots, Michael set the GPS cruise control. After checking everything to make sure it was on course and holding steady at speed, he turned to the inflatable dummy laying behind him. Finding the pump, he pressed the button and air began pouring into the plastic, inflating it rapidly. He watched as it quickly took on the shape of a person, complete with tactical headgear and goggles.

Viper hadn't been exaggerating. The dummy was fully inflated in less than a minute and the pump switched itself off. Michael disengaged it and sealed the intake valve. Then he looked at the life-sized dummy. It was uncannily life-like and he shook his head before wrapping his arms around it and hoisting it over the back of the driver's seat to place it at the wheel.

"There you go, Bob," he murmured. "You're the skipper now."

Grabbing some nylon cord, Michael quickly secured the dummy to the seat. By the time he was finished, it appeared that the rubber person was actively driving the boat. Sparing only a quick grin at the sight, he turned to the back of the boat and crouched down, peering under the back seat. He pulled a thin flashlight out of one of

Next Exit, No Outlet

his pockets and shone it under the bench, illuminating the explosive set up against the back hull.

He glanced at his watch. It was time. After a moment of natural hesitation, Michael took a deep breath and reached out to lift the clear, hard plastic cover protecting the timer. He pressed the button and a digital display popped up, counting down from five minutes.

He switched off the flashlight and slid it back into the pocket. Then, turning to the side of the boat, Michael switched on the tank in the bag Viper had given him. He strapped it onto his back and pulled the mask over his face. After taking a few easy breaths, he glanced at his watch again.

Without another hesitation, he hopped over the side of the boat and plunged into the dark, endless waves of the Atlantic.

Stephanie looked up as Blake joined her, tucking a phone away in his pocket. Before boarding the plane in Philadelphia, Rob had pressed a pre-paid phone into Blake's hand. Rob was the only one with the number and Blake had taken it gratefully. The lack of communication devices was driving both of them crazy, and Stephanie wasn't even irritated that Blake was the one with the phone. She was just glad they had one.

"Rob just got off with the Commander," he told her in a low voice. "He doesn't want to commit crews to this until he's sure all the civilians are off the yacht."

"Agreed," she said. "That's what we said from the beginning."

"Yes, but what he considers off the yacht and what we consider off the yacht appear to be very different things. He's talking about waiting until morning."

Stephanie's mouth dropped open. "That will be too late!"

He nodded grimly.

"I know. Rob said that he was assured that they are monitoring the yacht via satellite and at the first sign of trouble, the Commander will re-evaluate." Blake looked at his watch. "There is one thing in our favor though. The Lieutenant meeting us was a Marine."

Stephanie raised an eyebrow. "How does that make a difference?"

Blake grinned at her. "Semper fi, my dear. Semper fi."

The door to the large recreational room where they had been

left to wait opened and a broad-shouldered man with dark hair entered, a clipboard in his hand.

"Agents Walker and Hanover?" he asked, looking across the room.

"Yes."

"I'm Lieutenant Miller," he said, striding forward and holding out a hand. "I understand you're here to see about the yacht hovering offshore."

"Something like that," Blake said, grasping his hand firmly. "I'm Agent Hanover and this is Agent Walker."

Miller nodded to Stephanie and held out his hand. "Nice to meet you, ma'am."

"Have you received any new information about the *Sea Queen*?" she asked, shaking his hand. "There's a civilian being held onboard and I'm worried for her safety."

Lt. Miller nodded soberly.

"So I've been told. As of an hour ago, there's been no sign of unusual activity. No boats have approached the yacht and no one has left. It's all quiet." The Lieutenant looked from one to the other, his dark eyes probing. "My briefing gave me the layout, but why don't you tell me what you know."

Stephanie glanced at Blake and hesitated.

"That's not much, I'm afraid," he said calmly, his expression neutral. "All we know is that Angela Bolan was kidnapped by the cartel and taken to that yacht. We have no idea why or how."

"How do you know she was taken aboard?"

"I pulled satellite footage from yesterday morning."

The lieutenant nodded and walked over to lean against a ping-pong table. He set his clipboard down and crossed his arms over his chest.

"And you have no idea why?"

"No," Stephanie said a little too quickly, "but I'm sure you understand my concern."

"Yes, and I share it," he agreed. "Unfortunately, my hands are tied right now. We're under orders not to approach the vessel. All we can do is monitor and be prepared to move if needed. The problem is that they're staying in international waters. We need a clear and present danger to be able to approach, and even then it's a diplomatic nightmare. Do you know who's on that yacht?"

Stephanie and Blake glanced at each other.

"The Casa Reinos second-in-command, for one," Blake finally said. "Who are you referring to?"

Next Exit, No Outlet

"Colonel Harry Shore," the lieutenant said bluntly. "As I'm sure you're aware, the Coast Guard falls under the jurisdiction of the Department of Homeland Security. Essentially, our boss is on that yacht."

Stephanie swallowed hard and sank into a seat. "So you know."

Something like a smile crossed the lieutenant's face.

"Yes. We know." He studied them for a moment, looking from one to the other. "I understand that you want to make sure that the civilian gets off safely, and that the cartel is apprehended. Trust me, I'd like nothing more than to see the same thing myself. Right now, though, we're in a holding pattern until further notice."

"What does that mean, exactly?" Stephanie asked, looking up at him.

"It means all we can do is watch and wait," he said. "Now, I can set you guys up in an office to work from, but there's not much that can be done yet."

Blake nodded.

"I appreciate that," he said slowly. "When you get confirmation that Angela is off the boat, what then?"

The lieutenant shrugged. "Then we can approach if there are indications of danger or illegal activity. Until then, my orders are to stand down."

Blake looked at him steadily. "You don't like that anymore than we do," he said softly.

Lieutenant Miller met his gaze and shook his head.

"No," he admitted. "But those are my orders."

"I know about following orders. My company got ambushed once from following orders."

The lieutenant looked at him with a spark of interest.

"You served?"

"Fox Company, Second Battalion, Marines."

A rare smile crossed the lieutenants face.

"The Magnificent Bastards," he said with a nod. "I flew your company a few times."

Blake grinned. "I saw your bio on the way in. What made you come over to the Coast Guard?"

Miller shrugged.

"I wanted a change," he said easily. "The Coast Guard needed pilots, and I needed a break from deployment. It was a good move for me. How about you? How did you land with the FBI?"

"I just kind of fell into it. A good buddy of mine discharged and went into the Secret Service. You'd be surprised how many of us ended up in law enforcement."

Miller chuckled.

"No, I wouldn't. It makes sense, in a way." He looked at his watch, then seemed to hesitate for a moment. "Look, I'm about to make an observation run over the *Sea Queen*," he said slowly. "Nothing crazy. Just taking a chopper out and doing a pass to make sure they know we're watching them."

He paused again and looked from one to the other.

"I know you're concerned, and rightfully so. Why don't you come with me? Then you can see for yourself that everything's quiet?"

Stephanie stood up quickly, leaning on her cane.

"Yes, please!"

"That would be awesome," Blake said. "We'd really appreciate that."

Miller nodded and picked up his clipboard, turning toward the door.

"Hey, it's the least I can do for a fellow Marine," he said over his shoulder. "Follow me. I'll show you where you can leave your gear and then I'll take you up."

Chapter Thirty-Seven

Harry knocked once on the door to the bridge before opening it and stepping inside. The room where the captain spent most of his time was spacious and comfortable, resembling something closer to the command center of a spaceship than the bridge of a yacht. Located on the uppermost level, the large room was surrounded with windows that afforded a three hundred and sixty degree view of the ocean around them. Flat touch screen monitors lined the captain's helm, giving him instant and easy access to all the information needed to ensure a safe and uneventful voyage.

Behind the helm a comfortable sectional wrapped around a table, allowing the crew or owners to sit with the captain and take in the view. It was also where the captain liked to eat, and Harry found him seated with a plate of lasagna and a basket of garlic bread.

"How's it going, Tony?" Harry asked, glancing at the monitors. They cast a bright and cheerful glow against the blackness of the night outside. "Anything new?"

"No," Tony answered, swallowing and reaching for a tall glass of soda. "Everything is still quiet."

"Nothing at all?" Harry frowned and looked at the captain, seating himself across the table from him.

Tony shook his head.

"Nothing worth mentioning," he said with a shrug. "The radar picked up a boat about seven miles away, but it's been in the same spot now for about ten minutes. Someone's doing some night fishing."

Harry grunted and glanced at the monitors again. "That's it?"

"That's it."

He was silent for a moment.

"What about flights?" he finally asked. "Any planes fly by?"

Tony shook his head again and forked a mouthful of lasagna into his mouth.

"No. A flight plan was logged from a small airport on one of the barrier islands, but it's a private plane going down to Palm Beach."

Tony glanced up. "It logged a path over the water, so Roberto followed up on it just in case. It's carrying some rich playboy and his girlfriend down to Florida. Nothing to worry about."

Harry was quiet, watching him eat for a moment, then he got up and turned back toward the door.

"Well, let me know if anything changes. It looks like we're in for another quiet night."

"Yes, sir."

Harry left the bridge and made his way down the narrow stairs to the lower level. Where was she? He knew Viper would have marked the location of the *Sea Queen* by now. He couldn't have made it any easier for her. They were coasting along the same stretch of ocean constantly, not moving more than half a mile in either direction. He'd made sure that the marina cameras picked up Angela being taken offshore in the yacht tender. Viper knew she was here, so where the hell was she?

He went down the corridor and into the large entertaining area. A bar stretched across the back and large, comfortable chairs and sofas were arranged around a coffee table. A seventy-five inch TV dominated the front of the room while the sides offered floor-to-ceiling windows overlooking the water. The TV was dark and silent now, and Harry picked up the remote, switching it on and looking for a baseball game. Landing on the Phillies game, he set the remote down and went to the bar to pour himself a drink.

She was waiting for something.

The thought popped into his head as he poured bourbon into a glass and he paused, raising his eyes thoughtfully. That was the only explanation. Viper moved quickly, striking before her prey even knew she was on her way. That was her MO. The very fact that she hadn't come after Angela yet could only mean that she was waiting for something. But what?

Harry capped the bottle again and lifted the glass to take a sip. It wasn't backup. She worked alone. There was only one person she would ever trust enough to work alongside, and he was halfway across the world in Russia. No. She would be coming alone, of that he was sure.

He sipped his drink and watched the Phillies game absently. The only emotion Viper ever showed was for those two women, which was precisely why he'd targeted them. As soon as she found out Angela was on this boat, Viper should have come straight into his net. Yet she wasn't here, and he was running very short on time.

Roberto, La Cabeza's right-hand man, was getting impatient.

Next Exit, No Outlet

He had been entrusted with the *Sea Queen* and he didn't like how long they were idling in the same spot. He wanted to take Angela to Cuba, where Harry would catch his flight to Montenegro, then sail back to Mexico. Roberto thought La Cabeza would like her. Harry grunted to himself. He was probably right. Angela looked like exactly the type of woman to keep Martese amused, at least temporarily.

Harry set the drink down and turned to leave the room. Angela was the key, whether she knew it or not. Whether they stayed one more night or left in the morning was still to be decided, but it all hinged on her. And he hadn't checked on her since yesterday.

A few minutes later, he approached her room on the second level. Two men were seated outside the door, one with his phone in his hand, discussing the merits of one brand of phone over another. When they saw him coming towards them, they both stood up quickly and nodded to him.

"How is she?" he asked them brusquely.

"Sleeping," said one. "The doc was just here and gave her another dose. Before that, she was moving around in there, but she didn't try to get out."

Harry nodded and cracked open the door, peering inside. Angela was laying on the bed, fast asleep. He watched her for a second, then closed the door again.

"Did the doctor say anything about her condition?"

"Only that she's in a lot of pain," the second guard said with a shrug.

"Where is he now?"

"He's gone to the pool for a night swim."

He nodded and turned to leave, but paused after a few steps and looked over his shoulder.

"Stay awake," he warned them. "It's quiet, but if anyone comes on this yacht, they'll be coming for her."

Both men nodded and one patted the bulge at his side.

"We're ready," he promised.

Harry nodded and turned to make his way back up to one of the upper levels where a full-sized swimming pool offered additional recreation. He'd get a full medical report from the doctor and then go back to his baseball game. In the morning, he would re-evaluate. If there was still no sign of Viper, he would do as Roberto wished and leave, taking Angela with them. There was no rush. Viper would find him eventually and, when she did, he would finish what he'd started last year. It was time for the Organization to be destroyed.

And it would begin with Viper.

Harry had just reached the swimming pool when one of the crew members came running up behind him breathlessly.

"Colonel!" he gasped. "Captain wants you right away!"

Harry scowled and turned away from the pool as the doctor finished a lap and surfaced near the far end.

"What's going on?" he demanded, pinning the crew member with a ferocious look.

"I don't know," he stammered. "He just said to get you and be quick."

Harry exhaled and followed the young man quickly to the stairwell that would lead him back up to the bridge. Instead of accompanying him, the crew member continued down the corridor.

"Where are you going?"

The man turned to look at him. "To find Roberto."

Harry frowned and went up the stairs to the upper level. If the captain wanted both him and Roberto, something must be wrong. When he reached the bridge, he didn't bother knocking but opened the door and strode inside.

The captain was seated in front of his controls and flat screens, alternating between looking at the screens and peering out of the windows. The spotlights had been turned on outside, flooding the waves around the yacht with light. When he entered, the captain glanced at him.

"You wanted to know if anything changed," he said shortly.

"Yes?"

"That fishing boat is moving," he said, pointing to one of the screens. "It began moving a couple minutes ago. It's heading straight for us. I'm waiting for it to come into view now."

Harry strode forward and looked at the blip on the screen where the captain was pointing.

"How fast is it traveling?"

"About forty knots. Not fast enough to be alarming, but fast enough to make me think it's not a fisherman."

Harry raised his eyes and peered out into the illuminated ocean in front of them. After a second, he reached into his pocket and pulled out his phone.

"That's not a fishing boat," he told the captain, dialing. "It

Next Exit, No Outlet

wouldn't be coming straight for us like that."

The captain glanced at him. "You think it's what you've been waiting for?"

Harry didn't answer. Instead, he spoke into his phone. "Roberto, get your men ready. There's something happening. Get them to the front of the boat."

He hung up and watched through the windows, waiting for the boat to come into range of the floodlights. Below them, at the front of the bow, the helipad was empty. As he watched, Roberto ran out and across the open space, heading for the railing on the bow. Most of his men followed him, machine guns draped across their torsos, and Harry nodded faintly in approval. If Viper had chosen to hit them head on, she was in for a warm welcome.

"There!"

The captain pointed and Harry watched as a small speedboat came into view off the starboard bow. The figure at the helm was dressed in black tactical gear and Harry sucked in his breath. A part of him hadn't really believed it could be her. Viper wasn't reckless, and she certainly knew better than to come at them straight-on, but it appeared that that was exactly what she had decided to do.

"What are you up to?" he murmured to himself, watching as the boat skimmed across the waves, showing no indication of slowing down.

The look of interest quickly turned to one of disbelief as the boat sped toward them, drawing closer by the second.

"What the hell are they doing?" the captain exclaimed. "It's going to run right into us!"

Harry clenched his jaw as the boat drew dangerously close and the captain quickly spun the wheel, trying to turn the yacht and avoid a collision. Roberto's men opened fire, pelting the boat with a rain of bullets, yet the craft continued, the figure at the helm not moving.

The explosion was sudden, lighting up the water and night with a brilliant starburst of yellow and white. The bow of the small boat lurched up out of the water as flames engulfed the vessel, shooting sparks and debris into the air as the boom reached them in the bridge.

Harry stared, dumbfounded, at the burning wreckage of the speedboat as the aftershocks reverberated through the yacht, setting the whole ship trembling for a moment. While the vessel hadn't hit the yacht, it was close enough that they felt the explosion keenly.

"What the hell just happened?" he barked at the captain. "Did you see what happened?"

"It exploded."

"Yes, thank you," he snapped, turning to stride out of the bridge. "I want to know why!"

"Well, they were shooting at it," the captain called after him. "Maybe they hit the tank."

Harry scowled and moved down the stairs to the lower level, running along the corridor to the helipad.

"What the hell just happened?" he repeated his question to Roberto as he emerged onto the helipad.

"We stopped her," Roberto told him triumphantly. "We killed the Viper!"

Harry pushed past him and ran to the railing, staring over the side at the burning remnants of the boat. Parts of wood and fiberglass floated on the waves while flames devoured the structure of the boat. Something caught his eyes and he frowned. Turning, he motioned to the bridge, pointing to the area.

"Tell him to point a light on it!" he yelled.

Roberto pulled a hand-held radio out of his pocket and spoke into quickly. A moment later, one of the spotlights shifted, lending more light to the wreckage in the water. Harry sucked in his breath as he stared at what had caught his attention.

A deflated rubber inflatable wearing black tactical gear floated amongst the debris.

"Dammit!"

Harry spun around just as the sound of rapid gunfire reached them, coming from the stern. Roberto froze, staring at Harry in a moment of utter confusion.

"I don't understand," he began, but Harry cut him off as another burst gunfire erupted from the port aft.

"The boat was a decoy," he exclaimed disgustedly. "Viper is here. She came at the stern. She's already aboard!"

Viper reached up and cut the parachute lines away with her combat knife as a gust of ocean wind propelled her forward. The stern of the *Sea Queen* bobbed about ten feet below her, the flat deck deserted. She braced herself as she dropped, the black parachute disappearing into the waves behind the yacht. Her black boots hit the wood hard and she grimaced as the abrupt jolt sent shock waves up her spine. Gravity pulled her forward and she braced one black-gloved

Next Exit, No Outlet

hand on the wooden planks to stop from falling flat on her face. Looking up, she watched as another large black piece of nylon floated down to disappear into the waves. Hawk had landed on the uppermost level.

She straightened up and quickly undid the straps of the parachute pack on her back, pulling it off and tossing it over the side into the water. Michael's boat should be drawing attention to the bow of the ship, and that was where most of the security would be. She only had a few seconds. She swiftly unclipped the bag containing the diving tank and pulled it over her head. Looking around, she moved to a rattan chaise-lounge on the side of the deck and bent down to shove the bag under it. It would be safe there for now.

Then, glancing at her watch, she moved silently to the port side, moving along the outer railing of the yacht swiftly. She had just reached the outer steps to take her to the next level when the yacht lurched and the deck vibrated beneath her feet. A second later, she heard the explosion. A small, satisfied smile curled her lips and she ascended to the next level quickly. Michael should be getting on board now, if he wasn't already, and would start looking for Angela. It was up to her to make sure he had the opportunity to get her and then get to the tender boat in the garage behind the deck where she had just landed.

Reaching the next level, she turned aft and moved along the outer railing to the back of the boat. Coming to a wall of windows, she paused and pressed herself against the side of the ship, leaning forward to peer into the inner room. A huge TV flickered on the far end and she blinked at the sight of the Phillies at bat. Something pulled deep inside her. Viper wasn't a superstitious woman, but at the sight of Dave's favorite team hitting a home run, she felt a wave of peace go through her. It had to be a sign that Dave was watching out for her.

Shaking her head, she scanned the room and, finding it empty, moved quickly past the wall of windows. She was being ridiculous. Dave was dead, and she would be too if she kept letting things like a baseball game distract her.

Viper came to a stop suddenly as the hair on the back of her neck prickled and a shiver of awareness shot down her spine. Pressing herself against the side of the ship again, she glanced behind her to find the walkway empty. She turned her head back and listened, trying to hear something above the sound of the waves. There! Someone was moving toward the walkway around the corner ahead.

Pulling out her combat knife, Viper moved silently along the wall until she was next to the corner. She could hear the person breathing and smelled the acrid scent of cigarette smoke. A radio crackled and then a voice came over, loud in the silence.

"Pedro, go to the girl's room and back up Marcus and Jose," a voice barked. "A boat just tried to ram us. Make sure the prisoner is secure."

A heavy sigh greeted that and a cigarette butt flew past the edge of the wall to disappear over the railing.

"En camino."

Pedro rounded the corner, looking down as he clipped the radio back onto his belt. The last thing he saw was a blade flashing into his line of vision before it disappeared into his sternum. He opened his mouth, whether to scream or suck in air Viper would never know. Her gloved hand covered it swiftly as she wrenched the blade up to pierce his heart. A moment later, Pedro's eyes slid closed and she pulled the knife out as he slid silently to the floor.

She reached down and pulled the 9mm from his waistband before stepping over him and peering around the corner. Finding the adjoining walkway empty, she moved along it until she reached a door that would take her inside. Opening it, she slid inside and the smell of chlorine assaulted her nostrils. A full-sized pool stretched before her, surrounded by waterproofed teak flooring and several chairs. Someone was swimming underwater, heading away from her, and she moved silently to the side.

It was a man, and he was about halfway down the length of the pool. If he had gone under at the end, he would have to surface for air soon. She pulled one of the Ruger SR22s from its holster and reached into her inside jacket pocket for a suppressor. Attaching it with quick, sure fingers, she watched as the man continued underwater for a few more strokes. By the time he surfaced for air, she was ready, with the gun pointed at his head. At this distance, she couldn't miss.

After gulping some air, however, the man went back under and continued swimming. Viper made a face and lowered her pistol, moving alongside the pool and keeping pace with him, one eye on the swimmer and one eye on the other door to the pool room. He reached the end of the pool and this time when he surfaced, he was confronted with the end of a barrel.

"Who are you?!" he gasped, falling back a pace in the pool and staring up at her, water dripping down his face and neck.

"Who are you?" Viper returned softly.

The man visibly shuddered at the tone in her voice.

"I'm the ship's doctor," he said quickly, holding up his hands. "I'm one of the crew."

Next Exit, No Outlet

Viper tilted her head and studied him for a moment.

"Is that so? And what kind of illnesses do you treat on the high seas, doctor?"

"I...well, all kinds," he stammered. "Cuts, breaks, the odd gunshot or two." He shrugged and smiled weakly. "Water sports are a dangerous business."

"And are there many water sports going on right now?" she asked softly.

He shook his head, his hands shaking.

"No. Nothing. All I have is a patient that I have to keep sedated."

"How boring for you. So everyone is healthy?"

"Well, everyone except her."

Viper's eyes narrowed swiftly and she raised one eyebrow.

"Her?"

His eyes widened at the deadly tone in her voice.

"Yes. She has a dislocated shoulder. It happened before they brought her onboard. It's too swollen to put back into place, so I must keep her sedated to manage the pain."

Before Viper could press him for more information, a staccato of gunfire erupted from the direction of the stern. She stood up and ran swiftly to the door she had entered from, cracking it open and listening. Someone was shouting below and then there was a single shot, followed a second later by more rapid fire. Viper moved to the railing quickly and looked over in time to see Michael take cover behind the chaise lounge where she had hidden her bag. A figure lay prone on the deck a few feet away from him, a machine gun beside him. Turning her head, she saw another man advancing across the deck with an automatic in his hands.

Viper raised her gun and, a second later, the man fell backwards with a bullet hole in his forehead. Michael straightened up from behind the furniture and looked up at her. She touched her forehead in salute and he lifted a hand in thanks before darting out and disappearing from view along the port side.

Turning, she went back into the pool room in time to see the good doctor pull something out of a bag on the other side of the pool. He turned, a gun in his hand, and Viper fired. Blood appeared on his bare chest and the gun slipped out of his hand as he stumbled back, falling into the chair. She strode around the pool and towards him, her gun never wavering.

"Where is the patient with the dislocated shoulder?" she demanded, reaching him.

He stared up at her, his eyes glazed with pain. "I…can't…he'll kill me…" he gasped.

Viper looked down at him coldly.

"You're already dead. Where is she?"

After a few ragged gasps for air, he capitulated. "Cabin at the end…second level…"

Viper nodded, watching as he took his last breaths before she turned to leave the pool room. As she did so, her ear bud came alive.

"Satellite and electricals are primed. I'll detonate as soon as Michael and Angela clear the ship," Hawk said in her ear, his voice low and deep. "I'm heading for the lower level."

"Roger that," she replied, reaching the other door and cracking it open. Finding the corridor empty, she moved out of the pool room. "Tell Michael Angie is on the second level, in the cabin at the end."

"Got it." Hawk sounded out of breath, like he was running. "I'll let you know when the rest of the charges are set. Good hunting."

"You too."

Chapter Thirty-Eight

Michael moved down the corridor, his heart pounding. That had been too close for comfort. When he climbed aboard at the stern, he hadn't been expecting anyone to be waiting. They should have all been at the front of the yacht. Thankfully, as he pulled himself out of the water, he heard the shout from the other side of the deck and had time to fire before the first man pulled the trigger. His shot had been true, but another one had come around the corner just as he moved away from the edge of the deck. He managed to roll out of reach from the spray of bullets haphazardly sent in his direction. Luckily for him, the person firing clearly had no real experience in aiming his weapon. He just pointed in the general direction and pulled the trigger. Even so, it had been damn close. If it hadn't been for Alina, he doubted he would have made it past the stern.

He shook his head. When he looked up, an involuntary chill had gone down his spine. Even though she was on his side, the look on her face had been enough to make even the staunchest Marine balk. She looked like an avenging demon, standing near the railing dressed in full gear. He had been staring at her in shock when she raised her hand and touched her forehead in salute, breaking him out of his stupor. It was one thing to know what Dave's kid sister did for a living; it was something altogether different to actually see her in action.

There had been no sign of Damon, but Michael knew that if Alina was onboard, so was he. He had no idea how they got to the yacht, but clearly no one on the ship was aware of their presence. Yet. He had to locate Angela before that happened. Once the colonel realized what was happening, the cartel would spread out and tear the yacht apart looking for her.

He was halfway down the corridor when a door opened behind him and he heard an exclamation. Michael's heart sank, then started pounding once again.

"¡Eh, tú!" a deep voice called. "Stop!"

Michael sighed imperceptibly and came to a stop, holding up

his hands. Turning his head slightly, he looked behind him. A man was moving toward him, a Glock in his hand and a radio clipped to his belt. Taking a deep breath, Michael waited for the man to draw closer. He really wasn't having the best luck so far.

The man closed the gap between them and Michael waited, perfectly still, until he felt a hand touch his arm to turn him around. Moving swiftly, he reached behind him as he spun and grabbed the wrist of the hand holding the gun to his back. He wrenched it upward at the same time that his foot kicked the inside of the man's opposite knee. A sickening crack sounded and the man let out a howl of pain as his leg buckled at an odd angle. Michael moved behind him quickly and, a second later, the howling abruptly stopped as he twisted his neck. The man sank to the floor and Michael lifted the gun from his slack hand before stepping over the body.

He tucked the weapon into one of the pockets on his drysuit, annoyed to find his hands shaking. The long-forgotten movements from his active service days had come as second nature to him, but the adrenaline was something he hadn't had to deal with for a few years. It was rushing through him and he shook his head, taking a deep, calming breath.

He was just exhaling when his phone vibrated, making him start. Frowning, he pulled it out and swiped the screen, glancing at the brief message.

Target is in last cabin on second level.

Michael raised his eyebrows and looked around. Now how the hell had Damon discovered where they were keeping Angela? Putting the phone away, he moved along the corridor until he came to a narrow stairwell. Hearing heavy footsteps clatterring down, Michael looked around frantically and opened the door closest to him. Ducking inside, he just had time to note that it was a small powder room before he closed the door quietly. The door had just clicked shut when what sounded like two men emerged from the stairwell.

"Head aft!" one yelled in Spanish. "¡Prisa!"

The men ran down the corridor, their shoes echoing on the hardwood. Michael waited a second, then cracked the door open. The hallway was empty again, but he knew that wouldn't last. He could hear yelling outside and knew the gunfire had alerted the ship to Viper's presence.

Sorry, Lina, he thought, moving out of the powder room and into the stairwell. *Here they come.*

He went up the steps quickly and paused at the top, listening. He could still hear crew calling to each other outside, but the interior

Next Exit, No Outlet

seemed eerily quiet. Peering around the corner, Michael looked left, then right before emerging from the stairs. He was on the second level. Now he just had to figure out which end was *the* end.

The corridor to the left was clear and seemed to lead into a larger recreational room. He could see flickering not unlike that of a large TV. He turned right and started down the hall. It curved to the left at the end and he stayed near the wall, moving as quickly and quietly as possible. When he reached the corner, he stopped and took a deep breath, peering around the curve. There, at the end, two men were on their feet with guns in their hands, looking as if they would rather be anywhere but where they were.

Michael pulled out the 1911 Viper had handed him on the beach and quickly attached the suppressor. The two guards were about to be even more unhappy with their babysitting duty.

Taking a deep, calming breath, he peered around the corner again, gauging the distance and height of the guard closest to him. Then, without thinking twice, he rounded the corner as he aimed and fired. The guard cried out and grabbed his side where the bullet had torn through his ribs. Before he could do anything more, another bullet entered his skull. The second guard raised his gun and got a shot off in Michael's general direction, causing Michael to move to his right as he fired. His shot went through the guard's chest, throwing him backwards a pace. He followed up immediately with another shot to his head and the guard went down.

Michael strode quickly down the long corridor, impressed with the gun in his hands. Viper hadn't been exaggerating. The 1911 was one of the most superior pistols he'd ever fired. Tucking it into the holster on his leg, he reached the door, stepping over the body of the first guard. He tested the handle and raised an eyebrow when it opened easily. They hadn't bothered to lock her in?

He entered the room and closed the door behind him quietly, looking across the small room. Angela was sprawled across the bed, fast asleep and oblivious to the drama unfolding on the yacht. She was still dressed in the clothes she had been wearing the morning they took her, but they were the worse for wear. Blood stained her shirt and one look at her swollen bottom lip and scraped face was explanation enough. Her jeans were torn and crusted with blood where she had obviously fallen. The honey colored hair that was always so perfect lay tangled and matted, the hair tie that had held it in a ponytail that fateful morning long gone.

Irrational rage coursed through him at the sight of her and he strode forward quickly. She was a mess, but he had to get her up and out of here. Sitting on the edge of the bed, he leaned over her and shook her gently by the shoulder.

Angela came awake with a howl of pain and surged up, her eyes bulging open and staring at him in terror.

"Hey! It's me!" he exclaimed, raising his hands. "It's Michael!"

Angela gazed at him in glazed stupor then, to his consternation, her eyes filled with tears.

"Oh Michael!" she gasped, throwing herself into his arms. "I prayed someone would come!"

"Ssshhh…" Michael wrapped his arms around her and felt the violent tremors going through her body. "It's okay. We're here. I'm going to get you off this boat."

Angela pulled away and looked into his face. "We? Is Stephanie here?"

Michael shook his head and stood up.

"No. Alina and Damon are with me," he said, reaching for her hands, "but we have to move. Come on."

Before she could react, he grasped her hands and tried to pull her up. When she cried out again in pain, he dropped her hands and stared at her.

"What?" he demanded, his heart pounding. "What's wrong?"

Tears were streaming down her face and she shook her head.

"My shoulder," she gasped. "It's dislocated."

Michael dropped his gaze to her shoulders. Her left arm was hanging at strange angle and he exhaled, running hand over his hair.

"Oh my God, I didn't even see it," he said. "I'm so sorry. We're going to have to get it back in."

Angela shook her head violently and actually began backing across the bed away from him.

"No!" she cried. "It won't go back in! The doctor said it needs surgery."

Michael scowled. "What? What doctor?"

"The one who's been coming in here and dosing me with morphine for the pain."

"Morphine?" he repeated, feeling supremely out of his depth. "Well, that explains why you were dead to the world when I came in."

"I can't move my arm," she said, stopping in the middle of the bed now that he was no longer talking about forcing her shoulder back in. "I don't know if I can make it off the boat!"

Michael pressed his lips together grimly.

"Oh, you'll make it," he promised her, turning to look around the small room. Spotting the bathroom door, he strode toward it.

Next Exit, No Outlet

"Hang on."

He went into the bathroom and looked around. The shower stall had glass doors, so there was no shower curtain that he could cut into strips. It would have to be towels. Grabbing two full-sized bath towels, he carried them out into the bedroom and pulled out a utility knife. With Angela watching from the bed, he made a cut and then tore one of the towels into strips.

"What are you doing?" she finally asked.

"Making a sling."

She fell silent again and watched as he fashioned a sling out of the second towel. Using the knife, he managed to make two holes on either side of the towel to feed the strips through.

"It's not pretty, but it should work for as long as we need it to," he finally said, walking over to the side of the bed. "Come here."

Angela moved off the bed to stand in front of him. As gently as he could, Michael lifted the bad arm and placed it across her sternum. Angela lifted her right hand to hold it steady while he carefully arranged the makeshift sling around her arm, hooking two of the long strips of towel over her good shoulder and the other two around her neck. He shifted behind her and tied them into tight knots, then stepped back.

"How is that?"

Angela looked up at him. "I don't know how long it will hold, but it seems to be working."

He nodded and turned toward the door.

"All right. Let's go." Michael moved to the door with Angela close behind. When he reached the door, he paused and looked down at her. "Don't look."

"Don't look at what?"

He opened the door and heard a soft gasp as she caught sight of the two dead men in the corridor.

"D-D-id you do that?" she stammered.

"Yes. It was necessary. Come on."

Michael grabbed her right hand and pulled her out of the cabin, stepping over the one in front of the door. He turned in time to see Angela's face as she made a choking noise, stepping gingerly over the man, her eyes huge and glued to the bullet hole in his head.

"Hey," he said softly, reaching out and lifting her chin so her eyes were on his instead of the gruesome sight. "I told you not to look."

"How can I *not* look?!" she exclaimed in a hushed voice. "He's *dead!*"

"And that's what will happen to us if we don't get moving," he said, turning to go down the corridor. "Stay close to me and, for God's sake, don't scream."

"Why would I scream?"

"Because I'm sure there'll be a lot more dead people before we make it out of here."

Angela gulped and nodded, gripping his hand tightly. "Ok."

Michael glanced at her pale and resolute face and felt compassion roll over him. She was a civilian, a banker for heaven's sake. She hadn't asked for any of this. She'd been thrown into a maelstrom of Colonel Shore's making without any warning, gaining a severely messed up shoulder along the way. His jaw tightened when he thought of the amount of pain she had been in for two days. He'd known grown men who couldn't handle the pain of a dislocated shoulder for more than a few minutes, let alone days. And now he was asking her to face death as well.

They reached the corner and Michael stopped, pulling his own Beretta from the pocket at his waist. He would save the 1911 for when it was absolutely necessary. He had more clips for the Beretta than he did the loaner, and he had a feeling he was going to be doing a lot of shooting. With Angela next to useless, it fell solely on him to get them both out of here alive.

He glanced at her and she met his gaze, nodding slightly. He nodded back and looked around the corner. The stairwell was halfway down, centered between them and the large recreational room he had seen when he came up. The corridor was empty, but he could see shadows moving in the larger room and knew there was no way he and Angela would make it to the stairwell before the shadows made it to the corridor. There was one door between them and the stairwell and Michael took a deep breath.

He pulled Angela behind him as he swiftly moved to the door. Reaching it, he shoved her inside just as the first man came out of the room on the other end of the hall. He caught sight of him immediately, but Michael was already locked and loaded. The gunshot was deafening in the narrow corridor, but his aim was true, and the man fell back with blood spreading across his chest. As he did so, the automatic weapon in his hand fell with a clatter.

"Stay!" he said over his shoulder to Angela before charging down the hallway as another man emerged from the room.

Michael heard the shot and inwardly cringed, waiting for excruciating pain from some part of his anatomy, but there was none. The shot had gone wide, and he raised his Beretta and fired, catching the shooter in his shoulder. He stumbled back as Michael fired again, this time hitting him in the chest. He was just falling backwards into the recreational room as Michael reached the first body and grabbed the automatic weapon from the floor. Two more shadows moved, charging across the large room toward the door, and they were met with a stream of bullets.

Without stopping to see if there were more, Michael ran back to the room where he'd shoved Angela.

"Come on. We just lost the element of surprise," he gasped, grabbing her hand and pulling her down the hallway to the stairwell.

They clattered down the stairs to the lower level and Angela gasped at the sound of gunfire on the outside walkway. Michael tightened his fingers around hers and they ran down the corridor toward the stern. More gunfire erupted above them and Angela let out a choked sob.

"Oh my God, is that for Alina?"

Michael didn't answer. Seeing men running for the upper levels, he ducked into a galley-style bar area, pulling Angela in behind him and closing the door until it was open just a crack. He watched as two men with automatic rifles ran past, heading for the stairwell to go up. His lips tightened as frustration threatened to choke him. It was either Alina or Damon up there, and he couldn't help either of them. Instead, he was hiding in a galley, waiting for the area to clear so he could run away. Instead of running to the fight, he was escaping from it.

What kind of Marine was he?

Cold fingers stirred in his and Michael glanced down into Angela's brown eyes, wide in a white face. In that instant, he knew that his battle was getting her to safety. Lina was counting on him. If he failed, they all failed. He wasn't running away. He following a different path, and it was the path chosen for him by Alina.

Once the men had disappeared into the stairwell, Michael pushed the door open and got them moving again. They were almost there. Just a few more feet and they could move outside onto the stern where he could access the garage. Just a few more feet.

Angela called out a warning as they reached the end of the corridor and Michael swung around, shoving her behind him to trap her between him and the wall. He fired at the same time as a dark-skinned man with a gold front tooth who had come down the stairwell they just passed. Michael's bullet went into the man's forehead just as he felt searing pain streak down his right arm. Sucking in his breath, he glanced down and saw a hole in the arm of the drysuit.

Flexing his right arm, he grit his teeth at another flash of pain. The bullet had hit his bicep, but Michael didn't think it was that bad. He could still move his arm. He'd only been winged.

Turning, he pushed open the door to the back deck using the wounded arm, refusing to release Angela's hand with his other. They stepped outside and he moved to the right, pressing them up against the wall under the overhang from the upper deck. The sound of fighting above them was clear, and he kept them pressed along the wall and out of sight. Angela gripped his hand and pressed up against his side as if she could crawl behind him and Michael glanced down at her. She was listening, as he was, to the deadly scuffle taking place directly above them. A decidedly female grunt and moan was followed suddenly by a sharp crack and deeper howl of pain. Michael winced when the howl was cut short by a muffled pop. A thud above them left no doubt as to the result of the suppressed gunshot.

"Aaaggghh!"

A man let out what sounded like a battle cry and the sound of a fist hitting skin made its way to the pair in the shadows below. More hits, another female grunt, and then a sudden cry of pain cut through the night. Michael pulled out his Beretta, fear coursing through him. Alina was getting her ass kicked up there. He couldn't just stand here and do nothing.

Before he could move, a man bellowed in agony and, suddenly, a large figure dropped from above to hit the deck in front of them with a sickening thud.

Angela jumped and Michael clapped his hand over her mouth just as she let out an involuntary cry. He shook his head, willing her to stay quiet, then turned his eyes to the man on the deck before them. His leg was bent at an impossible angle and he could just see the white of a bone sticking through the canvas of his pant leg. Before he could react, the sound of a muffled shot came from above and the man jerked on the deck as a bullet went into his throat. Immediately, a second pop preceded another bullet in the middle of his forehead.

Michael turned Angela into his shoulder, pressing her face against him to shield her from the gruesome sight. Silence fell above, and Michael knew the dead man in front of him was the last of that fight. He took a deep breath and moved them along to the end of the wall. Letting go of Angela's hand, he turned and opened an electrical box set into the wood. After studying the buttons inside for a second, he pressed one and looked at the flat deck that stretched to the railing. Nothing happened.

He frowned and turned back to the panel, pressing another

Next Exit, No Outlet

button. A low hum started in the bowels of the stern and Angela gasped.

"Michael!"

He turned and watched as the flat deck slowly began to move. It was raising upward and he pulled Angela away from the wall as that also began to move. They both stared as the deck lifted up like a platform, exposing the ocean beneath. The wall they had been pressed against moments before was shifting and sliding to the side, disappearing into itself almost like the old pocket doors of years past.

"What on earth…?" Angela breathed. "What is it?"

"A boat garage."

The deck reached its full height and stopped, the low hum ceasing as the walls also finished sliding. Behind the wall, in the cavern now exposed, bobbed a speed boat.

"Well, I'll be damned," he murmured. "She said it was here, but I don't think I really believed her."

"Who said?"

"Lina."

He took her hand again and they moved into the garage, walking along a narrow walkway that ran parallel with the boat. He stopped and looked down at her.

"Hold on."

Releasing her hand, he gripped her around the waist and swung her effortlessly into the boat. As soon as her feet hit the floor, he released her and turned to untie the mooring at the back of the boat. Tossing it onto the platform, he jumped in and moved around her to the helm. Angela sat down in one of the leather bucket seats and cradled her arm in her lap, watching as he checked the instrument panel.

The engine roared to life, almost deafening them in the enclosed space. Michael pressed the throttle forward and the boat began to move out of the garage, water lapping at its sides. The bow had just moved out of the garage when someone ran onto the side deck, a gun in their hand.

Michael aimed and fired as the boat pulled out of the garage, hitting the man in the chest. A bullet whizzed past the bow and he increased the throttle, guiding the speedboat out into the ocean waves as another bullet hit the side of the small craft.

Letting out a curse, he reached into the holster on his leg and pulled out the 1911, turning to locate the threat. There were two, and the one closest to them was on the starboard side of the yacht, holding an automatic rifle. Michael's first shot went wide when the boat bobbed, but his second was true. The man wavered, then pitched over the side of the deck into the water.

Another bullet hit the leather chair next to Angela and she cried out, ducking.

"Get down!" Michael barked. She dove to the floor as Michael spun the wheel, trying to turn so he could get a better angle on the shooter. Raising his weapon, he aimed, and froze.

Colonel Harry Shore was standing on the upper level, a rifle braced against his shoulder, and his eye to the night scope.

Michael knew exactly who he was aiming for and, from that height advantage, he wouldn't miss again.

Without thinking, Michael let go of the wheel and threw himself over Angela.

Chapter Thirty-Nine

Viper ducked behind a half wall that separated a dining area from a sitting room and ejected the clip from her .22, sliding a new one in. This was the last one and then she was out of ammunition for the .22. Inhaling, she waited a second, then straightened up, firing across the room at the figure reloading his 9mm. The gun dropped out of his hand as he fell back, a bullet hole in his forehead.

She moved out from behind the wall and towards the door at the other end of the room. So far, she had heard Harry yelling orders, but had yet to lay eyes on her quarry. Instead, she was making her way through the ranks of the cartel that crewed the yacht. They were like cockroaches, coming from everywhere as soon as she got close.

Viper wasn't a fool. She knew what Harry was doing. He was buying time while she used up her ammunition and energy on the cartel thugs protecting him. At least, that was how he would have begun this game. By now, he must have realized that there was more than just her onboard. While she had been doing everything in her power to make sure that Michael had as much time to get Angela off the boat as possible, she had heard gunshots more than once in other parts of the ship. Some of those could have been Hawk, but she knew some were Michael. It was unavoidable.

And now Harry knew someone was going for Angela.

She moved outside on the port side walkway and started to head back towards the stern. When she was there a few minutes ago, there had been no sign of Michael or Angela. The yacht tender garage was still closed.

Viper glanced at her watch and her lips tightened. If they didn't get there in the next few minutes, they would be in serious trouble. They were running out of time.

A single gunshot rang out from the stern and she broke into a run. As she drew closer, she heard the sound of a speedboat engine and she exhaled silently. Reaching the railing, she watched from the shadows of the port side as the boat pulled away from the back of the yacht, Angela seated in one of the front seats. Relief washed through her at the sight of her friend, alive and moving away to safety. He'd done it. Michael had come through for her.

"The gunny is clear," she said in a low voice.

It was a moment before Hawk answered in her ear, "And the package?"

"With him."

"Stand-by."

Another gunshot rang out then and Michael turned in the boat to fire back at the yacht, hitting a figure standing on the lower deck. Viper frowned as she heard another shot and Angela dove to the floor of the boat.

She swiftly scanned the lower deck. Not seeing anyone, she moved along the walkway, crossing to the starboard side. She was mid-stride when a sudden, low hum vibrated through the yacht followed almost immediately by a loud crack. The yacht trembled as if it had been shocked, and then plunged into total darkness. The engine stopped, the lights went out, and in an instant, they were in pitch blackness with only the light of the moon above. Deathly silence reigned.

"Com check," Hawk whispered in her ear.

"Received."

Viper pulled a pair of goggles out of her jacket and pulled them over her head, pressing the button on the side to activate the night-vision. Everything took on a greenish-blue tinge and she moved forward silently until she reached the end of the walkway. Peering around the corner, her heart surged into her throat. There, a few feet away, Harry had a rifle trained on the speedboat.

Fury, instant and fierce, surged through her and propelled her forward. She fired one shot, but not at his head as was her habit. Her bullet tore into the forearm of the hand supporting the long barrel just as he pulled the trigger, sending the deadly shot harmlessly to the left of the speedboat. The rifle flew out of his hands and over the side of the railing as Harry let out a startled cry and grasped his arm, blood pouring through his fingers.

His eyes widened briefly as she advanced toward him, anger making her strides long and deliberate. She slid her gun into her leg holster and, as she reached him, her right hook drove into his jaw. He fell backwards and stumbled, hitting the railing. His eyes closed briefly, then he shook his head and straightened himself up with effort. Releasing his bleeding arm, he pulled a thin, deadly blade from his pocket and lunged toward her.

Next Exit, No Outlet

Viper side-stepped quickly and the blade caught the outer fold of her jacket. She brought her elbow down sharply, slamming it into his wrist, and the blade went skidding across the walkway and over the side. Before she could land another hit with her punishing right, Harry let out a sound like a growl and slammed his bald head forward, hitting her squarely on the forehead. The force of the blow sent starbursts through her eyes and her head snapped back painfully. Stumbling back a step, her vision was just clearing when Harry looked at something directly behind her.

Viper spun around just as a man slightly taller than herself swung a metal pipe at her head. Throwing her hands up, she grabbed the end of the pipe with both hands, stopping it. With a heave, she used his forward momentum to rip the pipe out of his hands. Feeling Harry behind her, she rammed it backwards, burying it solidly into his gut as she swept her leg out to catch the man off balance. A painful grunt told her that her aim had been true, but she didn't have time to feel any satisfaction. Raising the pipe swiftly, she cracked it against the temple of her attacker as he stumbled sideways.

As he sank to the floor, Viper swung around to face Harry again. He was just straightening up from the blow she'd dealt him below his sternum and, as she came around, he pulled one hand out of his pocket. She caught sight of the gun even as the pipe flashed and slammed into the wrist holding it. The gun fell from his fingers, but before she could take advantage of his disarmament, a streak of awareness went down her spine.

Viper didn't think, she just moved. Diving to the side, she hit the wall as searing pain went through her side. Her jaw tightened as Harry backed up, then turned to disappear through a door a few feet away. Ignoring the pain, she spun around to face the new threat and found herself confronting a face she knew from surveillance photos only.

Roberto, La Cabeza's new Second-in-Command, stood before her, and the long, deadly blade he held in his hand was stained with blood.

Michael killed the engine and grabbed the line, moving to the side to secure the small craft to the cleat on the dock. He had pulled the speed boat to the end of the farthest dock, where it was dark and quiet.

He tied it up and glanced at Angela. At some point on the way here, she'd passed out on the back seat. Obviously, the morphine was still strong in her system. He didn't know how else she could go to sleep after the hair-raising escape from the *Sea Queen*.

Michael still didn't know quite how they managed to make it off the yacht alive. By all odds, they shouldn't have, especially when the colonel had a perfect shot. When he lifted his head to try to take a shot himself, knowing that it was near impossible at that distance even with the range of the 1911, he hadn't had to fire after all. Viper had beat him to it. As he watched, she shot Harry Shore and saved both his and Angela's lives. Without wasting any more time, he had jumped up and turned the boat toward the coast.

Looking back, his last sight of Alina was of her fighting both Harry and another figure on the upper deck of the yacht. He had almost turned the boat around and gone back, but one look at Angela had reminded him what Lina was counting on him to do. And so he had opened the throttle and left the yacht behind.

Now, all he could do was pray she survived.

Glancing toward the dark marina, he took off the leg holster and removed the 1911. Setting it on one of the seats, he removed the dry suit that covered his clothes and carefully folded it before strapping the holster around it, creating a neat and tight package to return to Viper. He tucked the 1911 into his jacket pocket, glanced at his watch and looked at Angela again. It was time to get her moving. They were on time, but they wouldn't be if they waited any longer.

Michael moved to the back of the boat and crouched down beside the sleeping woman. Careful not to jar her shoulder this time, he gently shook her leg.

"Hey," he said quietly. "Wake up. It's time to move."

Angela stirred and opened her eyes, peering at him groggily.

"Huh?" she murmured sleepily. Then she gasped as she came fully awake and struggled to sit up. "Oh my God, are we safe? Where are we?"

Michael put an arm behind her and helped her to sit up.

"We're at a marina on St. Simons Island in Georgia," he told her. "We're not out of it yet. Transportation is waiting, but we have to get to it."

Angela nodded and tried to stand. She grimaced and tears of pain filled her eyes.

"Oh God it hurts," she moaned.

Michael helped her up and glanced at the dock. The dock wasn't high, but there was a gap between the boat and wooden planks

Next Exit, No Outlet

and Angela had no way to steady herself.

"I'll get out and then lift you onto the dock," he said. "It will hurt, but I don't see any other way. If you slip climbing out, you can't catch yourself."

She looked at the space between the boat and the pier and nodded.

"It wouldn't be a problem except I'm not feeling right," she muttered. "I'm having a problem just standing. I feel like I've been drugged."

"You have." Michael jumped out of the boat and turned around to face her. "Get as close as you can."

She moved to the edge of boat and tried to balance herself as it bobbed with her shifting weight. When it settled down again, he reached out and put his hands under her arms. He looked into her face.

"Ready?"

She nodded and he lifted her out of the boat and onto the pier, remorse washing over him as she let out an involuntary cry. He dropped his hands quickly and watched as she cradled her arm against her body. The makeshift sling he had made on the yacht was holding up surprisingly well, but it was starting to sag.

"Let try to tie these a little tighter," he said, reaching for the knot over her shoulder. "It might give a little relief."

Angela nodded and stood still while he retied the knot on her shoulder and then the one around her neck. When he was finished and stepped back, she caught sight of his arm and let out a gasp.

"You're bleeding!"

Michael glanced down. The sleeve of his jacket was soaked with blood and he could see the hole where the bullet had gone through.

"Yes," he agreed, glancing around the deserted pier. He turned toward the marina and took her hand. "It's fine. Just a scratch."

"That's more than a scratch. What happened?"

"I got caught with a bullet."

"When?!"

"On the yacht, before we got to the boat."

"You didn't make a sound!"

He glanced at her, amused. "I was a little busy."

"Am I the only one who hasn't been shot in this whole mess?" Angela demanded after a moment of silence. "Is this seriously everyone's life except mine?"

"It's not a bad thing. You say it like there's something wrong with you."

"Well, I'm starting to feel left out!" she exclaimed.

He looked at her incredulously. "Says the woman walking around with a jacked up shoulder that will need surgery to repair it."

"Yeah, but there's nothing sexy about that. At least you have war stories."

Michael saw a shadow move ahead on the main walkway and slid his hand into his pocket to close it around the 1911.

"Honey, you've got some war stories of your own now," he said, shifting closer to her so that he could shove her behind him if needed. "How did your shoulder get dislocated, anyway?"

Angela started to shrug then let out a groan of agony. "Ugh. I tried to escape."

The shadow ahead moved again and Michael's eyes narrowed. He scanned the rest of the area but couldn't see anymore. Was it friend? Or foe? Alina hadn't told him how many people would waiting, or even what the transportation was. All she said was that someone would be there.

"How?" he asked, trying to keep her talking. The less she noticed right now, the better. If she panicked, he would have another issue on his hands.

"I woke up in the back of a truck at a rest stop. I was alone. The bastard stopped to eat. Can you believe it?"

"And he left you in the truck?" Michael glanced at her. "Really?"

She nodded, completely unaware that he had moved even closer to her.

"My hands were zip-tied behind me. I think he drugged me and thought I was out for the count."

"But you weren't."

"No. I got out of the truck and ran. It was dark and there were a lot of tractor-trailers and I couldn't see very well. I tripped and fell and landed on my shoulder. It hurt, but I was so scared I got up and kept going. I didn't know it was dislocated."

The shadow moved again and moonlight glinted off something in its hands. Michael eased the gun out of his pocket, keeping it close to his side.

"And he caught up with you?"

"Yes." Her voice cracked. "When I woke up again, I was on the bed in the room where you found me."

"No wonder your shoulder is so messed up," he muttered, his eyes on the shadow. "You popped it out with your hands behind you, and then it stayed that way."

Next Exit, No Outlet

"Can we not talk about it? I'm trying to ignore the pain. Talking about it makes it worse."

The shadow shifted again, moving out from behind a moored boat as they drew closer and Michael saw that it was a man dressed in jeans and a hooded sweatshirt. He raised his hands and the moonlight illuminated the barrel of a sawed-off shotgun swinging towards them.

Releasing Angela's hand, Michael shoved her behind him and raised the gun, steadying it with both hands. He fired three quick shots as Angela let out a startled cry behind him, gripping the back of his jacket with her hand. The shadow lurched and then fell, the shotgun skidding out of his hand toward the edge of the pier.

"Stay behind me!" Michael commanded, moving forward quickly, the gun trained on the prone figure a few yards away.

He wasn't moving and Michael scanned the shadows for more as he drew closer. Not seeing anyone, he continued until he reached the shotgun laying near the edge of the planks. He kicked it off the pier and it splashed into the bay. Bending down, he felt for a pulse on the would-be attacker. There was none.

"Is he..." Angela's voice trailed off.

"It was us or him," Michael said grimly, straightening up and taking her hand again. "Come on. Stay close to me and, for God's sake, if you see something, tell me."

She nodded and stumbled as he started across the wide pier. His fingers tightened on hers and she gained her balance again, moving closer to him. The main pier ran for about fifty yards until it met the marina proper. Buildings lined the shore, and Michael knew they were exposed on the pier. There was no way around it, though. Angela couldn't swim and there was no other way to the marina.

He moved her quickly past boats moored along the dock, keeping in the shadows as much as possible. His eyes never stopped moving, and it was only because of that that he saw the shadow in the distance suddenly lurch out from behind a bench and fall to the ground. Michael's hand tightened on Angela's and he frowned, straining to see in the dim light. There was no other movement. Yet someone was there. Men didn't just go down on their own. He checked his stride, briefly wondering if he should continue, then kept going. Aside from going back to the boat and breaking the plan, there was no other choice.

They had just reached the marina when a stifled cry echoed from one building over, then silence. Michael's brows drew together sharply. What the hell?

"Michael!" Angela hissed, her fingers gripping his in a death clench. "Look! Up there!"

Michael followed her nod and his blood ran cold. A shadow was on top of the building to the right of them and he could see the rifle in the moonlight. He let go of her hand and pushed her behind him again, lifting the gun. While the 1911 had surprised him twice with its exceptional range, he knew this was a hail Mary shot.

He never had to pull the trigger. Before he could, the shadow suddenly lurched and a bullet went wide, hitting a trash can about five feet away from them. Angela let out a cry and grabbed his jacket, pressing against his back, but he was staring at the rooftop, dumbfounded. The shadow had turned and, as he watched, a second shadow appeared. They struggled for a moment, then the second one wrenched the rifle out of the first one's hands and slammed him over the head with it. For a sickening moment, the first shadow swayed on the edge of the rooftop. Almost in slow motion, he froze, suspended in the air, before tipping backwards over the edge.

Michael sucked in his breath and turned, wrapping his arms around Angela as he swiftly moved her down the sidewalk, keeping her face pressed into his chest. A second later, there was a thud behind them, accompanied by an awful crunch.

Angela trembled in his arms. "Was that...did he..."

"Don't think about it," he said grimly, "and don't look."

He turned her around and pulled her up against his side, hustling her down the sidewalk toward the parking lot. He didn't know what was going on, or who these people were, but they were clearly on their side, and he wasn't about to look a gift-horse in the mouth.

"I don't understand," Angela stammered, gagging. "How does someone pitch someone else off a roof?"

"I said don't think about."

"How can I *not* think about?!" she cried. "A man just went splat! How are *you* not thinking about it?!"

"How? Because if he hadn't gone splat, chances are high he would have put a bullet in one or both of us. So no, I'm not really concerned that he just nose-dived four stories."

"But...but..." she stammered, a violent shudder going through her.

"Stop. Think about something else."

"Something else? Like what?"

"I don't know. Think about puppies. Kittens. Think about Bella."

"Oh my God, Bella!" she gasped. "Where's my cat?"

"She's fine. She's at Alina's. Stephanie's taking care of her."

Next Exit, No Outlet

"Oh, thank God!"

Michael glanced down at her. After everything that had happened, and was still happening, the woman was worried about her cat. Something akin to respect rushed through him and he shook his head. Angela had been through a hell not of her own making and was still standing. He wasn't sure he knew many people who would be handling this as well.

They reached the parking lot and a tall, stocky man moved out of the shadows near a black Escalade. Michael raised his gun, but the man held his hands up to show he was unarmed.

"There's no need for all that," he said, his voice low and deep. "I've been waiting for you."

"So have others," Michael retorted, not lowering his weapon. "How do I know you're not one of them?"

"We have a mutual friend," the man said with a shrug. "She said you'd want proof."

"And?"

The man sighed. "She said for you to go to Arlington. She left something there for you. Said you'd know where to look."

Michael's heart skipped and he slowly lowered the gun. "Is that so?"

The man looked at Angela and shook his head.

"I think maybe we better get her to a hospital," he said, opening the back door of the Escalade. "She's not looking so good."

Michael glanced down at Angela, then back at the man.

"Do you have a name?"

"Stefan."

Michael sucked in his breath and felt his lips tremble suddenly. Of course! Stefan Delgado. That was why Alina had been adamant about him not mentioning his profession.

"Nice to meet you, Stefan," he said, moving forward and gently pushing Angela toward the SUV. "I'm Mike."

Angela looked at him dubiously and he nodded. She turned back and climbed into the SUV with difficulty, biting her lip in pain. Michael waited until she was inside, then moved to get in beside her. Something made the hair on his neck stand up and he turned his head, scanning the parking lot. His eyes lit on a black town car near the entrance. Idling partly in darkness, the back of the car was under the glow of a street light and he could just make out that the back window was down. As he looked, the tinted window slid up slowly, but not before he recognized Frankie Solitto in the back.

Michael looked at Stefan, startled, and Stefan smiled faintly.

"He wanted to be here personally, to make sure you're taken care off," he said. "Anything you need, it's yours."

Michael studied him for a minute. "Our mutual friend?"

Stefan nodded. "Our mutual friend."

Michael's lips twisted into a smile and he got into the Escalade. Stefan closed the door and he looked at Angela. She was exhausted and looked like she was about to pass out.

"It's over," he said quietly. "We made it."

Angela was silent for a moment, then she raised eyes swimming with tears to his.

"We made it, but what about Lina?"

He stared at her wordlessly. He had nothing to offer her, no words of comfort or encouragement. He had no idea what was happening on the yacht, or if Alina would survive. All he knew was that he had done what he promised her he would. Angela was safe.

And in the process, he had failed to keep his promise to her brother.

Chapter Forty

Roberto smiled coldly, his eyes glinting in the moonlight. "You picked the wrong boat, bitch," he snarled. "Do you have any idea who you're messing with?"

Viper didn't answer. She looked at the blade in his hand and raised her hand to touch her side. It came away sticky with blood but the wound, while deep, appeared to be essentially harmless. Confident that it hadn't hit any major organs, she smiled.

"Oh, I know," she said softly, straightening up. "I would have thought you got the message when Jenaro's head arrived in Mexico. I don't think *you* have any idea who you're dealing with."

At the mention of Jenaro, Roberto growled and lunged at her with the knife again. This time, Viper was ready. She blocked the blow easily and swept her leg to the side, knocking his plant foot off balance as she followed up with her right hook into his gut. Roberto grunted and doubled over as he fell against the wall. Recovering quickly, he moved the arm holding the knife in a slashing motion towards her neck. She parried the blow easily, closing her fingers around his wrist and squeezing the pressure points until his hand went numb and the knife dropped to the floor. Kicking the dagger to the right, she heard it slide across the deck and over the edge.

Robbed of his weapon, Roberto drove his other hand into her gut, robbing her of breath and causing her to double over. Pain shot up her side as her muscles contracted and Viper sucked in air as stars exploded behind her eyelids. An involuntary grunt escaped her lips, and then fury took over. The anger that had been simmering beneath the surface ever since John died boiled up inside her, filling her with an intense rage the likes of which she hadn't felt in years.

Completely unaware of the pressure keg that had just been tapped, Roberto raised a beefy fist to drive it into her head. It never made it. Still doubled over, Viper raised her hand, grabbing the fist and holding it at bay. There was a moment of stunned silence as Roberto realized that the hand blocking his blow was much stronger than he had given it credit for. Rage had given Viper new strength and she pushed his arm back as she straightened up, driving her left fist into his jaw. He stumbled back and let out another grunt of pain.

"Is that all you've got?" he demanded, looking at her as blood dripped from the side of his mouth. "It'll take a lot more than that."

He charged her and Viper side-stepped easily, grabbing his shoulder and slamming him into the wall, using his own forward motion against him. His face slammed into the paneling and she heard a decisive crunch as his nose broke. Before he could recover, Viper kicked the inside of one of his legs, sending it sideways as he let out a bellow of pain. Still refusing to go down, he spun around and used the wall for support while he stared at her. Blood was pouring from his nose and his mouth now, yet he smiled.

"You'll never win," he gasped, spitting blood onto the deck. "We've already won. Your friend below deck? He's dead. I killed him myself. Those bombs that he was setting up? They'll never go off."

Viper ignored him, blocking out his words as she reached into her back holster and pulled out her .45. Before she had a good grip on it, he swung his arm and knocked it out of her hand. The pistol fell to the floor and slid a few feet, stopping a little further down the walkway.

Roberto tried to follow up with a defensive punch, but Viper borrowed a page from Harry's book and slammed her forehead into his face. Roberto's head snapped back and cracked against the wall. His eyes rolled back and Viper pulled the .22 from her leg holster. Without hesitation, she fired a round directly into his forehead. Then, for good measure, she fired a second one into his heart.

He slid down the wall slowly, a look of stunned anger on his face as his eyes stared sightlessly ahead.

"You talk too much," she said dispassionately, turning away.

"And he lied," Hawk's voice spoke in her ear, deep and low. "Not only am I still here, but I'm setting the last two charges now."

Through the anger Viper felt a wave of relief and she smiled faintly.

"Good to know."

"That's it?" he asked, amused. "What would you have done if he was telling the truth?"

"Set the charges myself."

A low chuckle sounded in her ear. "Now that's cold."

The faint smile turned into a grin as Viper bent down to pick up her .45.

"If you're looking for sentiment, I'm a little busy right now," she murmured. "And so are you. Get those charges set. I'm going after Harry."

Next Exit, No Outlet

Hawk finished attaching a slim, round explosive to the underside of part of the engine and straightened up, turning away. One more to go and the explosives would be spread out throughout the entire lower level of the yacht. He glanced at his watch and left the engine room, moving down the narrow hallway until he reached the crew room at the end.

Now he knew who the man was who had been watching him about ten minutes ago. Hawk had turned around and saw him, but the man disappeared before he could draw his weapon. Whether or not Roberto had plans to come back was immaterial. He had missed his only shot, and now he was dead. Damon shook his head and pushed open the door to the crew room. It was empty, as expected. Those of the crew who were left were busy trying to protect Harry.

Damon pulled the last explosive charge out of his weapons bag and walked over to attach it to the far wall, on the hull of the back of the ship. Like the others, the spot had been chosen to ensure that the yacht went down quickly. Each charge on the outer walls was placed strategically to cause maximum damage, and the ones placed in the interior would cause explosions to rip the ship apart.

It was almost time.

Fixing the device to the hull, his lips tightened. Viper was going after Harry and if he had an ounce of sense, he would realize that it was Hawk that had accompanied her and then disappeared below deck. He would be getting desperate now as he realized that his carefully laid plans had blown up in his face. That would make him even more dangerous and unpredictable. With nothing left to lose, he would play with Viper, extending the game as long as possible. But once Hawk set the charges, she had only five minutes to finish what she'd started.

Damon's hand came away from the device and he pulled out the remote detonator that connected them all. The rectangular handheld box could detonate immediately or on a timer. He had already set the timer, and all he had to do was press the button to activate it. Hawk's finger paused over the button.

Viper was one of the best. Aside from that one time in Cairo, he had never known her to fail. But she had never gone up against their mentor and teacher before.

He looked at his watch again, hesitating. Once he hit that button, the clock started, both figuratively and in reality. There was no turning back once the charges were set. Right now, if something went wrong, he could still have time to help Viper.

But that wasn't the plan. The plan was that he would set the charges and then get off the yacht. She would follow once Harry was dead. That was the plan.

And Viper's plans never failed.

He turned away from the last explosive and strode out of the crew room, moving down the narrow corridor. For the first time in his life, he felt uncertainty. It wasn't just about Harry now. Things had changed; he and Viper had changed. The prospect of losing her caused an emotion that Damon had never felt before. The knowledge that the odds were not in her favor simply compounded the feeling. And yet, he knew that she would have it no other way. If this was where her story ended, he knew that she had planned it to end the way she wanted it to.

She would go out on her own terms.

Yet still he hesitated, holding the detonator in his hand as he strode down the corridor. Everything was in place, just as they'd planned, and timing was key. It all hinged on timing, and if he delayed any longer, it would be thrown irretrievably off. He had no choice. He had to hit the button.

Viper looked down, following the blood trail down the corridor with her .45 in her hands. Her side throbbed where Roberto had stabbed her and she was running low on both time and ammunition. The faster she found Harry, the better all around.

She passed a galley kitchen and noted that the blood trail went in and then came out again. Harry had grabbed something to try to stop the bleeding and, a little further along the corridor, the trail became significantly lighter. She let out a soft curse, picking up her pace. She had to find him before he stopped the bleeding altogether. There was no time to tear the ship apart.

The pain in her side and the rush of fear she had felt when Roberto claimed that Hawk was dead combined to fan the flames of fury burning inside her. Harry had started this, and she was damn well finishing it now. She wanted her life back.

The blood trail stopped and Viper looked into the open

Next Exit, No Outlet

doorway to find a stairwell going up. She was placing her foot on the bottom step when awareness streaked down her spine. She spun around just as a tall and heavy figure came out of a door to the left of the stairwell. Without hesitation, Viper raised her gun and fired. The figure fell backwards into the wall and slid to the floor, blood pouring out of his head.

Viper turned and checked both ends of the corridor before disappearing up the stairs. A few steps from the top, she paused, listening. In the silence, she felt rather than heard a presence outside the stairwell. Tucking her gun into the holster at her back, she reached down to pull her combat knife from the sheath on her ankle. Then, taking a calm breath, she moved up the last couple steps and braced herself.

Emerging from the stairwell, she immediately had a tall man swing something in the direction of her head. There were two of them, one on either side of the entrance to the stairs. She went low, almost to the floor, avoiding the blow aimed at her head, and braced herself on her left leg as her right leg swept the first attacker's feet out from under him. As he lost his balance, the weapon in his hand flew towards his companion, causing him to duck with a sharp exclamation.

Viper surged up swiftly and whipped behind him, placing her gloved hand over his mouth. Before he could react, her knife had sliced across the front of his throat. As he began to fall forward, blood pouring from the wound, she threw the knife unerringly at his companion. A strangled noise escaped him as it lodged in his neck and she reached into her leg holster, pulling out the .22. She fired into his head, stepping over the body in front of her. He fell back against the wall and Viper reached out to pull her knife from his throat as she passed.

A moment later she moved into a large room with panoramic windows lining each side. It was the recreational room she had glimpsed earlier, but now the huge TV was dark and silent. As she came through the doorway, Viper glanced to her left where a bar ran the width of the room. No one was behind it and she paused, scanning the area. Between the bar and the TV on the far wall were a sectional and two recliners, none of which were concealing anyone.

Pursing her lips, she moved further into the room, heading for the entrance on the other side. As she did, something moved out of the corner of her eye and she snapped her head around in time to see Harry emerge from behind a tall, potted fern. He raised a gun and fired.

She dove to her right, landing on her knees behind the recliner closest to her as his shot hit a vase on the wall to the side of the door.

"Still quick on your feet, I see" he said, his deep voice carrying across the room, "even after being stabbed. You never were one to let pain get in your way, I'll give you that."

Viper was silent, listening as he spoke. He was moving to his right, trying to get into a better position to take a shot when she moved, but he wasn't there yet. Raising the .22 in her hands, she ran out from behind the recliner, firing in his direction as she crossed the room to take cover behind the other chair. One of her shots caught him in the shoulder as he was firing at her and he let out an expletive, stumbling backwards a pace. His shot went wide, hitting the TV, and she rounded the recliner before he could get another one off.

There was a moment of silence, then Viper peered around the back of the chair to see Harry ducking behind the bar. A cold and deadly smile crossed her lips. He was shot in the opposite shoulder from the arm she'd winged earlier. With both arms shot, his effectiveness was seriously hindered, tipping the odds in her favor.

"Pain is just the body reacting to a trauma. I can let it control me, or I can control it." She pulled the clip out of her gun as she spoke, checking the amount of bullets left. "How's that shoulder?"

"I'll live."

"Oh no you won't," she muttered to herself, sliding the clip back into the gun with a click.

"It was poetic, you bringing O'Reilly along and having him rescue Angela." Harry's voice sounded muffled from behind the bar. "I'm sure Dave would have appreciated the effort to include his best friend."

Viper's lips tightened briefly and she glanced around the edge of the recliner. There was no sign of Harry. He was still concealed below the bar. The shoulder wound must be giving him trouble. It obviously hadn't affected his tongue, though. How predictable of him to try to bait her with her dead brother.

"Dave's dead. I don't think he really cares what goes on down here," she said, her voice even and flat. "I needed someone I could trust, and Michael was available. Nothing poetic about it."

"Charges are activated. You have five minutes."

Hawk's voice was low in her ear and Viper glanced at her watch, pressing the button to start the countdown. There was no more time for conversation. She had to finish this now.

Straightening up, she swiftly moved towards the bar.

Next Exit, No Outlet

Hawk heard Harry's voice through his earbud and rage rolled through him, catching him by surprise. It was the same voice that had barked orders at them over a loud-speaker on the training grounds. It was also the same voice that Hawk had had long conversations with over the past few years, a voice that had offered both wisdom and encouragement when it was needed. It was the voice of a hero and teacher, and now, the voice of the enemy. The smug bastard had gotten away with too much for far too long. Not only was he a traitor, but he'd compounded that felony by going after Viper.

Surprised by the anger rushing through him, Damon paused in the corridor. For the first time, he suddenly understood and appreciated why Alina had been so angry when John was killed. Gunshots popped in his ear and his jaw clenched. The thought of losing Viper tonight filled him with an almost uncontrollable rage. Harry could not be allowed to win.

Hawk's thumb moved over the button and he pressed it without any further hesitation.

"Charges are activated. You have five minutes."

With that, Hawk reached the stairwell leading up to the stern. He jogged up the stairs and moved down the walkway until he reached the small closet where he had concealed the bag with his breathing tank. He had just strapped it on his back and slid the mask over his face when Viper spoke.

"Why do they always try to justify themselves?" she asked in a low voice, surprising a low chuckle out of him.

"To make themselves feel superior," he replied. "Or to distract you. Be careful. He perfected that years ago."

"Tell me when you're clear."

She sounded breathless and no sooner had she spoke then there was the sound of breaking glass. A few seconds later, he heard her gasp and then let out an involuntary cry of pain. His heart stopped for second and then thudded heavily in his chest. He wanted nothing more than to go back and help her, but he knew he couldn't. One of them had to make it off the ship. He had to stick to the plan.

He was striding down the walkway towards the stern when a shadow moved out at the end, holding a rifle. Without breaking stride, Hawk pulled out his own weapon and fired rapidly in succession. The figure fell backwards and the rifle dropped harmlessly onto the floor.

Hawk strode past the body without a glance, heading for the edge of the deck. Reaching the railing he looked at the black waves lapping against the stationary ship.

"The ship is all yours," he said, gripping the railing with one hand. "Make it count."

"You know I will."

Damon smiled faintly. "I'll see you soon."

And with that he vaulted over the railing and into the ocean.

"Out of curiosity, when did you know it was me?"

Harry called the question from behind the bar as Viper moved silently across the room. She smiled faintly. He was trying to determine where she was, just as she had when he spoke.

"I suspected when I was in Singapore," she answered, diving to the right as soon as she finished speaking. She had just slid across the smooth wooden floor when a bullet tore into the back of the sectional near where she had been seconds before. "Not bad for being shot twice," she commended him, moving along the base of the front of the bar.

"I've been shot more times than years you've been alive," he retorted. "Don't patronize me."

"I plan on doing worse than that, don't worry."

Harry grunted. "When did you know for sure? What gave me away?"

Viper moved around the corner of the end of the bar, pausing against the heavy wood.

"John's hard-drive. My brother sent the missing piece twelve years ago."

"Of course he did," Harry muttered. "I knew there had to be something. John was too damned persistent, right up until I had him killed."

Viper shook her head, her lips twisting. And there it was. His probe with Dave hadn't worked, so he was pivoting to John. Hawk had been right the other night, and she was honest enough to admit to herself that that jab would have hit a nerve a few days ago. Now, it only served to irritate her.

She hesitated, her desire for answers warring with her common sense. She didn't have the time or inclination to chat, but there was one

Next Exit, No Outlet

thing she needed to know.

"Why did you allow me into the Organization when you knew you killed my brother?"

"You were Charlie's pick. I had no say in it. I tried to get rid of you in training, but you're a stubborn woman and refused to fail." Harry's voice was calm and unemotional, as if they were discussing the weather. "In the end, I had to accept it."

Viper was silent, feeling somewhat deflated at the rather prosaic answer. Somehow, she expected something more intricate than that.

"Don't you want to know why I did it?" he asked after a second of silence. "Everyone always wants to know why."

"Honestly? I don't really give a damn," she said bluntly. "Money, power, some kind of enlightened higher moral consciousness: I've heard it all. None of it matters. You went after my country and my family, and then you came after me. It's time for you to pay."

"In my defense, we're talking about an awful lot of money," Harry said. "I already had power, my Army career provided that, and I was content. But then Charlie and I had a philosophical disagreement over what direction to take the Organization. It was *our* brainchild, but *he* won the President's favor. It should never have been allowed to function without oversight. We were no better than the lawless bastards we hunted."

"Why do they always try to justify themselves?" Viper muttered into her mouthpiece to Hawk. She raised the .22, gripping it firmly and sliding her finger over the trigger. Then, raising her voice, "I really don't care, Harry."

Spinning around the bar to fire, she squeezed the trigger just as something flashed toward her. Sucking in her breath, she dove to the side as a knife flew past her head. Hitting the wall hard, Viper felt the gun slip from her fingers and she clenched her jaw as pain shot up her wounded side. Her eyes fell to the timer on her watch and she grit her teeth.

"Tell me when you're clear," she muttered to Hawk, forcing herself to straighten up. Her whole body seemed to be throbbing from that stab wound and she was running low on energy and time. She inhaled, turning resolutely to face Harry.

He was about a foot away with a bottle of vodka in his hand. Blood poured from the gunshot wound in his shoulder, but he didn't seem to notice as he brought the bottle down on the edge of the bar. The glass shattered and vodka poured out over the floor as he pivoted swiftly, wielding the deadly sharp, fragmented bottle neck in an arc toward her throat.

Viper threw up an arm to block the blow, but he changed direction at the last second and the makeshift blade sliced down into her thigh, narrowly missing her artery. An involuntary cry ripped out of her as her leg buckled under the sudden onslaught of pain and the damage to her quad muscle.

Lurching to the left, she fell against the bar, her weight falling on the stab wound in her side. Viper bit her lip in agony, reaching under the bar for something, anything she could use as a weapon. Her fingers found nothing and she twisted out of the way just as Harry swung for her neck again with the broken bottle. As it hit the wood instead of her, she reached out and grabbed his wrist, slamming it against the edge of the bar. The glass weapon flew out of his hand to slide across the smooth surface and disappear over the opposite edge. A second later, it hit the floor on the other side of the bar and shattered.

Disarmed, Harry turned to resort to hand combat, raising his injured arm to block a blow from her right hook. He grunted in pain as her fist slammed into his gunshot wound and stumbled back a step.

"The ship is yours. Make it count."

Hawk's voice was deep in her ear and a fresh surge of adrenaline flowed through Viper. She straightened up as much as her battered body would allow and raised deadly eyes to Harry's.

"You know I will."

She lunged forward on her injured leg, using her other foot to kick the inside of one of his knees. He wasn't expecting the move with her injured thigh and she caught him unprepared. Ignoring the pain shooting up her leg, she reached behind her back as Harry let out a scream of pain and his leg buckled. As his leg went out to the side and he fell, Viper pulled out her .45 and fired.

The bullet went through his forehead, blowing the back of his head off. She watched as he fell back, his eyes still open in stunned shock.

"That's for Dave, you son of a bitch," she snarled.

Harry's body hit the floor and the rage that had been simmering inside her for the past month dissipated, expelled from her on the tide of a long exhale. She waited for the heavy feeling of coldness to settle in her gut, as it always did when she killed a target, but there was nothing. There was no feeling of emptiness this time, no sense that part of her had been killed along with Harry. Now, there was only relief. It was over.

Dave and John had been avenged.

Next Exit, No Outlet

Turning away from Harry's body, Viper limped out from behind the bar and glanced at her watch.

2:45.

With a low curse, she broke into a run, forcing her injured leg to move. Darting into the corridor, she went to the stairwell and held onto the smooth railing as she started down the half-spiral. At the midway point, she leapt over the railing and landed at the bottom of the stairs, biting back a cry of pain. She forced the emotion away; there was no time for it. She had to make it to the deck and her dive bag under the chaise lounge.

Her breath came fast and labored as she ran down the walkway to the stern. A moment later, she hit the outer door and emerged onto the back deck where she had landed less than an hour before. Instead of silence and pitch darkness, she was greeted by the rhythmic churn of propeller blades as she stepped into a flood of unnatural white light.

Despite her pain and the pressing need to get to the bag, Viper's lips curved faintly. Ah Stephanie. Always so predictable. She knew she wouldn't stay put in Medford. She had gone to the Coast Guard, just as Viper knew she would.

Crossing the deck to the piece of furniture where she had stashed her bag, she wondered if Blake was with her in the chopper. Probably. He wouldn't leave her side, not until he knew she wasn't going to get a bullet in her head.

At least that wasn't something either of them had to worry about anymore.

She bent down to reach under the rattan chair, grimacing as her thigh buckled. She grabbed the side of the chair, narrowly missing the leg of a corpse draped over the back, and pulled the bag out. Using the chair as support, Viper managed to straighten up without her leg going out on her again. She swung the pack onto her back, tightening the straps as she turned to stride towards the railing. The mask was attached to the outside of the bag with a D-ring and she released it with one hand so that it hung free, ready to be slipped on when she hit the water. It was already connected to the tank and ready to go. All she had to do was get into the water before the charges went off.

Glancing up and into the light, Viper paused when she reached the railing, looking at the helicopter. A sudden wave of remorse crashed over her. She never even said good-bye, and now it was too late. Even if she raised her hand to wave, it could never be nearly enough. What kind of person had she become that she could just leave without saying farewell to her best friend since kindergarten?

Viper pushed the thoughts aside and glanced at her watch.

She was out of time.

Next Exit, No Outlet

Chapter Forty-one

Stephanie felt Blake's fingers close around hers and she looked at him in surprise. He was sitting next to her in the back of the Coast Guard helicopter with a headset covering his ears. They had been airborne for about five minutes now, and she was just getting used to the vibrations and noise that came with the helicopter. She gave him a questioning look and raised an eyebrow.
"What?"
"It's going to be all right," he said, speaking into the headset.
She smiled tremulously and squeezed his fingers before releasing his hand. She knew he was trying to help, but she seriously doubted that anything could make her feel better right now. Her stomach was tied in knots and her chest hurt from anxiety. She didn't know which was worse: not knowing what was going on, or realizing that she was about to see firsthand what was happening. She turned her attention out the window and stared into the black void, broken at regular intervals by the flashing lights on the side of the helicopter.

Her headset crackled again and Lt. Miller spoke from the cockpit in front of them.
"A small craft was just seen leaving the area where the *Sea Queen* is coasting," he told them.
Stephanie's heart raced and she looked at Blake hopefully.
"Any word on how many people were in it?" she asked.
"Two people, possibly a man and a woman. Sounds like your civilian made it off."
Blake sent her a grin as an acute feeling of relief swept over her.
"I told you everything would be fine," he said. "Michael doesn't know how to fail."
"It wasn't Michael I was worried about. It was everyone else." She leaned forward and looked toward Lt. Miller in the front. "Any word on anything else? Do we have any idea what's going on onboard?"
"There's a report of shots being fired. I'm waiting for

confirmation and more information."

Stephanie sat back, her lips pressed together tightly.

"How long until we reach the area?" Blake asked, seeing the look on her face.

"Another ten minutes."

Stephanie shook her head and gazed out the window, her jaw clenched. At least Michael had gotten Angela off the boat. That was half the battle. Hopefully he got her off before the shooting started. Stephanie didn't want to know how Angie would react if she saw someone get shot.

"How do you know shots are being fired?" Blake asked, drawing her attention back from the darkness outside.

"We have a satellite feed. The images are being passed on sporadically, but the last one showed a small boat leaving and indicated shots still being fired onboard."

"And you still don't have authorization to send in a team?" Stephanie demanded incredulously. "What the hell are they waiting for?!"

"I wish I knew, Agent Walker," he replied, the frustration clear in his voice.

Stephanie looked at Blake and saw that his lips were pressed together thoughtfully.

"What are you thinking?"

"Something's not right," he said, shaking his head. "Someone's pulling rank somewhere."

Stephanie pulled her headset off and motioned for him to do the same so that Lt. Miller couldn't hear what they said. Once he had, she leaned toward him. He met her halfway.

"You think Lina's boss is preventing the Coast Guard from moving in?" she demanded into his ear, raising her voice against the sound of the propellers. "Why? To what purpose?"

"Are you kidding me? This is a political and diplomatic nightmare for the White House. Not only is Harry Shore a prominent figure on Capitol Hill and a national hero, but he's the sitting head of the Department of Homeland Security. Do you have any idea what this scandal will do to the administration if it gets out?"

Stephanie stared at him speechlessly. She had been so focused on the fact that someone was trying to kill her and Alina that it never occurred to her that there were other repercussions to Harry Shore being behind everything. She had certainly not considered the fact that this was something the administration wouldn't want made public, let alone Alina's super-secret organization. No one came out of this

Next Exit, No Outlet

looking good.

"Oh my God," she finally breathed. "I never even thought…"

"If Viper's boss doesn't contain this, the backlash will be ungodly."

Stephanie sat back in her seat, stunned. Her mind was spinning. While she hadn't considered the ramifications of this entire situation before now, she knew without a doubt that Alina would have. Everything was starting to make sense now. Her and Damon's insistence that they be the ones to take care of Harry, Michael's reluctance to argue against them, and even Alina's ultimate decision to have Michael extract Angela: they all took on a new and disturbing meaning. Over the past few days, Alina had been systematically setting everything up and moving everyone into place so that she could contain this whole situation with the absolute minimum of public exposure possible. By having Michael be the one to get Angela off the yacht, she had even ensured that a member of the Secret Service was the only witness to what was happening, knowing that his very oath of service bound him to protect the White House. Even if he wanted to talk, he would be unable to do so.

"If you're right, then why are we up here?" she asked, leaning forward again. "I mean, why let us get near the ship if they don't want anyone involved?"

"That's what I've been trying to figure out for the past five minutes," Blake admitted. "I have no idea."

He pulled the headset back over his ears, and Stephanie did the same with a frown. If Alina's boss was holding the Coast Guard back, why would he allow them to do a flyover? Her lips tightened and she turned her gaze out the window again, chewing the inside of her bottom lip.

Now that Michael had gotten Angela to safety, any and all restraint that Viper may have been exerting would be gone. Her mind flashed back to that day in the bedroom and she felt a cold chill go through her. Alina was more than ready to face her death, and Stephanie was uncomfortably aware that her old friend wasn't particularly concerned about going out of her way to prevent it. She thought she deserved it.

Alina had been very clear about feeling responsible for everything that had happened to John, Angela, and Stephanie since she came back last year. Her priority would be to end this nightmare, and Stephanie knew that Viper didn't care if that meant she died in the process.

Miller interrupted her thoughts when he let out a startled

expletive. Stephanie and Blake glanced at each other, then Blake leaned forward slightly to look at their pilot.

"Everything okay?"

"Sorry. I forgot I had the intercom system on," Miller said, glancing over his shoulder at them. "Hold on."

Blake sat back with a frown as Miller switched to one of the other radio frequencies that he'd been using to communicate with his base. He looked at Stephanie and she met his gaze, her frown mirroring his. Blake dropped his gaze and glanced at his watch.

"We should be getting close," he said, looking out his window. "I wonder where Michael took Angela?"

"The closest barrier island is St. Simons," Stephanie said after a moment. He looked at her in surprise and she shrugged. "I looked it up before we left. You never know what will happen. If something goes wrong and I end up swimming in the Atlantic, I want to know where I have to swim for."

Blake stared at her for a beat. "Are you being serious?"

"Yes."

"Steph, we're on a Coast Guard chopper!" he exclaimed with a laugh. "You wouldn't have to swim. They rescue people every day. It's what they do!"

She made a face at him. "I just like to be prepared."

He was still laughing when Lt. Miller switched back to the intercom system.

"Well, we have a development," he said, "and it's not a good one. We lost our satellite."

"What?" Stephanie sat forward. "How?"

"No idea. We're not getting the feed anymore. They're working on getting it back, but right now we're blind."

"Well, we still know where the boat is, right?" Blake asked. "We can be the eyes until it comes back online."

"That's the other problem. We have a crew waiting just inside territorial water and they've been holding steady radar contact with the *Sea Queen*."

Stephanie felt a wave of apprehension go through her and she swallowed.

"And?" she managed to get out around the sudden lump in her throat.

"They've lost radar contact. It's almost like the ship just disappeared."

"How is that possible?" Blake demanded.

"In theory? It's not," Lt. Miller said grimly. "It's like they

Next Exit, No Outlet

disappeared into a black hole."

"So we don't know where they are?"

"We know where they were twenty minutes ago. That's our starting point."

"What can cause a blackout like that?" Stephanie asked, her voice sounding strained even to herself.

It was a moment before the Lieutenant answered her. When he finally did, his voice was somber.

"Complete mechanical and electrical failure."

Stephanie felt her chest tighten and she gripped the arms of the seat tightly. Lt. Miller was trying to be diplomatic, but it was clear that he had shifted into search and rescue mode.

Blake reached over, closing one strong hand around hers, and she took a deep breath.

"How far are we from their last location?" he asked Miller.

"Two minutes out." Miller looked over his shoulder at them. "I'm turning on the lights. It's going to get bright out there."

A moment later, Stephanie looked out the window and blinked. Miller hadn't been exaggerating. The dark waves below were suddenly illuminated with a bright light, an endless expanse of ocean that looked strangely calm given the drama unfolding on its surface.

"What's the plan when we find the yacht?" Blake asked, looking out his window.

"I radio back a sitrep."

Stephanie shook her head. "That's it? And then what? You just fly away and wait?"

"I'll circle and get footage and send it back," Miller replied. "Until I get different orders, the original plan stands. We observe and report and then head back."

"What if it's sinking?!"

"Then a rescue crew will launch."

Miller's voice was absurdly calm and it grated on Stephanie's already raw nerves. She looked at Blake in frustration and he shook his head, his jaw clenching. He didn't like it any more than she did, but there was nothing either of them could do.

She turned her attention out the window, searching the ocean below for some sign of the missing yacht. Her heart pounded against her ribs and she felt her palms getting damp as her stomach clenched. Alina and Damon were still on that ship, and now they had lost all communication with the outside world. Even if the yacht was still afloat, which Miller seemed to think was increasingly unlikely, they were alone in the middle of the ocean with one of the most vicious cartels in

Mexico.

God, I'm not a praying woman, but if you save Lina and Damon, I promise I will be, she prayed silently, her eyes fixed on the waves below. *It's too late for John, but it's not too late for them. I'll even go to mass. Just don't let them be dead.*

"Hey," Blake said, squeezing her hand.

She looked at him, knowing he could see the fear on her face. She didn't care. It wasn't something she couldn't hide now even if she tried.

"Remember what they do," he said softly. "More importantly, remember where and how they served their country. They're squids. If anyone is qualified to handle a situation at sea, they are."

"What the hell is a squid?" Stephanie demanded after a minute.

Blake grinned. "A Navy wuss."

She choked back an almost hysterical laugh.

"I can't think of anyone less wussy than them. Except maybe Rambo, but I think she even has him beat."

"After the parking garage, I'd probably agree." He squeezed her hand once more and then released it. "Have some faith."

He turned his attention back out the window and Stephanie took a deep breath, returning her gaze to the waves far below. Blake was right, on both counts. Damon had been a Navy SEAL, and Alina had joined the Navy after being on and around boats since she was a kid. She had to have a little faith, not just in their ability to survive but also in the fact that their training was far superior to anything she could even imagine.

"There she is!" Miller called out suddenly, breaking into the intercom. "The *Sea Queen's* still there!"

Stephanie strained to see from her window, but all she could see were empty waves. She looked over to Blake's side and then leaned forward between Miller and his co-pilot to look out the front windshield.

The bright spotlights from the helicopter lit up the superyacht in the night, making it look very small and insignificant in the vast expanse of waves. It bobbed far below them, dark and silent.

"They've lost power," the co-pilot said. "That's why there's no signal for the radar to pick up. Look. Her lights are out and there's no wake behind her."

"She doesn't appear to have any structural damage from this angle," Miller said. "I'll circle her. Maybe there's something on the other side."

Stephanie stared at the yacht, straining to see any movement

Next Exit, No Outlet

on any of the decks, but they were just too far away. They flew around to the right, placing the yacht on Stephanie's side of the helicopter. She sat back in her seat and peered out her window, picking the boat out of the waves a minute later.

"Can you see anyone?" Blake asked, leaning towards her to look out the window.

She shook her head. "No."

The helicopter circled around, and Stephanie lost the ship until Miller approached again, this time from the front. The yacht was still on the left, and she and Blake both peered down at the motionless ship, searching for movement.

"I don't see anything wrong on this side either," Miller said. "I'm going closer."

"I don't even see the distress flares," his co-pilot said. "They should have them lit by now."

"I don't like it," Blake murmured. "What the hell is going on down there?"

Stephanie didn't answer as the lieutenant brought the helicopter closer to the stranded vessel. The lack of light on the ship was eerie and she repressed a shiver of foreboding. Now that Miller had brought them in closer, she could see the top decks more clearly. A second later she inhaled sharply just as Blake let out a low curse.

"Are those bodies?!" the co-pilot exclaimed.

"Looks like it," Miller said grimly. "There's our confirmation of the shots fired."

Stephanie's chest tightened and she was having trouble breathing. Bodies were strewn throughout the upper and lower decks, spread over the ship and giving a macabre picture of just how many shots had been fired. She scanned the decks, desperately searching for movement, any sign of life at all.

Miller circled around to the other side again, once more approaching from the stern. Because they were lower and closer now, Stephanie clearly saw the back deck and an open and empty alcove that looked just big enough to fit a small boat. More bodies littered the deck, and one was even incongruously draped over a chaise lounge.

"It's like a ghost-ship," Blake said, his voice low. "It's something you'd expect to see in an old pirate movie."

Stephanie could only nod, not trusting her voice. The bright spotlights lit up the side of the yacht as the helicopter began to move forward along the side, and she let out a gasp as her heart surged into her throat.

"There!" she cried, pointing. "On the back deck. Someone's

still alive!"

Miller hovered in place as they all turned their attention back to the stern of the yacht. Sure enough, caught in the white wash of light from the helicopter, a door opened and a figure appeared on the deck. They limped out, slightly hunched over, and one arm clutched the favored side. Then, as if forcing themselves to move, the figure went toward the chaise-lounge with the body draped over it. They pushed something out of the way on the deck and bent to pull an object from underneath the chair.

"What the hell is that?" Blake asked, staring. "Is that…is that a bag?"

Stephanie shook her head and they all watched as the figure hooked the bag over its shoulders like a backpack, turning toward the edge of the deck. Relief robbed Stephanie of breath and she grabbed Blake's hand in a death grip. The light illuminated Alina's face as she turned toward the helicopter, glancing up towards them. She seemed to hesitate for a second, staring up at the chopper, then she looked at her watch and moved to the railing.

"She's alive!" Stephanie finally found her voice, her heart racing. "She's okay!"

Blake squeezed her hand. "I told you there was nothing to—"

He cut off abruptly as the pitch dark yacht was suddenly filled from within by a strange, white and yellow surge of light. The yacht lurched and almost seemed to contract in the middle as if it was taking a deep breath. It was eerily still for a split second before multiple explosions ripped through it, sudden and fierce in the darkness.

"Pull up!!!"

The helicopter rose swiftly as the yacht blew into pieces below them, the force of the explosion propelling flames, glass and wood into the air. A piece of what looked like metal streaked past the window and the helicopter shuddered from the air pressure pushing upwards below them.

"LINA!!!" Stephanie screamed, staring at the blazing inferno in horror as the helicopter pulled higher and away from the debris flying in all directions. "Wait! Go back!"

"Are you crazy?" Miller demanded. "It's a damn miracle nothing hit us!"

"She's down there!" Stephanie cried. "We have to help her!"

Silence greeted that and she tore her eyes away from the flames and splintered ship below. The look on Blake's face made her catch her breath and she found herself shaking her head even as tears filled her eyes.

Next Exit, No Outlet

"We can't just leave her!"

Blake gripped her hand.

"Steph, we have to," he said, his voice strained. "Even if we could get down there, there's flames and oil all over the surface of the water. There's no way to get to her."

"A rescue crew is on its way," Miller said, glancing over his shoulder. "I...I'm sorry."

Stephanie looked back out the window, straining to see the flames that were rapidly growing smaller as the distance between them grew. Tears streamed unheeded down her face as anguish welled up inside her, constricting her chest and choking her. Gasping for breath, she stared at the receding wreckage where Alina was still trapped in the water.

Blake's arm went around her shoulders and she realized she was violently shaking as he pulled her close.

"She's still down there," she sobbed, "and we're just leaving her there!"

Blake had no answer. He simply held her close to him as the flames faded into the night behind them.

Chapter Forty-Two

Jack glanced at his watch and sipped from a mug of hot tea, raising his gaze back to one of the monitors on the wall. It displayed the position of *HMS Trident*, one of the Royal Navy's nuclear submarines, in real-time. The screens on either side of the main monitor were also running information in real-time, one from a designated satellite feed and the other from a sonar relay from the submarine. It was the satellite feed that had him scowling. It had gone dark twenty minutes before and, so far, all attempts to get it back up had failed.

"Sir?"

Jones spoke quietly at his shoulder and Jack turned his head questioningly.

"It's the Prime Minister, sir," he said apologetically. "He's on the line for you."

He nodded and set his tea down, turning to follow his assistant out of the situation room. Once in the corridor, he took the cell phone from Jones.

"You're getting an early start, sir."

"I have you to thank for that, Jack," the Prime Minister said cheerfully. "I've just finished reading the report you sent over a few hours ago."

"Ah yes, I thought that would get your attention."

"Is the information credible?"

"Very."

"Do you mean that we might actually be able to get a resolution on this?" he asked incredulously. "According to your report, this has been ongoing for over twelve years!"

"Yes, sir."

"And the weapons were sold to the insurgents? OUR weapons?"

"Yes, sir."

"And we have the proof? The money trail?"

"Yes, sir."

Next Exit, No Outlet

"Well, how the bloody hell did you manage it? None of your predecessors had any joy. I'm told it was relegated to a filing cabinet years ago."

"I can't take credit for this one, sir. The information was offered to me by an American agent and her organization."

Silence ensued, then the Prime Minister cleared his throat. "CIA?"

"To be honest, I'm not sure," Jack admitted. "I think they're part of an elite outfit within Washington, but which umbrella they fall under is a mystery."

"How is that possible? I thought we knew everything about the US and their covert teams."

"So did I, sir, but obviously we don't."

"Well, that's unsettling."

Jack chuckled. "Yes, it is. But to be honest, I'm very grateful so little is known about them. The agent saved my life, sir. Twice."

"Afghanistan?" The Prime Minister asked sharply.

"Quite."

"Well, that's something," he said, mollified. "I'm assuming this is tied in with the operation I approved earlier?"

"Yes, sir. Thank you for that, by the way. I know it was very short notice. It's underway now."

"Yes, well, how's it coming?"

"I'll know more in the next hour."

"Then I'll let you get back to it. Whatever you need, you have it. I don't want this getting out any more than they do. The press on it would be nothing short of disastrous. That's the last thing we need right now."

"Understood, sir."

Jack disconnected and handed the phone to Jones, turning to go back into the darkened room filled with personnel. Admiral Jessup looked up as he re-entered, his sharp eyes meeting Jack's.

"We're making contact with the *Trident* now," he said, nodding to the monitors. "We got the satellite back, at last. It confirmed that the yacht is gone."

"Gone?" Jack demanded, his eyes flying to the satellite feed. "Where did it go?"

"Ethan?" Jessup addressed one of the senior officers a few feet away.

"I don't think it *went* anywhere, sir," that man said, turning away from a computer monitor to look at Jack. "I think it sunk."

Jack turned his attention back to the large monitor. "How the hell would that happen?"

"My best guess is some kind of explosion." The man turned to look at one of this techs. "Mandy, play back that section just before we lost the feed."

The young tech nodded and pulled something up on her screen.

"Put it on the big screen."

A moment later, Jack was watching a playback of the satellite feed of the *Sea Queen*. The yacht was dark and still on the waves.

"It doesn't look like it's in distress," he said.

"Exactly. Keep watching."

Jack obediently continued to watch. After about twenty seconds, there was some kind of flash throughout the inside of the yacht, then the screen went dark. His head snapped around.

"Where did it go?"

"That's where we lost the feed," Jessup answered, standing. "We went through the sonar relay from the *Trident*, and there is no vessel there now. Whatever happened, it happened quickly. That's why we think it was an explosion."

Jack pressed his lips together thoughtfully and picked up his tea again.

"Sir? We have the *Trident*."

The Admiral nodded and strode over to a phone, pressing the button to put it on speaker.

"Captain Fletcher? This is Admiral Jessup."

"Admiral."

"I've got a room full of people here trying to determine what happened to that yacht," Jessup told him. "What can you tell us?"

"Not much, I'm afraid," Capt. Fletcher said. "There was an explosion, but what caused it, we don't know."

"Captain, this is C," Jack said. "Any word on the package?"

"Not yet. I...oh, just a moment!"

The Captain stopped abruptly and they could hear a muffled discussion in the background. While they couldn't make out the words, they could clearly hear the urgency in the low tones. Jack glanced at the Admiral, and he shrugged. When the captain came back, his voice was even brisker than it had been before.

"The package just arrived," he said, "but there's a problem."

Jack frowned. "What kind of problem?"

"My doctor says one of them is critically injured. It's beyond his abilities. He's recommending transport back to the carrier."

Jack let out a low curse and set his tea down. "How long will

Next Exit, No Outlet

that take?"

"There's an aircraft carrier with a surgical team close to them," the admiral assured him. "Captain, have they dispatched the transport?"

"We're just contacting them now, Admiral. Stand by."

He looked at Jack.

"The carrier will send a helicopter to rendezvous with the submarine. The *Trident* will meet them halfway, where they'll surface and the package will be transferred to the helicopter," he explained. "They'll be on the carrier within an hour."

"And once they're on the carrier?"

"The ship has a full surgery. Your agent will be in good hands."

"Transport is on its way, gentlemen," Captain Fletcher announced, coming back onto the line.

"Thank you, Captain. What information do you have on the injury?" Jack asked.

"From what I'm told, there are multiple injuries. The most serious are a deep laceration and shrapnel impaled on a leg, and a puncture wound to the torso. A long piece of metal is embedded in the chest and has punctured one of the lungs. It's a bloody miracle the package made it to the pod for the rendezvous at all."

Jack's lips tightened.

"Thank you." He turned away and went to the door, glancing over his shoulder at the Admiral. "Excuse me. I have to make some arrangements."

Admiral Jessup nodded and Jack left the room, closing the door softly. Once in the corridor, he exhaled and rubbed a hand across his eyes. This whole operation was a suicide mission from the beginning, but Maggie was certainly no stranger to supposedly impossible tasks. She had taken on an entire Taliban camp single-handedly just to get him out alive. But, perhaps, this was the mission that was just one too many.

He lowered his hand and pulled out his phone. Until the surgeon on the carrier declared her dead, he had to assume she was still alive. He'd made both her and Charlie a promise that he intended to keep.

And that meant getting some people out of bed on both sides of the pond.

When Angela opened her eyes, she winced and squinted in confusion at the bright, white light. Where the hell was she now? The last thing she remembered was being in the back of a Cadillac Escalade with Michael, and it had been night. Now, she was in a bed and it was very clearly, and very brightly, day.

Fluorescent lights shone above her and bright sunshine streamed through a window, reflecting off the white blanket that covered her. She was in a hospital. The realization came to her suddenly and she let out a soft gasp. Squinting against the light, Angela turned her head slowly on the pillow to look at the heart-rate monitor next to the bed, and the IV stand next to it. IV? With a frown, she lifted her right arm and looked at the tube running from her hand to the clear plastic bag.

Dropping her arm back onto the bed, Angela stared at the ceiling, trying to concentrate. She and Michael got into the back of the SUV and...and then what? She didn't remember anything after that. Panic began to set in and she looked around the room frantically, looking for some sign of Michael. Where was he? What happened? Why was she all alone in a hospital room?

She was just working herself up into a cold-sweat when the door opened and Stephanie walked in, a large paper cup wrapped in a heat sleeve in her hand.

"Stephanie!" she gasped. "Oh, thank God!"

"You're awake!" Stephanie said, going over to the empty chair next to the bed. "You've been out cold since I've been here."

"Where is here? And how long have you been here? For that matter, how long have *I* been here?"

Stephanie sat in the chair and sipped her coffee before answering. Angela frowned, noting the big sunglasses that covered half her face.

"You're in a hospital in Charlotte, Georgia," she finally said, lowering the cup. "Michael brought you here last night. He said you passed out on the way in and when he got you here, they rushed you straight into surgery."

"My shoulder?"

She nodded.

"The doctor will tell you more, but they were afraid of nerve damage. I'm not sure how extensive it is, but apparently the surgeon was optimistic. Michael stayed with you all night. He just left about an hour ago when I got here."

"How is he? Why did they let him go?"

Next Exit, No Outlet

"Why wouldn't they?" Stephanie asked, startled.

"He was shot!"

"What?"

Angela frowned. "He didn't tell you?"

Stephanie slowly shook her head. "No. He didn't say a word."

She studied her friend for a long moment. Stephanie was being uncharacteristically quiet and her voice seemed almost void of emotion. While she was always the calmer one, Angie would have thought that she'd show more reaction to Michael being shot. And she was still wearing her sunglasses.

"Steph, what's going on? Why did Michael leave? And why are you here?"

"What do you mean? I'm here because you're here," Stephanie said, looking at her. "You were kidnapped, rescued and then rushed into surgery. You're my best friend. Where else would I be?"

"At Lina's house in Medford, where you'd be safe and, I might add, where you were when I was taken." Angela frowned as a thought occurred to her. "While we're at it, what happened last night? Where are Alina and Damon? Did they get off the yacht?"

Stephanie visibly blanched and her hand with the coffee started shaking. Angela watched her, a deep sense of foreboding stealing over her.

"What is wrong with you?" she demanded with a frown. "What's going on?"

Stephanie reached over and put the cup of coffee down on the side table near the bed. Taking a ragged breath, she clasped her trembling hands in her lap and looked at Angela.

"I...oh God, I don't want to say this," she said, her voice strained. "The boat that you were on, there was some kind of explosion. It...it blew up."

Angela stared at her, stunned, and felt all the blood draining out of her head.

"What do you mean, it blew up?" she whispered. "When?"

"Not long after Michael got you off." Stephanie took a deep, shuddering breath and sat back in the chair, rubbing her face.

Angela felt as if her whole body had been shocked and her muscles went wobbly as her breath caught in her throat. She tried to suck in a large gulp of air as her heart pounded in her chest.

"And Lina?" her voice came out in a raspy gasp. "Was she..."

Stephanie lowered her hands, her lips trembling.

"She was on the deck when it happened. The Coast Guard is looking for..." she broke off abruptly and Angela felt her stomach drop out of her.

"For what?" she demanded, her voice sharp. She needed to hear Stephanie say it.

Stephanie looked at her hopelessly. "Her body."

Michael buried his hands in his jacket pockets as he walked along the wide path through the meticulously manicured lawns of Arlington Cemetery. The sky was overcast and there was a chill in the air, Mother Nature's reminder to them that it was still Spring. A gust of wind blew into his face and Michael's eyes smarted with the blast of cold air as his cheeks tingled.

He walked along the well-known path, feeling numb. When Blake called in the middle of the night, he almost hadn't answered it. Not recognizing the number, he had been about to ignore the call when something made him take it. Michael was a sensible man, not given over to excessive flights of fancy or superstition. Yet some sense of premonition had compelled him to take the call.

He still couldn't believe it, didn't *want* to believe it.

His jaw clenched and Michael felt his chest tighten again, as it had been all day each time he considered the probability that Alina was gone. Even now the Coast Guard was pulling what bodies they could from the ocean at the site of the wreckage. Blake was with them, on hand to identify who he could, and he was waiting for the call to say that Alina was among those recovered.

The hollow feeling that had been with him since Blake described the explosion weighed heavily in his gut as he walked. Somehow, somewhere along the line, he had managed to convince himself that Alina was invincible, that *Viper* was invincible. Time after time, she had survived against overwhelming odds through pure and unadulterated luck. Last night, on the shore, she had been focused and all business, and he had never truly considered the possibility that her luck would run out.

Michael inhaled deeply and felt his gut clench. Even though the SEAL was there, he hadn't wanted to leave her on that boat. She had left him no choice by making him responsible for Angela, but he couldn't help thinking that if he had stayed, perhaps things would have ended differently. Maybe he could have extended that incredible lucky streak of hers and she would still be...

Next Exit, No Outlet

His mind blocked the thought even as it formed. There was no point in thinking like that. His lips twisted humorously. He could almost hear Alina's voice saying that thoughts like that were counter-productive and a waste of time. She had been nothing if not absolutely grounded in reality.

Looking around the cemetery, Michael wondered what he was doing here. When Stephanie showed up at the hospital, he had all but run out the door. Unable to sit helplessly in a chair while others were searching the Atlantic in a perfunctory and useless rescue effort, he had told Stephanie he would check in later and left. It wasn't until he got outside that he remembered Stefan's message from Viper. He caught a cab to the airport, booking a seat on the next flight to Ronald Regan Airport from his phone, and landed in Washington, DC, three hours later. Her last message to him had brought him here, but he wasn't sure if he wanted to know why.

There was only one place they both had in common here, and Michael stepped off the pavement to move along the grass towards Dave's grave. As he drew closer, his brows came together in consternation. Something was hanging on the headstone. He glanced around as he closed the gap, looking to see if anyone else was nearby. There was no one, and he returned his gaze to the grave.

Reaching out, Michael lifted the chain off the stone and turned one of the dog tags over, sucking in his breath. All at once, tears blurred his vision as his gut tightened painfully. His fingers closed over the metal plates and he blinked away the tears, trying to regain control over himself. She had left him her dog tags. There was only one reason she would have left them behind.

Alina knew she wasn't coming back.

He dragged in a ragged gasp of air and stared down at his best friend's grave.

"Dave, I'm so sorry," he said, shaking his head. "I tried. I really did. And now..."

His voice cracked and Michael looked up to the sky, willing the hollow feeling of sorrow to go away. It was a futile effort, and he knew it. After a long moment spent staring up at the overcast sky, he lowered his eyes to his fist and opened his hand to look at the dog tags.

"Your sister was one hell of a sailor, Davey," he said, dropping to his knees before the headstone. "You would have been proud of her. And her gear! Holy crap, what we would have given for just one of her rifles. She made us look like amateurs."

Michael raised his eyes from the metal in his hand and looked at the tomb stone in front of him. He'd been to see his old friend many times over the past couple years, but never had he felt as alone as he did now. Yet he couldn't stop himself from talking to the cold marble that couldn't answer back.

"She managed to make me believe she was invincible. Hell, she had so many close calls the past few months, it was only a matter of time before her luck ran out. I wanted to be there with her, you gotta believe that. She made sure I was well out of it, though. Your sister was just like you, you know. She made sure everyone else was taken care of, and then she went after the bastard who killed you. Did you see that up there? After all these years, she found out what the hell happened in Iraq. You were right, by the way. There *was* something fishy going on out there with our weapons getting sold to the insurgents. It was Colonel Shore behind everything."

Michael exhaled and shook his head.

"It's probably stupid of me to be talking like this. If anyone could hear, they'd think I was crazy. Maybe I am. I just like to think that you can see us from where you are, and that you understand. I wish I could have saved her, Dave. God, I wish I could have saved her!"

Michael's fingers closed around the dog tags again and he dropped his head as anguish rolled over him. There was no stopping the grief, no plugging the hollow hole that had taken up residence inside him. The past nine months had been a whirlwind as he got to know the woman who had saved them all from more than anyone could ever know. Not only had she saved her country, but she had saved each and every one of them individually in one way or another. They all owed her so much, yet no one would ever know about any of it. It was all classified. Her extraordinary life would pass into oblivion, no one knowing her name or what she had sacrificed for their peace and safety. She would become just another identical headstone in this sea of military recognition, known only to those who knew where to look for her.

It was a long time later when Michael slowly got to his feet and turned away to head back. He tucked the dog tags into the inside pocket of his jacket. It was time to go back to Charlotte, and back to Angela. He'd promised Alina he would make sure she was safe. Until he was satisfied that Harry hadn't left any outstanding orders, he could still fulfill at least one of his promises to the Maschiks.

Michael left the cemetery as he had arrived: feeling numb. As the cab that he'd called pulled up to the side of the entrance, a fat raindrop plopped onto his hand and he looked up. The rain that had been threatening was finally here. He paused, vividly remembering

Next Exit, No Outlet

another overcast day nine months ago when he'd been caught in the rain here, with Alina. That was the day he had unknowingly become part of a parade visiting Dave's grave, arranged by Viper to throw off anyone looking for her.

A feeling of amusement tried to break through his anguish. It failed. But as he opened the door to the taxi and got in, Michael suddenly knew that someday, he would come here and be able to smile about the past. He would be able to remember her without this gut-wrenching agony of loss, and he would once again appreciate the extraordinary person he had grown to know and love.

That day just wasn't here yet.

Chapter Forty-Three

Arlington National Cemetery - 1 month later

Stephanie stood on the grass next to Angela and stared at the flag-draped, empty coffin. Alina's parents were standing in front of the small group and Stephanie shifted her gaze to them. Mr. and Mrs. Maschik didn't know what really happened to their daughter. They had been told that there was a tragic boating accident off the coast of Georgia when the superyacht she was on suffered a mechanical failure that resulted in an explosion. As far they knew, Alina had been on the yacht with several others from her security firm, enjoying the successful acquisition of a lucrative client. The importance of neither of them ever knowing what really happened had been pressed forcefully on all of them, and Stephanie knew that not one of them would ever speak of the true events to anyone but each other. And so, Alina's parents would never know what a hero their daughter had been, or that she'd died the way she had lived her life: on her own terms.

Stephanie turned her gaze back to the coffin as the priest opened a prayer book to begin. She had never thought to ask Alina what her parents thought she did for a living. Now she knew that Alina had told them she worked for an international security firm in Paris. She even had a Paris phone number, which her parents used frequently to contact her. They spoke to her on the phone and emailed her regularly, but neither of them had physically seen their daughter in over five years. They believed it was because she was so busy. Stephanie knew it was because Alina wouldn't risk their safety. Now they would never see her again.

They had flown into DC last night, and Stephanie and Angela had met them for dinner. Over rich food and red wine, they had shared memories from the past and caught up on the present. The Maschiks were handling the death of their daughter as well as they could, as well as they all could. The shock had worn off, as had the initial grief. Now all of them were in the same place emotionally. They had accepted the

Next Exit, No Outlet

reality that Alina was gone and were moving forward with that as the new normal. This funeral service was the last formality to give them closure, and it was long overdue.

Blake's fingers closed around hers and Stephanie was grateful for his solid presence beside her. He and Michael had done everything they could to make this past month as painless as possible for both her and Angela. It hadn't been easy for them. Neither Alina nor Damon's bodies had been recovered, causing both women to cling to a sliver of hope that their friend had survived. As the days turned into weeks, that hope slowly died and the two friends clung to each other for support. Through it all, Blake and Michael had checked in regularly, offering what support and comfort they could.

Stephanie glanced over her shoulder to where Michael stood near the back, sunglasses covering his eyes, his hands folded in front of him. He was dressed in a black suit and, with the sunglasses, look dark and forbidding. He had taken Alina's death just as hard as they had, but he refused to talk to them about her. While he was more than happy to listen and be a friend for them, Michael had made it clear that he would mourn alone. Blake said it was just his way and that he would be fine, but Stephanie wasn't so sure. He was distancing himself from it, and that was a recipe for mental disaster.

He stood next to a man in dark charcoal suit whom she didn't recognize and she frowned, realizing that she didn't recognize any of the people at the back of the small group with the exception of Michael. Turning her head back to the priest, she pressed her lips together, wondering if any of them were Alina's boss. If so, she would love to go give him a good punch on the nose.

The priest finished reading from his Bible and closed the book, offering his own words of support and encouragement in a clear voice. Stephanie tried to concentrate on what he was saying, but her mind refused to cooperate. Who was Michael standing with? And why wasn't he up here with them? After everything they had all been through, they should be together right now. Yet he had chosen to remain in the back, at a distance.

Angela's fingers touched hers and Stephanie gripped her hand tightly as the priest finished speaking. She jumped at the first of three rifle volleys as the honor guard fired blanks into the air. Angela's fingers tightened on hers and Stephanie glanced at her. Tears were streaming down her face and Stephanie swallowed hard. Angela's left arm was still in a sling, a constant reminder of that night. She blamed herself for Alina even being on the yacht in the first place. Stephanie had told her repeatedly that it wasn't her fault, but it didn't ease Angie's feeling of guilt. She wasn't sure anything could.

As the sound of the rifle fire faded, Stephanie inhaled deeply. Two Navy officers stepped forward in full dress whites to remove the flag from the casket and fold it. Shee felt her chest tighten and tears filled her eyes as they carefully and solemnly folded the last flag to fly over Alina's memory. Even though she was no longer active military personnel, she had died in service of her country. Stephanie knew that the only concession Alina's mysterious Organization was making to her silent death was the burial with military honors. In all other respects, it was as if Alina had never existed. No one outside of the four of them knew anything about what, exactly, Alina Maschik had done for her country over the past year alone, nevermind what disasters she may have averted before that. As far as the world knew, she didn't exist.

Except that she had existed, and Stephanie and Angela would never forget her or her sacrifice to keep them safe and free. The honor guard was the least her agency could do to pay tribute to a woman who had given so much and asked for so little in return.

The tears spilled over her lashes as the tightly folded flag was presented to Alina's mother and Stephanie took a deep, ragged breath, willing them to stop. It was done. It was time to go about picking up the pieces of her life and moving forward. Alina wouldn't want them to cry forever. She had fought and sacrificed so much so that they could live their normal lives in relative peace.

It was only right to honor that sacrifice by getting back to living the life she had fought so hard to preserve for them, and that life could continue now. It was over.

Now it was time to move on.

Amsterdam, Netherlands - One week later

Alina moved through the crowds in the open market square, pausing to look at the offerings at a fruit stall. After looking at the variety thoughtfully for a minute, she smiled at the vendor and moved on. A moment later, a man dressed in jeans and a zippered sweatshirt passed her, going in the opposite direction. As he did so, his hand brushed hers and she took the phone he pressed into her palm. Without turning her head, she slipped the phone into her jacket pocket and continued to the next stall. Once again, she paused, examining the

Next Exit, No Outlet

wares for a moment before moving on.

Five minutes later, she had left the market behind and was crossing an old, arched bridge that stretched over one of the many canals winding through the city. Stopping at the apex of the bridge, she leaned on the railing and gazed out over the water. She could see why Damon loved this city. It was not only beautiful, but it's long, rich history virtually seeped from every narrow building, brick and cobblestone. It was truly different from any of the other cities she had been to.

Taking a deep breath, she pulled the phone from her pocket and powered it on, watching as the security settings began to load. Raising her eyes, she glanced into the canal as the bow of a longboat emerged from the bridge beneath her, moving languidly along the waterway. There were several of these boats moving throughout the canals, and she wondered briefly what it would be like to cruise Europe's rivers in one of them, carefree and relaxed.

The phone in her hand vibrated briefly, drawing her gaze from the receding boat. She swiped the screen and opened the secure message from Charlie. It was an image and, when it finished loading, Alina stared at it for a long, silent moment. It was a photo of the headstone in Arlington, etched with her name and rank, date of birth, date of death and then a single line: FREEDOM ABOVE ALL ELSE.

She knew it was coming. She had planned it herself, along with the entire operation. It was the only way to end it cleanly. With her anonymity gone and her cover shattered over multiple continents, Viper had two options: to die or retire. She opted for death over retirement, at the unabashed urging of Charlie. It was the perfect plan. That is, until it almost became a reality.

When she climbed out of the underwater delivery vehicle and into the hatch of *HMS Trident*, Alina had no idea how she was still conscious. Sheer will had propelled her to the rendezvous with the pod underwater where Hawk and the Royal Navy driver were waiting. When she was close, Hawk saw the blood in the water and got out to help her the rest of the way. If he hadn't, she wasn't entirely sure she would have made it. Her chest had been on fire and simply drawing air through the breathing tube attached to the tank on her back had been a laborious ordeal. Ten minutes later, they were attached to the hatch of the Royal Navy nuclear submarine.

And that was the last thing she remembered until she woke up on an aircraft carrier. When she went into the water as the yacht exploded, debris had hit her, resulting in a long piece of metal penetrating her torso and puncturing her lung. Another piece of debris had embedded itself in the leg already torn open by Harry and his vodka bottle. As soon as the submarine doctor saw the severity of the damage, she had been airlifted to the carrier where the ship surgeon had performed two separate surgeries, as well as stitching up the stab wound in her side. When she woke up, Damon was beside her, looking as if he hadn't slept in days. That's when she learned that the surgeon hadn't expected her to survive the surgeries.

One week later, she had been transported again. This time she'd been flown to London, where she alternated between convalescing and debriefing with both Charlie and Jack. It was there that she balked at continuing the charade of her death. After such an up close and personal brush with it, she was reluctant to tempt fate by going forward with the original plan. It took the combined efforts of both Charlie and Hawk, and ultimately Jack as well, to convince her that it was necessary. She would never be free. Harry had made sure of that. Viper had to die.

And so she did.

Now, looking at the proof in white marble, surrounded by rows of identical markers, Alina felt a sense of numbness steal over her. Below the image, Charlie had typed a single line.

Your funeral was last week. Operation was a success.

No one questioned her death. Her parents, Stephanie, Angie, Michael: they all bought the deception and believed she was dead.

Instead of feeling relief, Alina felt an overwhelming wave of sorrow crash over her. Her parents had lost both their children now, both in service to their country. Except, they had no idea she had still been serving her country. They thought she had been a civilian for the past five years. It was better for them to believe she had died in a tragic boating accident off the coast of Georgia, and that was the end of it. They could never know the truth. For them to do so would be to expose them to danger from the many enemies who wished pain upon Viper and all who knew her. And so they had to believe a lie.

Michael was the one she and Hawk had been the most worried about. His clearance gave him access to information and, if he decided Alina was still alive, there would be no stopping him from digging until he found the truth. Luckily, that didn't need to be a concern any longer. Charlie's note confirmed that Michael didn't suspect anything.

They all believed she had died in the explosion. Just weeks after losing her partner, Stephanie had now lost her oldest friend. Worse, she had been there to bear to witness to her death. It had been necessary to sell it, but now Alina felt nothing but remorse at the pain and grief her friend was going through.

Next Exit, No Outlet

It wasn't fair that it had to end this way. Harry had left them all no other choice but to play the game until the very end, forcing her to choose between herself and the safety of the only friends she had ever known. There had never really been a contest there. Alina had chosen the safety of her friends and her country over her own life, almost making her fictional demise a permanent state in the process.

And now it was over.

Harry was dead. Angela and Stephanie were safe now, Michael and Blake could go back to their work in Washington without looking over their shoulders. The remaining assets spread across the world working for the Organization could resume business as usual. It was over, and they were all free.

Freedom above all else.

Alina slid the phone into her pocket and turned away from the railing. She had done what she had to do, what her duty and honor required. Now she had an opportunity to start over and do what she wanted to do for her. 'Self-care' Angela had called it. Her lips curved faintly as she made her way off the bridge and along the ancient paving stones towards a hotel a block away. If nothing else, Angela would be happy that she was finally taking the time to focus on herself and her future. She inhaled deeply, looking around with wondering eyes. It was time to set the past behind her and look to the future.

It was time to find out just what it meant to be free.

Damon walked across the hotel lobby to the only concierge desk with someone behind it. The woman looked up as he reached it and he smiled at her, balancing his rolling bag on its end in front of the desk.

"Welcome to the Hotel Pulitzer, sir. May I assist you?"

"Good afternoon. I have a reservation," he told her in German, slipping his carry-on from his shoulder and setting it on the floor between him and the desk wall.

She smiled and switched effortlessly into German.

"Very good. And what name is it under?"

"Becker. Hans Becker."

The woman typed on a flat keyboard, turning her eyes to the monitor. A second later, she smiled.

"I have you and one other guest for five nights, is that

correct?" she asked, looking up.

"Yes. My wife and I are on a long-overdue honeymoon," Damon said easily, smiling. "Tell me, if we decide to extend our stay, will that be a problem?"

"It shouldn't be a problem, Herr Becker," the woman assured him. "I'll just need the card you made the reservation with and your identification, please."

Damon pulled out his wallet and handed over a credit card and identification card.

"Will your wife be joining you later?" she asked as she entered the information into the computer.

"Oh, she'll be along in a few moments. We passed a market on the way in and she insisted on walking through."

The woman looked up with a laugh.

"Ah yes. The market is very popular this time of year."

"I hope she doesn't tire herself," Damon said. "She's convalescing from quite a bad car accident. It's why we had to postpone our honeymoon."

"Oh my!" The woman paused and gave him her full attention. "How terrible!"

He nodded solemnly. There was no need to fake being a husband who had just almost lost his bride. The gut-wrenching terror was still a vivid and fresh memory, and one that still woke him in the middle of the night.

"I almost lost her before our life together had even begun. So how can I deny her time to wander through the market?"

"I'm sure she will be fine," the woman assured him. "The market is just around the corner." She paused then, looking at her screen before turning her dark eyes back to his face. "I have you in a suite on an upper floor. Would it be preferable for you to have a ground floor suite? I have one available that is very accessible for individuals with restricted movement."

Damon pretended to be horrified and shook his head.

"Oh no. She would be furious with me," he said with a laugh. "She's determined to make a record recovery. Oh, that reminds me! Does the hotel have a fitness center?"

"Yes, indeed. It has state-of-the-art equipment and a swimming pool for laps. We also have bicycles for hire to explore the city."

"Very good. That's excellent."

The woman went back to checking him in and Damon turned to scan the lobby, noting the security cameras and the positions of exits

Next Exit, No Outlet

out of habit. He was just turning back to the desk when the front door opened and Alina entered the hotel.

Damon watched as she paused to look around, leaning heavily on her cane. His lips tightened. He knew the walk through the market would be too much for that leg, but she'd not only insisted, she'd also refused to allow him to accompany her. Her face was pale and drawn, evidence of the physical and emotional trauma that she'd been through in the past six weeks. But when she spotted him, she smiled and started towards him, the weariness leaving her face.

Damon exhaled silently and felt his chest tighten at the sight of her. She had lost quite a bit of weight over the past month and had added several new scars to her collection, yet to him, she was beautiful. And she was his.

And he had almost lost her.

Damon knew he would never forget the absolute helplessness of watching her get loaded onto a helicopter from a submarine, not knowing if she would even survive the trip. Then, once they arrived on the aircraft carrier and the surgeon took a look at her, the prognosis had been grim. He was told that she probably would not survive the surgeries and to prepare himself to say goodbye. Damon wasn't a man given to prayer, but he had prayed that night and every night following for the next two weeks. It wasn't until they were in London that he finally allowed himself to believe that she had, once again, cheated death's reaper.

Watching her limp across the lobby towards him now, Damon felt a profound sense of relief. It was over.

His heart filled with joy and his blue eyes met hers across the distance, his lips curving into an answering smile. They were embarking on their tour of the cities they wanted to explore together, starting with Amsterdam. For the next few months, all they had to worry about was where to go next and where they would settle at the end of it.

Viper and Hawk were dead. There would be no more ops and no more suicide missions. The future was no longer an ambiguous possibility that they would face if they were lucky enough to get there. It was here.

And they were free.

Epilogue

Washington, DC - 6 months later

Michael looked up as a shadow fell across the scarred, wood tabletop in the back booth of the bar. He nodded and watched as a man dressed in a charcoal grey suit seated himself across from him, setting a pint of dark ale down on the table. Grey eyes met his and Michael raised his own beer to take a sip.

"Did everything go as you expected?" he asked, setting the half-empty pint glass down.

The man across from him nodded.

"Everything is in place. You'll arrive in Dubai two days before your asset, giving you time for surveillance. Your ticket is under the name Josef Carnelucci." The man sipped his ale. "Are you sure you're ready for this? Once you get on that plane, there's no turning back."

Michael looked at him steadily.

"Did you tell Alina that before she flew to Cairo?" he asked softly.

The man smiled faintly.

"There was no need. She knew the risks. She had trained for them."

"So have I."

"Yes, but in a different capacity." The man studied him for a long moment. "I arranged for a twenty-four layover in Italy, as you requested. What do you think you'll find in Sorrento?"

"What do I think I'll find? Nothing." Michael reached for his beer again. "What do I hope I'll find? A newlywed couple living the life Dave always wanted for his sister."

"You still believe she's alive?"

Michael's jaw tightened and he stared at the man across from him. "Yes."

The man was silent for a long moment, then he lifted his beer and drank, his eyes never leaving Michael's. Finding the scrutiny

Next Exit, No Outlet

unnerving, Michael reached for his glass again.

"When you approached me seven months ago, was it because you wanted to serve your country again? Or was it because you wanted to hunt for a ghost?" the man finally asked.

"To serve my country again."

There was no hesitation in his answer and the man nodded slowly. Michael was aware that those sharp eyes missed nothing, and he was conscious of a feeling of relief when the man accepted his answer. It was the truth, but even so, his new boss had a way of making him feel as if he were lying when he wasn't. He supposed it came with the job. After Harry's treachery, they were all a little skeptical these days, and rightly so.

"And the hunt for the ghost?" the man asked softly.

Michael swallowed. "You know when that began."

There was another long silence as those grey eyes studied him some more and he resisted the urge to shift in his seat.

"Michael, do yourself, and me, a favor: let it go. Let *her* go. She's earned the right to rest in peace."

"And if she is truly dead, I will do that."

The man sighed softly.

"Fair enough." He reached into the inside pocket of his suit, pulling out a sealed envelope and slid it across the table. "A parting gift," he said in explanation.

Michael took the envelope, raising an eyebrow in question. "What is it?"

The man smiled and stood up, buttoning his suit jacket.

"Open it on the plane."

He turned to leave and Michael frowned.

"Charlie?" he said, stopping him. "Why did you approve Sorrento if you think I should drop it?"

Charlie turned back to face him, a faint smile on his lips.

"Have a safe trip, Michael," he told him. "I'll see you when you get back."

Other Titles in the Exit Series by CW Browning:

Next Exit, 3 Miles

Next Exit, Pay Toll

Next Exit, Dead Ahead

Next Exit, Quarter Mile

Next Exit, Use Caution

Next Exit, One Way

Available on Amazon

About the Author

CW Browning was writing before she could spell. Making up stories with her childhood best friend in the backyard in Olathe, Kansas, imagination ran wild from the very beginning. At the age of eight, she printed out her first full-length novel on a dot-matrix printer. All eighteen chapters of it. Through the years, the writing took a backseat to the mechanics of life as she pursued other avenues of interest. Those mechanics, however, have a great way of underlining what truly lifts a spirt and makes the soul sing. After attending Rutgers University and studying History, her love for writing was rekindled. It became apparent where her heart lay. Picking up an old manuscript, she dusted it off and went back to what made her whole. CW still makes up stories in her backyard, but now she crafts them for her readers to enjoy. She makes her home in Southern New Jersey, where she loves to grill steak and sip red wine on the patio.

    Visit her at: www.cwbrowning.com
    Also find her on Facebook, Instagram and Twitter!

Printed in Great Britain
by Amazon